TIC TOCK

THE

OFF

SWITCH

A JAKE HARPER AND TJ ALVAREZ NOVEL

THE WAR AFTER THE WAR SERIES

BOOK III

2

I am the master of my fate.

I am the captain of my soul…

Invictus

William Ernest Henley

Do not go gentle into that good night…

Dylan Thomas

This book is a work of fiction. Certain locations, restaurants, bars, marinas, and other businesses are used fictionally. Any resemblance to real people, living or dead, and events is coincidental and unintended by the author. The techno "facts" may or may not be as depicted.

First Edition Copyright 2021 by Ronald K Marshall.

ISBN 978-1-7334517-3-4

ALSO BY

RONALD K MARSHALL

Spy Op A Taste of Paradise

Fragmentary Evidence

For all who support the Arts and Sciences

And all those who sacrifice for their sake.

<u>*IN MEMORIUM 9/11*</u>

FOR ALL THOSE WHO LOST THEIR LIVES ON 9/11,
THE SURVIVORS AND FAMILIES
AND THE VETERANS WHO SERVED AND DIED
AS A RESULT

Gulf of Mexico
Holbox
Contoy
Is
Muj
Progreso
Cancun
Cancun Airport
Merida
Puerto Morelos
Chichen Itza
Riviera
Playa del Carmen
State
Puerto Aventuras
of
Coba
Cozum
Yucatan
Akumal
Tulum
Yucatan
Peninsula
Campeche
Punta Allen
Caribbe
Sea
Sian Ka'an
Preserve
State
of
Quintana Roo
Costa Maya
Majahual
State
Bacalar
Banco
of
Chetumal
Chinchorro
Campeche
Xcalak
BELIZE
Map by Magnolia W

AUTHOR'S NOTE

The idea for this series began with an observation: I noticed with the rise in portable computers, the internet and cell phones, dependence on the latest and more advanced technologies, for better or worse, had taken hold and was changing humanity. I jokingly surmised someday chips would be inserted into our children's heads at birth which would eliminate these extraneous devices. Little did I know, and through research I discovered, the idea was not a joke, the technology is being developed.
I asked myself what does this mean, what are the social consequences, other than political and military exigencies? Thus, The War After The War Series, a fictionalized account of what I foresee this will mean.

PRELUDE

"How do I turn this thing off?

"Off? Why on earth would you want to turn this thing, as you call it, off?"

"Privacy. Some people, me being one of them, enjoy privacy. I have to have it."

Doctor Perkins, his nametag said, shook his head, a confused look on his face. "Privacy?" He pronounced the word with a soft I, not the hard I, Jake was accustomed to. Had to be a transplant, British maybe, perhaps a New Englander.

"Look Doc, when I'm alone, all by myself, or, with certain people, doing things most decent people don't talk about, making whoopie, or whatever-- things I don't wish to share with other people if I choose not to, that's called privacy. So, now I ask you one more time, how do I turn this damn thing off?"

"Oh. I see," he said with a chuckle. By the look on his face, Jake doubted it.

"Mr. Harper, the NM0099 is programmed so you can censor such thoughts and actions. You helped program it. It is a part of you. It knows when you want privacy. You could consider this your device's on and off if that is what you wish. The NM0099 is learning this as we speak. Concentrate, give it a name, if you like. Give it key words for these commands. You and your device are teaching each other. I say again, the NM0099 is part of you. Give yourself time. Give the NM0099 time. Before long you will take it for granted and would no more want to be without it than you would an arm or leg.

THE OFF SWITCH

CHAPTER

1

The Farm, York County, SC
Jake and Ariel

Jake's demons had been held at bay. His too oft disturbing awakening thoughts given a respite, failing to take him to those places he had been trying hard to forget, the darkest dread of darkness, the heart-rending voices not - there echoing following the too real images of his fallen veteran brothers, their bodies torn and disfigured, their lives no more--nightmarish reminders of his own personal brush with death, the resulting failed marriage, and children alienated by lies from his now deceased ex and her family.

Elena, his second, now estranged wife, a practical nurse, had termed it PTSD. He wasn't sure that was true, nor that there was any one certain cause for those unwelcome episodes. All he knew was he had awoken feeling refreshed.

He did his best to keep from disturbing Ariel, his childhood sweetheart, his only true love. He had gently rolled over, tried unsuccessfully not to wake her.

Jake lay back, his heart was pounding. He stared up at the hundred-year-old yellow-brown, heart-pine ceiling, watching the ceiling fan, as old as he was, spin the morning sun's light. Its shattered rays crept across the ceiling. The stirred air was refreshing, invigorating, titillating, his skin, moist with sweat and their love juices.

He took a deep breath, inhaled the stimulating scent, a pleasant reminder of the lust-desire-fulfilled feelings, far beyond mere memories from youth and the unsatisfying substitutes since. His hope, that it would never end. Almost. If only…

Their lovemaking had been a much-needed reprieve, an intense burn, that was slowly dying down from its feverish pitch--the troubling thoughts pushed aside. No way would they, *It*, rob him of this postcoital bliss that he and Ariel both deserved. No way. Wow. If only this dream-like reality could be all there was. But Jake knew hell had no place and heaven only gave people like him a fleeting glimpse.

"You seem distracted?"

Jake looked down at her. Her luxurious auburn hair, mussed from their love making, framed her lightly freckled face which contrasted with the deep pools of her emerald-green eyes staring up at him from his chest. She smiled, then her tongue lightly flicked a nipple. She playfully tried to revive his limp penis, swinging it, twisting it gingerly back and forth in her long delicate fingers. Her hands were soft, the hands of a professional news anchor person, which is what she had become. This was one of only a few times she had stayed over, and they had made love since his release from the clinic. Quarantined, so she was told and never questioned since she too, like the rest of his contacts, had been quarantined due to the seemingly never-ending coronavirus pandemic.

Looking down at her brought more pleasing thoughts, going back to their youth when her hands had been less soft, the hands of a farm girl who had had farm chores and animals to tend to, especially her horse which she rode religiously every day. Jake accompanied her many times on his horse as they walked and galloped down dusty country lanes and ventured across plowed-under fields after the crops were harvested.

Ariel knew nothing about the neuro-implant. Jake wished he could stop thinking about *It*. Was *It here now?* (He had decided to call the thing *It-- Stephen King's invasive, threatening Pennywise It.*)

Was this thing recording his private thoughts and actions? Had *It* learned the commands and meaning for on and off? Their lovemaking was not the type of action he wanted *It* to participate and learn about. This was a distraction. Was *It* listening to his thoughts, doing as he wished--butting out, turning the signal off, vanquishing rather than resending those unpleasant memories? Distracting? Absolutely.

Had *It* paid notice to their discussion last night about the ghosts, the ancestors' appearances, his curious thoughts of their seeming disapproval of his ex-wives? Did *It* feel threatened? When he told Ariel, leaving out any mention of *It*, she had laughed, saw Jake's face, and replied, "Why shouldn't I believe you, you think they approve of me?" He hoped so, felt certain they did. "They haven't shown themselves yet. So far, so good." She had laughed some more. Jake loved hearing her gaiety.

If only he could tell Ariel he thought his ancestors would kick *It*'s ass. Had *It* picked up on that? Perhaps the intermittent web service, mostly nonexistent in this part of his home, kept *It* at bay, prevented *It* from hearing the challenge. Perhaps *It* had not been the reason for his wakening nightmarish thoughts. Jake hated having *It*.

He felt her playful attempts at reviving his penis halt. She raised up and was staring at him.

"Jake, you listening? There you go zoning out on me. Does this have anything to do with Elena? Kind of bothers me being in the same bed you and her shared. Maybe we should have waited. If you want, I can leave."

He reached up and tickled her. Her laughter. Like sweet chimes. She grabbed his hands and flopped down beside him.

Jake turned toward her. She was staring up at the ceiling.

"Guess I'll have to get a whole new bedroom suit. We could have slept at your place. Then I could ask with whom you shared your bed and body."

"And you would have been deeply disappointed." She sighed "The only bedmate was my dog, who now is with my brother's family. I hope Elena isn't causing your wandering thoughts." She turned to face him.

Jake reached out and gently laid his right hand on her cheek.

"Elena isn't here, in my mind or in any other way. Elena and I both knew our marriage was a mistake. Seeing you made me realize that more than anything. He hesitated, gathering his thoughts, trying not to think about the implant. He traced his fingers down and circled them across her arm onto her left breast. For so long he had dreamed of moments like this, having Ariel back, making love—this was a dream come true.

"You ever feel any guilt about us?" Jake asked. He felt her tense, wished he hadn't said that.

"What? Where did that come from?" Ariel pushed his hand away, her eyes met his, imploring, searching for where this was headed.

"You know, you being young, me a little older, a cousin, distant, but a cousin, nonetheless? In today's way of thinking, many would point an accusing finger, say this was wrong, that I took advantage of you." He saw the squinty look leave her face. Saw her posture relax.

"Yeah. You dirty old man." They both seemed to let out captured breaths. She laughed, he laughed--their laughs harmonized.

"As I recall, it was me who made the first move. Are you feeling guilty? Is that where your mind is?"

Ariel lowered herself, kissed his chest and once more teased his nipples with her tongue. She both felt and heard his breath catch as she slid her head down, her hair followed as she kissed her way down across his stomach and flicked her tongue over what Jake called little man's head.

"I guess little man has a mind of his own. What's wrong, don't you want to be wrapped inside me anymore?" She was talking to his penis.

Jake pulled her up and kissed her, the taste of their comingled juices fresh on her tongue.

"Maybe he doesn't have a long memory. Believe me, this has nothing to do with you or feelings of guilt. You are beautiful and the whole time I was in the clinic I thought of this happening. Hoping you wanted me as much as I wanted you."

If only I could tell you about "It".

She rolled over and lay down on top of him, her body became molded to his. She nestled her head on his shoulder, felt his heartbeat, fast, but steady. Her voice was slightly muffled. Her breath sweet and soft, like a feather across his face.

"I came by the clinic again after your arrest and my quarantine period ended. I tried calling, but they refused to let me talk to you. I thought you might not want to have any more to do with me. Then you called. I hope you don't think I just hop in bed with anyone. In fact, this is the first time in a long time I wanted to."

Jake pulled her up. They rolled over onto their sides facing each other. Jake ran his hand down and began massaging her pliantly firm derriere.

"Twenty some years--another lifetime."

"Yeah. Back then we tried everything. I've never repeated half the things we did. No way. From what I remember, two times would not have been enough. And your penis seemed much larger and harder from what I remember."

Ariel chuckled, then quickly leaned over, brushed her lips over Jake's, moved down and took him into her mouth. "Mmm, "she purred, bringing little man to attention.

After they made love again, Jake raised up, his hands pressed down on the now wrinkled cotton sheets bunched up on each of her sides—their eyes locked.

"I was worried all you wanted me for was to further your career. Guess I was wrong, it was my body you were really after. Stick around, might be surprised at what this old man is capable of. Just don't go disappearing on me again."

She pushed him over and sat up.

"Don't even go there. I tried to tell myself interviewing you would only be a professional move. Hate to admit, I was curious. Then I wondered if that was all it would ever be. Now, here we are again, you're the one getting ready to leave once more."

He raised up, brushed her hair aside and kissed her on her neck.

"A part of me wishes I wasn't. Being here with you makes leaving difficult. But I am obligated. If I hadn't accepted what they offered, I would probably be in jail. I would have lost everything, and you and I would not be enjoying each other's company."

"Where are you going? How long before you leave?"

"I don't know yet. I have to meet with them today. Ariel, I promise you I meant what I said. I do love you. I always have."

Jake slid up, swung his legs over and eased down beside her on the edge of the bed. She looked over at him, then looked down.

"The night after you called asking for my help, I wondered about you, about us. Then I saw you, made trying to be professional difficult. It was like a dream. That was until I heard that noise coming from up on the tower, I was petrified. All I could think was you really had taken Elena. That you and your fiend TJ were the sadistic domestic terrorists the York County DA accused you of being." She hesitated. "Then you said those words and I looked at that sad expression. I didn't know what to do, guess part of it was journalistic curiosity, but mostly it was hearing what I had wished to hear. All those years, I wondered what happened to you, why you left me without any attempt at an explanation."

"You left first. Wanted to get away from me. At least that's how it seemed. Your father said you had gone to live with your aunt overseas, told me to leave you be. I had come by your house to tell you that I had joined the Army. I was going to ask you to wait for me, two more years, then we could get married. You were gone. Didn't bother telling me why. Imagine my shock, when Bitch told me you were back here and a news anchorwoman in Columbia. Then when I saw you again…"

"Oh Jake, my father wasn't just upset about us being cousins. He and mama were, maybe a little bit, but… Daddy thought you were a hooligan. I told him how smart you were, could've been in the Honor Society, chose Beta Club instead because you thought the Beta Club was cooler—he thought that made you stupid, not smart. To him you were never going to amount to much because you were always getting in trouble with the law—he thought you were too wild, drugs, alcohol, fast cars, and the guys you hung around with, said you got it honest. Afterall, your great grandfather held up moonshiners, called it collecting a toll, your grandfather urinated in the teacher's gas tank, and burned down the school's outhouse. Shall I go on?" Before Jake could reply, she hastily added, "I tried to tell him that wasn't all there was about your family and that you weren't like that—to me you were real, still are-- what you see is what you get, and I've always liked what you've got."

"Wait a cotton-picking minute. My ancestors are your ancestors."

"On my father's side, once removed, he never failed to add when mama or we kids reminded him." They both laughed.

Jake shook his head, stood up and pulled her to her feet. They held each other.

"I don't deserve you."

Her emerald-blue eyes sought his.

"How soon before you have to leave? I would like to see you as much as you can manage before then."

Ariel finally took note of the sun's orangey-glow pouring in over the pull-down blinds. She looked over at the clock on the bedside table. Quarter till seven.

"Oh shit, I've got to go. I'm to meet with the station manager this morning. She's worried I might take one of the other offers that have been coming in since I broke your story and helped bust Thurmond Tindal."

"What are you going to do?"

"Depends on you. Let's talk about it over dinner tonight. Call me when you can. I need to shower." She brushed his lips with hers and hurried out of the bedroom before he could react.

"I'm going to make coffee. You still drink yours with a taste of honey? Jake asked, not certain she heard him.

He handed her the to-go insulated container, she pecked him on the lips and hurried out the door. He followed out onto the porch, watched her Jeep Grand Cherokee disappear as the sun danced its flickering light across the green-leaved, gnarly limbs of the ancient oaks, silent sentinels, recorders of his family's continued presence on the land. Other than the birds singing and the squirrels chattering, it was quiet. No whining of saws, no crashes of trees, no hunter's vehicles or blasts, deer season was over, turkey season had yet to begin.

Jake inhaled, took in a breath of spring, the fragrances of sweet olives and gardenias wafted up from the base of the oak around which the drive circled, mingled with the sweetness of his and Ariel's lovemaking, reminding him of what he would miss, the end of the spring, and Ariel.

Memories. Standing here, in the same spot where not long ago he had watched his estranged wife Elena heading out on her morning jog with their dogs Maisy and Dusty. Memories: awaiting their return, the sound of his friend TJ Alvarez' truck roaring past the house, up the drive, Elena's tear-streaked face in the rear seat, her sweats covered in their dog Dusty's blood, his entrails lying exposed on the seat.

His life, TJ's, their families' lives, forever had been changed by that incident.

Colonel Thurmond Tindal, a neighbor, owner of Tindal Industries, weapon manufacturer, developer of a drone called The Hive--its Bumblebee arsenal had done the damage to Dusty. Tindal had tried to cover up the cause of the supposedly errant shot, then had his COO Bud Jenkins frame Jake and TJ. They were forced to go on the run to clear their name; and, to find Elena who had been kidnapped by the Gonzalez brothers, front men for the Juarez Cartel who, among others, were conspiring with Jenkins to steal The Hive.

Jake and TJ with Ariel's help managed to elude the authorities and the Mexican gang members and implicate Tindal Industries' involvement with the cartel gangbangers.

Unfortunately, Jenkins had managed to escape, and took Jake's wife Elena with him. He also had taken the source codes, specs, and blueprints for the Hive along with military satellite information and a version of the NM0099 neuro implant. Somehow, apparently with the help of her father, which she had yet to be forthcoming to Jake and the authorities about, Elena had managed to get free. Over the phone, she told Jake after he and TJ had been captured and were being held in DHS's clinic waiting to be implanted, that she had decided she could no longer live at the farm with him and had decided she was going to remain with her family in Louisiana or Texas--Jake didn't know where exactly and didn't care to know—the marriage which shouldn't have been, was over. They no longer talked.

Jake and TJ were held in the clinic for over a month. Authorities were told David Gonzalez had infected them with the coronavirus—the same story told to any others who needed to hear a reason for their isolation. Deane, Ariel, and many others they came in contact with, spent two weeks in quarantine. Who knew if this was true or necessary? Jake figured it was so the news stories would die down.

As a result, he and TJ became experimental government test animals. Once more Homeland Security agents. Once more playing a part in the government's ongoing Operation Pink Flamingo, or whatever it was currently called. The mission: determine the whereabouts of Jenkins and the intel he stole. Their choice had been do this, or go to jail and await trial for any number of federal and local charges resulting from their previous actions. For Jake that would have meant losing his ancestral farm, his refuge, and Ariel.

Uncle Sam's offer seemed the better option.

TJ, who was and had been, an undercover member of Charlotte Metro SWAT, had been part of the original joint task force headed by Homeland Security. Due to their attempted raid on Tindal's property, TJ ended up in the same boat as Jake. He too could not afford to be convicted, lose his job, and go to prison, where, undoubtably, cartel members would have made sure they never left alive.

As Jake thought about his never-ending troubles, he couldn't help but worry Elena would, knowing about Ariel, join hands with Tindal in his continued attempts to force him to sell the farm. She had intimated suspicions, mentioning Ariel after he asked about the emails from her daughter Jennifer's biological father. He had to be careful until the one-year separation date was up—when, hopefully, the divorce could be finalized.

The farm, both ex-wives felt he thought more of it than he did them. They each had pleaded then demanded he sell and leave, move closer to their friends and families in Louisiana and Texas. At first, they appeared to like the solitude, then, for them it became solitary confinement—he the warden.

Now there was Ariel. Ariel started life as a country girl, he wondered and hoped her life and experiences in the cosmopolitan world had not changed her? Could she be happy here with him? Would she and he have to choose?

Time to stop dwelling on the past. It is what it is. He had to get a move on. Shaking off the morning chill, he took his cup back in, poured a hot refill.

Maisy was ready to come out of her pen—the pen she had used as a pup— the pen which was once more her refuge. With Dusty still at Doc Hunter's Veterinarian Clinic and Elena no longer here, Maisy had lost her vitality, seemed depressed. He was going to ask Doc Hunter if she could stay in the same space as Dusty or next to him while he was away on the mission. Damn sure a good thing the judge ordered Tindal to pay the vet bill. Jake and TJ had lawyers breathing down their necks to sue his greedy ass. They still had time to decide.

He looked at the clock, time to get going. He would stop by the vet on his way to his meeting with Homeland Security Undersecretary Robert Hardy at the field office clinic on the other side of Rock Hill, part of the NFL Carolina Panther Owner's new training and multi-use complex.

Would he have more time to spend with Ariel before going away on the op? He would know before the end of the day.

He needed to get moving. He had animals to tend to before he hit the road. Thankfully, the advancing spring meant less work tending to the animals. It was a good thing that he had foregone planting his usual large garden. Whoever watched over the farm would not be overburdened. Speaking of which, he would have to check to make sure his neighbor's family were okay with watching his farm once more while he was away. After the last time and everything which happened since, he wasn't sure.

His neighbor, like most in the community, tended to straddle the line when it came to Thurmond Tindal. The news and gossip had spread concerning Jake's involvement in his wife's disappearance and Tindal's arrest. Current rumor had it Jake was an undercover government agent. The locals had a history of being antiauthoritarianalistic, fueled by local, state, and federal office seekers' hate-baiting rhetoric. Jake, who had never been much for socializing, a non-churchgoer, had become an easy target for the locals. Like one of his grandfather's employees used to say, "ain't nothin' I ain't heared before. Long as they's talkin' 'bout me, they's leavin' other peoples alone."

He loaded Maisy in the truck, drove down the drive, locked the gate and headed down the tree-lined gravel road where all but a couple of the modest few homes were hidden, set way back out of sight, their owners the type who kept their own lives secret, made do entertaining each other, sharing stories heard about others. Doc Hunter was the rarity. He seemed to keep his head above the fray, listened to the gossip, and wisely tended to stay neutral.

CHAPTER

2

York County, SC
Colonel Tindal

From a chair on his marbled terrace, Colonel Thurmond Tindal was attempting to enjoy the morning's quiet. He stared transfixed, his thoughts elsewhere. Two days of relentless questioning before he saw his attorney, then two more days repeating the same story. They were determined to bring him down, no matter what he or his attorneys said.

"I am the victim here, Jenkins' duplicity shouldn't be allowed to destroy my reputation," he declared over and over to his interrogators.

He had to remind himself how good it was to be back home on this fine late October morning, enjoying the warmth of the golden sun's rays that descended the distant tree line, looking like phantom fingers moving toward the shoreline, starting at the treetops then descending downward, pointing toward the site of what was to become his manufacturing facility—once historic Pinckneyville—soon to be his UAV and weapons research and development facility. When operational, it was his sincere belief that it would make him one of the wealthiest men in the area, the king-daddy of them all, as big or bigger than the former cotton kings of his youth.

Bud Jenkins, former COO of Tindal Industries, had temporarily delayed his plans by running off with the specs, blueprints, and most importantly, the source codes for The Hive and a neuro implant device, leaving him holding the bag. His offer of one million dollars for the capture of Jenkins and the stolen bounty should have given the feds pause. Would a guilty man offer that kind of reward?

The looks on their faces said they had not believed he was serious about Jenkins' capture. Why would he be involved, what could they possibly think would be his motive?

And Jenkins, the duplicitous bastard, why had he taken his neighbor, the Harper man's wife with him, then abandoned her somewhere in Mexico? She escaped, so her now estranged husband claims she told him. She was refusing to cooperate with his attorney and the feds. What was she afraid of?

Could it be the Harper man and his wife were involved in the theft along with Jenkins as some thought? Had all the things Jenkins did to Harper on his own behalf to obtain Harper's land—had it all been a coverup? The Harper woman's father Sam, an old friend and fellow intelligence operative, why would he not tell his daughter to cooperate? Was he somehow complicit in Jenkins' scheme also? Too many unanswered questions. His wife claimed he was paranoid, among other not-so-loving things. Then she left, was suing him.

He had every reason to be paranoid—his dreams, and his freedom were at stake. Jenkins needed to be found. He needed the Harper land. Half-million for Harper, a million for Jenkins—the rewards were well worth it. He wanted revenge. Jenkins, the Harper man, and his journalist whore, they would soon learn, they messed with the wrong man.

But for now, Tindal Industries needed a new COO. Someone who could be trusted to do his bidding, get things back on track, and not divulge his and the company's secrets.

Dr. Lisa Guthridge was the leader of the technical team for The Hive. She had top security clearance. Surely, she could get the damn project back on track quicker than a new hire. Tindal wondered if she had been cleared by the feds. It stood to reason the whole team would be questioned and under scrutiny. He needed to know if Jenkins had given her any reason to suspect him of having knowledge of the crimes for which he was accused. Best to keep her close. How close was the question? Would she? He dared not risk a sexual harassment claim.

He buzzed the lab. She was there--a good sign--the feds probably had not talked to her yet. He asked the egghead who answered to ask her to join him on the terrace. This would be their first time since his arrest for them to meet face to face to discuss the future. He needed to find out, if she was willing to carry on, and whether she could be trusted.

Lisa Guthridge was a tall, willowy woman with high cheekbones, who carried herself well--would have made a great runway model. Tindal watched her as she approached from the elevator. Loose-fitting lab clothes, head held high, she moved like an athlete, androgynous, yet feminine, not stodgy the way Tindal expected a research scientist to look or move. He gave her his most beatific smile. She did not return the smile. Her expression was stern, inquisitive.

Look at him, dressed like he's expecting some pompous-ass dignitary.

"Hello Lisa. May I call you Lisa or do you prefer Dr. Guthridge?"

She stopped well over an arm's length away, hands clasped in front like a school marm. He figured her standoffish posture was a carryover from the COVID-19 crisis. She answered in a businesslike manner.

"You wanted to see me?"

Not the deference he expected.

"Lisa, I wanted to thank you for the work you have done since joining Tindal Industries. The Hive would not have happened except for your perseverance and your teams' outstanding efforts. I am sure you are aware of the situation facing me and my company. Bud Jenkins tried to sabotage the program. Were you aware, or should I say, suspicious of what he intended?"

"Not in the least," she answered abruptly. "I was proud of The Hive's performance. It exceeded my teams' expectations, other than that one programming error. In retrospect I'm not certain Mr. Jenkins wasn't the one responsible for what was called an error. I checked the program myself. As did Dr. Perkins. The tech who was fired was a scapegoat in my opinion. That was the only time I suspected Mr. Jenkins' actions."

"That unfortunate error nearly killed the Harper family pet and has become a PR nightmare. Have you talked to the FBI yet?"

"No sir," she replied. Locking eyes--she hoped this would convince this pompous, over-bearing jerk of her feigned truthfulness.

"You know they arrested me and questioned whether I was complicit in Mr. Jenkins' actions. I assured them and I assure you, what he did shocked me. Why would I sabotage my company, my dreams?"

"Can't think of any reason sir." She saw the wary look he gave her.

"Lisa, I would not." Tindal went to the side bar and poured himself a coffee and a shot of Brandy. "Would you care for coffee? Maybe something stronger?"

"No sir. Thank you."

"Relax. Have a seat."

She continued to stand. "Sir, was there some reason you summoned me?"

Tindal took a drink of the Brandy, then the coffee and walked back over to the edge of the upper terrace.

"Look at all this." He swept his arms around in an arch. "Believe it or not, I came from nothing. My mother was a live-in-nanny for a wealthy merchant in Charleston. Never knew my father. And now I'm living the American dream. How about you Lisa, did your family have a comfortable life?"

"They got by. I had scholarships. Took out loans. They couldn't afford college for me."

Tindal turned and studied her. Her seemingly haughty attitude bothered him. He was about to offer her the opportunity of a lifetime. Was it a mistake?

"You asked why I summoned you. Is it possible you have backup specs and plans for The Hive and the Bumblebees?"

You know we do. "If I may sir, why do you ask? You should know DoD has requested our set." Lisa had received a memo from DARPA, asking her if she wished to continue her work. When she answered in the affirmative, they informed her the work would be performed under their direction. Tindal was not to know.

"Sir, DARPA has issued a cease-and-desist order regarding The Hive. They copied you with the order. Did you not see it?"

Tindal was beginning to wonder. Perhaps he should have second thoughts about Lisa. She was a regular girl scout. Then again, maybe naivety was what he needed. He could hire another person to do the off-the-books necessities.

"My attorneys will be looking into this. I need to know if you'll be staying with Tindal Industries. I hold the patent. I expect to have The Hive back in production shortly. I want you and your team to stay with me. You will be rewarded for your work. I am offering you Jenkins' COO position on an interim basis. I hope you will accept."

Lisa had not expected this. This would give her greater access. McDab and Poponovich would think they struck gold. Seem reluctant, her inner voice cautioned.

"I don't know sir. I'm a scientist. I don't know anything about being an operations officer."

"You're intelligent. I'm willing to bet you can learn to do what it takes. Mostly I need you to continue with what you've been doing. Tindal Industries must produce products for the military and our private companies' future needs, make the existing ones better. Our government is determined that we do not lose the tech advantage to the Russians and the Chinamen. Our contributions, these products will help insure this. The COO is my go between. My technical mouthpiece. You are well-suited to lead our efforts. The paperwork won't be much more than what you already do. Just give it a try, see how it goes."

"And if I decide it's not for me?"

"You continue as before. And you get to keep the salary, stock options and performance bonuses."

"This is sudden. I'm not certain how I could even begin."

"Start by putting together a package for my attorneys. We need DARPA to back off."

"Also, I have offered a million-dollar reward for the capture and return of Jenkins and the source codes he stole. When this is announced, there will be a slew of people, mostly cranks, calling hoping to collect. I need a dedicated hotline set up and manned twenty-four seven."

"Tindal Industries' government security contract requires that I purchase or lease the Harper land. That means we need the land so The Hive and other future projects can become reality. You want this, don't you?" He didn't wait for a reply. "I need you to find a way to smooth things over with the Harper man. Jenkins tried the heavy hand approach--without my knowledge. I want you to use your best judgement to persuade him to come to a mutually beneficial agreement." He paused for a response. None. Hm?

"His weakness is his estranged wife and his current girlfriend, the news woman Ariel Gaspard. Hire an investigator to help you find a way to bring him to the table. Also, his wife needs to be convinced to cooperate. Her father is an old associate and friend of mine—this could be beneficial for everyone."

Tindal saw her eyes drift.

"You were in the military, Air National Guard, correct?"

"Yes sir. I served six years. Did a tour in Iraq."

"A junior officer knows how to do what it takes to accomplish the objective--prepare and execute, use team-work and lead by example. That is why I chose you. Can I count on you?" She hesitated, briefly closed her eyes, seemed to reach a conclusion, finally, she seemed to struggle to give a less-than-reassuring reply.

"Yes sir. I'll do my best."

'What is wrong with the woman?' Tindal thought. 'Her attitude did not reflect the enthusiasm he hoped for. Had the feds put the fear of God to her?'

Lisa was thinking she needed to get away from Tindal. Some military brass was due to arrive this morning. Colonel Hunter had contacted her. He was sending some personnel to talk with her in private, away from Tindal he said.

Dr. Perkins, who resigned after Jenkins fled, was DARPA's project lead man in charge of the NM0099 Neural Implant and The Hive approval team. A congressional oversight committee wanted counter measures developed for the implant and The Hive, a way to shut them down, an on-off-switch Leonard laughingly said. She was reminded of her top security clearance, forbidding her from discussing this with anyone, including and especially her boss Thurmond Tindal. Apparently, Tindal did not know this. Or did he? He was giving her too much scrutiny. She had to be careful.

"Forgive me sir, I should be getting back. The tech staff will be wondering why you summoned me. I need to put their concerns at ease--keep them working."

"Use Jenkins' old office. It is yours now. There is an elevator that comes up to my office. Think about my offer—I hope you and I can continue our work together."

Tindal was not satisfied. He needed a man to keep an eye on her. Someone who had worked with him and was not afraid to get his hands dirty. Colonel Hunter would be a good candidate. Except the Colonel had not liked how Tindal coerced him to approve The Hive. Had this Jenkins' fiasco caused the Colonel concern for his future with DARPA? Doubtful he would get the star he so coveted. Tindal still had a copy of the videos used as persuasion for the DARPA approval. Money and potential scandal should be incentive enough to bring him on board--the carrot and the stick approach. He would need to be contrite, sound desperate and plead. Something he was not good at doing. He did, would do so, with the FBI; he could do this with the Colonel also. Screw the Colonel. Screw Jenkins. Screw Harper. Screw them all. He was better at this game than all of them.

Mark Poponovich was wary. The Gonzalez brothers, David and Arturo, had been forced to flee back across the border to Juarez. He should have fled with them. Jenkins had screwed everyone. As the financial planner for the cartel to acquire The Hive with laundered funds in conjunction with Jenkins, the failure had caused Mark to be looked at in a whole new way by the cartel. The questions increasingly became accusatory.

His CIA Section Chief, General McDab, wanted to pull him out. His career would have ended with a fizz instead of the bang he wished. Over twenty years undercover brought him to this point. He wanted to bring down the Juarez Cartel. Jenkins was to be the way to do this. He needed to continue the charade. The other agencies were all in.

Lo and behold, Homeland was sending his old buddy Jake Harper and the Alvarez man as part of their team. He would have to keep his eye on them. He liked the Harper man, despite their last encounter. Funny how their paths kept crossing—Cuba, the Carolinas, and now wherever the search for Jenkins would lead him and his team. There were other questions about the cartel's zip files which never showed up in the evidence that was confiscated. What had Jake and TJ done with them?

Mark wondered what kind of woman would be next for the Harper man. Had some nice ones in Cuba: Amy, Blakely, then there was his estranged wife, she too had been a looker, and now this newswoman. Hm? Maybe there was a way to use the news woman to keep tabs on him. Would make some interesting moments if nothing else. She certainly made watching entertaining. Could it be she knew something about the files? He had nothing on his plate for today. Maybe he should pay her a visit.

CHAPTER
3

Homeland Station, Rock Hill, SC
Jake and TJ

The farm chores were taken care of. Maybe for the last time by him, Jake thought. He hoped not. Homeland was paying him so he could pay his neighbor to take care of the place while he was gone. The neighbor suspected his story about travelling to be fabricated—he had to wonder how Jake's well-publicized arrest warrant and manhunt suddenly seemed to go away, as did most people in the area. He didn't ask, Jake didn't volunteer to explain.

Jake stopped off to see how Dusty was doing. Doc Hunter said leaving Maisy there would probably be therapeutic for Dusty's continued recovery. Seeing Dusty was difficult. He lay wrapped like a mummy, still slightly sedated. He seemed to know when Jake was there, his closed eyes would flutter when he called his name. Jake wondered if he would ever be able to live a normal life. Many wounded human and animal vets he had known never seemed to become the same, physically, or mentally.

Jake was one of them. Hardy had promised there was a way to heal his painful, stiff neck using gene therapy. He had read up on it. Seemed promising, but there were also reports of turning the wrong bio-sequence off allowed cancer cells to grow. He was allowing himself to once more be a test animal, and someone else was profiting from the experiment, at his expense. 'Screw me once shame on you, screw me twice shame on me'--a cliché--like all clichés, there was some truth in it.

The Homeland clinic was thirty minutes from Doc Hunter's Veterinarian Clinic, give or take, depending on the traffic. When Jake first moved to the farm, he could drive the route in less than twenty minutes and rarely encounter more than a handful of other vehicles. Progress—people in a hurry going nowhere fast. No time for viewing the disappearing beauty of the countryside. Perhaps he was the anachronism.

He wondered about Ariel. Did she still appreciate the country, or would she become like his exes, want a more social life?

He and Ariel had rushed into their newfound passion as though they were stranded on a deserted island. From experience, Jake knew physical ardor was up against the mundane everyday habits and the emotions created by life's curveballs. Sooner or later, you have to get real. What was real for Ariel? Jake wasn't sure what was real for himself anymore. The neuro-implant, how would that change reality for him? Would he ever be able to tell Ariel? What would she think? Secrets could kill a relationship. Jake wasn't sure what relationships with anyone would be from now on.

Wonder what TJ thinks about all this? Fortunately, he had a soulmate. In TJ's case, soulmate had always been a reality. Deane and TJ were as close to having the perfect relationship as any couple he had ever known. She knew TJ had work secrets and that didn't appear to bother her. His career and long absences had not seemed to affect their relationship. He was a lucky man and knew it.

'Damn right I know it bro,' TJ 's device's meme shocked Jake. 'How 'bout getting your mind out of the gutter and your ass in gear. I'm outside the clinic waiting.'

TJ was at the end of the lot. Jake saw him looking his way.

'Really? Maybe you are trainable after all. Deane has probably gotten tired of the same ole same old you. If you need some pointers, let me know.'

'You do realize Deane knows a good thing when she sees it.'

'Is that why her eyes light up every time she sees me?' Jake memed.

They both laughed.

Jake pulled up next to TJ's truck. When he got out, TJ started walking toward the entrance of the nondescript office/warehouse building without waiting for Jake.

"Come on Romeo," TJ said, no longer meming. "Hardy been waiting. That damn sore neck shit getting tiresome to hear, maybe you should get the treatment. Oh, that's right, then you have to find something else as an excuse."

"Excuse for what?"

"Being a Chickin Little complainer."

"Nothing like catching shit first thing in the morning from mucho macho ghetto man, mister serious, kill 'em all, let God sort 'em out, lone wolf sniper dude, now a company man, gone all social, moved uptown kiss-asser, who's scared of water. Screw you. Chicken Little? Kiss my ass."

"Yep. That be me. Better watch out cracker man—might end up working for this darkie's ass. Been gittin' my water wings, I can now swim Chickin Little Crackerman."

"Yeah and Superman survived by killing himself."

They clasped and bro hugged.

"You lookin' like the cat that caught a mouse. Guess you finally got lucky."

The elevator took them down to the lowest level. Before Jake could snap off a reply, the doors opened, Dr. Perkins' lanky, balding, television-doctor-looking figure stood there, a stern look on his face, creased by a forced smile. Hardy stood off in a corner, he was dressed like the preppy Homeland company-man, bureaucrat he was—his face grim, like a card player not sure if he had the winning hand.

Hardy spoke up, "Jake, TJ, Dr. Perkins and I have been patiently waiting. He's here to answer any concerns regarding the NM0099 you might have."

Jake responded. "Is that what this thing is called?"

He followed TJ into the stark white room. The only furniture was a stainless-steel table and six computer-print-formed plastic chairs. Hardy nodded to the table and Jake and TJ sat on opposite sides. Hardy remained standing at one end and Dr. Perkins moved to the other end.

"Where is the spotlight? Don't you want to turn off the other lights to add more drama? Reminds me of the X-Files. Just call me Mueller," Jake retorted.

The smile slipped off the doctor's face, Hardy frowned, TJ shook his head. And Jake shrugged.

"Jake, I don't have much time and patience for nonsense. For some reason you failed to listen when the NM0099 was explained to you prior to the implanting. Dr. Perkins is here to rehash the info. You seem to have a problem with privacy issues. Listen to him, ask what you need to allay your fears. We need to move on to the briefing for the impending mission."

Dr. Perkins jumped right in.

"NM0099 is the nomenclature for the neuro implant you received. The device is what Jung would call the collective unconscious. NM0099 is more than that, and less. It is limited to each recipient's available information. The NM0099 takes your information and draws conclusions based upon all information available within the realms of human physiology, psychology, even mythology, the collective unconsciousness of humanity, based partially on DNA and part mystical for lack of a better term."

He paused. Jake sat with his best poker face wondering what in the hell he was trying to say. TJ seemed to remain bemused. Hardy not so much.

"NM0099's algorithms are written to learn each individual's thoughts and interpret its relevance. In other words, it learns who you are, your habits, your normal if you will. It knows when not to communicate. Non-pertinent information, thoughts, bio-signals are kept private. You are training it as you use it—think of it as an "Alexis" of the mind."

"Alexis on steroids is what you are describing. So, if I heard you correctly, this AI device is now physically part of me and knows when I want it to shut up or shut down?"

"That is one way of thinking—in actuality, the NM0099 is an IA, intelligence augmentation device that links you to the universal web. It is often referenced as Intelligence Advanced Technology, thus IA. You can receive information to your inquiries, but you are not some god who knows everything. This device was developed by DARPA as a tool for military intelligence and specialized combat personnel to give them a leg up on the enemy."

"But this IA, AI, whatever, knows most everything about me—open book—hackable open book is that not so?"

Hardy put his hands down noisily on the table. Jake looked from the concerned face of the doctor to TJ's grim stare to Hardy.

"That will be all for now Doctor. Thank you."

Doctor Perkins abruptly turned, went to the elevator, and disappeared.

"What about answering questions?" Jake asked as the elevator door closed.

"Anything is hackable Jake, Hardy said. "You think there is anything out there about you, that a hacker can't access. Think again. The government has known about you even before you joined the Army. Your paranoia about this implant is unreasonable. Get over it."

"What about the leg up on the enemy the good Doctor said this device provides. If it is hackable, how is it a leg up?"

"No one knows about us. There are very few people who know you, and TJ and I have this. Since Major Jenkins has the device, there is a reasonable expectation that the device's existence may be known. The Russians claim to have so-called "super spies", capable of using mental powers to hack into our computers, communicating mentally with one another. The Chinese could be Jenkins' customer. Given their tech superiority it's just a matter of time before they learn about it, then improve upon the technology. Could be Iranians,

Saudis, any number of enemies, or, from what we know, any number of our so-called allies. No one knows if any of them has acquired the implant and plan to use it against us. It's just another tool in a country's modern-day arsenal. As of now, we *are* the advantage."

"Meaning, once more I'm a guinea pig and I'm stuck with this thing. Seems to me this is another way for Big Brother to own me. What if I want to remove it, is that possible?"

"Possible? Perhaps. Not many qualified to perform the operation, be very expensive, most likely fatal."

"What a pal. I don't recall you mentioning that before I was coerced into doing this."

"Look at this as an opportunity to do your job better—catch those who would destroy what we believe in and took an oath to protect. I chose you two because I knew you shared these values. Plus, you have a personal grudge against the man we seek. I know you value your independence and privacy. I hate to burst your balloon--as I said, you never had complete privacy, those days were gone before you were born. Not only that, you and TJ have become personal enemies for some powerful groups who will be looking for revenge."

"You should take that dog and pony show on the road. Perhaps you should consider hosting a reality show. You could call it "Screwing Friends For Fun.""

"My next job maybe. Moving on. Our mission is to make sure none of our tech ends up in the wrong hands. To that end we need to locate Jenkins, recover The Hive source codes, blueprint, specs, and military satellite location info, and not least, the NM0099 that Jenkins also possesses. At the same time, we need to find and stop any Russian technology, including the amphibious UAV we failed to capture, along with any other threatening technology available for sale--our mission includes preventing any of these from getting into the wrong hands."

"And how are we supposed to deal with Jenkins, behead him?"

Hardy looked Jake in the eye. "If necessary," He stated matter-of-factly. "Less drastic means would be preferred. You will have defensive weapons at your disposal, in addition to some technologically upgraded weaponry connected via the implant. You will receive smart weapon training at Fort Hood—it will be on you in this training to figure out ways to utilize the implant defensively regarding these weapons--the instructor knows nothing about the implant—make sure it remains that way. We will leave out early, day after tomorrow. Your itinerary will be made available to you--use the implant to access it. You are not to tell anyone anything concerning your itinerary or the mission. Jake your news lady friend concerns me in several ways. You are still married, and you know the risks. Getting away is what you need."

"Also, Jake when we questioned your estranged wife, she said Jenkins left in the company of four men. Why would they have left your wife behind?"

"Estranged, soon to be ex-wife or you plan to be a Mormon?" TJ quiped.

"Good one TJ, hadn't thought of that." He turned back to look at Hardy. "I've wondered about that myself. She and I haven't talked since I left the clinic. She made it clear she wanted nothing more to do with me."

"What about the Gonzalez brothers?" TJ asked. "Heard anything? My SWAT commander he put me on leave, says he's not very happy with the situation, refuses to tell me what there is he knows."

"From what I have been able to find out, they have gone dark. Could be they are dead. David seemed to be at death's door from the diabetic coma, possibly has other health issues. And the cartel boss can't be overly joyed at their failure to obtain The Hive—failures are not well-treated in their world.

TJ started to ask Hardy why the Gonzalez brothers were let go—no trial—no home in Supermax—not taken off the board? His device had failed to find out.

"What about Mark Poponovich? Jake asked before TJ could ask.

"Nothing. The CIA's counterintelligence is not being cooperative. Hopefully, he hasn't gone rogue. He could be another one on a list of operatives, domestic and foreign, out there looking for, even working with Jenkins."

Hardy's supervisor told him to not worry about Poponovich and crew—"let it be," were her words.

He was surprised Jake didn't ask about Thomas Devereaux, Blakely Carmichael, Toby Tobolokov, James Dean and the others. He didn't need or wish to discuss them with Jake or TJ at this time. Better they didn't know what he knew, they would most likely find out soon enough. Special Agent Swanson, now retired, had said he had not shared the info with TJ. Hardy hoped it stayed unknown. With the implant, this was not a given.

"Gentlemen I have other duties I need to tend to. I will see you day after tomorrow."

They got in the elevator together. Hardy went to his Suburban and drove out of the lot headed toward Charlotte. Jake and TJ got in their trucks. They decided to catch lunch at the newly reopened Rock Hill City Grill.

They took a seat in the far corner away from the glass where the waitress initially attempted to seat them. Two tables spaced out from theirs and nearest them had been pulled together by a group of students, Jake guessed they attended Winthrop University. They acted, looked, and sounded like typical college kids which suited Jake fine. They were all into their own little protected world, engrossed by their laptops and cell phones—their fingers gliding over keys-- tuned in, turned on—the death of normal, physical social skills. Not realizing two infonauts were seated next to them. Infonauts--where did that come from?

On the drive over Jake tried to get in touch with Ariel. He reached an answering service instead. The robot-like woman said Ariel left on an assignment, asked if he wanted to leave a message. Jake replied he would call back. He tried her cell—went straight to voicemail. He didn't leave a message. She should see his missed call.

He had been attempting to stay offline with his thoughts and wasn't sure if he had been successful. After the waitress took their order, he asked TJ if he had been listening in on him on the way to the grill.

"Didn't know that what you want bro."

"Yes or no?"

"No. You trying to reach me? Was talking to Deane, let her know the scheduled departure."

"You seem to be at ease with this whole damn thing. Doesn't it bother you that we're putting ourselves out there—I mean totally out there?"

"Look around bro. These kids and most people they putting themselves out there—privacy cease to exist back when we sniffing little girl bicycle seats."

"Girl's bicycle seats? You did that?"

"Borrowed that from you." TJ gave his big *got-you* grin. "The Doc he right- - withstanding that collective conscience Jung shit--this where the world going. We ain't the first. Seen lot of technological shit come down the pipe since I came of age, joined the Army and police. This just another one of those things. If it give me a leg up on the bad guys, I'm all for it. Just another tech weapon, the way I see it. Get with it Chickin Little."

"You always were more gung-ho than me. I guess when I look around, I see Big Brother, you see kindly ole Uncle Sam."

"Never bite the hand that feed you my mama always say. I am where I am because of good ole Uncle Sam. We had food on our table because my father served, then died in Nam. If I die, Deane she have the same."

"I get that. What I don't get is, why me? You, okay, maybe. But me? If you were an employer and you had hundreds, thousands, millions of people, employees, soldiers, whatever, that you could pick and choose from—why me? I'm a medically discharged veteran, a subsistence farmer and renovator who is virtually technologically challenged with limited experience in this kind of cat and mouse adventure. Why me? This is what I keep asking myself. Something doesn't add up." Jake sat back shaking his head.

Before TJ could respond their food came—two plates of chopped beef brisket, slaw, and a plate with a mixture of fried okra, French fries, hush puppies and onion rings. They had reordered two beers and she had brought them water and failed to bring their beers. She apologized and hurried off to get them. Jake doused his food with hot sauce—he always ate everything with the sauce. They dug into the food without further talk. Both thinking about Jake's question.

Once they finished and were out by Jake's truck, TJ said, "Don't know the answer to your question. Do know I'm glad it's you has my back. Even though you a pain in the ass most of the time, wouldn't want anyone else."

"Does this mean you'll be sending me flowers? I prefer chocolate."

A non-TJ sounding chuckle disrupted Jake's thoughts. 'What the…'

'Don't go getting bitchy with me, listen to Hardy.'

Jake was about to protest but Hardy interrupted.

Hardy: 'I don't know why you doubt your abilities or question my choice. We are here because I, more than you two, failed to stop Jenkins. This was and is my op, I own the failure. TJ tried to tell me, and I acted too late. Some of that was you two's fault. Jake, you and TJ had me waste time and resources looking for you, to save your asses. Jake, you should have come to me, rather than going after Jenkins on your own.'

'TJ is right to trust you. I chose you because you alluded capture and because I owed you one from our little Cuban adventure, where you did a commendable job with little training or direction. I trust you to cover my back as does TJ. You two are part of our team and I'm glad to have you with me.'

'Several issues we need to deal with: there is still the question of your wife Elena's involvement; Jenkins disappeared into Mexico and all our sources find no concrete answers to his location—one credible source says he left Mexico, went to Venezuela and is now in Cuba. Your girlfriend, the newswoman, is at this time. reported meeting with a man named Paul Pierre Alperts, an agent of a mercenary group called DICE. All these Issues are connected to you, directly or indirectly. You need to help us get some answers. This is vital for our mission.'

'Damn. How do you know Ariel is meeting with this Alperts man? Are ya'll spying on her too? You're beginning to really piss me off.'

'Hold on Jake. Homeland has nothing to do with this. We received an inquiry because of your past escapade and the op--that's my guess. I have not been able to confirm the source. If it's true, you need to find out what this is all about. DICE is a renegade organization that makes Blackwater look like Boy Scouts and this Alperts dude is one of the worst.'

'You know Hardy, you're beginning to make me think you're like every other upper echelon officer, political bureaucratic hacks, glory boys, sending others out to do your dirty work, then come riding in to take credit.'

'I've been right there with you Jake. And like it or not, I take responsibility and blame for my screwups. As well as yours.'

'Yeah, well the way I see it, you got me into this shit from the git go, and here I am again.'

TJ looked at Jake with a lopsided grin and shook his head.

Hardy was using his implant to watch via Jake's and TJ's devices. He didn't need this crap. He had to keep the op on track. He moved on past Jake's rant.

'TJ, you need to try to find out what happened to the Gonzalez brothers. Be nice to know if they're still alive and if the Juarez Cartel has Jenkins. Check with the gangs in Miami, maybe their rivals know something. You two better get someone to keep an eye on your families. The cartel will want their revenge on you and Jake.'

'Whatever happened with Double D Diego and Renaldo? Any follow up on the info Deane obtained?' TJ asked.

'As you know, the FBI took them during the shutdown. My guess, they ended up with the CIA in some max, perhaps Gitmo. I requested their file, received nada. Our beloved Secretary gave me the runaround. The former President may or may not have been briefed. Seems his obsession with the wall was made HSI's top priority. Our mission could prove the border wall is of little importance to the cartels. That would provide political fodder on both sides of the aisle--become election campaign slogans. Most in congress have not been told about this technology—have no idea what it means for national security. These are the ones that want to put a lid on it, before it comes to light—they are inclined to refuse funding. The other agencies would like nothing better. We...'

Jake and TJ thought they had lost him somehow—bad connection, interrupted service.

'Gotta go. See you two morning after next.' The connection broke again.

CHAPTER
4

University of South Carolina
Alperts [DICE operative] and Ariel

"**A**nd I should hire your little bunch of merry men to find Jenkins. Why, when Homeland Security, the NSA, CIA, and every other government agency, with arguably the most sophisticated resources at their disposal are doing so for free? Not to mention I have placed a million-dollar bounty for the retrieval of the stolen information's return and for him—dead or alive—which you are more than welcome to collect if you are successful."

Thurmond Tindal was standing behind his ornate mahogany desk wondering why he was wasting his time talking to this frog from across the pond whose face looked like it had been pinched by forceps at birth and his Adams Apple kept bobbing up and down as he spoke.

"Bollocks. Those bloody nitwicks couldn't find their arse with a map and a guide. They have too many rules and protocols--bureaucrats watching and directing their every move. Your million dollars will bloody well remain safe unless you hire someone who knows how this kind of operation must be done. We operate quickly and discretely, thus the name, Discrete Intelligence Contracting Exigencies, DICE, if you would. We are not beholden to any government—we produce results while others do procedures. Their kind is the reason Osama bin Laden stayed alive so long."

"Nevertheless, the SEALs got him."

"Righto. Had it been us, he would have been taken care of a lot sooner. You want your problem taken care of fast—we deliver."

Tindal needed someone to make sure he was the sole possessor of his information. If anyone profited it should be him and him alone. He didn't care what happened to Jenkins. Dead would suit his legal situation better. He needed someone to do his dirty work for him. Also, the Harper man, his sidekick and the news bitch need to be made to go away--but two million.

"Tell you what, I have several minor problems that need to be handled that would have to be included in any deal that cost me two million. They are related to this problem and need to be handled very discreetly."

"That is what we do—whatever has to be done, we can make it happen without anyone being the wiser."

Alperts knew, heard, and saw all he needed to know about this self-absorbed, Jew hater, former intelligence piece of wasted breath, Colonel Tindal, and his career connections with the man Jenkins, his attempts at having the Russian do the Harper man, and the failures. Tindal was an easy score, the kind used to having others do what had to be done, making sure he covered his arse, leaving others to take the blame. There would be no shame in making him pay. And pay he bloody well would, one way or another.

"I take it you are agreeing to include the extras?"

"Do you believe in God?"

Tindal didn't know where this was going. Was he a religious fanatic, a hater of Christians, as well as Muslims? Could he trust him?

"I don't see what my religion or my beliefs have to do with this. You came to me. I'm offering you a huge sum of money. All I want to make sure of is whether you're willing to do what I'm paying you for."

"Right you are," Alperts replied, thinking he had him, let him think on who he was dealing with.

"As long as they are not current clients and do not require unpaid-for collateral damage."

"The first case is highly unlikely, the second is outside my control, that's on you."

Good, the Colonel did not suspect his prior arrangements. Doesn't hurt to ask for payment for extras--collateral damage rarely created a problem for his organization.

"Then we shall be in agreement. We require a thirty percent retainer wired to our account and you tell me who or what is the problem, and we shall make it go away."

"Twenty-Five percent. A half million should be more than adequate."

Paul Alperts was pleased, another payment for making problems go away—two birds with the same proverbial stone, and the potential of an additional million-dollar bonus. Good thing he had done his homework prior to meeting with both. Amazing what a group of dedicated intelligence operatives could uncover about any person in this modern connected world. He had learned about the Harper and Alvarez men and their new employment as Homeland Security agents tasked with locating Jenkins. He knew about the newswoman and her rekindled relation with the Harper man. What was surprising, pleasantly surprising, was what was discovered about their earlier connection and her life overseas. This gave him leverage. In a bloody short time, he would put that leverage into action.

Ariel told the front desk to hold her calls. She went in to see the Station General Manager Susan, (Suzie) McDermot, concerning her future employment. She had expected an offer of a new position, perhaps in management, and a substantial raise, at least a willingness to match any other offers. What she didn't expect was to be accused of trying to undermine Suzie--getting her fired in hopes of taking her job. No matter what she said, Suzie refused to listen. Ariel tried to find out who or what made her think this. To no avail. Instead of a promotion she was reassigned to field reporting while the allegations were being investigated. Suzie told Ariel she would not give her any recommendations and would ruin her if the accusations were found to have merit. Ariel considered resigning but decided to do nothing until she had a chance to talk to an attorney.

Sitting at her desk, she felt miserable. How could this have happened? She took out her cell phone and looked up attorneys, then thought what good would that do. The station was part of a network, any lawyer she hired would be up against a major legal team. It could cost a fortune. She would be out of a job with no way to afford the fight. She saw two missed calls. One was Jake, he had not left a message. She wanted to have him hold her, tell her everything would be okay. She wanted to call, but she didn't want to talk about this on the phone.

The other caller had left a message. A man, foreign, British from the sound of it, told her he could make her personal legal problems go away. *What personal legal problems? How could he know?*

He told her he would be at the Starbucks in the Thomas Cooper Library of The University of South Carolina at one if she was interested.

What was going on? Her first thought was to call Jake. He would be busy getting briefed, and she feared what he might do; the police--highly unlikely they would do anything. She thought of asking another reporter, but there was no one she trusted well enough to hear what could be personal, or incriminating information. Incriminating? She had done nothing wrong, why did that word pop into her mind? Her inner voice said to ignore the call. But Suzie had accused her and threatened her career—what if this person knew something that could clear her name. Could this be the person who was attempting to frame her? She couldn't ignore this. The Starbucks would have other people-- only a deranged person would do anything with witnesses. Lots of crazy people out there. She had met her share, and, like everyone else, had borne witness to many other crazoids daily.

When she entered the Starbucks, she saw many of the USC students in groups at the individual cubbyholes created by open shelves with volumes of books. There were some older people, some in casual attire, probably professors, others in suits and ties—more than likely, administrators and businesspeople. No one seemed out of place or paying much attention to her—guess most of them didn't watch her newscasts. She walked through, turned, and started back toward the end she came through. A tall lanky man with a prominent nose and pinched face dressed like a professor in sockless loafers, Khaki cargo pants and a garnet and black knit shirt with USC emblazoned on it, stepped out from behind a column and approached her like he knew her.

"Mrs. Gaspard. Glad you could join me." He handed her a cup.

Black with a taste of honey. How could he know?

"Shall we be seated?"

"Who are you? How is it you know about me? I don't believe, no, I know we've never met. I know and remember faces."

"You may call me Paul. If you will, have a seat, and I will explain. I promise you will not be disappointed deary."

Ariel hesitated. She stared into his eyes. Nothing. No sign of emotion. A cop or bureaucrat perhaps. She chose a table where they could be seen by the people behind the counter and anyone who was waiting in line. He pulled her chair out. After she was seated, he took the chair across from her.

"What is the nature of your business concerning me? And don't address me with a familiarity…"

"No need to be alarmed. I came here to talk to you about your situation. I may be able to help."

"What situation would that be? I'm sorry but you seem to know more about me than I feel comfortable with a stranger knowing, a foreign stranger no less.

Who are you, what is your business and why have you been snooping into my affairs?"

Alperts ignored her demand. "I know a great deal about you. Never ceases to amaze what's out there about anyone. That is if you know how to look and have the resources to do so. I'm sure you are well aware of this. What I learned about you made me curious. I wanted to see you, meet the person to get some answers to questions that the information raised. The same as you would. Think of this as an interview."

"An interview? For what?"

"I wanted to know what would make a mother forsake her child." A shocked look came onto her face, before she could respond, he continued. "I was an orphan. My parents were French and Polish of Jewish descent. I was raised in Israel on a Kibbutz. Amazing what you can find on an ancestral DNA search. What I didn't find were my parents or how I ended up an orphan in Israel. So, you see when I discovered you had forsaken your daughter, I became curious. I wanted to meet you, ask you, maybe get some insight into my own question."

"You're mistaken, I never had a child. If you came here hoping to ruin my life with this fabrication, you have made a big mistake, a slanderous one—screw you."

Ariel stood to leave. Alperts pulled out an IPad Mini and held it up so she could see the screen. On it a live video showed a young female strolling through a square, lined on each side by tree-shaded cobblestone sidewalks in front of shops with signs whose titles displayed were written in French. Ariel stood frozen watching as Alperts made the image zoom in. The young woman stopped in front of an outdoor café at a table occupied by a dark-skinned young man, either Mediterranean or Middle Eastern descent, A carafe of clear liquid was on the table in front of him with a glass that dripped condensation. He took a drink and motioned for the woman to sit. The image zoomed in closer to the woman who looked familiar. Ariel knew she had never met the woman. Her breath caught in her throat, she almost gasped, she struggled to remain calm—the young woman resembled pictures of herself at that early age. The age when she had lived outside London with her mother's sister and family, sent there by her father when they discovered her pregnancy. She was given little choice: have an abortion or have the baby and give it up for adoption. She never saw the baby and, despite later efforts, never was able to find out what happened to the child. Not knowing left a big hole in her heart. Could this be her daughter, hers, and Jake's daughter?

The young woman stood her ground behind the wrought-iron seat facing the man, her face twisted in anger. The man came into view. He wore a cap and designer sunglasses. A snide smirk was plastered on his handsome face. He sat calmly, occasionally taking a drink, his lips moving. She was animated, gesticulating, struggling with her emotions—fear and anger written upon her face.

Ariel took the proffered mini and sat back down. Alperts reached across and pulled it from her fingers.

"What do you want?" Ariel tried to keep her voice under control.

"In due time. Amazing resemblance wouldn't you agree? Must make you regret your decision."

"Wasn't given a choice. Why are you showing me this? Why are you trying to ruin my career? What are you up to? If it's blackmail, I don't have much of value."

Ariel reached down and pulled her bag into the chair closer to him. Inside was her phone, a microphone attached, set on record, she hoped it had picked up the earlier conversation.

Alperts sat back. "You haven't touched your coffee. Would you rather have something different? Tea, juice, water, something to eat perhaps?"

"Can you get to the point. What do you want from me?"

"Ironic isn't it. You and this young lady both married Spanish Aristocracy, yours mainland, hers Cuban. Your marriage ended in divorce, seems hers is headed that direction. For her this will be more devastating. I'm sure you can understand. You see she has a son and this man of means is going to take the young boy with him and his parents on a trip to Mexico, then on to Cuba. That is why your daughter is so angry. She is helpless to stop him."

Ariel couldn't keep the shock off her face. Could this be her daughter? That meant she was a grandmother—Jake was a grandfather. Ariel took a big drink of the coffee. The hot liquid almost choked her. Ariel wanted to reach across and slap the smug look from this man's ugly face. What was going on here? The problem with her job seemed less important—that poor woman—possibly her daughter—she wished she could reach through that phone to help her.

"Please tell me why you're doing this?"

"Please. That's more like it. The young lady's name is Elizabeth. Her husband has a long titular name, he goes by Pablo. Their child's name is Gabriel. Oh, look she threw her drink in his face." He held the phone so Ariel could see.

The man he called Pablo stood from the table, took his napkin, wiped his face and shirt in a vain attempt to dry it. He said something to the woman then stormed off. The woman, he called Elizabeth, sat down heavily, tears ran down her cheeks. Ariel felt her pain as if it were her own.

"Have you not wondered about how we are viewing this tragedy? Perhaps you would like to hear your daughter's voice."

He took the mini and spoke rapidly in a language Ariel did not recognize, sounded like Hebrew. He handed her a mic-set, he slipped the audio portion of the mic-set onto his ears and held the phone where she could see.

Ariel hesitated before putting the other proffered set on, only doing so, when she heard the man on the other end say in a foreign accent to this woman that her mother wished to speak with her.

Elizabeth hesitated then slowly reached for the other man's mini, the man held it back from her hand. It was on Facetime and Ariel saw the shocked look on her supposed-daughter's face when she saw Ariel.

"That is not my mother. My parents are in Zurich. Who is she? Who are you?"

Alperts spoke up, "Elizabeth take a good look at this woman. She is your biological mother. Like looking at an older version of yourself, is it not?"

Elizabeth said, "Did Pablo put you up to this? If you don't leave me alone, I will call the police." She tried to stand. The man's hand appeared on her shoulder.

Ariel heard him tell her if she wanted to see her son Gabriel again, she would remain seated and do as she was told.

Alperts nodded to Ariel.

"Elizabeth, that is your name, so I was told. I had nothing to do with this. I don't know you and you don't know me. I have no idea what these men are up to. They say you are my daughter. I cannot say that I know that to be true."

Alperts spoke up, "This can be verified by a DNA test. The people you know as your parents, ask them if they adopted you from St. Agnes School for Unwed Mothers in Scotland."

"I have never been there," Ariel said, "if that is your proof, I know that is not true."

"That is where the infant, you Elizabeth, was taken, after you Ariel gave birth," Alperts replied. "If you both demand more than the obvious, you may elect to have the DNA test as confirmation. Now that you both have met, we need you to understand your position. If you cooperate with what we propose, you can have a grand family reunion. Otherwise, this will be as far as either of you will go, and neither of you shall see Gabriel, you Elizabeth again and for you Ariel, well you will never have the opportunity for a first time. My comrade will explain to Elizabeth what we expect, and I will do the same for Ariel. Ciao"

He shut the mini off and put it back in the pocket of his cargo pants.

Ariel never ceased to wonder at how much cruelty there was in the world. To use, abuse or kill a child always struck her as the lowest form of life. She had witnessed children with bombs strapped to them, children whose parents chained, starved, and beat them to death--their own flesh and blood. Parents who sexually abused or allowed others to abuse their child, selling their body and robbing them of their souls. Ariel did not want to believe in capital punishment, but, after witnessing such evil, she had no problem thinking these animals did not deserve to stay above ground. At this moment if she had the power, she would not hesitate to do what she had to do to keep this man from what she felt was a threat to her, the woman Elizabeth and the infant Gabriel. But all she had was pepper spray. That would not stop him, possibly insure the worst.

"I believe you are cruel and capable of doing diabolical acts that shame the human race."

Alperts smiled. "So quick to judge. What happened to objectivity?'

"You have threatened me and what you claim are my family, that takes away objectivity. What is it you want from me to make the threat go away?"

"A mother who abandons her child has no right taking the high ground. If not for me, you would never have had the opportunity to meet your offspring. I am the sole person who can make this happen. If I were evil, as you have stated, I would have made you disappear as I was instructed to do."

Ariel was taken back. She had done some hard-hitting investigative reporting during her time as a journalist. There had been numerous threats— never any attempts--that she was aware of—until now.

"Who hired you?"

"My organization prides itself for our discretion. When we accept a contract, we use all haste to fulfill the terms. Often the terms are specific. In your case, we were instructed to make you disappear."

Ariel watched his Adam's Apple bob up and down as if some small animal was trying to escape. Normally when listening to someone she would watch their eyes or their lips if they spoke softly as he was doing. She glanced around. No one was there she could turn to.

"While doing my homework, I discovered there were many options regarding your case, one of which included your abandoned child and her child. I learned your family unit was being threatened. To fulfill other terms of the contract, this turn of events offered me an opportunity. In my line of work, opportunities often have to be created, rarely are they fortuitous. Now that I have met you, I decided your contract terms can be fulfilled, and we could help your family problem go away at the same time. Mercifully humanitarian, don't you agree?"

"Not sure you fit into the saintly category."

"Righto."

He smiled at her. "Mrs. Gaspard, I appreciate your attempt at humor. Nevertheless, I guess you are anxious to hear what part you must play in this production of mine. Very simple really. You will play an investigative journalist following the trail of your grandson's other grandparents."

"To what end? Are they fugitives, criminals, or, are you planning on doing them harm? If this requires me to break any laws or be complicit in any crime, you can forget about it."

"I am offering you the opportunity to help solve one of the great mysteries of our time and meet your grandson while doing so. Before you ask what mystery, I must tell you, you will have to wait for the answer. I am afraid this offer is the best one on the table, especially with regards to the alternative. I feel certain you would jump on this offer, as would any journalist, if you knew the subject of the mystery."

He looked at his gaudy watch. It looked like one Jake had, but never wore. Was this guy a soldier? One of those soldiers of fortune, a mercenary Ariel would bet. There was no doubt his threat was real. Jake was going to be leaving soon, she couldn't expect him to be able to protect her. There was no one else. There was her daughter and grandson, Jake's daughter, and grandson he knew nothing about, how could she explain this to him without destroying any chance at continuing their relationship. She couldn't keep this from him. But if she let anything happen to them, he would never forgive her—she could never forgive herself.

Alperts stood. "You will need to pack lightly, be sure to include two pairs of comfortable hiking boots and desert attire. Any other clothes you can purchase as needed. Bring your passport, other ID, including press credentials and cash, no credit cards. We will depart from Charlotte Douglas, the day after tomorrow. I will text you the itinerary. Tell your boss you need a leave of absence, I'm sure she will be willing to grant it. Tell no one where or what you will be doing—especially your boyfriend Mr. Harper. Expect someone is watching you. They will be."

He turned and left without hesitating to see if she had any questions. Ariel reached in her bag and turned off the recorder. She would download the recording and leave a copy in her safety deposit box and store one in a file on her computer. If anything happened to her, Jake and the authorities would have something to start with. A terrible way for Jake to learn her secret.

She started for the exit, stopping to throw her half full coffee cup away. As she went out the door, the sounds of the busy campus suddenly became apparent. Students and faculty were moving along, going about their lives, everyone had their challenges, most were not so great a mystery as hers. What had happened on this day was greater than anything she could recall happening on any other day--none so personal, other than when she gave up the privilege of being a mother, or when Jake came back into her life as a fugitive.

It was a beautiful day. The sun sparkled off the walkways, shadows of the huge oaks playing their dance across the green grass of the common area. Any other time after an interview Ariel would sit down and go over her notes while enjoying a day like this. She loved her job—discovering things, creating a story, reporting the dramatic events that make or change people's lives--often making them uncomfortable. But this was her life, her dramatic events, this horrid man had robbed her of any normal sense of well-being.

Lost in her thoughts, looking down and not watching where she was going, she was shocked when she felt the contact that upset her balance. An arm gently grabbed her keeping her from falling. She glanced up to see the nice-looking face of her savior, he smiled and said, "beware the Ides of March", turned and walked off, back the way she had come. Jesus. What was that all about? His face. She had seen him before. He had been in Starbucks. She had met his eyes briefly before he looked away when she was thinking about seeking help while listening to the man called Paul. But she was certain she had seen him somewhere else.

She couldn't go back to the news station. She had to. She would tell Suzie she needed to take a leave of absence while things were being sorted out. The man was right, Suzie would not hesitate in giving approval. Then what? She would go by her condo and pack, download the recording, go to the bank. She wanted to see Jake, but she was afraid her emotions would spill out. She needed to tell him the secret. How could she? Jake, I've been meaning to tell you, you have another daughter, and a grandson. Oh God please help me. What to do? If she didn't go and something were to happen to him during his mission, she would never forgive her cowardice. She was going to have to play her assigned role. "Beware the Ides of March". Indeed.

CHAPTER
5

The Farm
Jake and Ariel

The trees were bare boned, their skeletons in full display. Fields of tall fescue had been mown, raked then rolled, covered in white plastic lining the edges of the stubble-speckled land. A breeze bringing a cold front had started to sway the trees breaking the sun into fingers of sparkling light as Jake drove down the McConnells Highway. It was a little over a mile to the turnoff to Brattonsville, the historic Revolutionary site made nationally famous in the film titled *The Patriot*. He turned into Doc Hunter's Animal Clinic parking lot. A quick stop to check on Dusty and see how Maisy was handling being near him and if he was responding to her presence. It was the first time going on a year since the two dogs had been near each other.

Maisy started her pitiful yapping, her body shaking with excitement upon seeing Jake, even though it had been only hours since he dropped her off. Doc's wife, who was also a vet thought having Maisy there went well.

"His pulse quickened somewhat when I brought Maisy near him. Keep your eyes on the monitor. See it is slowing some since you picked up Maisy. Even now it is slightly elevated. I believe he knows you both are here."

"That's great. So how long before he will be taken off the sedatives and pain medication?"

"Possibly we can reduce the dosage within a week or two. His wounds will have to be where he can be out of quarantine first. They're beginning to heal. It's amazing, this dog has one helluva will to survive. Did anyone ever determine what kind of bullet did this?"

"The information can't be disclosed pending the trial. Maybe never. The possible person responsible is at large. No one knows where he is."

"Good thing Thurmond Tindal is picking up Dusty's bill. I didn't know you two were friends." She looked at Jake, a bemused look playing across her attractive face.

"Good thing yeah. I guess Doc told you Maisy will be staying here while I'm away on business. Maybe that will speed Dusty's recovery. Thanks for everything Doctor Hunter."

"Call me Susan. No problem. It's what we do. I hear you and your wife have parted ways," she said with a twinkle in her blue eyes as she moved closer to him."

Jake handed Maisy to her. He patted Maisy and made a quick exit. He managed a hasty thanks. Rumor was Doc and his wife had an on and off relationship--whatever that meant. Jake remonstrated himself—like TJ says, I'm always letting the little head control the big one. Another fact--the gossip mill was alive and grinding. Guess I'm the new grain on the wheel.

Fifteen minutes later he was on the road to his home. His stomach still clinched when he reached the spot where Dusty had been shot. The dust and gravel had settled back hiding where the bullet had pocked the ground and had created indentations streaked with blood and pieces of Dusty's entrails.

When he came over the hill where he could see the hill his house sat on, he saw a truck parked on the road out front. He accelerated. Two people came rushing out from his fenced in yard, jumped in the truck and took off slinging dust and gravel as they shot out of sight headed downhill toward Turkey Creek. Jake floored his truck. By the time he got through the ninety-degree bend in the road at the bottom of the hill, all that was left of their departure was the dust stirring in the breeze.

Back at the house, Jake walked around trying to figure out what they had been up to. He saw no signs of any attempt at breaking in. He went down to check on the animals. The chickens were moving around, scratching, and pecking at the remains of the hay he had put in the tin covered feed trough for the few cows he had. The heifer was licking and nudging her months-old calf. Flies were buzzing and dive bombing the prostrate calf. Jake hurried over.

The calf had been hogtied and someone had used a knife to carve *screw you* into its hide. The blood dripped onto the hard-packed red clay floor.

"Damn you!"

Jake rushed into the barn and grabbed the bottle of antiseptic blue ointment and strips of an old sheet that he kept in an airtight metal first aid box. He administered the ointment and struggled to get the strips wrapped around the heavy calf while having to push the mother out of the way.

He had a good idea who did this. Maybe tomorrow he would pay Tindal's former yard dogs Butch and Billy a visit. He hoped he could find them.

He untied the calf and made sure it was able to stand, then led it into the barn where he put leather cinches over the sterile sheet strips to keep the calf and Betsy the mother from reopening the wound or licking the ointment. Betsy was not happy. It was too early to be shut up. She pushed at the stall door. Jake threw some hay in the stall feed chute, topped off the water barrel and went to look in on the two hogs. They appeared fine.

Tomorrow assholes. He went back to the house. Took a shower and tried Ariel to see if they were still on for dinner. She answered sounding less than enthused to be talking to him.

"Something wrong?" he asked.

"Today just wasn't my day" was all she said, a tremble in her voice.

"I don't like how you sound. You're on your way here I hope."

"I'm not sure if I'll be good company."

"All the more reason to be with me. We can stay here, not go out for dinner. How does that sound?"

"I love you Jake."

She sounded like she was crying. Jake had never been good dealing with a woman's tearing up.

"Ariel you're one of the strongest women I've ever known. You kneed me in the balls. No other woman has ever done that to me. Don't ever give in to whoever brings you pain. Get here and let me help you feel better. I'll run you a bath, that should make you feel better—maybe I can join you and we can play up periscope, I believe that was your magic word."

He heard her snuffle a chuckle. "I should be there in less than an hour. That bath sounds great. A little wine maybe."

"You got it."

Jake memed TJ. 'Got a problem.'

'What's new bro?'

'Call me. Don't trust this implant.'

Jake's phone trilled.

"I believe friends Butch and Billy were here." Jake told him what had happened.

"Hey bro, don't go jumping without proof. Need to slow it down. You hearin' me, bro. Let our lawyer know. Call Deputy Coulter."

"So, I'm supposed to let someone carve a permanent obscenity into my helpless calf and do nothing. Can't do that."

"Let the law handle it. You work for HS now. We leave day after tomorrow. You get tangled up in something, Hardy, and the rest of them will hang you out to dry. I'm going to call Deputy Coulter. At least let him go with you."

"This *will* get handled one way or another. Ariel's upset, this Alpert's dude, we're leaving, I don't need this shit right now, I won't be fooling around."

"Don't go there. Deal with Ariel. Find a way to talk to her about this Alperts dude. I checked him out. He's bad news. Damn mercenary. Need to know 'bout his meet-up with Ariel? Let the law handle this thing with your cow."

TJ's thoughts jumped back to what he had been thinking when Jake memed him. "Talked to Leon, my brother in Lil Havana. He's checkin' up on the Gonzalez brothers and keepin' an eye on mama. He's getting' too old for the gang thing and mama she getting too old to be by herself—thought maybe they should move up here--don't want my niece and nephew caught up in The Hood's gang shit--sounds like he might do it. I hate asking, but seeing as how we goina be gone, thought maybe they could stay at your place--watch your animals and such. Deane says she could see 'bout helpin' find him a job and mama could stay with her here. HS goina put security people watching our places. If you say no, that's okay."

"What does he know about taking care of a farm?"

"Leon's smart. Even though he's a banger, he has a good heart. Maybe you could get your neighbor to help until he knows what to do. I mean it's not like there is that much to do this time of year. And you can bet your ass ain't no one goina come messing around while he's there. But if you say no, I'll understand."

"Forget about my neighbor having anything to do with him. He's willing to help me once more, despite the problems his family encountered when I was in the Bahamas. But wouldn't do any good asking him to do this. He and I don't have much in common when it comes to politics and social issues, no way would he help your brother. Sorry man, but that's the way most of these people are, you of all people should know that. Look, you are closer to me than family, but the idea of anyone living here besides me is not something I can deal with right now. Tell you what, when we get back, I'll help you get your brother up here. You said he has worked with some of the groups fixing up homes down there, maybe I can use him or get him some work up here."

"Alright, we'll figure somethin' out. You need leave those ass wads alone, let Deputy Coulter deal with them. Spend some time with Ariel--don't go screwin' this one up bro. Oh yeah. That thing about Elena and her connection to Jenkins--you say her ole man a friend of Jenkins and Tindal--come up here and she didn't tell you. Think he may have something to do with Jenkins' disappearance? You should look into that tomorrow and let the locals deal with your animal abuse shit."

"Gotta go, ask Deputy Coulter to come see me in the morning."

Jake wandered back through the house to the master bath. Master, one of those words left over from ancient times when there were slaves and servants. Not much different today, everyone was enslaved by those who controlled the wealth. Most people lived in debt. Death often didn't change things. The Great Recession and the recent natural disasters and epidemics proved that. Nothing is settled until you die and your presence is only memories for the very few who care to remember.

He started the water running slowly into the huge sunken garden tub whose skirted edge was made of oyster shells. The flat surrounding portion, like the floor, was broken tile--pieces left over from a lakefront home he built for a wealthy real estate developer. He lit some scented candles inside decorative glass containers left by Elena. She had liked the atmosphere. Early in their relationship, they would share the bath and make love by the light of the candles.

While the tub slowly filled, Jake went to the kitchen and took some gumbo from the freezer and put it in the microwave to defrost. He put a pot of water on the stove and put the burner on high to bring the water to a boil for the rice. He went back turned off the water with the tub half full. He would top it off with hot water when Ariel arrived. Then he went out to the mailbox for the mail. Normally he took it out of the box before turning into the drive. Today that other truck had disrupted his routine. There was a Netflix movie, a couple bills and a fancy looking envelope. The address bore some name he didn't recognize. It had come from Natchez, Mississippi and was sent to Mr. and Mrs. Jackson Harper.

Jake opened the envelope as he walked back toward the house. A wedding invitation—his son Jacob Connor Harper was marrying Teressa Penelope Ayers at St. Stephens Episcopal Church in Natchez the last Saturday, three weeks from tomorrow. Nothing like a half-decent notice. No mention of him being included in the wedding. Jake was surprised, but he hated to admit--it stung. Why did they bother sending him an invitation? His son's future wife must have done this, certainly would not have been his ex-in-laws' doing.

Jake was torn. He hadn't seen his kids since their mother died, nearly four years ago. Her parents had taken custody while he was financially helpless, strapped with medical bills, waiting on the VA to pay up. They had poisoned his kids' minds, blaming him for her death—organ failure due to alcohol and opioid addiction. Never mind that she had left him while he was at Bethesda in a drug-induced coma, as a result of the IED satchel bomb attack, while serving as a trainer with the Philippine Scout Rangers—his neck had been broken.

He didn't want to see his ex-in-laws, but he would love to see his kids. Maybe he could renew his relationship—maybe this wife-to-be was reaching out to him. She could be the conduit to the renewal. Whoa. He would be at Ft. Hood doing smart weapon training at Homeland's behest. Maybe he could leave the following week to be there ahead of the wedding.

He memed Undersecretary Hardy. Hardy said he would put in the request. He then asked Jake about the issues he was supposed to investigate. Jake told him he was working on them. He added that going to the wedding would give him the opportunity to stress the danger the cartel potentially put his children into.

Hardy said he would let him know.

Jake had to boil more water for the rice he had forgotten was cooking. He pulled the gumbo out of the microwave and put it in another pot to let it simmer until they were ready to eat. He made a simple salad and was opening a bottle of his home-brewed muscadine wine when he heard, then saw, Ariel's car enter the drive.

He went out on the porch to greet her. The breeze had picked up, a chill was in the air. A taste of fall weather. The sun had almost set, its last rays touched Ariel's auburn hair making the reddish colors shimmer and shine. Jake went down the steps and walked out to meet her. Her face had a forced smile. They hugged, she held onto him tighter than normal, he could feel her trembling. After a brief time, she pulled back, the forced smile back in place, her eyes moist, he tilted her chin up and kissed her.

"Come on inside. Your bath awaits."

"Let me grab my bag."

"I'll get it. Go on inside. It's getting cold out here. Oh, and if you don't mind, stir the gumbo, and add rice to the boiling water. I need to go shut the cows and chickens up, then I'll be in."

Ariel had poured herself a glass of the wine and was fluffing the rice when Jake came back inside.

"I need to top off the tub. Why don't you take the wine and get into the bath? I think I'll start a fire."

"I'd like you to join me."

"Wouldn't dare miss it. I'll get the fire going then join you."

"You make a great man to come home to."

"Thanks. Now go."

They stretched out in the tub. Ariel rested her head back on Jake's hairy chest. He rested the side of his chin on top of her head. His arms were wrapped around her, and she rested her chin on his arms.

He told her about the wedding invitation.

"Are you going?"

"If HS will let me. I have mixed feelings. It's been four years. I'm not sure they expect or want me to be there."

"You would think your son would want you to be there. You are his father."

"Sperm donor. That's probably how he thinks of me."

"Do you wish we could have had children?"

She turned slightly to look at him.

"I wish you had been with me instead of the other two. They were poor substitutes. That's how I think of them now--has nothing to do with how I feel about my children, only about how I feel about you. Ever since I saw you again, I realized I never stopped loving you. To answer your question—yeah—I wish you had been my wife and as much as we like making love, we probably would have had several children. Do you regret not having had children?"

Ariel turned back around her gaze dropped, seeming to avoid eye contact. Jake sensed something was wrong.

"I hadn't thought much of it until lately. I made my career my life. You did the same. Maybe this was the way it was meant to be. Who knows, if we had stayed together, maybe we would have grown apart?"

"What happened today? Why were you so upset?"

"The station manager called me into her office and accused me of trying to take her job."

"Wow. Did you get it straightened out?"

"No. I'm taking a leave of absence."

"You thinking of taking one of those other job offers you were telling me about?"

Jake felt her stiffen.

"Think I'll take some time off, maybe do some travelling. After all, you're going to be gone and I need to do some thinking about what I want to do."

"About us?"

"Not so much. I mean if I were to go to Washington, Seattle or New York where the other jobs are, how would we handle that?"

"I don't know. Have I thought about what your moving there would mean? Yeah, I have."

"And?"

"You mean more to me than anything. Could I be happy in one of those cities? No. I'm a country boy. I have to have open space, greenery, meadows, trees that kind of thing. But there is farmland near those places and with these new suborbital plane jumpers, if you made enough money, we could stay here. Your commute wouldn't be much different from here than it is for the auto commutes outside the major metros."

"Not there yet. I know you don't want to leave here. What if I were to go back to being a travelling reporter? This could be our home base and you could travel with me."

"Probably wouldn't mind that. As of now, I'm with HS. At least until this mission is complete. After that who knows. I do know I don't want to be without you."

Ariel turned her head and they kissed. The kiss grew more intense. She reached down.

"Hm. What do we have here?"

She raised up and slid Jake into her and began a slow back and forth. Soon Jake felt her quiver, her breathing grew rapid as did his. She raised up and pulled him down then stood and turned around to face him. He looked up enjoying the view. He reached up and helped as she eased him back inside and they began kissing again as she raised her hips up and down in an erotic squat. Their kisses became slurping slips of tongue in and out of each other's mouths. They both moaned and Jake arched up as they both felt the day's tensions surrender to their other selves.

Jake thought, *the little head always wins. Asking about Alpert would have to wait.*

Ariel thought, *this may be one of the last times they would ever do this. She wanted to tell Jake. She didn't know how. What would him knowing mean?*

CHAPTER

6

The Farm
Mark Poponovich—CIA Clandestine Unit

Mark had killed the lights and quietly coasted his hybrid electric SUV down the road, stopping just out of sight past the front of Jake's house. He now had the video and audio equipment trained on the house, listening, and watching the silhouettes of Jake and his latest squeeze, Ariel. Damn they had put on a stimulatingly imaginative show. He would have to visit Lisa later.

After their lovemaking ended and they were laid back in the tub talking, neither Jake nor his lady friend had talked about the DICE operative, Paul Alperts. And nothing about their troubled daughter or grandson either. That was puzzling. He would hang around until they went to bed. He couldn't imagine the elephant in the room not rearing its head at some point. He wasn't sure what they would be doing tomorrow, hopefully a repeat performance before they headed out. After dark he would need to find a place where he could be inconspicuous when he came back from seeing Lisa.

Jake had a camper out back he noticed from the views he had seen using Google Earth. That should work, he would check shortly. Damn they were going to stay sans clothes. Must be nice. That damn Jake certainly was a player. Bet he tells them all how much he loves them.

A couple hours passed. It was a moonless night. So dark, Mark would have had a hard time moving had he not had his night vision capable tactical headgear. Good thing the darkness worked in his favor. He settled into the camper, watched, and listened. They ate and made small talk. Jake was telling her about two guys that had been in front of his house, chasing them and then finding his calf carved up. Ariel asked him not to go off half-cocked.

"TJ made me promise to let the local law handle it."

They moved to the sunken tv room and watched a movie.

Come on. Come on, Mark wanted to shout, talk it out, need to know how this was possibly going to play. Would Jake get to keep this gal? What had happened to the zip drives with the cartel's financial files that supposedly only he himself and David had the passwords to? He couldn't imagine Jake or TJ keeping them. Could Ariel have them? Didn't seem likely. Maybe she had them and didn't know she had them? He needed to know. The other need to know was did Jake, TJ and HS know something about Alperts that the agency didn't?

Come on lover boy and gal stop leaving brother Mark all hot and bothered. He could hardly wait to see Lisa. Afterwards, she could tell him what she had learned from Tindal.

Lisa had been an easy recruit. She had fallen for his Lothario moves. Not bad either, lots of pent-up passion, eager for release. Too bad Jenkins fooled them all. Lisa had told him about what she called a neuro-implant, said Jenkins had the specs. She tried to explain what that meant, Mark listened, pretended ignorance. DARPA supposedly possessed the only other data set. Or did they? No wonder the agency was so determined to get their hands on Jenkins and the info he stole, and why they were determined to know if Harper and his women knew anything about it.

Movie over. Jake and Ariel went to the kitchen for more wine. Jake asked her if she wanted to see the stars. Oh shit, they're coming out back. Mark eased the camper door closed and pulled out his stun gun. The camper was parked under a shed seventy feet or so from the back screened porch and the small deck. They had donned heavy robes and Jake brought a blanket. They sat in a love seat swing. He could hear the metallic grind of the swing, and their voices came through, loud and clear.

They talked about the stars being so bright without all the light pollution of the city. Jake told about flying up the coast from Miami in a commercial jetliner on his way home from Havana. How everything was lit up all the way up except for one area. Jake said he had been waiting to see if he could pick out the area where the farm was. It and the immediate area were one of the few dark spots along the whole east coast.

Ariel said how beautiful the sky was. Then, she threw Mark a shot past left field. She asked Jake about the guy he shared the house with in Cuba. "I think I saw him today."

"Where?" Jake asked.

"I was leaving USC's main campus student center after conducting an interview. I was outside the library's Starbucks, I wasn't watching where I was going and ran into someone. He caught me to keep me from falling. I turned and looked him in the face. I thought I recognized him. I thought he had been in the lounge watching me when I was doing the interview. When you mentioned Cuba in the house earlier, it hit me, I'm certain he was in the pictures you showed me that you said were from your trip to Havana."

Jake was quiet.

Ariel asked, "what is it? Why do you have that look on your face?"

"An interview? I thought you took a leave of absence?"

"I decided to do that after the interview. That's not it. What is it?"

"That interview, wouldn't happen to be with a man last name Alperts?"

"Why does it sound like you are accusing me of something?"

She stood up and was facing Jake. He shrugged off the blanket and stood. She stared out across the yard. Jake hated having to bring it up and ruin their evening. It couldn't wait.

"Homeland was told by some source that you met with this Alperts' man. He is a mercenary that works for a foreign agency called DICE. They make what used to be Blackwater look like a bunch of school kids. This guy is one of the worst, so what did you talk about?"

"Jake you know that's privileged information."

"Bullshit. Is something he said why you took the leave of absence?"

He took her by the shoulders and turned her to face him.

"Tell me."

"No. I needed to get away while the station manager sorted things out. It was either take a leave, quit or possibly get fired."

"Ariel there's something you're not telling me. I can see it on your face. I thought you trusted me."

"Trust. Why were you spying on me?"

She tried to shrug his hands off. He held on.

"Don't make me knee you again."

Jake turned his hips.

"I knew nothing about the surveillance until after the fact. You can believe me or not. It's the gods' honest truth."

"Oh Jake, I don't want us to lose the trust. I want to tell you. I can't. Not now. If I do, you might do something crazy. Then I would blame myself. Please. I would never do anything to hurt you. After you come back, I'll tell you everything. We don't have much time left. I don't want you to leave here angry with me."

She moved in and hugged Jake.

"You're shivering. Let's go inside."

"Let's go to bed. I need you to hold me."

How touching, Mark thought. She recognized him. That meant watching her was going to be problematic. He could handle it. Jake might be another thing.

Jake now knew he was in the area. No matter. Another day and they would all be out of here.

Mark started to exit the camper. He heard a noise. Turning he saw two figures outside the camper. Oh shit. Who could this be? He quietly opened the door and watched as they hurried to a window that was lit inside. The bathroom. He could see Jake's image inside. They moved on toward the roadside of the house. Mark moved after them. They stopped outside the master bedroom. Ariel was coming from the master bath. Were these a couple of peeping toms? Whoever they were they stayed there watching until the lights went out. They turned and started back toward him. He moved back behind the camper.

When they went by him, he heard one of them say something that sounded like getting gas and burning them out. Their hard-to-understand lingo told him they intended to mess Jake up and possibly rape Ariel, then burn the house down.

Mark followed them down to a metal building where Jake had his farming equipment. They went inside. Mark saw a faint light from around the door and heard a low metal banging sound. He waited. Shortly they came back out and he zapped the nearest one and then the other one as he turned to swing what Mark took to be a gas can. He was scared the charge would ignite the fumes. Fortunately, none spilled. He went inside Jake's building, found some zip ties on a work bench, along with some rags. He zipped their hands and feet together and zip-tied rags in their mouths.

It took him almost an hour to carry them one at a time down the road to a camp building he knew belonged to Thurmond Tindal. He didn't want to kill them. Too messy. But they didn't deserve to go unpunished. Mark thought about castrating them. Taking their smelly pants off didn't seem like something he wanted to do. He decided to do a little carving. He remembered Jake talking about someone cutting *screw you* into his calf's side. The punishment should fit the crime.

Mark carved pig lover into the forehead of the bigger one, and sheep lover into the other one's brow, then took some purple ointment that was on a bench and dabbed it into the cut. He stood back admiring his handiwork. When they appeared to have regained their mobility, he cut their legs loose, tied them together and marched them moaning, and undoubtably cursing, muffled by the filthy gags stuffed inside their mouths, down the road out of hearing range of Jake and Ariel. He then cut them loose, and told them to keep going until they could crawl back into whatever hole they had come out of. He would be watching and if they came back, he would start carving them into something their mama wouldn't recognize.

It was getting late. He needed to see Lisa. Good thing he carried a change of clothes.

CHAPTER
7

The Farm
Jake and Ariel

Jake lay there holding Ariel until he heard her breathing grow steady, then he eased her head off his aching shoulder onto the pillow. He couldn't sleep. What Ariel said and didn't say bothered him. Trying to see what had happened and where it would lead was like looking through a telescope and not seeing very far. What did the fates intend?

He needed to take care of business with Butch and Billy, figure out what this Alpert asshole was holding over Ariel which kept her from telling him what was going on, check to see if Elena and her father were somehow involved with Jenkins, and decide, if given the go ahead, whether to attend his son's wedding. Too many things and too little time. He needed to sleep.

Seemed like he had just dozed off when he was woken by the incessant woe-begotten sound of a damn whippoorwill outside in a tree not far from the bedroom window. He was making his plea for a mate and warning other males to stay away from his territory. The sound wasn't as raucous as it would have been had the outside door or window been open, but it was loud enough to keep him from going back to sleep.

Ariel had one leg and an arm draped over him. Normally a light sleeper, amazingly he had not woken when Ariel deposited her limbs over him. He turned his stiff neck to check the clock, seven twenty, he was usually up by six. He gently shifted Ariel's arm and leg off him. She moved closer. He rolled away and shifted his legs then his body off the bed.

Quiet as he could he went out of the bedroom and down the hall to the kitchen to make the coffee. The house had a chill to it. He switched the thermostat over to heat and set it to 69 degrees, his favorite number. Like most normal men he was always thinking about sex. He wondered if Ariel would be amenable. Did he have time before Deputy Coulter arrived? Most likely TJ would be awake. He memed him, asked if he talked to the deputy.

'That's affirmative,' TJ responded, 'said be 'bout midmorning. Not planning on being there so behave yourself.'

'Don't need you to worry about me. I'll behave however the situation plays out.'

'Be cool bro.'

Jake had time. The coffee was ready. He went back to the bedroom.

Ariel didn't need much prompting. They made slow passionate love.

She insisted on making breakfast while he went about his morning chores.

He kept Betsy and her calf in the stall so Deputy James could have a look. He let the chickens out and slopped the hogs. Soon he would need to decide on whether to gilt the boar, and slaughter him in winter, or see if they mated and produced a liter. Since he would probably not be here, the boar should be given a reprieve was his thinking.

During breakfast, Jake told Ariel about HS's concern with Elena and her father. She volunteered to look into it since she had nothing else to do.

"Elena's computer is still here. Maybe she left some clue on it," Jake said. "I was thinking, if I am allowed and decide to go to my son's wedding, would you be willing to go with me? They never met Elena so you could pretend to be my wife."

"You gotta be kidding. I would never pretend to be your wife. I don't think my going there is a good idea." Ariel couldn't tell him she would be elsewhere.

Jake started to argue with her answer. The sound of a vehicle stopping in front of the house, interrupted his attempt.

Deputy James and another deputy were walking up the steps when Jake opened the door. He had been expecting Deputy Coulter.

"Good morning deputies," Jake said.

"Morning. I hear you had some kind of animal abuse here yesterday. Would you show us?"

"Let me grab a jacket."

Jake led them to the barn. He told them about the two men, the truck, his attempt to catch them and the subsequent discovery of the mutilated calf. He showed them where the calf had lain. There was a small amount of dried blood stains covered in flies. Inside the barn, he took Betsy out of the stall, then uncovered the carved obscenity. They took pictures and entered a report. Jake redressed the wound and led Betsy and her calf back into the stall.

"Any idea who might have done this?" Deputy James asked.

"My bet would be Tindal's yardmen, Billy and Buster. I'm not sure about their last names."

"What makes you suspect them?"

Jake told them about the incident at Turkey Creek Saloon where he and TJ had a run in with them and their subsequent threat to get even. He also mentioned Elena's description of a truck out on the road prior to her receiving heavy breathing telephone calls.

"I would like to accompany you when you question them."

"We can't allow that. Besides, we've already talked to them. They say you probably did that to your own calf."

"That's crazy. Why would I do that?"

"Where were you late yesterday afternoon?"

"I just told you. This is crazy."

"Can anyone verify your whereabouts at that time?"

"I got here about four thirty. That's when this happened. My friend Ariel arrived just before dark, about five thirty. Oh, and I talked to TJ around five, told him what happened."

"According to these men, they came here to deliver a message from their boss, Mr. Tindal and you used a stun gun on them, hog tied them then used a knife to carve obscenities into their foreheads. Afterwards, you marched them down the road threatening to cut them up into pieces their mother wouldn't recognize if they came back. I have to say they've got the cuts to add weight to their story. Care to comment?"

"What did the carvings say?"

"Why don't you tell us?"

"How would I know? Their story has obvious problems. How did they get here, walk? I doubt that. And then there is the time factor. I can prove I was here at the time I said I was and that I was in my house. I have a game camera in my house that monitors my front door with time and date registered. I'm sure it will verify my claims. Any missing time would mean I am damn fast and a helluva knife man to have done that in the short amount of time unaccounted for."

Deputy James took his cap off his head, ran his hand across the stubble then put it back on.

"You get all that?" He asked the other deputy, a young, pinched-face, jug-eared rookie, his name tag said Deputy Yates. He was busy, punching the keys on his mini tablet. He said he had.

"Jake. This matter is under investigation. Until a determination is made, I am instructing you to stay away from those men and not to leave the state without the DA's approval. Do you understand?"

"I'm leaving tomorrow. I don't know when I'll be back. I have no desire of notifying the DA. Not after what he accused me of before. If you were me, you'd feel the same way. I suggest you tell those two jerkoffs my place will be under guard and, if they come back here, the next cut will likely be done by someone called Bubba. Oh, by the way, what was carved into their foreheads, so I can tell the people who are watching my place who to be on the lookout for?"

"Pig lover and sheep lover. Whoever did them could have done your calf. That would be my guess. Be bad news if we've got some nutcase out there doing this."

Jake laughed. "I'm not laughing about the knife cutting. I find it almost poetic justice for those two lowlifes."

The deputies walked off shaking their heads. Deputy James called over his shoulder, "Jake, it would be better if you let the DA see your camera files."

Jake went around and checked all his game cameras to make sure they were still in place. He down-loaded, then reactivated them remotely using the implant. Sure beat the hell out of having to crawl up a ladder. He emailed the file attesting to his whereabouts to the DA's office. He wanted to add," go screw yourself", to the email. It was tempting.

He found the fuel can outside his equipment building. The ground was scratched like some big animal had squirmed around, as if there had been a couple animals in a scuffle. Inside he saw footprints in the dust of the floor. The zip tie bag was open on his work bench, as was a stained rag next to the blue antiseptic ointment from the new bottle he forgot to take to the barn. "What the . . . .? Who had been here? When? Why the fuel can that contained diesel? Who had scuffled? Buster and Billy? Then who had caught them and carved them?

He went back in the house and told Ariel what was said and what he found in his building.

"That makes no sense. Who and when would this have happened? This creeps me out." She thought about Alperts saying she would be watched. Had he or one of his men been here and done this? "Do you think whoever did this could still be out there somewhere?"

For their sake they better not be. But who was the good Samaritan? His implant *It* could have told him. He could have been monitoring the cameras if Jake had thought to tell him. He told *It* to do so from now on.

He saw Ariel's concerned face. "Doubt they'll come back. Not after what happened to them." He shook his head, had a brief thought, then it was gone.

Ariel noticed. "What about whoever cut them?"

"I can't see him hanging around, too risky. Just wish I had had all the outside game cameras on. They are all activated now. I'll be notified if they pick up anything while I'm gone."

He called TJ and they had a good laugh. He told him what he had found at the shed and that he had turned the other cams on.

"Yeah. Lotta sick mothers out there, could be they had plans to burn you out. Don't think they be back anytime soon. Need to let Homeland know to be on the lookout. Shouldn't be hard to spot. He laughed again."

"Deputy James wanted me to go to the DA's office for questioning. I told him no way in hell. I emailed footage from the interior cameras to Deputy James instead of the DA. Should prove my being here at the time in question. They may question you to verify the other part of my story."

"TJ told Jake not to worry about the DA. "Notify Hardy and fill him in on the happenings. Let HS handle the DA."

Jake said he would. "What worries me is who did the carving? What was he doing here in the first place?"

"Don't know, bro. Doubt they'll come back since you'll be gone, and HS will be hangin' around. Best tell Hardy."

Hardy wanted to know why he called instead of meming. Jake told him Ariel was there. Hardy was not too happy with having to notify the DA.

"The man, like most locals resents us feds, and he is backed by your buddy Tindal. They both are under investigation. This may pose a problem. Guess I'll let Washington handle this one. We may have to say you are a federal witness being summoned to another jurisdiction--that's what I will suggest. Jake how about trying to avoid any more issues. Concentrate on the mission at hand, okay? I'll tell the team that will be watching your place about what you said. Oh, did you ask your lady friend about the Alperts man?"

"Yes. That is a negative from her. Did you ask about my son's wedding?"

"That's being left up to me. And that depends on your training and our mission, hard to say right now everything depends on the intel that comes in concerning the files and what we find out about Jenkins."

There was little doubt in Jake's mind about Buster and Billy having been the two assholes fleeing his house yesterday. But who was responsible for what happened to them? If he knew, he would congratulate him or them. If there was someone else out there who also did his calf, then he had a much bigger problem. If that was the case, that person or persons would strike again. If that was not the case, someone else had been here, watching them. He would keep monitoring his cams using the implant, that should make monitoring a cinch. Had to be good for something.

He walked to the door of Elena's old office. Ariel was on the computer.

"Anything interesting?"

She shifted the screen to another screen. He had caught a glimpse of a young woman on the other screen.

"Who were you looking at?"

"Just someone I was supposed to interview before I took the leave of absence. I was curious. I'm considering doing some freelance work." Ariel quickly changed the subject.

"Anyway, as for your wife and father: Elena has a checkered past. Before she became a nurse, she worked as a waitress and bartender for an upscale bistro in San Antonio. The bistro's owner was busted as a big-time coke dealer. He also ran a high-class call-girl service, was indicted, but not convicted, of illegal gun running. He was murdered in prison. Elena left there about that time and nine months later she had her daughter. Kind of makes you wonder."

"Her father, Sam McIntyre, has a lot of holes in his service record. You said he retired from the Marines after thirty years of service. That is not what his records show. He had twenty total years as a Marine, yet his retirement benefits show thirty-years. That makes no sense."

"I told you, he admitted he was a CIA agent. He served in Vietnam and was there when Saigon fell."

"Maybe that explains the gap. Did you know he testified in the Iran Contra investigation? Guess who he testified for?"

"Thurmond Tindal?"

"No. Close. Major John Wade Jenkins, Bud Jenkins father, who resigned to prevent receiving a dishonorable discharge. The reason I said close is because his Commanding Officer was Colonel Thurmond Pinckney Tindal. Jenkins father was later exonerated—posthumously. Talk about motivation. Tindal goes onto NSA then becomes a weapons merchant, later a manufacturer with government contracts. Warrant Officer Samuel L McIntyre retires, moves to San Antonio, becomes a weapon merchant. Elena worked for an accused gun runner. No wonder Homeland has an interest in Elena and her father."

"No connection to a Pierre Paul Alperts?"

"Come on Jake. Please. I'm not going to go into that again. Not now. Don't ruin our last day together by giving me the third degree."

"Did you look?"

"No."

"Why not?"

"Jake, do you want me to leave?"

"No. Ariel, Homeland and other feds are looking at him. You met with him. I was told to ask. This is not going to go away. Avoiding questions, not being able to give them a reasonable explanation, looks suspicious. Makes this a problem for us. I know you would never do anything illegal or traitorous. Makes me think there is something personal from your past he is threatening you with. I don't care what it might be. But I do care that you don't feel you can trust telling me. Whatever it is, the feds will find it, and, unless it has something to do with national security, I will be told. Would you rather I hear whatever it is from you or from them?"

Ariel clicked back on the screen with the young woman. Jake leaned in close, looking over her shoulder. "Who is she?"

"Look closer." She zoomed in.

"Is that a picture of you when you were in Europe?"

"Her name is Elizabeth Jean Alonso de Castro de Oro de Espanoche."

"And?"

"She lives in Spain. She is 23 years old. She was born in England and her adoptive parents have homes in London and Sweden. Her husband's name is Pablo. They have a son named Gabriel. Pablo's father is the Cuban Ambassador to Spain."

"Again, and? Oh, I thought you and your ex didn't have any kids? Is this what this is about? What does this have to do with Paul Alperts?"

"Jake I was not married at that time. I wasn't even 17."

Jake leaned in closer. "Oh Jesus. She's your daughter?..." He stood back. "Our daughter?... And she has a son...I am a grandfather...we are grandparents. Oh, wow."

Jake plopped down in the Queen Anne Chair next to the desk. Turned the monitor and stared at the woman.

"She's beautiful, like her mother."

He kept staring. He looked at Ariel. She sat stone faced. Something was wrong.

"There's something else. Something about this wonderful news that is not so good. Has something happened to her? No. To her son, our grandson? Oh no. What is it?" He stood back up. "What does Alperts have to do with this? Tell me Ariel why are you so sad?"

"It's not what you think. Her husband is leaving her. He is taking her son, our grandson, and leaving with his parents. They are going to Mexico then Cuba. She can't stop them. She may never get to see her son again. We may never get to know her or him."

"Jesus. I'll talk to Hardy. Our State Department, maybe the embassy can do something."

"They have left. There is nothing the government can do. Why would they?"

Jake started pacing.

"What does Alperts have to do with this?"

"I don't know." Ariel looked down.

"What did he tell you? There is more to this. Why did you think you couldn't tell me this?"

"Oh Jake, I thought you would hate me. I had her and I didn't know what happened to her. No one would tell me. I didn't tell you. I swear I didn't know anything about her, where she was, not even if she was alive. I tried. Nothing. Not until this man Alperts somehow found out and showed me this. I talked to her. She was as surprised as I was, am. Please don't hate me."

"Hate you. You've been carrying this guilt by yourself all these years."

He pulled her to her feet and hugged her tight.

"I could never hate you. You and I didn't know where each of us was all those years when all this other stuff happened. I'm upset because you thought I would blame you."

He felt her tears wetting his shirt.

"So, what else is there? Alperts threatened you, what is the threat?"

"His organization has Elizabeth. He told me if I told anyone, I would never see her again or our grandson."

Jake looked at the woman on the screen again. She did look a lot like Ariel, the young version he remembered from way back then, before their long separation. But photos could be faked, impersonators created that have been used to fool people, to blackmail or swindle the people afraid not to believe, even the strongest of skeptics.

"This could be a hoax. What does he want?"

"It's no hoax. I spoke to her. I recorded everything. Here." Ariel took her phone, found the recorder and hit play.

Jake and Ariel sat back down. Jake listened to the conversation. He hoped the implant was recording this. Could there be a multitask recording? He attempted mental notes as he listened. Alperts' DICE Organization had been contracted to make Ariel disappear, possibly the so-called daughter also. Contracted by whom? They wanted Ariel's assistance for tracking the grandparent. What is that all about? DNA, a possibility there—would need to locate the other woman. Jake recognized that Alperts spoke Hebrew to the other operative. The signs indicated France, why not Spain? This was getting weirder by the moment. Something wasn't right. When the recording ended Jake had Ariel play it once more.

CHAPTER

8

The Farm
Jake and Ariel

Mark slipped into the camper before daylight. He listened and watched Jake and Ariel. Daylight made watching ghostlike. Nothing new from the recording, he had been there.

He was tired. Not much sleep from the night before. Lisa had been shocked when he had shown up at her door--the blood still not dry on his clothes. After he showered and changed, she briefed him on Tindal's and Alperts' conversation and Tindal's requests to make the Harper man and Ariel go away.

She said nothing about the conversation with NSA's DARPA concerning the implant and the Hive. She wanted to but dared not.

"You need to be careful. Alperts left one of his men there you say. He will be sweeping the place regularly and will plant his own recording devices."

"I recruited the head of housekeeping. I got her the job when Tindal and his wife cleaned house of all former employees. She will be a roaming recorder and will place and remove devices as needed."

"The man is naturally paranoid. Remember he worked for the agency, then NSA. Alperts' man will be well trained also. If she gets caught, she will give you up. And no matter how tough you are, everyone eventually talks. You should remember that from your training. We need you more than we need recordings. Don't stick your neck out, play it safe. I need to get some rest."

She led him back to her bed and undressed him then herself. It amazed him how much enthusiasm she exhibited and how well she learned what he liked the most.

Thinking about the brief relief didn't help much to relieve the claustrophobic feeling from being stuck inside the camper. He needed to move around and didn't for fear of being discovered. He thought Jake was going to come in on him when he came out to check his game cameras were in place and on, right after the local law-dogs left. One of the cameras was in the eave of the camper shed roof. Shit. This was going to be a problem when he had to exit.

"**Y**ou don't know that is our daughter. This man is up to something. No great mystery here--needing your journalistic skills, don't tell anyone, especially me--bullshit. Ariel, the man is a dangerous soldier of fortune. HS checked him out. I checked him out. You can't go with him."

"Don't tell me what I can and can't do. I *know* that is our daughter. Call it woman's intuition or my journalistic truth meter, that woman was not play acting. She was as much at a loss as I was. And even if she isn't our daughter, she is in trouble, I'm in trouble, this Alperts man and his organization have her and they were hired to make you and me disappear, looks like they intend the same for her, her son, our grandson. Believe her or not, I do. You are leaving tomorrow—you can't do anything yourself. I'm her only hope."

"Ariel, listen to me. This contract—think—there are two entities who come to mind who have the motive and means to take out this contract. One is Tindal. You exposed him. The other is the cartel. They will do whatever they can to get back at me—they're in Mexico--he wants you to go to Mexico. You'd need to be crazy to go there. If they are the ones he's working for, then…It doesn't matter--they find out you are there I'll never see or hear from you again, unless they intend to use you to lure me into their trap. Think about it. They could kill two maybe three birds with the same stone, or more—you, me, Elizabeth, her son, and TJ. You talk about intuition, journalistic smell test—well, this stinks. Okay, I shouldn't have said you can't. I should have said you shouldn't. Please listen to me."

"And do nothing. Who is going to protect our daughter and grandson? Who's going to protect me once you're gone. Remember he said someone would be watching me. For all we know they are right now. We don't know who he's working for. It could be some organization that has any number of capabilities. Tindal, the cartel, who knows maybe it *was* them. Remember, they tracked you before. Someone had to have helped them. TJ said there was a drone. Who sent that? There was satellite surveillance you said—that means they could be watching and recording us as we speak. Maybe this mission is a way to get you and TJ out of the country to make you disappear. Like you said, no one is safe no matter who or where they are. The cartel and Tindal want you and TJ out of the way more than they would me. I just report what I know. You were part of what happened to bust their plans, much more than I was. Yet, you're going. And I'm supposed to stay here, keep looking over my shoulder, try not to think or care what may be happening to you, our daughter, our grandson, is that what you think I should do?"

"I'm going to run this by TJ and Homeland. Maybe I can get them to let me work on this and join the mission later."

Hardy listened to Jake as he took the Netflix envelope to the mailbox. He needed to notify the post office to hold his mail. Not much, mostly garbage, his bills were on auto draft. He would notify Netflix and put his service on hold, maybe he should do streaming, he could play the movies in his head. Hardy reminded him to stay on track, and no, he probably shouldn't consider streaming movies while on HS's time.

He strolled around outside looking to see if there were any vehicles out on the road or at Tindal's hunting camp. There were several vehicles at the camp. bow and black powder seasons for deer were open. Occasionally Jake heard distant shots in early morning and late evening. The four-wheeler traffic had picked up. He didn't see any vehicles he had not seen before—not that that was a surety for one of them not belonging to a spy buddy of Tindal's or DICE's.

Hardy said he had no choice—Jake had to leave for weapons training the next day. This was a special session just for the neuro implant testing and training. He promised to put a team on investigating Ariel's story. He stated the same things about the validity of the people and the possibility of it being a hoax or a trap. He also surmised Ariel's involvement. This angered Jake, he told Hardy in no uncertain terms that he should have left that one unsaid. Hardy told Jake Ariel should go. He would put a team to watch her.

'Concentrate on the upcoming mission. The surveillance team will be bringing a mobile unit there to watch your place. They'll make sure no one bothers your neighbor while he tends the animals. We've got a lot invested in you and TJ. I need results. This mission is a top priority. Who knows maybe this Alperts and his DICE team will lead us to Jenkins? Maybe whoever they're working for is connected to his disappearance. TJ, you and I may end up being part of the team watching your girlfriend, and maybe this *supposed* daughter and grandson. I'm also going to see about a team to watch your wife and ex-in-laws. This could end up being a family affair for you. Also, could be we'll end up back in Cuba. From what you said and other intel, everything seems to be pointing that direction. You and I back in Cuba. And TJ, his ancestral homeland, wouldn't that be something. Keep cool Jake. Be sure to check your itinerary. Stay off the phones and shut that computer down, remove the hard drive.'

'One more thing. Pull up the FAA Part 107 Preparatory Course for UAV Training. You and TJ will need to be able to pass the test at your training session. Should be a cinch for you since you flew small planes.'

Jake wanted to tell Hardy he and TJ had utilized drones overseas. Hardy had cut the connection.

TJ took a break from studying the UAV material. Nothing new. His spotter had used them on missions in the bush and had given him a briefing.

He had been enjoying the downtime with Deane and his dogs, when Jake memed telling him what he had found out and what Hardy said.

'He's right. Ariel's right. My mother's coming up here, and brother Leon, he's coming also. As will Homeland's team. They own us bro. Uncle Sam once more your daddy. I can't see Alperts doing anything to Ariel. Sounds to me like he needs her, and your daughter and grandson. Big mystery be about Jenkins, the intel he stole. My bet Alperts going to use her to get close to them. Don't see anything happening 'til Jenkins found and/or the shit he stole recovered. Ariel, like you say, has been in hotspots—the Middle East, and interviewed that drug cartel madam, so-called Queen of The South, Theresa something or other, even took a chance interviewing your sorry ass when we were called domestic terrorists. Better odds down there than up here if that where Alperts headed. Betcha it is. And we goina be right there also. Nothing else to be done bro.'

'If and when I get my hands on this froggy asshole, he's going to wish he never messed with me and my family. I have a feeling he's working for Tindal.'

'Leave that be. We know once we catch up to him.' TJ paused, before Jake could reply, he changed course. 'Hardy tell you 'bout studying for this UAV testing? Lot of crap on there. Know most of it from overseas' deployments. They done added some new ones to the arsenal. Looks like we'll be checking these babies out. Don't see nothin' 'bout The Hive though. Guess they got it under wraps. Catch you later.'

When Jake joined Ariel, she was looking at a recipe online and writing down the ingredients.

"Thought we could cook a nice meal and eat in tonight since this may be our last bit of time together before you leave." And before I leave as well. She dared not say that to Jake and get another argument started.

The long periods of silence from Jake seemed strange. Brought back memories, the rumors, questions, doubts, from experiences when he and his crew were at Guantanamo. The big question was about Jenkins--not answered in his briefing. Jake? Not likely.

He heard Jake tell Ariel he was going to talk to Homeland and his friend TJ. Mark had focused the listening device on Jake when he walked around. He heard nothing. Except him entering the house and speaking to Ariel, he picked their voices up fine. Did he have a blocking device? When he had visual, Jake's lips didn't appear to move. Hmm? Strange. Could it be?

Mark was beginning to feel even more claustrophobic. He needed to get out of here if he was going to follow Ariel. He had to wait, right now it was too risky. He would leave if an opportunity arose before nightfall, hope Jake didn't monitor his cameras and see him. He had preparations to make. Alperts' and Ariel's departure was set for tomorrow. That meant he needed to be back here before daylight. He decided he would use the afternoon time for resting up. No telling when he would be able to do so again.

CHAPTER
9

Fort Hood, Texas
Jake, TJ and HS Undersecretary Hardy

The departure for Jake, TJ and Hardy was scheduled for 0700 from the Air National Guard Field outside Rock Hill. Too early for anything but a quickee, leaving Jake less than satisfied. Ariel said she wasn't feeling well. Jake figured it was nerves. Understandable. He hoped she would reconsider her trip with Alperts. She was noncommittal.

They boarded an executive jet on loan from a retired Air Force General who worked for Boeing at their Charleston facility. Jake had never been on a private jet. This was a Cessna Ten, one of the fastest private, nonmilitary jets in the world, Jake was informed via the implant connection to the web. The layout was like an executive board room with comfortable lounge type seats laid out on each side facing a bar on the left aft side and a large screen on the opposite side. Behind the bar was a fully apportioned bath, noticeably larger than Jake's camper's bath but far more luxurious.

Hardy took one of the seats at a table to the side of the screen and indicated Jake and TJ should sit facing the screen. They were told to buckle up and within minutes taxied away from the hangar and were airborne. Shortly the jet banked heading west and levelled off, there was little air noise.

The Air Force Major asked if they cared for drinks or anything to eat. Hardy shook his head. She turned and looked at Jake who had been studying her. He looked up at her, smiled and requested a black coffee and sweet roll. No returned smile, just a stone-faced nod. TJ rolled his eyes at Jake. She gave TJ a brief smile when he asked for green tea.

While they were eating, Hardy asked if they had studied for the UAV test. They both had. The giant screen on the wall lit up. On it was the UAV they recognized as the one which they encountered during their failed raid onto Tindal's estate.

"That looks familiar," TJ said leaning forward.

"That gentlemen is called The Hive. You had a less than favorable skirmish with the prototype. Which is how you ended up here and one of the reasons we are engaged in this mission."

Hardy went through the specs and explained The Hive's arsenal of Bumblebee smart weapons capabilities.

"Jenkins made off with the source codes along with DoD's military satellite positioning and capabilities." Hardy switched to meming. 'As we all now know, he has an earlier version of what we each have.' He nodded toward the Major, who was serving as their hostess, her back to them and memed for them not to say anything about the neuro implant.

"The reason you were asked to study up on drone flying is so you can learn how to not only be able to fly the newer models but also learn the other side's capabilities and limitations. The threat of being surveilled or attacked by these aerial dervishes is a distinct possibility, almost a certainty. Our learning time is limited. We need to make the most of it."

Hardy summoned the Major over and asked her to give them privacy. She went to a wall and pushed a button. An almost invisible screen surrounded them. She left and went forward to the cockpit.

"Our implants give us a tremendous advantage. You and your devices will learn the information about UAV capabilities and limitations. You will be able to use your device's surveillance communication capabilities to help warn you when a UAV is detected by satellite or, in some instances, your own drone's surveillance capabilities."

"Our drones?" TJ and Jake asked almost simultaneously.

"Yes. Your own drone. Where possible, we will have a high-altitude UAV deployed along with satellite access. Other times, there again, where possible, you will have smaller drones at your disposal, such as the ones you are familiar with that were used in the Middle East."

"What you mean, where possible?" TJ asked.

"They will be available on a moment's notice where politically feasible. Many countries forbid us to deploy drones in all or certain areas within their borders. You must follow directives from the chain of command--the go ahead must be given by them. Depending upon your location, you will need to allow time for the drone to get within range. There are other high-altitude surveillance UAVs which will be monitoring from a distance when satellite imagery is sketchy. The drones, you have access to, will not be armed. If we go to the land of the Castros or other noncooperating countries, getting access will be problematic."

"Our situation is going to be fluid. Rely upon your implant's memory storage. You will not only need to learn and teach yourself, therefore the implant, how to utilize and fly various drones, when we reach Fort Hood you will also be given hands-on instructions on how to use the latest non-lethal and smart weapons. We should arrive at approximately 0900. That gives you one and a half hours to study.'

The table in front of them opened and screens appeared.

"These are simulator trainers. Using your implants, you will begin your training. No controllers. Your thoughts will serve that purpose while we are onboard. Once we reach our destination, you will demonstrate you and your device's synchronicity and astound your testers with your capabilities."

Learning to control the flight pattern was easier for Jake due to prior flight simulator training. TJ was better at engaging a target because he was better at meteorological variables, learned as a sniper. They shared their individual knowledge with the other via their implants. Both were amazed that they were able to fly and outmaneuver simulated enemy attacks with the accuracy of air combat veterans by using their implants instead of the simulator joy sticks. They knew this was a simulator and not live combat situations where others they may be up against had actual experience with these other drones. Still, it was exciting and made Jake feel better about having the implant.

"Jake, you keep this up and you just might be allowed to attend your son's wedding," Hardy remarked after Jake beat him in a game of drone combat. Jake bested TJ narrowly, only because his aeronautical skills proved better than TJ's firing skills."

"Still not certain I should attend the wedding. I would probably be less than welcome by my kids and not welcome at all by my ex-in-laws."

"I've been told your ex-father-in-law is connected. Does business with the so-called Dixie Mafia."

"So, it seems. He and I never got along. Instant disliking. Went to shit after Joanna's overdose death. He blamed me. The son of a bitch has done everything he can to poison my kids against me."

"Why did you marry his daughter, if you don't mind my asking?"

"I loved her, mostly—nothing like Ariel—that could never be equaled."

"Started when I came home, in between tours, I was stationed at Fort Campbell in western Louisiana. Another ranger I became friendly with invited me to go to New Orleans for Mardi Gras. There was a Mardi Gras Ball and his family insisted I attend. Tony set me up with a friend of his girlfriend whose date had cancelled on her. I figured why not. What a party. Joanna was damn good looking and we hit it off. One thing led to another. I started spending my downtime in Baton Rouge. She was attending LSU and her ole man had set her up in a nice condo near campus. Anyway, two months later Joanna informed me she was in the family way and insisted I marry her. I thought that was the honorable thing to do. I mean I was fond of her; she was fun; I had lost touch with Ariel—a lot of reasons."

"We had a big wedding, then her ole man found out she was pregnant. The shit hit the fan between he and I. Jo got pregnant twice more, I got deployed to the Philippines, she went from being a party drinker to a full-fledged alcoholic, started messing around. When my injury happened and it wasn't certain I would live or might be paralyzed, she took the kids, left, then divorced me. Within a short time, opioids and alcohol killed her. Her father Hank blamed me, took custody of our children. I couldn't afford to fight him."

"Good ole Jake, always letting your dick do the thinking. Wonder if that implant can control that one. Don't look like it." TJ said laughing. "Jake his definition of nice girls are ones that puts it in for you."

Hardy joined in the laughter. Jake just shook his head side to side. He wanted to deny, but felt he'd be opening himself up for more ridicule. He turned and gazed out the window behind Hardy.

They had started their descent. The screens disappeared and the consoles slid back in place. Down below was Ft. Hood, like Ft. Campbell, named for a Confederate officer, one who had lost both major campaigns he commanded. Yet here his name was honored, bestowed upon one of the largest military posts of the United States. Probably not for long, Jake thought, not if the current anti-Confederacy political activists had their say. In this, unlike some of the other get-rid-of-history cases, he agreed with their political correctness.

They were met on the ground by two men, neither in uniform, nor did they carry themselves with military posture. They were ushered into a black, tinted window van with no signage or military nomenclature. Almost fifteen minutes later they entered a domed, hangar structure. Giant doors slowly slid closed sealing them off from an area that looked like a barren firing range. Off in the distance Jake had seen two hills, appearing like two giant mounds on a flat open plain.

Inside the hangar were numerous UAVs of varying size and shape. A few men in mechanic suits were performing what Jake figured was routine maintenance. They worked on rolling tables. Computer monitors were lit up and an assortment of instruments and tools were scattered on the table and around the drones. Overhead cables snaked down from hanging grids mounted on tracks.

They were ushered into an elevator that descended to another level. When the doors slid open, a blast of chilled air hit them. Stepping out, Jake saw they were in what appeared to be a military command center. Wall to wall monitors surrounded the room and in the center was an octagon tower reaching to the ceiling that was covered in more monitors, like something NASA would have.

They were greeted by a stern looking, block-headed man with insignia of a Bird Colonel shining on his collar. Introductions were made. He was Colonel William, call me Bill, Hanson.

"Welcome gentlemen to DoD UAS Training Center and Homeland Security Southwest Command Fort Hood Station for Smart Weapon Training." Jake thought, what a mouthful.

"Sergeant Major Richard Otis Offmeyer will be handling your training. Anything you need, that we can accommodate, he will be the man to come to."

The Sergeant Major stepped forward and shook their hands. He was a straight-backed, bear-like man slightly shorter than the Colonel, with a weathered face and a crook in his lips, probably from chewing on a stogie Jake guessed. His uniform looked stiff and starched, suited what Jake knew of the Sergeant Majors he had come across.

In a hoarse, gravelly smoker's tone, he said, "You can call me Dick. Not Dickhead, just Dick." He turned, nodded, and gave a quirky smile looking TJ up and down and barked, "If you will, follow me, I will show you your quarters."

Jake looked at TJ who smiled and shrugged as did Hardy. They turned to follow the Sergeant Major.

He led them to another set of elevators that ascended back to ground level. Next door was a two-story barracks where they were led into a room filled with rows of bunk beds.

"Welcome to the Fort Hood UAS Hilton. At the other end is the head with all the latest fixtures for your bathing needs. Next door is the dining hall. Meals are served twenty-four-seven. We man this facility twenty-four-seven. Any questions?" He barked this out as if they were new recruits.

TJ stepped forward getting in the Sergeant Major's face.

"We not in the military and you had oughta treat us with respect. Your attitude beginnin' to piss me off and you don't want to piss me off Dickhead."

The Sergeant Major moved closer, locking eyes with TJ. "Son, I told you to call me Dick, not Dickhead. We can take this outside if you like."

Hardy and Jake stepped forward expecting a fight. TJ and the Sergeant Major glared at each other. Jake saw TJ's crooked grin. Uh oh. They moved into a fighter's stance—stayed that way longer than was comfortable to watch. Then they lunged at each other, laughed, and did the man hug thing.

"You old son of a salty dog, good to see you," TJ said.

"You too TJ. Damn been what, twenty years?"

"Nah man. More like forever." TJ turned to look at Jake's and Hardy's stunned faces. "This man my first weapons' instructor. One of the best. Got all kinds awards. Beat the hell out of everybody 'cross all branches of military." He turned back to Dick. "Now you doing the smart weapons' training?"

"Yep. Eyes got old. With these things you can be half blind and still score. Shocked me when I saw your name on the list. Looks like we both have become Homeland men."

"Dick, these two men here my new team. This Undersecretary Hardy, careful with him, he big chief, soft from riding a desk, he claims he been there and done that. This other fellow my closest friend, Jake. Jake and I served together overseas in 'Stan and Iraq and were trainers in the Philippines when an IED attack messed him up. So, if he acts funny, humpin' a hole in the ground or whatnot, don't worry, he can't help it."

"Screw you." Jake said.

"See what I mean. Be careful, don't bend over with your back to him. 'Having your back', got a whole new meaning for him."

Everyone laughed including Jake.

Hardy spoke up. "Sergeant Major, I don't know how much you know about what training we need…"

Dick held up his hand interrupting Hardy. "Sir, please call me Dick. And yessir I know a little about your special capabilities, don't understand the technical shit, but I have seen the flyboys' use of what I figure is something like it. I don't have to know much about how you trigger the weapon, your smart controller some call it, to teach you what these newest non-lethal and smart weapons are capable of and not capable of. I don't know everything about how they're put together, but I can teach you how to use 'em. A lot of the techno-speak, you can learn from watching the videos, but, 'ain't nothing like the real thing', as the saying goes. I'll let you get up close and personal with the real thing. Shall we get started? Your gear will be brought to the hotel. This was just for show. In case someone gets curious."

They watched videos and were shown the various smart weapons after each session.

"The next two days, or however long it takes, you are going to be hands-on. When I'm satisfied you have command of these smart boys, you'll be on your way. Wish I was going with you, but I guess my old lady would find me, and beat the tar out of me if'n I did. Anyway, I don't know if any of you've been to Texas, doesn't matter. There's a steakhouse here serves a 64-ounce piece of cow, that, if you can eat it with all the trimmings, it's free. Have big cold mugs of beer that'll take the sweat off your ass and make you feel like you can lick the world. I feel it my duty to take you there, then you can mosey on over to your hotel and get some beauty rest before the real thing happens tomorrow How's that sound?"

Jake's mind was hundreds of miles away—where are you Ariel? *God don't let anything happen to her.*

CHAPTER
10

In flight
Ariel and Alperts

Ariel was aboard a chartered private jet. They took off from the same airport outside Rock Hill as Jake had a couple hours earlier. She had hardly slept wondering about Jake and her future. He wasn't happy about her continued refusal to discuss her impending plans for leaving with the Alperts man. The unspoken truth lay heavy upon their moods--created tension. She hadn't felt well, nerves she guessed. Their lovemaking was done in silence. Before they parted, there had been only a clinging hug and farewell kiss, strained-sounding I love yous.

She felt she had no choice. She investigated Elizabeth's and Gabriel's backgrounds. She had to know if she was being deceived. The video could have been doctored. Until there was proof of deception, she would do what she felt was necessary. This was her job. Her duty as a reporter and, more importantly, as a possible mother and grandmother. The truth lay with Alperts' and DICE's connections.

She promised Jake she would do her best to avoid being put in danger by Alperts and his organization. She wished she could. She couldn't. Too much was at stake. Jake, as was his nature, felt she should leave everything up to him. This was her daughter and grandson also.

Alperts sat in another seat across a table from her, his pointy face lit up with excitement. She wished there was a way to make that smug look disappear. She might be in his company, but she damn sure didn't have to pretend to enjoy it.

"I should have told you to pack for the beach, but perhaps like most women, you take pleasure in shopping. Although we may not get to enjoy the beautiful Caribbean surf and sand. I bet you turn most men's heads when you are in a swimsuit."

"Don't really think about it. Nor do I care. Since you mentioned the Caribbean, would you mind telling me where we're going and what exactly I will be doing?"

Ariel looked at him with a cold hard stare. She had participated in some shaky assignments. Only with Jake, again like now, had they been this personal.

He continued his know-it-all smirk.

"Cancun my sources discovered is where your grandson and family are headed. You may get to meet your grandson sooner than anticipated."

"And how do you intend on this happening? I'm sure they will be surrounded by bodyguards, and I doubt very seriously you have an invitation to join them. Perhaps you will enlighten me as to how they fit into whatever scheme you and your colleagues are being paid to perpetrate. And what do my family and I have to do with making this happen? I know you aren't doing us any favors. This isn't about helping me."

"Perpetrate. An interesting choice of words. Sounds ominous, perhaps implying nefarious. Do hope for everyone involved that is not the case. I prefer nonviolent cooperation. This is where you come in. I expect you to use your journalistic skills to get an impromptu interview with the ambassador, if not with him, perhaps his wife. You can use this opportunity to meet your grandson. So, you see, I do intend to help you."

He nodded to the Hispanic woman who was serving as hostess. She had been making Ariel uncomfortable with her deadpan eyes locked on Ariel's every time Ariel glanced her way. She made Ariel think femenista, guerrilla from Soldier of Fortune Magazine. Out of costume playing hostess. Alperts ordered a gin and tonic. Ariel declined. She wanted a coffee but was afraid of what might be put in it. The hostess never spoke. Her movements led Ariel to wonder if she could be a male transvestite, her features said she was female, could possibly be pretty if she tried. Ariel wondered why she was here. Was she another agent with DICE?

"I guess I could call them and tell them I am an anchorwoman with NBC's affiliate in Columbia, South Carolina on my way, hoping for an interview because viewers will be interested to know…What exactly is it the viewers would like to know?"

"Clever. Not bloody bad. How about this: your viewers would be interested to know that the ambassador is meeting with the Russian Ambassador to Mexico and a top aide to the Mexican President. They will be discussing America's President's ongoing threat to cancel NAFTA which threatens Mexico's sovereignty, intending to force them to pay for his constituents' desire for his wall. A wall they know, and the rest of the world knows, he wants built by companies he will profit from."

"Former President."

"I do believe that is still being debated." He saw the frown on her lovely face. "As you will, former President who still holds sway over your country's legislative agenda."

Ariel nodded. She was in no mood to discuss politics with this man.

"You can say you believe the Russian Ambassador is meeting to discuss the possible purchase of military weapon secrets stolen by a traitor, Major Bud Jenkins, formerly COO of Tindal Industries. And, you wish to know if the rumors are true that her husband may be looking to sell the Cubans and Mexicans a little Russian technology also."

Ariel was shocked by this disclosure. Was he lying?

"Where do you get your information? Sounds improbable to me. As I'm sure it would to them."

Alperts gave her his not-so-charming smile and continued, "your new president will be having his first meeting with his friend Russian President Putin in a few weeks. If we are correct, the Russian Ambassador's gambit, this bargaining chip if you will, will have a huge bearing on the outcome of that meeting. Your president has told you people the meeting is scheduled to denounce Russia's Ransomware attacks and discuss some few issues upon which they can agree. I believe your viewers will take notice, as will your old station manager. If this gets broadcast, your government will be scrambling to catch up, they will be too late."

Ariel sat there trying to keep her mouth from dropping open from the shock. Could this be true? How did this man know so much? Jesus, what had she gotten involved in? Most journalists would be delighted. Ariel would be also if this didn't involve her family. And the feds—he's right--they will be all over this. She could be charged with all kinds of things. The Patriot Act—her own government possibly would want to make her disappear--Cuba, Guantanamo, who knows where? Was this what whoever his employer wanted when they hired him to make her disappear. Now she was really scared—his last statements—"if this gets broadcast--they will be too late."

"Aren't you going to thank me? You said I was trying to get you fired. This is a journalistic coup. I doubt any other news organization has a clue. Think on it, you will get to see your grandson. I'm sure when you drop this knowledge bomb on the ambassador, you will be granted a meeting. A simple thank you, will do." He downed his drink, raised his glass for another. "You sure you won't have one? You look like you could use one." Even the feminista smiled.

Mark watched the jet carrying Ariel takeoff. He rushed into the terminal. A man was seated behind a desk. He looked up from a computer monitor sitting in front of him.

"The jet that took off a few minutes ago, what is its destination?"

"Can't tell you." Was his short reply.

"Can't or won't?"

"Same thing. That's privileged information and I can't give it out unless you have a court order."

Mark didn't have time for bullshit regulations. "I'm a federal agent," he flipped open to his ID, "unless you want me to get my boss to get the FBI and FAA to take a close look at your operation, I suggest you honor my request. This is a matter of national security and you just let a federal witness charter a plane and fly out of here." Sounded good, Mark thought.

The man quickly looked back down, tapped the keyboard without daring to look back up. "I'm a federal employee also. This is not my operation. I just work here. If I could help you I would. Rules are rules. Since you are here and I need to go to the restroom, would you tell anyone who comes in I'll be right back."

He rolled his chair back and walked toward the hallway where a lit-up sign said restrooms. Mark swiveled the monitor around and read the screen. Cancun.

When the man came back, Mark asked, "can you look up flight information for me to book a flight to Cancun?"

The man, his name tag said Roy, sat back down and rolled back under the desk. "Sure, we're part of Douglas International in Charlotte." He tapped on the keyboard, looked up and said, "there's a flight in an hour, arrives around noon. Next flight is around five and arrives at eight. They're both booked up. Tourist season, lots of people head south to escape the autumn and winter blues."

"Give me the number for the airline with the flight that leaves in an hour. Guess someone's going to get bumped. Hate it, but…"

Mark rushed back out to his rental, speed dialed General McDab, filled him in on what was happening and requested he get him on the flight and have someone meet him to get him past security and take his rental car.

CHAPTER
11

Fort Hood, Texas
Jake, TJ and Hardy

No one seemed to be hungover. The information Hardy dropped on Jake put a damper on any conversation he and Hardy might have been inclined to have. TJ and Dick hardly noticed their silence; they were too caught up in getting caught up. That left Jake in the corner booth next to Hardy. Hardy's meme asking if Elena's father possibly knew or contributed to her kidnapping, surprised him.

Jake memed, 'What's with you and TJ? I find it highly unlikely her father Sam would have been party to her kidnapping.'

'What if she wasn't being held hostage, was Jenkins' guest? She did leave with Jenkins, and I find it strange she managed to escape unharmed. Furthermore, Elena and her father have lawyered up. Usually that indicates, in my experience, people have something to hide. We ran background checks on them—found connections and possible connections between them and the people being investigated. Then there are the video cameras we found. The computers, all the information gone, wiped clean, viruses installed. Our techs are working to get what they can. Looks like Tindal's going to come out clean. We need Jenkins. He's the key.'

Jake sat twirling his mug on its coaster. He nursed his beer, cold but not dark enough for his taste.

'We catch him. He comes back, gets immunity from prosecution if he testifies. Seems like you could hack his neuro-implant, find where he is, everything he knows without all this effort.'

'That's just it, his implant has gone dark—like he dropped off the face of the earth. Could be he is where the satellites can't find him. He knows the system--he's staying offline.'

'Or, he's being held somewhere by some entity that knows how to block our attempts to locate him. There are other possibilities I'm sure you and these other *experts* have thought of--possibly he had the implant disabled or removed—could be he's dead. In which case, finding him doesn't matter.'

Jake and Hardy paused to take a drink. TJ kept glancing their way. Dick seemed not to notice their presence and their apparent silence as though they were listening to TJ's and his conversation. He was on his second mug, which may have helped.

'The information he stole does. It's worth a small fortune to our enemies and poses a threat to national security.'

'What about the Russians and Operation Pink Flamingo?'

'Ongoing. This is part of the same op, they are major players—stealing, buying, and selling technology is a top priority for them—as Putin said, "once KGB, always KGB," most of the oligarchs came from that camp. Our job is to stop them and whoever else threatens us and our allies' security. However, in this case, everyone, friend, and foe, wants Jenkins and/or what he stole.'

Jake looked over as a tall man dressed like a construction worker entered, had the impression of a hard-hat pressed into his mussed, dark hair--may or may not be what he seems. Jake hated being paranoid about other people. The war and everything that happened since had made his natural distrust worse.

The crowd made him feel trapped. The bathrooms were behind them, cold water might help. The place was filling up, the bar area packed with soldiers in fatigues and other construction workers, very few women, all possible threats. Middle of the week, hump day, no social distancing—come on get a grip, Ariel's got you all wound up.

Hardy was watching him. TJ kept stealing glances.

'Okay, okay. So where do we start?'

'Intel says Jenkins may be in Cuba. Humint has not confirmed this. That's where we come in. Other interesting information was sent to me before we arrived here. Our missing CIA man, our old pal Poponovich, has *a follow but do not detain order* for Ms. Gaspard and him sent out to all agencies. Interestingly, *he* has been declared a fugitive from justice by every agency, except the CIA Counterterrorism Unit.'

'What do you think that's all about?'

'Initially I thought it concerned his role with the Tindal investigation. However, our agency and the FBI believe he was, and could still be, the money man for the cartel. The information TJ and you provided seems to point that direction, which means he has gone rogue. There is nothing conclusive that can be relied upon, but my bet is, he's been, and still is, operating undercover for the CIA Clandestine Unit. General McDab, head of the unit refuses to answer my requests about him. Furthermore, I have been told the team watching Alperts, saw someone fitting his description at the Rock Hill Airport this morning. Seems after we took off, Alperts boarded a chartered jet and departed from there and our friend rushed out of there jumped in a rental car and hurried north to Charlotte. Our team asked the controller some questions. Reluctantly, he divulged Mark was headed to Charlotte Douglas for a flight to Cancun. He was booked and boarded using a passport bearing the name Marcus Zedekiah Osborne.'

'This is where it gets more interesting. The private jet with Alperts contained other passengers, one we are trying to ascertain, care to guess the name of another passenger?'

Jake almost choked on his beer. Why? She seemed to agree she would stay away from Alperts.

'Thought you warned her off. Guess she didn't listen. We're scrambling a team to go there. She will be detained, hopefully when they arrive. As will Alperts and Poponovich. That's the plan.'

Jake pursed his lips drawing a longer look from TJ. 'Why Cancun?'

'We're working on that. I hope to hear something shortly.'

'Sounds like that is where we should be going.'

'Soon as I know something, I'll make the call. As it stands, we have the training tomorrow and that is not going to be cancelled. Hate to tell you, as of right now, it no longer looks like you'll make your son's wedding. Better stay sharp. Don't overdo the drinking.'

Don't worry, stay sharp, Jake told himself upon awakening. He hardly slept. Why would Ariel have accompanied Alperts? Why had she not listened to him? That one seemed obvious; she didn't want to renew their argument. Seems she had already made up her mind. She was going to do what she had to for their newly-discovered family.

Jake felt frustrated. He had to force himself to concentrate. He figured his implant was learning the use of the smart weapons.

They shot smart bullets, which made it impossible for even someone with no experience to miss the target. There was a conventional looking M4, called a VKS launcher which used kinetic energy, loaded with a magazine or drum that fired paintball looking ammunition that exploded releasing PAVA, a pepper chemical to disable or immobilize the recipient. Relatedly, was the TCP semiauto pistol that fired VKR rounds using the same kinetic delivery system and was effective up to fifty yards. Both weapons cartridges used CO2 or nitrogen as the propellent.

"Kinetic energy, where have I heard that before?" TJ asked.

"The Navy has the Railguns and the Airforce has tungsten projectiles called "The Rod of God" weapon that we threatened to use on North Korea. That is probably where you heard about it. These systems use hypersonic, nonchemical propelled sabot projectiles that have a shotgun effect, disabling or destroying men and machine in an apocalyptic manner. They rely on speed and density rather than explosive payload. As you saw, especially useful in a small or broad targeted area. The VKS and PCP are nonlethal elements of the system. As is 40 LMTS, 40 mm "sponge gun," Dick did air quotation marks. "Single round has a range of a football field, delivering blunt trauma up to 250 feet. There are three to twenty shot bandoliers which deliver the same debilitating affect at five or one hundred feet. These are similar to the nonlethal beanbag weapons you have probably seen or used. Unfortunately, I only have the VKS, which you just fired. There are lethal chemical balls available to certain combat units, as well as some explosive balls for the VKS and PCP. Those are restricted, you didn't hear about them from me. Although I have heard you three may be given access. I wouldn't know."

They moved on to another area.

Dick said, "Several of these weapons can't be demonstrated due to the painful effects upon the victim. You will be provided a training video to view the consequences." He moved over to the first one. "This is a PEP, pulsed energy projectile, weapon. It produces short laser bursts creating plasma on the surface of the skin, then fills the plasma with laser energy which explodes. Kinda like mini flashbang grenades on the skin. Scares the hell out of the victim. Next up is the ADS, active denial system, uses millimeter waves of energy to heat the water under the skin, worse than any sunburn you may have ever experienced, so they tell me. This one here is called the Plasma Shield. Another shock and awe weapon designed to create pockets of plasma in the air. Another laser ignites the plasma, more flashbangs, ten explosions per second. And then we have the oleoresin capsicum dispenser, TJ and Jake you're probably familiar with this one." He turned his attention on Hardy. "These projectiles cause agitation to the skin, sinuses, the whole respiratory system. Makes you cough and cry like hell. The tear gas effect. Any questions?" No one said anything. "Like I said, you can watch the training videos later."

They continued with their field training firing rocket propelled missiles and grenades their implants guided, "smelled out", using detection-integrated-radar and infrared to pinpoint the target. They took out a vehicle, simulated enemy forces, mines and IEDs. Utilizing their implants, they directed an explosion in midair which sprayed an area with what could have been lethal pellets. Jake and TJ didn't care to spend much time on these weapons. After all Jake and TJ had been soldiers, this was just a variation which improved accuracy.

Jake and TJ added to the implants' repertoire, sharing their knowledge with Hardy's implant about reinforced personnel carriers and other mobile mechs they had used which allowed a drone operator to sit inside and direct their fire support without having a gunner exposed on top to weapon fire or IEDs. Hardy apparently knew something about what the Sergeant Major demonstrated. His implant didn't add anything to the shared info Jake's and TJ's implants imparted to his. Jake still remained skeptical Hardy had any previous military experience.

They spent most of the day flying drones. The drones varied in size and tactical capabilities. Some were capable of visual only, others had audio and visual capabilities and infrared, then there were the ones armed with various types of ammunition, chemically debilitating or lethal, like The Hive--he and TJ were all too familiar with that one.

The Sergeant Major was amazed at how adroit they were at flying them.

"Normally it takes weeks, months of training for anyone to reach this level of competence with no prior experience. I think you men have put one over on me." He shook his head in disbelief. "You ever decide to, you could join my team as instructors."

They walked back to the staging pickup point where the van waited.

Jake had to ask, "these smart weapons, why don't we equip our troops with more of them?"

"I've asked the same question. The masters of our universe have treaties, rules of engagement that say the playing field must be balanced, no unfair advantage given in how we kill each other. Our enemies don't have such compunctions, as we are all well aware. These supposed masters of our tribal realm are slow to adapt changes. Part of that is cost, but the major reason seems to be that politicians, here and abroad, have lots of constituents who make a living off the fruits of war."

"Soon old instructors like me will be put out to pasture. From what I hear, the next generation of weapons read like something ole Joe Haldeman or Isaac Asimov dreamed up. Getting' too sophisticated for me. I'm sure you boys know more about that than I do."

TJ replied, "You'll be here until they take you out of here in a box or urn. Gotta have someone to keep 'em straight around here until then."

"War ain't the same anymore. These young recruits don't care. All games for them. Not many good leaders out there either. Keeping these weapons out of the hands of terrorists and others who don't live by the rules is a huge factor. We have a history of deploying then withdrawing and leaving behind too much ordinance which often ends up in the wrong hands continuing the threats, wasting taxpayer money."

Hardy began looking uncomfortable. He quickly added, "That's why Homeland and trainers like you exists, why we came here, and the reason we are allowed access to the latest technology forbidden to others. And the reason we need to put a move on. We have some of those bad ones on the move, and we need to go enjoy ourselves somewhere else. We appreciate your time, but we're on a tight schedule."

The driver of their van was standing by the open passenger door. The other doors were open.

"Our plane awaits. We'll drop you off Sergeant Major."

"Beautiful day. I'll walk, just the same thank you Undersecretary Hardy. If you need a hand let me know. It's been a pleasure. Maybe someday, you can tell me how you did it. Jake take care of TJ for me. He was one of my star pupils."

Once they were airborne and the screen was in place with the Major forward out of earshot, Hardy filled them in on the latest developments.

"DICE agent Alperts and party didn't arrive at Cancun Airport. I've been told Alperts' plane filed a flight plan for El Paso. We believe this is a diversion since they have reservations in Cancun. Our team spotted Poponovich, or Osborne as he now calls himself. He caught a flight headed to El Paso. Someone is feeding him good intel. Perhaps Alperts suspects Poponovich and others are following him. The CIA locals claim they know nothing about Poponovich or his movements."

This worried Jake. "Is the team that was following Alperts and Ariel going there? You gave me your word she would be watched and detained."
"One of the border teams will take over. You need to concentrate your efforts on our mission. I'll keep you posted about the Gaspard woman. When I hear something, you'll be informed. We now know the Russian Ambassador to

Mexico has joined the Cuban Ambassador to Spain, they are at the Cuban Embassy joined by a friend of the Mexican President, who has a hacienda down the coast toward Playa del Carmen, less than an hour south of Cancun and not too far from where your lady friend and company are booked to stay."

Hardy watched Jake. No reaction. Hmm.

"The presence of the foreign ambassadors means something is up. Jenkins may be there or could show up. There is ample reason to expect other foreign nationals seeking our man will be there, along with numerous operatives, and of course our cartel buddies. The feds Joint Terrorism Task Force, of which we are part, will be operating out of our embassy as well as from the Cancun airport. Things could get interesting fast."

"Our team is scrambling to find suitable accommodations in the area for you and company. So far, no luck, tourist season is making things difficult, and they are trying to keep your presence unknown. Seems that proposition failed, looks like they will be expecting us, which means getting close and personal, problematic."

"You will be given tactical gear, the nonlethal kind. You must avoid lethal action, don't want to create any international fallout. Mexican prisons aren't the best place to enjoy tourist activities. With relations between our countries at a low point, you get in trouble, there may not be much anyone can do. No diplomatic status for you two, understood?"

"Us? What about you?" Jake asked.

"I will be operating out of our control center near a private airport, as well as the embassy. Unless we can arrange something, you will have to bunk out in a warehouse."

"You will be given disguises, appropriate clothing, including baseball caps. They are very touristy looking, hopefully helping you to blend in…"

"Blend in? Two guys? What are we supposed to be? Gay? I don't think so." Jake said. "TJ's crack about backdoor was a joke."

"Aw sweet thing you goina break my heart," TJ laughingly quipped.

Hardy interrupted. "You will have two female agents working with you. The major will be one of them."

"Whoa," TJ said, "Jake and I are a team. I don't need to have to worry about anyone else."

"Worry? When have you ever had to worry about me?" Jake replied.

"You've been known to get a little carried away sometimes, especially with the women folks."

"Me?"

Hardy broke in again. "These women have years of experience in the field, they can handle themselves. You will need the cover to help you blend in."

"Deane goina kill me, you too Jake, if she hear 'bout this. So we clear, ain't goina be no "in the room in bed with me at night happenin'.""

"We will attempt to have you in adjoining rooms wherever it can be arranged. Then you two lovebirds can have one room and they can have the other without anyone knowing."

"The other issue is the cartels. Like most areas where there are tourists, the cartels ply their trades: drugs, robbery, kidnapping for human trafficking, and so on. And, as usual, they have their turf wars. I need not remind you; your cartel buddies have their members here and it would be a good bet that they know you are coming. You have targets on your backs. You must be on the lookout, another reason you need the major and your other pseudo mate. There will be other operatives watching also including me. I will be watching using your implants and the UAV surveillance team's eyes in the sky, which you will have access to as well. No lethal action—we are not registered to operate there."

"Really? Give me a break. From what you've said everyone knows we're coming. And our only defense is eyes in the sky. Good to know our possible demise will be seen without offending anyone." Jake looked at TJ. He was smiling. "Glad to see you're enjoying this."

"Just like old times bro. If you're getting screwed might as well enjoy it."

Hardy said, "You'll have weapons, they will be nonlethal. Better than ending up in a Mexican prison."

"Did our cartel buddies get the memo about nonlethal weapons?"

Hardy ignored the quip.

"Jake, one other thing, you are not to spend time locating Mrs. Gaspard or your grandson. Or, going after the Alperts man."

"What are we supposed to be doing down there? If you have all these teams there, what exactly is our mission? I can't see Jenkins showing up there. You said Cuba. That makes more sense."

Hardy once more ignored Jake's comments—was beginning to piss him off.

"The other Homeland team is already there for surveillance and support only. The other task force members are there to coordinate their part of the operation, technically we are under State Department and the Ambassador's Command."

"Meaning the CIA?"

"They have their team, as does the DEA, FBI and NSA. None of them have the advantage that we have. They don't know anything about our implants. We should be ahead of them because of that. The mission remains what it has always been: get Jenkins, the information he stole and keep our enemies from getting their hands on either of these things while keeping our eyes and ears open for any other enemy technology we discover."

"Why do I feel like we're the bait in a stocked pond of piranhas?"

"Like I said, smile bro. Helps ease the pain."

They sat there in silence each thinking about the situation. Not sharing their thoughts.

Hardy was worried Jake or TJ might try to access the major's and the captain's info. If they tried, they'd find it blocked—on a-need-to-know lockout.

Jake's mental landscape contained too many personal landmines--Ariel, the Alperts man, the reality of, the dangers to another daughter and a grandson, on top of his son's wedding. More than likely he would not be missed at the wedding—after this any hope for reconciliation would likely not be a possibility. Now two women dumped into the field of foley. Jake felt his world was set to blow up, jeopardizing him and everyone else. He had a nagging feeling there was something Hardy was holding back, felt like another ticking timebomb.

TJ wondered why they were going there. Seemed the key thing was the ambassadors—why put themselves in jeopardy? Why there? And Jenkins, Jake was right, why would he be there? Everything pointed to the cartels. Did they have Jenkins? Did David Gonzalez recover and how much did he know? The fat morphodite's computer burned up in the cabin fire when their gang buddies tried to burn him and Jake out. Damn. He forgot about the bag of zip drives. With everything that happened since their capture…where had they gone? They were in his truck. Had Arturo found them before fleeing? Or had the feds. Did Hardy know about them? Screw me running, that why they headed there?

Hardy removed the shield, went to the bar, made himself a gin and tonic.

"How about a cocktail, a beer? Help yourself. You two need to get more acquainted with the Major and your other companion, I'll send them back."

TJ looked from Jake to Hardy. "Where this other one been? Never saw anyone board with us other than the major. You see any other one Jake?"

"The other one has been our copilot. We don't have much time, so I need to summon them. Have a drink. Might be a while before we have another free moment for introductions."

Jake had been half listening. "You didn't answer me, what about the intel indicating Jenkins was in Cuba?"

"Not confirmed, but that was the latest. Why?"

"Doesn't make sense. Why he would go there? You said it was likely everyone looking for him was there or headed there."

"Okay. What's your point?" Hardy asked.

"Seems like a waste of time. If our mission is to find Jenkins and retrieve him and the stolen info, why go there?"

TJ spoke. "Thought we established that--we the tethered lambs. Come on bro, we goin' there 'cause everybody else there. Has to be a reason for it. Right? Perhaps we decoys. HS has other teams trailin' Jenkins."

Hardy remained quiet. He had debated with the HIS's Secretary about how much to disclose to them and when. Had to let it play out—not compromise the experiment—skew the results. But the op was the end all.

"Good one TJ, that tethered lamb thing. Seems everybody is trying to figure out where Jenkins is or what it is he has to sell. No Jenkins, no sale. Excluding perhaps the Russians and the Cubans, but then why would they be there if he is in Cuba? Perhaps the ambassadors are there to serve as his go-betweens or to meet with someone else. We never did locate Okneyev or that amphib UAV." He looked at Hardy. TJ did also.

"That is a possibility. Or, as you surmised, this could be a Trojan Horse, a sleight of hand. We must start somewhere. Why would they be his auctioneers? What if Jenkins and Okneyev are coming there to meet the ambassadors or others? There are a lot of possibilities. This is our mission, what we have to determine."

"I don't think these people or anyone else knows where Jenkins is. One way to find out. The tethered lamb—what if Jenkins were to be seen? Then everybody would have to show their hand."

"Like you say bro, Jenkins wouldn't go there, too risky.

"What if he were to be seen elsewhere? What if we produced a look-a-like who is seen and disappears? We chose what group we want to implicate. I say our cartel buddies. Have this impostor take bids. We feed the bidders, including other agencies in our government, enough info to make it seem legit. Create a Trojan Horse. Place a trace on all bidders. Whoever doesn't bid must know this scheme is bogus. Helps eliminate poseurs and gives our agency hackers an easy way to track the other guys' intel. Maybe we learn Jenkins is no longer in the land of the living."

"Jeezum. You come up with all this on your own?" TJ was smiling his what-the-f… smile.

"Better than what I've heard otherwise, what do you think Bob?"

Hardy paused seeming to think as he drank his cocktail. "Maybe? If nothing else, it would keep everyone busy trying to determine if it is legit. Put some heat on our cartel buddies. Although it could start a war with the other cartels, that could be nasty, lot of innocents would get caught in the crossfire. I need to run this up the chain."

"You think that is a good idea? What if this is a ruse run by some rogue person or group, within or with access to the task force, responsible for Jenkins' disappearance?" Jake asked. "Perhaps Alperts knows something we don't. The cartel could be behind this ruse. Jenkins could be in their hands, and all of this could be a smokescreen. Fake Jenkins seems to be one way of knowing who does or doesn't have him."

"Easy to be paranoid. Often times it pays. But I have no way to authorize a change in mission. I'll have to take it up with my superior. Meanwhile, you need to familiarize yourselves with your teammates in case we are told to continue with the mission as it is now."

Hardy finished his drink, set the empty glass down in the bar sink and headed to the cockpit. It worked. Jake came up with a good idea. The target—results were all that mattered. Had to be extra careful with his thoughts. Couldn't slip up—they might not like his method.

TJ grabbed a beer, as did Jake.

'Something come to me while you having your brain flush.' TJ memed. 'Remember David Gonzalez' computer—do you think it burned completely in that cabin fire? Somebody could have recovered the hard drive. Then, there's those thumb drives, I'm certain I left those in the truck when we pulled our Huck and Jim raid from Pinckneyville. The feds they recovered and searched my truck. Nothing been said about any thumb drives. Either Arturo took them, or the feds have them. I wonder what all was on them? You looked at them, was there anything on them you saw indicate how much David knew about The Hive and the other shit Jenkins took?'

Jake shook his head. 'Not really. But they wouldn't be buying a pig in a poke. Poponovich, how much did he know? You thinking, what I'm thinking?'

'Hardy holding out on us--Jenkins ain't necessarily the reason we here. For damn sure we the bait, not sure to what end. That about cover it?'

'Exactomundo. Makes you wonder how much Alperts knows. Is he using Ariel for bait? Which would explain Poponovich. He's going after Alperts and Ariel, possibly meeting with the cartel. Could be they have Jenkins?'

'Or both? We don't know who Alperts' employer is? My bet's on Tindal. Ever wonder what happened to Dean and crew or Devereaux? Carl, he was less than forthcoming.'

'As far as Alperts' employer. Could be the cartel or Tindal. Either way, you can bet Tindal figures his million-dollar bounty puts him in control. Yeah, I do wonder what happened to Dean, Devereaux and the others. All I know is what Hardy told me. He hasn't given me anything except lip-service credit for saving his op in Cuba. He promised me funds. I've been scrambling to stay afloat. As you know, it was touch and go during the COVID-19 Crisis and the economic nightmare hasn't let up for me. I haven't seen nary a dime of any of Hardy's promised money and I damn sure could use it.'

Jake got up got a beer. TJ declined.

'The guys with the brass balls never share, you know that. Hardy his tactics the same ole, same old, bro.'

TJ was told, threatened by the feds, not to reveal his ongoing part in the task force operation, especially to Jake. Left him feeling guilty, especially after transferring to Charlotte. He owned up to some of it with Jake when the shit with the bangers and Tindal went down. He and Deane weathered the subsequent coronavirus and economic tragedies better than most because they had government jobs. He offered to help Jake out. Stubborn ass refused. He hoped now wouldn't be no more keeping anything more from him. Hardy was just another fed, for him the op and his career would always come first.

'Gotta watch what you meme. Not just Hardy, who knows hackers, like our old buddy David Gonzalez, may be just able to tap in, you never know. Lots of these other government agencies have access to spyware. Supposedly, Jenkins has the implant. Got to assume there're others. Makes you wonder about these women we're being paired with. Be careful bro—women yo' Achilles' Heel.'

'That's behind me now. Being paired up with these women, I don't like it. We're a team. No way to know what to expect from outsiders. Heading out into enemy territory with a couple of unknowns usually spells disaster. I have enough shit on my mind as it is. This crap with Ariel and Alperts, us going on this damn mission blind, our dicks hanging out there, no way to protect ourselves, this damn implant, now this. Disaster after disaster waiting to happen.'

'Watch it, bro. Here they come.'

CHAPTER
12

Southeast of Juarez, Mexico
Ariel, Alperts and General Toraz

"This isn't Cancun." Ariel was looking out the window. The jet had flown over a large border town and was descending toward a road on a patch of ground in the middle of the desert.

"Right you are. A slight change in plans. I need to talk to someone. We will continue on afterwards."

He spoke to the other woman whose eyes stayed on Ariel. The woman's expression didn't change but her eyes seemed to say she was not happy. He abruptly stopped talking. She nodded and they took their seats as the plane made its final approach.

She and Alperts deplaned taking backpacks with them. Ariel had her toiletries and two changes of clothes including her other pair of hiking boots. The jet with the other woman still onboard, turned, taxied, then took off. There was scrub and cactus as far as Ariel could see. On top of a slight rise was a wooden building with a windsock hanging limp from a pole set on top. Alperts set out for this building. She followed. "Where are we?"

He didn't answer.

They entered the wooden building whose wooden floor was covered in sand. At the back was another door. Alperts opened it. Inside was an outhouse two-seater. Alperts took out his phone and entered something via the keypad. There was a hum and the two-seater slid down and off to the left revealing steps that led down to a tunnel dimly lit by bulbs hanging from an electrical wire. Ariel felt she had no alternative other than to follow Alperts down. He had to keep his head bent to keep from hitting the bulbs. Once they reached the tunnel floor, he punched in the code and the outhouse floor returned into position. They moved slowly down the tight sloping tunnel. After what seemed an hour, the tunnel began to slope upward and terminated at a door. Alperts punched in another set of instructions.

The door opened into a garden shed which opened out to a vine covered arbor with a decorative Mexican tile walkway bordering a patio area with a fountain in the center. At a decorative wrought iron table was seated an older distinguished-looking Hispanic man flanked by a young, swarthy uniformed Federales across from two less-well-dressed Hispanic men. Standing nearby was a young, pleasant-looking Indian woman in a loose fitting pleated white dress with frills at the top of the bodice and around the waist.

"Buenos Dios," Alperts said as they approached the table. The man did not rise.

"So glad you decided to join us Senor Alperts. Who is this beautiful Senorita you have brought to my humble abode?" He rose to take Ariel's hand which he kissed after Alperts introduced her.

Alperts told Ariel to please excuse them that he needed to talk to General Toraz in private.

The General turned to the Indian woman. "Isabella please take our guest inside while Senor Alperts and I discuss some business." Ariel followed Isabella into the white stuccoed hacienda with its red clay-tiled roof.

Ariel was shown into a well-appointed living area: floors of picturesque marble, furnishings a western rustic style motif—carved wood with animal hide coverings over sterile off-white cushions, walls colorfully painted and hung with wood framed autographed paintings mixed in with photos of her host with numerous well-dressed people. She walked around taking it all in. Isabella left to get her a glass of water and returned with a crystal glass of sparkling mineral water, accompanied by a young man in the uniform of the federal police who introduced himself as Officer Guippe Sanchez.

"Please be seated Senora Gaspard, you look tired. General Toraz and your friend will join you momentarily."

"Do you work for General Toraz, is he with the federales?"

He smiled and said, "No. I am here at the General's request." He didn't offer to elaborate, turned and went back out to the patio area.

Ariel sat in one of the fur-covered chairs, put her feet up on an ottoman and closed her eyes. She had not intended on falling asleep and was startled awake by the sound of voices coming from an adjoining room. She heard footsteps on the floor and turned to see Alperts walking toward her. She sat up and he stepped in front of her.

"General Toraz has invited us to stay overnight. I told him we needed to be on our way. He was not too happy. I believe he was looking forward to dining with us. I should say with you. He was quite taken by your appearance. He knew you were a journalist, said you had done an outstanding interview with an acquaintance of his, Teresa Mendoza. He has offered us safe passage to an airfield where a plane has been arranged to take us on to Cancun. Isabella is packing us lunch. Then we will need to be on our way. If you need to use the ladies' room, I suggest you do so."

Ariel went to the bathroom. Thank goodness her morning queasiness had subsided. Been a long time since she had roughed it as she suspected where they were headed could very well be. Doubly so, thinking of Alperts being there. Had she made a mistake? Her journalistic sense said yes--Too late now.

Isabella brought them a fruit basket with a picnic assortment of food. Isabella whispered for her to be careful that there were many dangerous men outside the gates. Ariel followed her back to where Alperts was waiting with General Toraz.

"I hate to see you go Senora Gaspard. I was hoping to have you as my guest, but Senor Alperts insists he needs your expertise to accomplish some business for my associates. Senor Alperts has promised to bring you here when our mutual business has been taken care of. I hope that is not to be exceptionally long. I am looking forward to seeing you again." He bowed and once more kissed her hand.

Officer Sanchez accompanied them out to a delivery van where three armed men waited with the doors open. She got in followed by Alperts and one of the men. The other two got in the front and they drove around a circular entrance area and out through a set of gates manned by more armed guards. Ariel started to speak and Alperts shook his head. Their fellow armed passenger sat rigid staring out a small window in one of the rear doors. Ariel tried to see out the back. The window was obscure glass. She focused her attention out the front windshield. Nothing but barren desert, distant dusty looking hills, and an occasional sprinkling of mesquite and cactus.

They passed through a few squalid looking communities with half-starved dogs seeking shade, chickens scattering out of the road accompanied by half-naked kids on the sides of the road whose dirt-smeared faces seemed to be taken-in by their hasty intrusion.

The van was going as fast as the uneven road allowed. Ariel clung to her seat, the seat belt bit in every time they hit a bump. Minutes after passing through one of the communities she heard the sound of motorbikes. The sound seemed to be coming from the sides and the rear.

Their armed escorts began speaking rapidly to each other. One of them spoke into a mic pinned onto his vest. As he was talking Ariel saw two bikers coming at them head on. Neither their driver nor the bikers slowed or deviated from what Ariel was certain to be a collision. At the last second the bikers split, there were loud thumps on the sides, one near the front quarter panel, another near her at the rear wheel area. Ariel felt certain the sounds had to have been caused by the riders' bikes having careening off the sides of the van.

She was turning her head when Alperts reached over undid her seat belt, grabbed her, and shoved her forward onto the floor. He landed on top of her. In the same instant there were two loud whumps, the van started swerving then began rolling.

Ariel and Alperts along with their armed escorts were tumbled like in a large clothes dryer. To her the seconds seemed like minutes until the rolling stopped, then the van began rocking back and forth on its roof. Ariel's ears rang. She saw Alperts struggling to get to his feet. He grabbed the automatic rifle from the rear guard who lay with his neck twisted in an unnatural way, his open eyes staring at Ariel, not blinking, or moving.

Before she had time to think, Alperts slid the side door open, leaned out and fired two rounds into the face of the closest biker. He rolled out and Ariel scrambled to follow holding tight onto her bag. Alperts grabbed her and they rolled. Then she felt the recoil of the weapon and the heat of the shells as Alperts fired across her. Another biker dropped a few feet away.

Alperts stood and yanked her to her feet, shoved her forward toward a low rise in the desert floor where he yanked her down. She felt the air pressure change and the heat from the van as it exploded. Alperts grabbed her and they began running, then he yanked her down again, as they dropped, he fired the rifle at two more bikers charging at them. One then the other was hit, their bodies going one way and their bikes continuing forward crashing to the earth sending up waves of sandy dirt. Alperts walked back to where they lay and shot each of them in the head like you would a fatally wounded animal. He stood there gazing off toward the direction they had come from. Ariel followed his stare. She saw dust disappearing over a rise. She still couldn't hear much.

During her time covering events home and abroad, she had seen more than her share of the aftermath of violence. Never had she been directly involved in the carnage. She started shaking, tears flowed down her cheeks.

The bikes were no worse for wear. Alperts picked them up and started each one. He tied her bag onto the back of one of the bikes with a broken bungee cord. He walked over to Ariel and pulled her to her feet.

Through the tears she saw his lips move. He was saying something to her. He shook her and shouted, "Come on girl before those blokes return with reinforcements." She didn't dare move. He took her arm and led her to the bike. "You know how to ride one of these?"

She reached up and touched his face. When she removed her hand, it was covered in blood. He bent down and looked in the tiny mirror. He had a two-inch muddy gash on his right cheek. He hadn't noticed the bleeding.

"Can you ride?" he yelled at her. She nodded. "Right. Then get on the bloody thing." He watched as she climbed on.

She had ridden her brothers' dirt bikes. That had been a long time ago. Several times she had rented bikes in England and Europe. This bike proved more difficult—the power far greater—she struggled attempting to not over-throttle--the bike jerked and jumped threatening to dump her.

Alperts watched, wondering if perhaps they should abandon each taking a bike and only use one. Finally, she seemed to get the hang of it. He grabbed another less-damaged one and they headed out, ran parallel to the road, slowing as they went up the rises and speeding up on the downhill side. Alperts would charge ahead momentarily to see if he could spot any other vehicles. They stopped and laid the bikes down out of sight the few times he spotted another vehicle. Several miles later they spotted a village. They approached slowly.

There were some Mexican/Indian looking adults with more potbellied half-naked children staring at them from inside open doorways. They stopped in front of a small, rusty tin-roofed shack with crates of potatoes, corn, and yuccas along the front wall. To her dismay, Alperts handed her the rifle after dismounting. He hitched his pants up and walked inside, leaving her there wondering if she had to, could she shoot anyone. She felt like all eyes were on her. She laid the rifle across the handlebars and looked in her bike's mirror. Staring back at her was a face she hardly recognized, reminders of assignments in the Middle East. She felt her filth. She craved a good hot bath and a change of clothes. This didn't look like a likely place for that to happen. What was Alperts doing? How soon before they would get to the airport? What would she do if anything happened to Alperts?

If anything happens to him, you're doomed, she thought as he came back out with two six-ringed holders of bottled water.

He handed her a cool bottle and she rinsed her hands of the dried blood and dirt, splashed some on her face and neck, then drained the rest, feeling the cool moisture as it found its way down her parched throat. Alperts drank most of his and took a wad of napkins and washed the blood off his face with some of his. He tore a couple pieces of napkin which he placed on the cut and applied a strip of duct tape to hold it in place. He looked more macabre--a monster from some B-rated horror movie. He handed Ariel some cellophane-wrapped crackers and told her to put them and the water in her bag.

"I don't believe they'll fit."

"Then make them fit. Better to have these bloody things than anything you think is so bloody precious. Those other bloody things are replaceable."

Ariel stuffed them in and used the straps to hold everything in. Her jean legs hung half out, draped down the scuffed bags' sides.

"When will we be at this airport?"

He didn't answer, took the rifle, slung it over his shoulder, and remounted his bike. They continued their ride down the street. Curious eyes followed them.

Less than a mile out of town was a rundown shack sitting on top of a rise. Alperts turned off the road and Ariel followed. They pulled behind the shack into a sliver of shade and stopped. Alperts laid his bike down and had her do the same. He walked over to a mesquite, pulled out a knife cut a limb and walked back the way they came.

Ariel was stunned. "Why are we stopping?" she shouted at his receding back.

"We need to make sure no one is following. Stay there."

He went back down to the road, walked a short-ways back and used the mesquite branch to sweep their tracks away.

Ariel's hearing was better--still some ringing. She faintly heard the popping of the metal of the bikes as they cooled. Her ragged breathing echoed inside her head. She took another bottle of water, rinsed, and spat, then drank more deeply. Alperts took one, poured some over his head and neck, drained the rest and tossed his bottle aside. Ariel reached down and retrieved his empty, crushed it, and put it back in the bag. He looked at her with a bemused look on his face.

"Good habit wasted out here," he said.

"How long are we going to wait? I need to use the facilities and there damn sure aren't any here."

"Country girl like you, know what's what, right? Best watch for centipedes and snakes."

"I've already done the deed. I need to get cleaned up, change clothes."

He chuckled. "First firefight. No need worry 'bout getting sorted out. Why bother, right?"

"How far to the airstrip?" she asked.

"I will check. For now, we need to stay put. The store-keep acted like he knew nothing. Believe the appearance of a blood-streaked gringo was not an everyday thing for him...Listen."

Ariel listened. She thought she heard a far-off rumble. The sound grew louder, came from the direction of the town, a dusty cloud floated in the air.

Suddenly two pickup trucks topped the last rise and came roaring down the sun-scorched road. They went past. There were two men in each truck and one man in the back of the rear truck holding onto a large-barreled weapon.

At the next rise, they slid to a screeching halt and turned around. The trucks slid to a stop on the road downgrade from where she and Alperts lay in the dwindling shade of their pitiful hiding place, which couldn't stop the breeze stirred sand, much less a bullet.

A man jumped out of the truck that carried the gun in the rear and started walking toward them. The large gun turned and took aim in their direction. The man stopped half-way. Part of his face and neck showed the inked work of tattoos that ran down inside his camo-colored tee shirt and snaked their way down his sinewy arm giving him a menacing appearance. The other man was tattooed with similar ink, his dirty tee shirt had the caricature of a man's face on it, perhaps Che Guevara or Bob Marley.

"Do not shoot Senor. General Toraz sent us. He want us help you get where you going."

"General Toraz sent you? I don't think so."

"Si. Is true. He call. We near, see wreck, come find you. We help."

"He try call? No get phone."

"I lost my phone. If you will, lend me your phone and I will call him."

"Si. I get phone." He started to turn.

"Stop! Stay where you are. Have your compadre bring you the phone."

The man called back to the truck. The driver in the gun truck got out holding a phone. He started up the rise toward the closer man. When he reached him Alperts told him to continue, bring the phone to him. He took the phone. From the phone came a voice, "Senor Alperts. Do not move. I come to you. We talk." From the other truck another man emerged, followed by the driver, who stopped and put his rifle across the hood pointed in their direction.

The man continued, "I need to speak to the Senorita."

"She's listening." Ariel started to rise and Alperts told her to stay down.

"Senorita. You have chosen bad company. Your friend Senor Harper and others come here make our people unhappy. I told to say we know your family, his family, we no want to harm you or your family. You must leave. I give safe ride to you, you go or you never live to see your grandson. Plane waits. You must go now. You stay with this man, you die."

Ariel looked up at Alperts. "How does he know about my grandson? I just found out from you. This had to come from you or your people."

Alperts kept his eyes locked on the other men. "Not from us. You have told someone."

"I told Jake. No one else. These people couldn't have heard it from him."

"Righto. Trust me. The information did not come from me or my group."

"I don't know who to trust."

"You go with these men, I promise you will never be heard from again. Even if they don't kill you, they will make you wish you were dead. These men are ruthless terrorists with no morals."

"And you? Seems you aren't much different."

"I don't kill innocents. Nor do I intend to die." Alperts, who had been sighting his rifle, shot the man with the M-50. Before he dropped, Alperts shot the man with the gun across the hood, his head exploding like a melon. He rose up and shot the man who had been doing the talking in an exposed leg as he was attempting to get back in the truck. He shot him again when he crumpled to the ground. He then shot the other driver before he could exit the truck. The two men who had come up the rise were about to reach their truck, Alperts dropped them both. In less time that it would have taken for him to try to convince Ariel not to trust these men, the discussion was settled.

Ariel had clapped her hands over her ears. She lay there stunned, her face covered in the gritty dirt, the smell of cordite hung in the air. Alperts pulled her to her feet. "Come on. Bring your bike." He grabbed his bike and started down the hill.

She stood there. "You murdered them," she yelled at his retreating back. "You have made me an accomplice in a mass murder."

"Right again. You should be bloody thankful it's them and not us. No one but their fellow bangers are going to give a shit. The authorities, including the ones that are too afraid to do anything and aren't directly involved, will be glad. They will call this another incident between rival cartels. We need to get on the move before more of these bloody sods or the local crooked police show."

Fear of going on with Alperts was only slightly less frightful than staying. Ariel rolled her bike back down and Alperts helped to load them in the back of the truck with the M-50 in it. First, he tossed the body out and used the dead men's canteens of water to rinse the drying blood out of the back and off the hood using a bandana that had been tied around one of the men's head. He instructed Ariel to gather the dead men's weapons and valuables including their phones. She helped with the weapons but refused to touch the bodies. Alperts staged the bodies in and around the other truck, then used the mesquite limb to cover their tracks and signs of blood on the slope up toward the dilapidated shack.

The inside of the truck had worn seats. Dust clung to all the surfaces. Odors: the musky smell of sweaty maleness competed with odors of onion, garlic and other pungent unrefrigerated smells wafting up from the trash that littered the floorboards. An empty tequila bottle stuck its neck out from under the seat. Ariel plopped her bag on the seat, wondering if the contamination would permeate its contents.

Alperts got in the driver's side. He placed a pistol on the dash. The rifle butt was shoved into the trash, its barrel resting against her bag, a reminder to Ariel of the carnage left behind and fear of what lay ahead. He laid a torn dirty shirt full of phones and other valuables from the dead on top of her bag. She wanted to protest but knew it would not change anything. He Googled a map of the area using one of the phones. He said out loud that there was an airfield a little over an hour away east of their position. He started the truck and continued the way they had been travelling. He made a call telling someone on the other end he needed a plane and pilot at the airstrip, he gave the coordinates. Ariel could see from the hardness of his face that he was not happy to hear what had been said. He told the person to make it happen and call him back on his stolen phone with confirmation.

"What about the plane General Toraz said would be waiting? Why not call him?"

"Toraz may have sent these men."

"We left with his men. They killed them. Why would he have his own men killed and why would he want to have us killed?"

"I told you he was unhappy about our business arrangement. He had partners who were unhappy. This is Mexico. That's all you need to know. No more talk about this. You need to keep your eyes on what's going on around us." He kept looking in the mirrors and scanning the horizon.

"I need to call Jake. He needs to be told about this threat."

"I'm sure your bloody friend Jake knows there are threats. In our business threats are a part of the life. I would think your business is the same. We need to keep these phones open, see who calls or sends texts to them."

"Aren't you afraid they will use these phones to track us?"

"A chance we must take. I need to find out who is behind this. These phones may hold the answer," he replied. There is not much light left. It is cold out here at night this time of year."

After what she had witnessed, she felt certain there was no way he intended to let her live. He had said someone had hired him to make her disappear. At this point, who his employer was mattered little. He would use her, perhaps for what he said, then Elizabeth's, perhaps Gabriel's, certainly her life, would no longer be of consequence. Ariel needed to get her hands on that phone. She wanted to know who he had been talking with. Maybe it was the man who had Elizabeth. If I can, I will save them, even if it costs me my own life. If only she could get in touch with Jake.

CHAPTER
13

Juarez, Mexico
Don Geraldo Francisco Gomez—Juarez Cartel Boss

Mark lost Ariel and Alperts. No jet fitting the description of theirs had landed in El Paso. He had to touch base with Arturo soon, let him know he was alive and not under wraps by the feds. He hoped the fugitive warrant would give weight to his innocence and keep Arturo from wanting his head, literally.

Arturo's brother David's passwords were needed to open the accounts—these were thought to be in the Alvarez man's or Jake Harper's possession. He would need Arturo's protection if he was going to survive until then.

Finding Arturo and David from Charlotte had been fruitless, from here, nearly impossible, this was their home base. Convincing them he was not a traitor, could prove difficult. He would feign incredulity, accuse them of taking off, leaving him to fend for himself. He hoped they would believe him. If not, he would most certainly suffer, what was left of him made to disappear.

He used the Border Patrol office phones, contacted his superior and let him know what had happened and what he planned to do. The General didn't need to know his true motive. As expected, he was against Mark's plan, warned Mark to avoid the risk—not pursue the Gaspard woman. He wanted Mark to go to Cancun and join the team there. For the agency finding Jenkins and the codes was more important than losing him to the cartel.

He felt certain from the intel his team had gathered, sooner or later, the Alperts man and the Gaspard woman would lead him to Jenkins. The cartel will want to believe this. Either they, or the Gaspard woman, will lead him to the Russians, Jenkins, and the files. If the general gets upset, so be it.

The codes Jake or his friend were thought to have, and which the Gaspard woman may know about, were the key for his way out--allow him a comfortable retirement. If they didn't have them, then, as his team suspected, Jake's wife Elena was in possession of Jenkin's stolen files, with the outside possibility Jake was biding his time and he and his wife were playing everyone. Getting his hands on Jenkins or the stolen files before anyone else, collecting Tindal's proffered reward, wouldn't give him the same comforts as the cartel's funds would, but it was better than what Uncle Sam was offering.

"They needed to eliminate the cartel as a possible contact for Jenkins," he argued, "they may be responsible for his disappearance." He promised the general, he would be heading to Cancun in a day or two.

He was given one day. Hopefully, someone in the cartel knew something.

If Arturo suspected anything, knew Jake cared about her, she would die in a most horrible fashion. It was entirely possible she and Alperts were in their hands at this very moment.

Arturo would kill him along with Jenkins if Jenkins was captured, and had recordings of the conversations they had about screwing the cartel.

Ciudad Juarez was a place caught in a time warp. Tin and tile-rooved, cinder block homes, some stuccoed, many painted in multi-colors lay next to factories of all shapes, like giant *Lego-Land* creations made from metal and glass. The result of an explosion of unplanned growth. In the last several years this had become a leader in development in the Americas. Before the pandemic, hundreds of thousands crossed through the four border crossings like automatons. Every day at the start and end of their shifts.

Intermingled were tourists, usually arriving later in the morning and leaving before the sun made being on foot unbearable. Their numbers increased during the late spring to mid-fall season, especially on weekends. The nightlife attracted the young and more adventurous to the nightclubs where disc jockeys spun the Latino recordings and the revelers danced and drank themselves into a frenzy. Many times, gunfire would pierce the darkness, rival gangs, members of the main cartels fighting to control the trades of sin.

Mark, riding in a taxi down Avenida 16 de Septembre, decided to go to one of the markets called Mercado Juarez. He went inside wandering past stalls of tourist trinkets, bright colored clothing and various Hispanic arts and crafts.

Out the back was an outdoor food and drink stand, he sat on a stool and ordered some tortillas and a Cuervo. Like most places in Mexico, the food was good and cheap, beer, not so much. Once he finished the red sauce-soaked tortillas and his first beer, he ordered another beer and asked the short, older looking bartender smartly dressed in clean, new field worker attire, if he knew where he could find David and Arturo Gonzalez. The bartender laid his other beer on the counter and looked hard at Mark as if he didn't know what to say. Finally, he said no. He threw Mark's red grease-stained paper plate and his empty beer bottle in the trash then went back to the kitchen area. Mark saw a young boy come out the back and hurry off down the shimmering street. Bingo.

Before he had finished his other beer, an older model Cadillac Escalade, white, darkened windows, with spinner spoked wheels, came up the boulevard, slowing down as it passed by behind Mark. Not long after, two men, one shorter and heavy, the muscle, the other skinny with a pock-marked face, the messenger, sauntered, out of a nearby side street and approached the place where he sat. They were both dressed in tight fitting white pants, designer tennis shoes and silky looking cut-collared shirts--like they had stepped out of a seventies disco club.

They took stools on each side of Mark. The bartender went out of sight.

"I'm not a very good dancer and I didn't come dressed for the occasion I'm afraid," Mark said without looking at either of them.

"You come. No need worry 'bout clothes or dancing," the messenger on the right said. Didn't sound like he was in the mood for conversation. They raised up off their stools and stood waiting for Mark. He finished his beer, put some pesos on the counter, stood up and asked, "Shall I lead or follow?" Muscle took his arm and pulled him forward. The taller talker fell in step on Mark's other side.

"My name is Jose Jiminez. I didn't catch yours." Neither replied.

When they reached the car, he was given a dark blindfold and placed in the back of the Escalade. The taller one got in beside him and made sure the mask was on tight. Mark was used to this routine. The first time he had been put in the trunk of an eighties model Chevrolet that smelled like gas, grease, and a hint of rotten meat. The ride was extremely uncomfortable. These escorts had a sense of humor. They had not come dressed like ordinary street thugs. Unlike the not so fancy-dan cabrones the first time.

The ride was stop and go. They made several turns. Then after what seemed like fifteen minutes, they picked up speed and the stops were less frequent.

Emerging from the auto, Mark, blindfold left in place, was led inside an airconditioned space. There was street noise, followed by the sounds of a metal door opening and closing, their footsteps echoed on concrete for a calculated distance of twenty steps, some metal scraping and clanging, air tool noise, another stop, then an even cooler room with carpeted floor. The room's odor reeked of cigars and an unknown spice smell. Once the mask was off, Mark saw a well-dressed gentleman seated behind an ornate desk, twirling a large caliber bullet casing between manicured fingers. He smiled at Mark.

"You must be the money man Mark Poponovich. I am Don Geraldo Francisco Gomez. Welcome to Juarez." He motioned for Mark to take a seat in one of two mahogany-stained wood chairs in front of the desk. His two escorts took up positions behind and to the sides of him.

"I was expecting to see David and Arturo. Will they be coming?"

"Arturo is away on business. David, he not feeling so well. I am uncle, their mother was my sister. Arturo was excited to hear from you. He wished to know why you have not contacted him before now?"

"I have been in hiding. The numbers I had for them were out of service, even the ones for the offices in Chicago and Miami. I figured the feds had moved on all the offices. I changed my phones regularly, so as not to be traced. Finally, I was able to make my way here."

"It is good that you have come. Arturo, he wants to know the money it is safe?"

"It should be."

"Should? You do not know? What is this should?" He leaned forward, the cartridge held still, both hands clutched together on the desk. Mark heard his escorts' feet move.

"The last time I was able to check was before everything fell apart. When I heard the feds were moving in after everyone fled, I locked everything down. I removed the hard drives and replaced them with blanks. I have no way to access the information. I dared not and could not do anything until I talked to Arturo and David. To access the accounts requires several entries for security reasons. I know some of the passwords, David, as far as I know, is the only other person with the other passwords."

He leaned back. His hands remained on the desk. The sounds from the outside were faint. Mark could feel the tension.

Senor Gomez reached inside his dress jacket and pulled out a cell phone. After a brief pause, Mark listened as he told the other person what Mark said. There were Si and Si and Si, then he put the phone on speaker. Arturo asked in an accusatory tone where Mark had been, why he stay gone so long?

Mark repeated the story he told his uncle. Arturo interrupted before he could finish. Arturo said flatly, "I no believe this shit. You and this Jenkins man play games with me. The Harper and Alvarez men soon see, they mess with wrong man. They hurt my brother, they pay, their family pay. The news whore, Harper, and Alvarez men, soon be mine, the grandson also. I find Jenkins, he be sorry. You lie, you be sorry. Uncle say he send you to me. We talk. I see if you tell lies."

Mark looked at the phone, it was dead.

Senor Gomez shrugged.

"You young people always in hurry never know what is possible if you do as asked. You have one week to fulfill what was asked. What was promised."

"I never promised."

Senor Gomez nodded. Mark was seized, a hood came over his head, and he was led away.

CHAPTER

14

Charter Jet over Caribbean
Major Duplantis and Captain Adams—US Airforce

The Major emerged from the cockpit area, followed by a slightly shorter, pretty, and fit-looking, Eurasian woman wearing an Air Force Uniform with Captain insignia on her collar.

"I am Major Marjorie Duplantis and this is Captain Jennifer Adams."

"I don't believe calling you by your rank is appropriate considering what our relationship is supposed to be, so what should we call you?" Jake asked.

"You may call me Marge."

"I prefer Jen or Jeni?"

TJ asked them if they wished to be seated? When they were seated, the Major asked TJ to tell something about himself.

"I go by TJ. I'm former Army Sniper and trainer, currently, civilian SWAT Team member, undercover gang and drug agent for Metro Charlotte and Homeland Security, happily married, no children. My family's originally from Cuba, grew up in the Hood, Lil' Havana in Miami."

Everyone's eyes went to Jake. "Whatever happened to ladies first? "

They appeared to bristle then insisted he go next.

"You can call me Jake or Harper. I served in the Army, as an officer in a Combat Engineer Unit. Became a Ranger. Did tours in Afghanistan, Iraq, then as a trainer in the Philippines which earned me a broken neck from an IED satchel bomb and a medical discharge. I briefly worked with HSI and

Undersecretary Hardy in the Bahamas on a mission. I grew up on a farm near Lancaster, South Carolina and currently live on a farm in western York County, South Carolina. I have been married twice, have three children I rarely see or hear from. My son is getting married next weekend. I received a last-minute guest invitation, which should tell you all there is to know about that. I am currently separated from my hopefully soon-to-be ex-wife. I recently discovered and hooked up with my childhood girlfriend, by whom I just found out we have a daughter and, also a grandson. FYI we may encounter my newsperson lady friend and our grandson, possibly the daughter also, in Cancun. I have been told not to make their status a part of our mission, but…Enough about me and my problems. I expect you know about us. We know nothing about you."

"Yeah," TJ added, "we could spend days listening to Jake's lady friend problems. Careful ladies, it's been said you can get pregnant from just being in the same room with him."

They laughed. Jake didn't.

"Jen," Margie said, "tell them about yourself." Jen sat up straighter.

"I am a military brat. My father is an Air Force General, who met my Peloponnesian mother while stationed on Guam. I had an older brother who was an Air Force pilot shot down over Afghanistan. My parents were not happy when I joined. And my father has kept me out of the cockpit as a fighter pilot. So, I volunteered to serve as an RPA pilot, not jokingly referred to by combat pilots as "desk pilots", "no fly shooters", "dronies" and other demeaning names. I have piloted the Global Hawk mainly, also have several missions with Predators and Reapers. From what I've been told, the stress of flying a kill mission with the latter two are as bad or worse than actually being in the cockpit. The RPA gets you up close and personal. I would bet you two know what that's like."

Jake and TJ nodded.

"Anyway. My father had me reassigned to a support unit where I met Marge and she got me reassigned to her unit. This is my first mission."

Marge smiled at Jen. 'Hmm?' Jake memed TJ, 'was something else happening here? She had not said anything about her marital status. She wears no ring.'

'Get your head out of the gutter bro. Remember, don't ask, don't tell. Besides, this way we don't have to worry about them coming on to us.'

Marge spoke up. "My upbringing was pretty ordinary. I grew up in San Diego. Big Padres and Chargers fan. Went to San Diego State majored in Poly-sci. Was on the debate team, thought about going to law school, want to go into politics. Joined the ROTC team my junior year, decided joining the Air Force would help my future political career. My recruiter had me take some tests and Air Force Intelligence, Surveillance and Reconnaissance liked what they saw. I have been in the unit for twelve years with tours in Afghanistan and Syria. Now I'm stationed at Lackland in Texas. Not married. No children. May hurt my political career, who knows. Any questions?"

Jake wasn't about to ask what he wanted to ask. TJ spoke up.

"What have you been told about the mission?"

"We were briefed back at Lackland. We knew about your previous experience with the perp, interesting reading. I would like to know why we are going to Cancun. Not that I object, never been there, hear it's nice. Have either of you been?"

TJ and Jake each replied "no". Jake added, "I have questioned why Cancun, was told numerous intel sources indicate a convergence of foreign officials are there, pointing to the possibility of Jenkins and/ or the stolen info being there, offered for sale. I have my doubts. I don't see Jenkins being or coming there. I think this is a smoke and mirror operation. And I hate to say it, but I think all of us are being put in unnecessary danger."

Marge spoke up, "isn't that what missions like this always mean. How else would you know? Perhaps your personal life is causing you trepidation."

"Absolutely. I won't deny that. Personally, I want Jenkins off the board. The crap he stole, I could care less."

Jeni stepped in. "You could care less about National Security? Then, I don't know why they have you here."

"Don't go wrapping yourself in any flag miss and don't get it in your head that I don't care about our country. I'll let my record speak for itself. But the info he stole is not some high-level secret. Any hacker can find out all there is to know about all most anything. National Security is a way for bureaucrats, politicians, and the Pentagon to peddle their influence for votes, money, and bloated budgets. We are here to play the game. They are sending you, your friend, me, and TJ unarmed out there into a den of murderers armed with lethal weapons to play by bullshit rules that the other side has no intention to play by. Your flag won't save you. It will only, and in all likelihood, end up covering your coffin. I would rather not have your lives, my life, and people I care about lives, be put in this situation. If I had my druthers, I would let me and TJ handle things our way. No rules. Winner take all."

"Sorry ladies. Jake tries, often fails, being subtle. What Jake's trying to say is having you two out there's going to make us vulnerable. No matter what.

No offense intended. Call it macho or whatever, we don't want to be responsible for what happens to you. You will be a distraction."

"I've put my ass on the line in combat zones and I have never been afraid to do what has to be done. I was picked for this mission because of my years of experience in the intelligence field, in far more dangerous situations than this. As for Captain Adams, she was chosen because she is an experienced RPA pilot and knows their strengths and weaknesses as well or better than her male counterparts, certainly far better than you two. We won't be in your way or slow you down, so take your macho bullshit and shove it."

Hardy came back from the cockpit. "Glad to hear you all getting on so well. Just as the honeymoon is getting started."

"Jake the big man liked your idea. In fact, he liked it so much that he's hired a company out of central casting. They are being flown in here on the earliest flight we could arrange. All of you will be given a couple of new faces which should keep anyone from guessing who you are. As for Jenkins, that is going to be slightly more difficult since they don't have his actual body, they tell me they can use older photos to scan his biometrics, we'll see. Maybe they can come close enough to fool our friends."

"Our operations center has had some additions. We will have the main two as was discussed, two more are being set up in two of the big box clothing store garage/ storage areas which will be used as work rooms for central casting. One is in Cancun and another is further south near a private airfield."

"There might be some discomfort due to the heat and humidity. I was told the newest material, could be used for the disguises, is breathable material used by those wimpy actors, so all of you should be able to suffer through."

"I didn't hear how you so agreeable couples decided to pair up. My suggestion would be you Major with Jake, and you Captain with TJ. That puts the two most experienced intelligence people with the two least experienced. For the most part, the ladies will do what vacationing ladies do, shop. Leaving the men to do what they are best at, people watching and finding good, strategic drinking establishments."

"As couples, depending on your disguise, you'll do sightseeing, dining and sitting at outdoor bars. All locations will be selected based upon where our friends are said to be or are determined to be going. Of course, you will be spending your evenings together as couples. We have been able to secure accommodations at a nice Bed and Breakfast owned by an expat couple that retired from one of our fellow agencies. It is in El Centro, the business center behind, but close to what's called Zona Hotelera, Hotel Row. I am told this is where the best shopping is and there are plenty fine dining establishments.

Intel says the ambassadors' wives will take advantage of the opportunity to go shopping, supposedly, sometime this afternoon. Seems they are older and too modest to prowl the beach. You ladies will be there waiting. Be a good training exercise for Jeni."

"Comments? Questions? Speak now or hold your peace."

'Not piece Jake,' TJ memed. Hardy almost laughed.

Jake asked, "Two things: Why are these two ladies' info blocked?" Everyone looked at Jake.

The women started to speak; Hardy held up his hand. "Same as yours, mine and TJ's, for security reasons. Second question?"

Jake hesitated, puzzling over Hardy's response, wondering what other info was being held back and who all knew what. The women were glaring at him, TJ had a crooked smile. Oh well.

"Yeah, any word on Ariel, Alperts, Poponovich or our cartel buddies?"

"We all know the cartels are here. Numerous bangers, some top lieutenants have been spotted, the DEA has key people in place. For the most part, they have been seen in the hotel districts, on the beaches and in clubs. Some petty crime in the city center. Mostly the violence is typical turf war crap. We must assume they are expecting you. Once we have the disguises, you should be only as vulnerable as any other tourist. Alperts, Mrs. Gaspard and Poponovich dropped off the radar. We are trying to locate them, but our resources are mainly being used for this mission. It is out of my hands. Last word from the border patrol was Poponovich was noted crossing into Juarez via a cab. They had nothing on your journalist lady friend and her escort. There was a report of bodies thought to be cartel members in the desert northwest of Juarez, east of Palomas. Other than that, nothing. All phone communication will go through Marge--better to coordinate through her, since she's more of an unknown." Hardy memed, 'these ladies know nothing about our implants, how we communicate.'

Hardy continued, "The other woman who flew into Juarez with your lady friend and the DICE operative is already in the Cancun area. By the way, you may have seen her at Tindal's estate. She is the Gonzalez brothers' cousin. I expect they will show up, hopefully, sooner rather than later. They will be detained when they do, I will be notified, and I will let you know. I suspect Alperts knows not to be seen. They too may already be there. You need to concentrate on the mission. Let it play out however it does. Remember Alperts is after the same thing we are. If he's in Cancun, you are as likely as anyone else to encounter him. No lethal action. Are we clear about that?"

"I hear you," Jake replied. He downed his beer, discarded the bottle, and sat back down across from TJ.

"Our crew on the ground reported numerous not so friendlies hanging around the terminal. Was advised we should wait for darkness. I felt that was a waste of time. If they are expecting us, they'll wait. I figure their teams, like ours, are there to see who is arriving and will be pulling shifts. Why not some razzle dazzle, ye old shell game. I have requested two low profile vehicles with tinted windows and a van from one of the companies that delivers to your B&B. We will park as far from the concourse as possible. The pilot and I will leave with the two ladies in the autos and you two will wait for the service men to bring you company caps and attire to help in your exit. We will meet at your B&B and I will have the delivery van take me to the Embassy."

"By that time, I should know when central casting possibly will have themselves in place and set up. This afternoon is my hope. The sooner we have your disguises, the sooner we can get on with the job at hand. TJ and Jake, you two will stay out of sight. The ladies will do some recce of the EL Centro shopping area. Major you need to give the Captain some quick tradecraft lessons: help her spot the other side, learn some evasion techniques, how to blend, how to lose a tail, teach her, test her. Check the businesses where the ambassadors' wives may go. Find a place or places where you would go for lunch or dinner. If it's safe and we don't have the disguises, think where all of you could go this evening for dinner. Otherwise, gentlemen we will have food delivered. And don't drink the water…advise bottled or filtered only…no ice unless the place has filtered water."

"Great. Hot mixed drinks…gotta love it," Jake grumbled. "And what are we supposed to do at the B&B until central casting calls?"

"The Captain will be your connection to the drones we have surveilling the area. We will do recce from the air. The tactical gear and nonlethal weapons are supposed to be waiting. Your host has a safe room set aside where you will be able to do your monitoring and check these ladies in action.

"Captain I believe you are wanted in the cockpit. We are approaching our destination. Enjoy your honeymoons."

CHAPTER
15

Southeast of Juarez, Mexico
Ariel and Alperts

The truck ride was as rough as the van ride. Alperts drove like there was no tomorrow. Ariel was feeling more than ever that could prove true.

"Where did you receive your training to be an assassin?"

"First off sweetie, I'm not an assassin. I was trained as a youth in Israel, later I joined the French Foreign Legion."

Alperts' mind was divided between what had happened and what lay ahead. He had not heard back from his contact. Tindal had assured him requests would be handled expeditiously. He was beginning to believe there was a saboteur somewhere within that pompous ass's network. It would be easy to believe Tindal had decided to cut his expenditures, but Tindal needed Jenkins to be caught to get his company and himself off the hook. His initial assessment of Senor Toraz did not add up either--perhaps pressure from one of his investors, angry enough with DICE to want him eliminated. The more he thought about the situation, the more he was inclined to believe someone was doing the bidding of the cartels. Officer Sanchez could easily be in their employ, as could any number of General Toraz or the other investors' employees. For that matter, any number of them could be controlled by the cartels. Perhaps someone was after his passenger, and either he or she needed to be eliminated. Most likely him; the cartels could use her as a bargaining chip in more ways than one.

They should be getting close to the airstrip. If need be, he could rent a plane. He knew how to fly small propeller driven aircraft. Whoever had sent those men, would be bloody well more determined than ever to stop them from getting away. They would cover all means of escape, the airstrip being one of them. He needed to pull over and let Ariel drive. Take the weapons and ammo, lay low in the rear, and be prepared for an ambush ahead. He pulled over.

"Why have we stopped?" Ariel asked.

"Get out. Stretch your legs. Use the loo if you need to. You need to drive. The airport is not far ahead, and our friends may be lying in wait. I expect there won't be a band or cheering crowds but lots of fireworks. I plan to add to the gala." He climbed in the rear with the rifle and extra ammo.

"If you're not going to use the loo, get in. Mustn't keep them waiting. When the airport comes in sight, stop while I get a lay of the land. If there is shooting, I will direct you to the best advantage positioning. In all likelihood will mean the truck perpendicular to them, passenger side toward them, allowing me to use the big gun and keep you further out of the fire. Stay low, be prepared to exit the truck. Then place yourself against the front wheel. That way the metal of the motor and the wheel rim will help protect you."

"How comforting," Ariel replied climbing into the driver's seat.

The sun was beginning its descent, the road and desert sand captured the fractured rays twinkling and shimmering, pinpoints of dazzling color beaming into Ariel's eyes. She wished this were a dream and she would awaken and none of this was happening. Hill after hill. Over which one did their destination await?

She was shocked when it did appear. Alperts tapped on the top of the truck and she stopped. There, off on the horizon. The buildings looked small, their image wavering in the light. Outside one appeared to be two matchbook size airplanes. Other than the refracted light, nothing appeared to be moving. Alperts tapped on her window, and she lowered the ass.

"Drive ahead slowly. I can't see much from here. Keep your window down in case I need to give you directions."

Ariel shifted into drive and let the truck lumber along at twenty miles per hour. She looked at the fuel gage.

"The truck is almost empty," she yelled hoping he heard her over the noise of the motor.

"Let's hope we won't need the bloody thing from here onward," he leaned over and said into her window opening.

A few minutes later, half-way there, she could make out the cement block and tin roof of one building and the rounded metal shape of the other building where the two planes were parked. Still no vehicles or people were in sight.

"Looks deserted," she said out the window to Alperts who was leaning on the bed of the truck, his head stuck around the side near enough she could have whispered if not for the noise of the truck.

"Quite right. Looks can be deceiving deary. In this bloody place people steal most anything, I don't believe those planes would be left outside unless someone is here to watch them. Take the road to the left just ahead. I want to get a look at the other side."

"Remember we're running out of gas."

"Right you are. Nothing to be done about that unless there is fuel here. Go slow."

They moved ahead and Ariel started to the left. Before they had gone a hundred yards, a bullet pinged off the passenger side front of the truck at the same time as the sound from its firing reached them. Alperts yelled for her to turn left, then yelled stop when she did. She heard a series of loud explosions and the truck shook, wobbling with the sound coming from the big gun. She looked back. The rounds were hitting the corner of the concrete building sending chunks of concrete into the air. Alperts then directed the weapon's fury into a desert mound off from the corner of the building where Ariel saw sprays of sand and pieces of color rising up then disappearing as more rounds hit the truck. She ducked down as one struck the rear window sending glass on to her and through the windshield. She covered her ears, her screams echoing inside her head, with the steady roar from the big gun punctuating the sound.

The gun stopped. Ariel had not heard her door open, she felt herself being drug out of the truck, sliding, on glass. Alperts pushed then pulled her by the arm. They ran away from the truck.

Ariel heard a loud screech and felt herself being pulled down then lifted after a loud explosion sent a shock wave out catching them and hurtling them over a low dune. It felt like her whole body had been invaded, rattling loose, her insides losing their moorings, her teeth smacking against each other, her eyes bouncing in their sockets, her breath pushed out of her lungs, then the impact pulled at her clothing sending dirt and debris in her mouth and across her skin, scraping, then burying her. She lost consciousness.

Once more the blindfold was in place. Mark was led out of the office, through the noisy warehouse and put in the back of the vehicle.

"My passports are in my pocket," he said to no one in particular. No one in particular did not reply.

He heard the tires over the payment intermixed with the echoes from the hustle and bustle of international commerce being performed by underpaid workers from both sides of the border. They were moving faster; the tires hum sang louder.

"Could we have some music. Maybe something we all could sing along with." Nothing. "Perhaps you two could do a tune and I could guess what it is," he remarked in Spanish. They chose silence. Maybe they had headphones on. He reached to take the blindfold off, his arms were seized.

"No music, no scenery. You guys make lousy tour guides."

What seemed an hour or more, the ride became rougher, the tires were singing less and the sound of grit pinging in the wheel wells took up the percussion side of Mark's divided thoughts. Obviously, they were not going to any major airport. The last intelligence he received indicated Arturo was in the Juarez area. So much for the intel. He wondered where Alperts and the Gaspard woman were. Were these two silent escorts taking him to Arturo? Was his fate sealed? Maybe David had been able to hack his computer and phone. If that was true, why had they not taken care of him back there? No. Arturo wants to see him, perhaps to do the deed himself.

Wherever here was, they had arrived. The vehicle stopped. He was taken out of the back and the blindfold removed. Mark looked around. It was a small airstrip. Two planes sat in front of a metal hanger next to where he stood. The acrid smell of smoke and cordite mixed with smells of blood and human destruction overwhelming. Desert dust hung in the air.

Turning around he saw a concrete block building pockmarked with large chunks torn away at the corner. Nearby were men scrambling around the remains of what had been some of their compadres. His escorts had walked over and were talking to two men. One held an assault rifle, an AR-15. Another held an RPG launcher. They pointed off to his right. Mark turned to see other men hovering around the burnout resemblance of a truck resting on its side, still smoking.

One of his escorts rejoined him. "Arturo will be pleased. The news woman and her friend are no more." He pointed out toward the smoldering wreck.

The men who had been at the wreck came walking around the smoldering remains. Mark watched as two pairs carrying something between them approached their position. His escort headed toward them, and Mark followed. Damn. This was going to be a major problem.

Mark saw the Alperts man was torn up badly. He watched as Ariel's body was carried by the others. The men took their bodies to the metal hanger. Mark knelt and felt Alperts' pulse. Nothing. When they set the Gaspard woman down, he checked her pulse. A slight flutter. He quickly brushed the dirt and debris from her face and started performing CPR. His escort and the other men stood back watching. He heard their chatter.

"Get some water. Aqua. She's alive," he shouted in English then repeated in Spanish. No one seemed to move, then his escort repeated his request. Mark heard feet hurrying toward the back of the building. Behind him he heard a muted voice say in Spanish, "He kiss her, feel her up, now he want to clean her, perhaps he want to do her." There was low laughter. Mark wanted to stop the CPR and kill them all. If only. Soon someone handed him a bottled water. He pulled off his shirt. There were intakes of breath and murmurs. His scars from being cut twice and shot lay exposed. He wet his shirt and gently began dabbing at the dirt encased cuts and scrapes on the Gaspard woman's once flawless skin.

"Echate. Vamose," he heard the escort say and the others left the hanger. He leaned down and asked in perfect English, "We must go. You think she live until we get her to a hospital?"

Mark looked up. "Perhaps." Mark picked her up gently and the escort helped him load her in one of the airplanes. "How far to the nearest hospital? he asked.

"Over an hour to any of them. Arturo has doctors at clinic where he have us come. I will call him. We must hurry."

Mark hated to delay but he had to ask, "Any computer or phones with them?"

The escort turned to the man nearest him and asked. The man hurried away then came running back with a sack and handed it to the escort.

The plane headed south. They were flying low, below radar. Mark knew any sudden downdraft and they were goners. Fifteen minutes or so later, the plane rose banking, heading east. The desert gave way to clouds through which could be seen a thick, green, forested, hilly landscape. His escort, who said his name was Eduardo, sat in the co-pilots seat talking to someone. Mark saw the sack of phones next to Eduardo's seat. He needed to know what was on them.

Mark kept checking Ariel. Her breathing was erratic, her chest barely moving. Her breasts were exposed, there were cuts, none very deep. He had tried to cover the exposure, but her shirt was too tattered. He could do no more than cover her bruised nipples. Not that he wouldn't have enjoyed the sight, not like this, not now. Jake Harper will not be pleased. He wished he could let him know. What would Arturo want to do now? He said he would soon have her. Now what? Mark, if Arturo let him have a say, would attempt to convince him of her value. He needed to keep her alive, she could be of use to manipulate Jake he would tell him. And the ambassador had Jake's and her grandson, there could be value in that. Maybe the ambassador knows something about Jenkins. That was, if Arturo intended to keep any of them alive, including him.

CHAPTER
16

Cancun
Blakely Carmichael--Interpol

Blakely Carmichael watched Hardy, another man dressed like a pilot and two women emerge from the private jet, get in two separate Audis, and depart the airport. No Jake or his friend TJ Alvarez. She wanted the reported intel to be true. She had her hopes up, was excited about seeing him once more.

It had been a while, too long. Their last day and night before Okneyev tried to kill them had been more than she expected. In the aftermath Jake disappeared and she was picked up and taken into custody by a Coast Guard Patrol Boat, questioned for days at Guantanamo, offered political asylum in exchange for her continued cooperation. Her Interpol control had not come to her aid. She was left with no option. She later learned Jake survived.

It hurt when she discovered he had remarried. She followed the reports of his run-in with Thurmond Tindal. Her enthusiasm built when Jake's wife disappeared with Tindal's man Jenkins causing their separation. Why hadn't she been told about his wife's presence with Jenkins when he was taken?

Worse had been reading news of Jake's interest in the newsperson, Ariel Gaspard, made more painful, when she realized this had been his first love, the one he mentioned to her long ago, and, to learn they had a lovechild and grandson. All these obstacles for an ask-for-forgiveness reunion were reported to her before coming here.

And here she was, ordered to perform this tortured assignment, shadow Hardy, Jake, and party. She had to continue to play her assigned role. Her control demanded her continued involvement. Where was Jake?

She texted Devereaux, 'No Harper or Alvarez.'

'Follow Hardy. Will continue surveille plane,' he texted back.

She wanted to argue. Devereaux was team leader. She drove like a maniac, horns blaring as she cut in and around vehicles until she spotted them, then maintained her distance, going with the flow. Tourist season, too many people, too much traffic. This was not going to be a picnic.

They stopped at a house. Blakely went past and stopped at the next block, keeping her eye on the vehicles via her rear mirrors. Shortly Hardy and the pilot emerged. The pilot got in a car, Hardy into a van. Both vehicles came her way. She slid down, turning her head when they drove past. She followed Hardy. His driver took him to the embassy. She decided it would be best to go back to watch the women, see who showed, hopefully Jake would.

She texted Devereaux. 'Anything?'

'Two men entered plane, four exited, following service van. Hardy?'

'Embassy. Women at B&B near Centro Business District. I'm watching home.'

'Gotcha. See service van, two men entering? Stay there. Observe only. Notify if move. Going to embassy.'

This was the part Blakely hated—sitting, watching, butt numbing boring. Fortunately, she didn't have to wait more than thirty minutes before the two women emerged. They walked past her car, oblivious to her presence.

'Women on move on foot. No men.'

'Follow.'

She eased out of the car, quickly moving to keep them in sight. Once they turned toward the Centro, the shorter Asian-looking-one reached over and took the taller one's hand after she stumbled on the broken concrete sidewalk. They continued, still holding hands. Lesbos, real or a cover? Blakely felt relieved. Jake was probably safe. Unless these two were into threesomes. She admonished herself, tried to convince herself that it didn't matter since Jake had hooked back up with the one he told her was his first love.

Her first love long ago ceased being her lover. He became her Interpol superior. Only spoke to her through Devereaux, which was fine by her. She needed to let this Jake fantasy go. There were other dicks, always another chance for love. If not, dangerous assignments would have to do, along with zipless sex.

The women no longer held hands when they entered the busy central shopping area. Real lesbos, she bet. They casually strolled along, stopping often to gaze in shop and restaurant windows. Blakely had to duck into doorways to avoid their moves. Seemed to be recceing the area for someone. Too conspicuous, amateurs attempting tradecraft in case they might be watched, which they were. The taller one received a phone call. Brief. Must have been her controller. Could be someone nearby. Blakely carefully let her eyes wander, looking for someone trying to appear not to be watching. No one stood out. Hopefully, there was no in-place camera or drone. She glanced up. Didn't see anything.

The women took a seat in the central square, ordered drinks, and continued their too obvious observations. Blakely went in a café and chose a corner seat near the window where she could watch without being seen. She ordered bottled water, much to the waiter's dismay. She quickly snapped off several photo shots of the twosome. Should help with determining their identity.

Thirty minutes later Blakely saw the taller one nod, the other glanced in the direction indicated. Blakely did the same. So, this is why they're here. She knew them from her briefing, the ambassadors' wives. The one from Spain, grandmother of Jake's grandson. She snapped off and forwarded pictures, then texted Devereaux what was happening.

'Stay with women. Ambassador women must be their target.'

No shit, Sherlock.

The next two hours the ambassador's wives ate, drank, shopped all over the Centro area. Blakely kept her distance. She had picked up on the four men hovering on the periphery—bodyguards. The Americans had picked up on them also. Became a hide and seek scenario, until the ambassador's wives had to summon two of their escorts to carry their packages. Blakely watched as the taller one moved like a drunk bumping into one of the men, knocking a package loose, then bumping into the one from Spain as the escort bent to pick up the package. The American had said something probably an apology then stumbled on as if a tipsy drunk. All eyes followed her until she plopped down in a seat.

Good moves. Blakely was impressed. Her tailee had placed some device on, or in her purse. Once the Russians were out of sight, the taller one stumbled along until she had exited the square.

Her friend rejoined her, they returned to the B&B. Blakely went to Devereaux' auto, told him what she thought.

"Damn. Who are these women?"

Blakely showed him the photos and he sent them to their contact to be IDed.

Right before dark, the two men and women came out, got in the service van, and drove past. They waited for another vehicle to pass, then dropped in behind it.

"That was Jake and his buddy. I recognize Jake's walk. His buddy is supposedly a hunk. So I've been told. Has to be them."

CHAPTER

17

Near Tulum, Mexico
Mark and Arturo Gonzalez [cartel underboss]

The plane banked, then made a stall-like dive and landed on a strip nestled inside a tropical forest. Mark was staring out a window, glimpsed an ocean during the maneuver. He hoped someone was able to pick up his GPS chip strategically placed under his perineum skin. He activated his phone recorder.

Two men with a gurney met the plane, loaded Ariel in an ambulance, and rushed off out of sight. Mark was kept from going with her by two men armed with AR15s. They escorted him to a limo. Didn't bother to search him. Arturo's tense face greeted him as he entered the rear compartment. Two more armed men sat across from Arturo. Their cold, dead-pan eyes stayed on him. He sat down next to Arturo, who said nothing until they were underway. Mark wanted to know where they were taking Ariel.

Arturo kept his head turned away from him and said, "The Yankee whore go see doctor. She live, depend on you."

"Your money is all where it's supposed to be, making more money, the stock market, Huawei and AT&T deal, check them out, many more. I would not have come here otherwise. Like I said on the phone." Arturo's stare was forward; the other men watched, expressionless. "I did not dare get in touch with you. I was questioned by the feds and now I am a fugitive. I'm sure you know all this. I did not hear from you or your brother. I figured you knew not to." Mark tried not to sound panicked. Feared he had not been successful.

Arturo turned his head, faced Mark. He simply stared. His eyes deep, dark pools. Mark bet it was the last thing many men saw before dying an excruciating death.

"Come on Arturo." Mark knew Arturo was seconds away from doing the dirty deed. "The man Jenkins screwed the deal when he disappeared. Word has it he put out feelers. It may or may not be him. From everyone I've asked, I hear the same thing, Jenkins is dead. I've been trying to find you, tried to get in touch with you and David, ask if you knew anything."

"Rumor has it the Harper woman saw four Hispanic men escorting him from where they had escaped to. Most think it was you or another Mexican group. I don't believe it. If you or another cartel had the information, I wouldn't be here. I believe you think you can make the purchase. I believe Jenkins is operating through the Russian Ambassador. Either that, or he is dead. Either way, I believe someone has the info and are the facilitators. Your money is safe. Like I said on the phone, I need the codes your brother has and with the codes I have, we can access your funds."

"You think I no have funds without you? You think this man Jenkins all there is? You big fool. I think. I have other people beside you. No. You here 'cause you know too much. I see El Chapo trial, learn it no good have man know too much."

Mark wondered what else besides Jenkins was the cartel involved in, could it be the cartel was working with the Russians on something else, perhaps the stealth sub deal? He had to find out. Needed to play along.

"Yes and no. Why would I talk. I'm not stupid enough not to know they would lock me up in a supermax. That is if I made it into the court room. I could have cut a deal--not bother to come here. I'm here because I want you to be the man. With the right purchases, you could take control of the border. With the Gaspard woman, you have a way in. I can help with this." Mark hoped Arturo had not been in cahoots with Alpert. If so, he would know he was lying.

"You lie."

Oh well. Hopefully, someone was listening and would get here in time to save the Gaspard woman. Perhaps when his name was added to the wall someone would recognize, pay homage for his sacrifice."

"Russians have better technology. Make super soldiers. American drone no good against this. You give brother codes; I no make you suffer." Arturo nodded, the soldier behind the driver tapped on the security glass and the limo moved on.

Mark felt some relief, he almost laughed. The Russians, like the US had been investigating the human mind's potential for reading and controlling other minds for over a half century. Rumor had it scientists had made breakthroughs. Rumors. No verifiable intel—Mark knew—he had been among the agents doing the investigating of the Russians. Was this a pig-in-a-poke the Russians were peddling instead of the amphibious drone? Had everyone been led here as a ruse while Jenkins, or whoever had the stolen US technology, were somewhere else consummating the deadly deal? If so, his death will have accomplished nothing.

Nothing wagered, nothing gained. Hope this shit works. Mark spun his ring around, backhanded Arturo across the mouth while, at the same instant he launched himself from his seat, catching the nearest, surprised soldier's weapon with his right hand as his left hand pushed the other soldier's AR15 down. Having deflected their weapons, Mark brought the ring up smashing it into the cheek of the one across from Arturo. Both Arturo and this soldier collapsed forward. The driver looked into the mirror; the limo swerved which caused the other soldier to lose his grip on his weapon. With a roar, he drove his freed fist into the side of Mark's head, stunning him. Fortunately, Mark caught the man's other wrist with the ring when he attempted to finish Mark off with another punch. He was able to land his elbow into his face finishing him off.

The limo driver slammed on brakes. Mark's addled mind heard the slight whine of the motor operating the window, separating the driver from the rear passenger compartment. He struggled with the last soldier, rolling him on top when the driver's revolver exploded. He felt the searing sting. The first shot went through his human shield. He felt searing pain in his left upper arm. With his remaining adrenalin-infused strength, he shoved the soldier up, deflecting the second shot. He felt the heat, his ears rang from the other soldier's blow to his head and the driver's weapon's roar. He trapped the driver's arm against the partition and rear window with the soldier's body. Barely holding on, he managed to twirl the ring with his thumb, the small tip scratched the driver's arm. Mark held on. Just as he thought the CIA's lab tech's super curare-like tranq shit was all played out, he felt the driver's arm lose its resistance. Turning his head, Mark saw the eyes had lost their motion. He jammed his palm up under the other man's jaw.

With a sigh, Mark rocked back into a crouch. Good thing that shit worked as demonstrated. He checked his shoulder. A slow, trickle of blood ran down his arm. His tee with "Just Do It" emblazoned on it was ruined.

"If you're listening, I'm alive," he gasped out. He pulled his phone out of his trouser pocket. No bars. Damn. They most likely hadn't heard a damn thing.

He tore off a piece of Arturo's expensive-looking white dress shirt and tied it around his arm. He checked Arturo's pulse, terribly slow heartbeat. He hoped he didn't die. He would need him. He pushed Arturo back into a sitting position. His eyes were now deep, bottomless canyons.

"Should have made me buckle up asshole."

Mark climbed through the open partition, hit the door-unlock-button, went out the back door, and pulled Arturo's three men out. Using a knife, he took off the belt of one of the soldiers, he cut their clothes off. Using their belts and strips of their clothing, he tied them together off the road down an embankment, out of sight. It was doubtful, he thought, that the one with the chest wound would survive.

He got back in the limo and headed off in the direction the ambulance had taken Ariel. He looked up in the rear-view mirror. From the waist up Arturo looked like a sleeping passenger. Mark had made a harness of the seat belts to act as restraints. The tranq should keep him sedated for at least another hour.

The tinted windows would keep outside observers from seeing in. The driver's clothes were a little big, but they would serve their purpose. Although it was doubtful any authorities would be stopping Arturo's limo—to their way of thinking, it would be unhealthy.

CHAPTER
18

In and Around Cancun
Jake, TJ, Major Duplantis and Captain Adams

"I hope I don't look like the kind of beach bum tourist people stare at wondering if he's a panhandler. I thought we were supposed to blend in, not stand out. Why not simply have us wear masks?"

"Executive thinkin'. You know bro you do look kinda like a red-bulbous-nosed, middle-aged, touristy pervert who spent his hard-earned money partying all night. Lots of those in case you haven't noticed. Look at me, I look like the guy should be down on the beach renting umbrellas or some other crap."

Marge and Jeni came in and stood off in the corner of the basement staring at a mini-tablet. Jeni glanced up.

"Wow Marge. They're going to make us feel like two hookers they picked up off the street."

Marge glanced up, then turned her attention back to the tablet.

"You two need to stop primping and be ready to roll. Our people monitoring intel traffic, picked up a broken signal which mentioned some names of interest, namely Ariel and Arturo."

Jake and TJ went over to join them.

"Gotta be the Alperts man. He and Ariel must have arrived and hooked up with the Gonzalez brothers," TJ said. "Do they have a fix on the signal?"

"Not yet. Hardy said we needed to be ready to move. I called him to let him know I put a monitoring device on one of the Russian Ambassador's wives' purse. I guess the signal is working."

"Wonder why Hardy didn't inform us?"

'Didn't want to interrupt your makeover,' was Hardy's immediate memed response. 'Intel believes the signal may have come from Poponovich. It was bounced around, ended up at Langley, the Counterterrorism Center. We can't confirm. The signal was weak and disappeared. It's back. We're trying to get a satellite fix. Last known tic was near a small private airstrip on a secluded piece of property about ten mics southwest of your location.'

TJ's throwaway phone chirped. It was Hardy. "Move out. Do not attempt a rescue—observe only—no violence. Will send in Federales if necessary." TJ told Jake and the women what Hardy said.

They exited the rear service entrance in a van bearing the logo of the ladies' fashion shop where the central casting makeover had taken place. The van was equipped with the latest surveillance equipment, including a monitor for Jeni to work her magic piloting a duo of small drones one which rested on the desk next to where she was strapped in. Another had been launched from inside the dock area. Jeni used it to surveille the area after they exited. She saw no suspicious-looking observers or tails. They hurried toward the target.

"Small Toyota Rav, man and woman occupants seem to be lagging back, tailing us. I've sent photo to intel." Jeni reported as she sent the drone higher over the treetops.

Immediately Hardy responded over the speakers. "Pursuers identified—Thomas Devereaux and Blakely Carmichael. Will attempt to block."

Jake looked in the rear-view, met TJ's eyes. "Thought Blakely had gone into witsec?" TJ said.

'Doesn't appear so. Take the next right and floor it,' Hardy memed.

Jake kept checking the mirrors. TJ kept his eyes on the monitor. Jake did as Hardy instructed. Soon as he floored their vehicle, a service truck pulled out of an alley blocking the road.

"Go right, take next two rights get back on road." It was Hardy. He was watching via satellite and Jeni's drone video feed. "Tail slammed on brakes, backed out, you're behind them, decoy van appears to have fooled them. Jeni send drone ahead to scout the compound. Should have our satellite feed showing on your screen--use as needed. Will arrive at property in five. Be alert. Seems to be major activity at compound. Jake let Jeni direct you. TJ, have tranq rifles under your seat--defensive use only."

"He wasn't kidding about activity."

TJ loaded tranq cartridges into the rifles. He stood to look over Jeni's shoulder. Plenty of trees. He could make out numerous buildings arranged in a semi-circle on each side of a larger structure. Several vehicles were immobile in the center. Little dots were converging on an approaching vehicle.

"Zoom in. There. Stay on that moving limo."

The limo stopped short of the approaching armed men.

"Heat signature indicates two bodies. Body in front is getting into the back." Jeni had the small drone hovering over the armed men. One man emerged holding a handgun, held up his hand to halt the others. He approached the limo, stopping at the rear driver-side door.

"Zoom in on him." The picture from the small drone changed angles. "Mark Poponovich. Jake it's your ole buddy Poponovich. Jeni move around see if you can get a shot of who is in the limo."

Once more the picture changed. "Can't see through the glass." She moved the drone, zoomed in so they could see through the windshield past Poponovich past the blood-streaked, part-the-way-down partition into the rear compartment.

"Hello Arturo--looks like he's out of it, not moving."

Marge spoke up. "Target is at this locale. Phone is on. Hardy says target is asking where Ariel is. Target offering a swap."

"Ariel is here somewhere. Need to locate her. Jeni scan the other buildings, see if you pick up heat signatures," Jake yelled back over the din of chatter coming through the speakers from command.

Hardy said, "Permission granted. Jake take next left. Will bring you to rear of property. One vehicle, two men. TJ it's a go. Take them down. Stand by after. Need to contact the federales."

Jake yelled, "No, too risky. The cartels probably scan their frequencies or have them in their hip pocket. Need to locate Ariel. Mark has what they want. Maybe Poponovich can arrange a swap."

Hardy memed Jake and TJ, 'Mexican Undersecretary of Interior has been notified by our ambassador, there are agents from their Naval Intelligence and CISEN Command Center monitoring all communications. Do not talk, meme only. They are assembling a contingent of soldiers. Approximate ETA in thirty.'

Jake looked up TJ nodded.

TJ put his phone to his ear. "Yes sir, copy" he said to dead air. He wrote a note telling Marge to cut the audio link to command. "Hardy says has ears on communications. Jeni, find anything?"

"Back of center building. Four hostiles—two armed at door, one near prone figure, possibly female, other side of room. Lost feed. Command has overridden my communication to satellite. The image zoomed out, then split. One image was over the compound, another showed soldiers at a naval yard loading into personnel carriers. Their vehicle came into view.

TJ told Jake to stop. He handed him a tranq rifle. "Two, around the bend. You go left, I'll take the right. Need to get in close. As you well know."

They climbed over another drone case and other accompanying equipment and slipped out the back of the van. Before they did Jake yanked off the fake nose, then told Jeni to bring the inflight drone over their position. When I give the signal, buzz those two mothers. Need to distract them."

"Need to bring the drone back soon. Needs recharging."

TJ was already at the bend when Jake moved in on the left. Jake couldn't see the men. He memed TJ, 'You have eyes on them?'

'Negative. Moving in to cover. Damn this shit's thick. Hope I don't run up on any no-shoulders. Got visual. You?'

Jake: 'No shot. Jeni will buzz them on my signal. No can signal.'

TJ: 'Hear drone. Eyes on it. They see it. Take closest.'

Jake stepped out. Darts caught targets in necks. Both went down. He and TJ converged on the soldiers. He chuckled. "Look at us. We look like beach bums. Damn sure not dressed for this shit."

Blood was trickling down Jake's leg from a scratch, making his sandal sticky.

They removed the darts, drug the soldiers into the shrub and disarmed them. TJ memed Hardy, 'Have the women move the van up to our position.' Before he finished the meme the van came into sight. He and Jake rejoined the women. Jeni brought the drone in, soon as they stopped, she told them to bring it to the back of the van so she could do the recharge.

"Twenty minutes."

"Don't have that much time. Estimate soldiers will be here by then," Marge said. "Any ideas?"

"I'm going in," Jake said.

TJ knew there was no use saying what a bad idea that was. 'Sure wish I had my sniper rifle. But Hardy said no weapons.' Jake didn't reply. He headed toward the gate.

"Hold on Jake, just a minute." He turned to Jeni. "Think that drone could maybe make it ten more minutes?"

"Maybe. Maybe not."

"We need eyes out there. We can monitor it from our phone."

"Not without special software."

"We have it." She started to talk, TJ held up his hand holding a phone. "Got it, okay? Going in and extract the woman, other targets if possible. You two move off down the road and observe only. Do as Hardy orders."

Marge yelled major expletives at them, mostly concerning male anatomical slang, asshole bullshit and not following orders--he waved her off, joined Jake and they jogged off out of sight. Soon they heard the buzz of the drone as it passed over their heads—a little too close for comfort.

"Believe they're pissed," TJ said.

"I would say screw them, but I don't believe they would. I definitely wouldn't."

"What's the plan?" TJ asked when Jake stopped. They had come to a razor-wire-topped fence—no guards visible. He inwardly laughed—their appearance was comical—not exactly what an assault team should look like—decrepit-looking tourists don't signify impending doom.

Jake had pulled up the drone view on his mental screen. "Looks like we have a definite Mexican standoff out front. Think Hardy will give Jeni Mark's number they acquired?"

TJ memed Hardy. 'Need to contact Poponovich to coordinate plan.'

Hardy: 'Told you observe only. Soldiers on the way. Need to leave now.'

'No can do. Will extract Gaspard woman. Need Poponovich to move, five mics once we enter fence, be ready to come to rear position for evacuation.'

TJ turned to Jake who had been looking for a way through or over the fence. "Need the jeep. Hope it's not too loud." He began jogging back the way they came.

The jeep was not exactly quiet, especially when TJ ran through the fence. Jake followed running straight for the back of the center building. TJ abandoned the jeep and joined him. Hardy memed, 'Door on porch, right side. Inside guards moving toward it. Texted Poponovich on phone we scanned. No reply. Has hands full.' Jake and TJ moved to each side of door. 'Guards wait each side. Weapons ready. Too risky. Abort.'

Jake went to window toward front of porch, memed, 'TJ through door in 3-2-1.' Jake broke the glass on 2. TJ broke through the door and rolled; he used the tranq to put down one. The other had turned from the window, giving Jake an advantage. He jammed a dart into the back of the neck of the other guard. TJ hurried to look out front as Jake sprinted down the hall to the room where Ariel lay. No sign of whoever had been at her bedside.

'Behind door in bath to right. Something in hand.'

Jake rammed into the door, surprised how little it pained his sore neck. A man in fatigues crashed to the floor. Jake tranqed him. TJ was in the bedroom when Jake came out. He retrieved the ARs they left on the porch. Jake brushed some hair back from Ariel's scratched-up face, she had a slow pulse. When he pulled back the sheet covering her, he saw her bruised, battered, cut chest and abdomen. He wanted to cry. Had to get her out of here, despite his trepidation at having to move her.

'Gotta go bro. Let me carry her.'

Hardy memed, 'Soldiers approaching front entrance. One carrier moving to rear. Poponovich on move. Get out of there.'

Before Jake could argue, TJ gently scooped Ariel up, the pillow cradling her head, Jake grabbed the weapons, they ran for the side door. Jake and TJ rushed down the steps, the sound of automatic fire hitting metal, mixed with panicked orders coming from the front and other side of the building. They ran for the jeep. The limo fish tailed as it slid to a stop next to them. TJ opened the rear door and quickly laid Ariel inside, he jumped in, followed by Jake. Mark Poponovich floored the limo, nearly causing the door to catch Jake's legs. Bullets hit the door, just missing TJ; it slammed shut amid the steady barrage of automatic fire. Luckily, the limo was bullet proof.

"She alive?" Mark asked after lowering the glass partition.

"Barely," Jake replied. He was holding onto Ariel's wrist with one hand, while trying to keep her on the seat with the other. Her head rested on Arturo's thigh. He wished he could hold her in his arms, kiss life into her. Please don't die. Save her, take me, he repeated over and over in his head, not caring if Hardy and TJ were reading his thoughts.

Hardy memed, 'Medvac on way. Go left out of side gate. Opening, mile down road.'

TJ relayed message to Mark. He looked over at Arturo.

"Damn man, what's with the get-up, you got a gig on the bus or something?"

TJ answered. "Called going undercover. Something you should know a helluva lot about. For now, let's concentrate on getting us safely away from here. We will all have much explaining to do if the federales catch us. Have to assume they have eyes on us. For now, shut-up and drive."

'Going to be close,' TJ memed. He tapped into the satellite feed. 'Big firefight 'bout to end. The Gonzalez' men are laying down their arms. Personnel carrier circling around to back entrance.'

A small, shrubless clearing suddenly emerged on the east side of the narrow road. Mark turned, went to the far end. There was a trail disappearing into trees, too narrow for the limo. He swung around, drove back to the edge closest to where the personnel carrier would come from and stopped.

TJ saw Jeni had landed the drone at the rear entrance blocking the carrier's exit. A passenger emerged, was talking into a handheld radio.

They heard, then saw, the med-vac chopper. It landed next to them. Jake and TJ jumped out to assist two men with a stretcher, loaded Ariel, followed to the chopper. Two medics began triage.

"I'm going with her," Jake said and climbed aboard.

Immediately the chopper lifted off and disappeared to the east. TJ ran back to the limo's front passenger side, told Mark to go left as Hardy memed him directions. Also telling him to look at his phone to continue to monitor the satellite view. After a series of turns they emerged onto a heavily trafficked highway, which Hardy said would take them to the far south-end of Cancun, where they would meet up with the Major and Captain. 'Ditch the limo. Major will take you and company to a safe house. The ambassador is not happy. Our new secretary in Washington will be less happy. You two are too valuable assets, you have put this whole operation at risk—our cover compromised.'

'Ariel Gaspard is an American citizen was being held hostage, her life in jeopardy. She's Jake's woman.'

'She is a journalist. She put herself in jeopardy. Personal relationships or not, Jake and you must follow orders. Get to that safehouse, wait for further instructions.'

'Where are they taking Ariel?'

'She will be flown out on a chartered flight to a hospital in Miami.'

'What about Jake?'

'He will be rejoining you. In cuffs, if need be. He has refused to communicate with me.'

'I don't believe that is a good idea. Knowing Jake, his energy and mind will be on being with her. You can't force him to do what needs to be done.'

'Then it is up to you to convince him otherwise. The alternative is spending the rest of his life locked away from her and everything he holds dear. Uncle Sam owns all our asses. Besides, he has a daughter and grandson whose safety, perhaps their lives are at stake. Mrs. Gaspard, if she survives, would not likely forgive him if anything untoward happened to them. Mrs. Gaspard will receive the best of care. What happens after is up to her and him. Convince him of this. It's not up for further discussion.'

Mark kept checking on Arturo in the mirror, glancing over at TJ, who seemed to be staring off into space, giving him directions as if he were obtaining them from his phone by osmosis.

"You got invisible earplugs or something? You seem to be off in space, calling out directions like someone's telling them to you or, is it somehow, you've been here before?"

"Something like that." TJ looked back at Arturo. "How is it you managed to get this guy and his limo?"

"Didn't like his old driver, so I took the job. How is it you and Jake showed up back there?"

"Those phones." TJ nodded to the bag sitting in the floorboard. "And yours. How is it you knew about Mrs. Gaspard. Jake says you paid her a visit back in the Carolinas. You working with the Alperts dude? Speaking of which, where is he and how is it a CIA counterterrorism guy, such as yourself, has ties to Alperts and DICE?"

"What makes you think that bullshit? I'm a businessman, not CIA and, I have no connection to the now deceased Mr. Alperts or this DICE. I was across the border on business, got careless and was taken against my will to a small airport between here and Juarez, where some of this man's cohorts had used a grenade launcher to blow up a truck, which I guess this Alperts man and the Gaspard woman had been passengers in. Arturo's men had carried their bodies into the maintenance shed where they took me. I ascertained Mrs. Gaspard was needing immediate medical care and the men were instructed by Arturo to bring Mrs. Gaspard and myself to the airstrip back there. Mrs. Gaspard was taken away in an ambulance and Arturo made it clear, he wanted ransom--he claimed he intended on buying the services of some foreign mind-reading, supermen or some such shit--made no sense to me—I thought I was in the hands of some lunatic and if I didn't come up with the money, I would never be heard from again. I have had some self-defense training and was able to surprise our delusional guest—and here we are."

"Seems you the one delusional. Jake knows you—housemates in Cuba, saved your sorry ass from getting blown up on a Russian freighter. You now our guest. Try any of that self-defense shit on me, you won't fare so well. Either cooperate, or things goina get nasty--seeing as how, by your own admission, you not under the umbrella of any American agency. Seems your business was with our friend back there, a deal gone bad, huh? Think you will find cooperating goina save time, whole lot of unpleasant questioning." TJ rested the tranq rifle across his lap aimed at Mark. Mark smiled. He twirled his ring, decided be better to not take a chance, might need it later.

CHAPTER
19

Cancun
Devereaux and Carmichael--Interpol

Thomas Devereaux and Blakely Carmichael soon learned they were following a decoy. The van stopped on the far end of Hotel Row and a young man got out carrying a box, entered a boutique, emerged in a few minutes, and made a u-turn, passed them by headed back to wherever.

Blakely who had been monitoring the local authorities' radio traffic, put the monitor on speaker. They listened to the reports coming through about a raid on a compound.

"Bet that's where they were headed," Devereaux said. "Might as well go back to the B&B. They'll return there at some point. Maybe you should go up and knock on the door. I bet Jake will be thrilled to see you."

"About as much as he would like to see you."

"Must bug the hell out of you that he was a player, that you, the trained player, got played. Mark tell you Dean said Jake balled that Amy chick. Did some young things in Cuba before you. Then went home, got married, now he's hooked up with his old flame."

"You and Dean are just pissed because you aren't getting any."

"Got that right."

Devereaux shifty eyes flashed. He would be more attractive if he didn't always have that lascivious, probing stare, Blakely thought.

"Ole wifey not too happy with my career path. But. Anyway, our briefing says Jake has a daughter in Europe somewhere, last known in Spain, and a grandson who is also the grandson of the Russian Ambassador to Spain, whose wife has been bugged by one of the women in Jake's party, whom you think might be girlfriends with the other female member of their party. Damn. Keeps getting juicier and juicier. Be great if we could be a bug on their wall."

"We have infrared imaging and remote audio."

"Like watching cartoon porn."

"You are a damn pervert."

They parked his rental car several blocks away. Blakely retrieved her rental, and they grabbed some takeout-for-the-stakeout. Darkness came, no one was seen entering. Lights came on in two rooms. They figured they were on timers.

"Have you spoken to Dean?" Blakely asked munching on some nuts.

Devereaux wanted to say if you only knew, instead he said, "He and his team are on my boat. Had to install new equipment after Homeland requisitioned theirs. The agency has better equipment, pays better for letting them use it."

"They share intel?"

"Only if I have something they want, just like our guys at Interpol. Speaking of which, why did they want you and I paired up for what is basically a one-man job?"

"Women are wary of men like you. Can't see you going in a fashion shop or ladies' room. I have more experience. Kind of galls me you are the team contact."

"Guess your charms weren't good enough for your old lover. You blew the op. Exposed everyone. Okneyev went into hiding. The damn amphib is still out there somewhere." Devereaux shook his head. "I mean, what the hell were you thinking. Attempting to poison Okneyev and those two Cuban generals. Did you think no one would find out? You were damn lucky to escape that freighter. After what you did to that poor bastard Mark and the rest of us, it's a wonder he pulled some strings and got you listed as wit-sec. The bureau wanted to make an example of you. The agency considered making you a resident of one of their budget hotels. This op is your chance to redeem yourself. If you must know, I also wish they hadn't paired us up."

"As I recall, you were part of the failed op."

"I was a prisoner—you damn sure know that—helped save your ass."

"You killed two Russians, put me under the scope of Okneyev, almost got Jake, Tobolokov and me killed."

"Really. Screw it. Let's just call a truce. Get this venture over with. Okay? At least we missed out on the COVID-19 virus shit."

"I don't know about you, but I knew some victims. Okay? And no more sexist remarks and no more talk of my past."

"Deal, sweetheart." Devereaux laughed. "You get the dykes. I get lover boy and his friend."

He quickly turned the radio on and volume up. "We've got company. Other side of street. Saw an infrared flash. Came from that window on the second floor." Devereaux put an infrared scope on the house. "Four bodies, woman and man up, two men down. Circle the block. Drop me off a couple blocks over, then come back here. They'll try to locate my presence." He checked the time on his phone: 9:08. "At 9:12, hold your phone so they can see it, call me, I'll tell you where to meet. That should draw at least one of them to the location. When I'm approached, slip behind and taser the bastard. You're good at this, as I recall."

"What if I don't get there in time."

"Make sure you do." He got out of the car.

It worked. One man came. Turned out to be Mossad, Israeli intelligence. He followed Devereaux, staying back in the shadows. Blakely got the drop on him.

"Hello David," she said moving in, keeping a safe distance.

"Hello Blakely. You learned well."

"Had a good teacher. How have you been?"

"Busy. Seems you have also. Why don't we join your colleague?"

Devereaux was flabbergasted when Blakely stepped out of the shadows with the well-built, angular man, his face scarred from a near-death encounter with a suicide bomber in Germany.

"Agent Devereaux, Levon Gerod, Mossad. He was about to explain to me, why he is watching us, weren't you Levon?"

"There's some people that must clarify the situation. Why don't we join them?"

Another man stepped out from behind Devereaux into the light from a streetlamp. He had his hand in his trouser pocket with something pointed in their direction, could have been his finger, a gun or, perhaps, he was turned on by Blakely's curvaceous body whose loose shorts and shirt did little to provide much cover.

"Yes. I believe Levon is right," the man said in a gravelly voice. "Your auto is back this way, shall we?"

"Everything is okay Yuri. I will handle this," Levon replied.

Without another word, Yuri turned and disappeared back into the shadows.

Once they were seated in Devereaux' car, the two men in front and Blakely in the rear, David turned so he could see both.

"Why were you spying on us? Devereaux asked.

"We weren't there for you. You appeared in our view. Naturally, we were curious."

"Care to tell us how you happen to be here?" Blakely asked.

"We have our sources same as you. At first, we thought you two were watchers for the others. When it was reported they gave you the slip, we had to find out exactly who you were and what your interests were in the others. Care to explain?"

"How long has Mossad been involved?"

They sat in silence several minutes listening to the radio.

"No need for the radio. I have an interrupter on me. No one can hear us."

Devereaux turned the radio off.

"We were alerted by the Americans when Major Jenkins disappeared with sensitive military techno-information. We had already taken note, when our intel was alerted to the teaser posted deep on the dark web. When the Russians and our sworn enemies, the Iranians, showed interest, we took note. Strangely, we were not officially notified by the Americans until after the major's disappearance. Seldom does someone like Major Jenkins work alone. DICE's Alperts name appeared recently, received word American's plan a big event—invitation only—naturally, we had to investigate. Your turn. Why is Interpol watching the Americans?"

Blakely and Devereaux exchanged eye contact. Devereaux nodded, took the initiative.

"The two American men have been directly involved in the investigation from the beginning. No prior agency training or affiliation. Seems that is why they were chosen. But, not quite. One of them is the neighbor of Thurmond Tindal, Tindal Industries, the company that Jenkins was employed by and stole the technology from. When Jenkins fled, he took the wife of this American with him, seems his wife's father has prior connections with Tindal and Jenkins. The wife was there when Jenkins was taken away by four unknowns. We recently learned our American has an illegitimate daughter, who is married to the Cuban Ambassador to Spain's son. The daughter is missing. Her biological mother was last seen in the company of the Alperts man in Mexico and the grandson is here with the ambassador and family, perhaps for this event, maybe Jenkins and friends show. Interpol and the FBI want to know how all these loose ends are tied together."

"Interesting story. Sounds convincing. We already discovered most of this frazzled tale. But. I don't believe that is the main reason you are here. You, Mr. Devereaux, perhaps you are looking for this Major Jenkins. Miss Carmichael, Blakely, we have many reasons to believe you know more than has been discovered. You forget we know your background."

"I have nothing to hide," Blakely said. "The real reason Mossad sent you here wasn't to check up on me. Your government, like every other government, and others who are here, want to know what he has to sell, want to purchase it. I'm just another side story."

"Our intel says otherwise. This has been personal for you. We both know this. What is curious is what Pietr Okneyev knew and how much did he share with you? We know he was in touch with Major Jenkins. There is considerable evidence he is the master mind behind the disappearance. We think he made it permanent after he purchased the information. There are those who believe you killed Okneyev and know where the information is. Some would say perhaps you are here to sell that information, possibly with your American friend and lover being set up to take the fall; that is if he isn't willing to join you. We have tried to find your cohort Toby Tobolokov, seems he dropped off the face of the earth. That leaves just you and perhaps the Harper and Poponovich men to shine light on our suspicions."

"You're wasting your time. That is, if you actually believe this? Makes me feel safer having Mossad watching my back. Same old story, no one trusts anyone, so we keep spying on each other--plays right into the hands of our enemies. Keep on keeping on Levon. Shalom."

"Keep your friends close, your enemies closer. Shalom." Levon exited the car. Blakely got out, took the seat up front.

"You believe that bullshit?" Blakely remarked.

"Had some interesting points. I can see where doubt concerning everyone's story makes everyone suspicious of each other. I have often wondered why so many people want harm to come to Jake Harper, his family, and friends. And why so much time and resources have been expended to protect him and his friend. Take you for instance, you put your ass on the line numerous times for him, why is that?"

Blakely said nothing.

"You've got the hots for him, is that it?"

Still no reply. She wasn't sure what to say. She knew this only added to the suspicions. Nothing to be done for it.

CHAPTER
20

Safe House
Mark Poponovich

Took three men to restrain Jake. He felt his duty was to stay with Ariel. The thought of her on that plane, lying in a hospital bed, possibly dying, without him there by her side, was not to be. They sedated him, cuffed him, and brought him to the B&B. When he regained consciousness, he was in the house den, music was playing, a lamp on a table at the end of the sofa, TJ sat in a chair, staring at him. Despite the music, he heard the two women's voices coming from another room. Everything felt disjointed. Before he was aware of his own presence, what he perceived, and some he knew as dead people visited him, some benevolent, others brought haunting memories.

TJ handed him a bottled water. He sat up and drank half the bottle.

"Welcome back bro."

He looked down at the floor, up at TJ. "What time is it?"

"Going on eleven hundred, local time. You feel up to talking?"

"Any word on Ariel?"

"Being kept in a coma. Kinda like when you were laid up. Neurosurgeon says she should come out just fine, no permanent damage. She has some broken ribs, punctured lung, which will heal, some stitches, a little scarring, may elect to have plastic surgery. No major damage to vital organs, maybe some hearing loss. All in all, she's alive and will survive. They'll keep her under until they feel she's ready. You know how it goes. She should be up and around no more than a month, two at the most. Deane's staying with her--took vacation time."

"I should be there."

"Bro, Uncle Sam owns our asses, just like being in the military. Duty comes first. You have a daughter and grandson to think about. Ariel expect you to do what you can for them."

Jake stood, twisted his neck out of habit—amazing he had not thought about it—his neck pain and stiffness had all but disappeared. One promise Hardy hadn't bullshitted him with. But. Ariel. Nothing else mattered.

"Had visits from the dead. Think it may be a warning. I'm not afraid for me, never feared dying. Not sure what it means--the dying visiting me. Don't know this daughter and grandson—not sure if the omen was about them—doesn't feel right. Scared me, especially when Joanna appeared, made me think it was about Ariel."

"Just your mind messin' with you bro. Took fear of losing Ariel into your unconscious subconscious, that's all. Ariel goina be fine, and we goina find your grandson. Staties issued a search request to Interpol to locate your daughter after Hardy told them Alperts bit the dust—he initiated the search—starting with anyone connectied to Alperts and DICE. Which brings up an interesting adjunct. I checked the phones we seized before I turned them over to Hardy. On one of Alperts' three, were several calls to a General Toraz in Juarez and several more were to an apparent burner purchased in the Charlotte area. I notified my SWAT team buddy in Charlotte to see what he can do to find out where it was purchased. He says it's doubtful he can find out who purchased the phone. Never know, could find surveillance video which will turn up something. Ariel may be able to fill in some pieces once she's able."

"What about Mark?"

"Right here Jake." Jake turned around. Mark was standing in the door to the kitchen.

Mark worried about the phone. He hoped it wouldn't get traced. Needed to warn Lisa.

"Being watched by your buddy here and those two lovely ladies. Got both doors covered, bars on the windows, seem to think I may be a threat to society. Glad to hear Mrs. Gaspard is going to make it. Got me to thank. If it hadn't been for my misfortune and her good fortune, who knows, probably would be lying out there with Alperts. On the other hand, could be Arturo Gonzalez only allowed me to live because of her. Makes me wonder, did I piss him off more, or was it you?"

"You have one screwed-up, gigantic ego—think everything revolves around your ass. Thank you? I ought to kick your ass. You knew all about Alperts, followed Ariel, yet did nothing until it was almost too late."

"Got it wrong buddy. I was taken hostage by some of Gonzalez' men. The incident happened just before I arrived. I had no idea Ariel or Alperts were there. If you want proof, talk to Hardy, he has Arturo--I'm sure they have him talking by now." Mark stood up straight. Someone had given him clean clothes. He passed a hand back through his wavy, brown hair. "Have you people got any kind of alcohol here. I could use a drink--drink to Ariel's good health. I don't know how you do it buddy—you sure do end up with some fine women. What say, we have a few—you can tell me your secret."

TJ had a big grin on his face. He stood back, ready, expecting Jake goina take his anger and frustration out on Mark. He wasn't sure how soon he would step in. They needed to get Mark talking, maybe alcohol would work better than kicking his ass.

"I'll ask the ladies to go. They need to see if there are any eyes on the house. Give you two a chance to come to a truce."

TJ memed Jake, 'why don't you get cleaned up. Alcohol will hopefully loosen Poponovich's lying tongue. Need touch base with Hardy. Man concerned about your state of mind.'

Jake looked at his image in the mirror. What he saw was a droopy-eyed caricature with a bald spot reflecting the overhead light beam. He carefully peeled the mask off and set it aside, did his kidney and bowel cleansing business, showered, and shaved. He still felt listless. He didn't want to converse with Hardy. Might as well get it over with.

'Jake. Good to hear you decided to communicate.'

Jake didn't respond.

"Look man. I'm sorry about Ariel. We have provided her with the best care available. She's going to be fine I'm told. You'll be able to be there shortly. Be angry. I don't blame you. Direct that anger at those who did this to her. Let's catch these motherfuckers.'

Hardy had been briefed about pending neuro-implant upgrades. He was forbidden to share this info with Jake and TJ.

Jake stayed unresponsive.

'You still there?'

'Yeah. I will do whatever I have to do until my grandson is returned to his mother. If that doesn't happen satisfactorily, there won't be any rules of engagement bullshit. Just so we're clear.'

'We're working on that. We have Mrs. Gaspard's, Alperts' and cartel phones, the FBI and Interpol are following all possible leads on finding your daughter. Your grandson is here with his Latino father and grandparents. He has been spotted. We're keeping eyes on him. There is nothing we can do unless the parent breaks international law. If we can prove a connection to your daughter's disappearance, your grandson will be taken into protective custody.'

"I heard a recording of Alperts' threats, check Ariel's phone."

'Her phone was mangled by the blast, the sim card heavily damaged. The FBI has an expert working on trying to recover the data. They're doing all they can to catch the supposed kidnappers.'

'No damn supposed, I heard the video. The husband was there. An accomplice of Alperts was there with her at an outdoor café, somewhere in Spain. Alperts coerced, blackmailed Ariel into going with him using threats to our daughter. They were in Mexico. Has to be a connection to the Juarez Cartel and the Gonzalez brothers.'

'I'm in the middle of reading the initial statements provided by Mr. Gonzalez. Not much we didn't already know. Nothing about Alperts or DICE. We'll give him the treatment overnight, maybe soften him up. TJ has been at Mark--says he needs you. You've been around Poponovich, maybe you can open him up. We know he is connected to the Gonzalez brothers and TJ says Ariel told you Mark witnessed the meeting between her and Alperts. You two need to work on him tonight. Some agency, almost certainly a group within the CIA, will be checking in with him. They find out we have him, we could be forced to release him. Someone may be looking for him—may be watching now. Jeni put in a request for satellite surveillance in your area. Just handed a note—images show man and woman, second floor house across street, equipment trained on your house. Home beside you has four, three men and a woman, equipment trained on you and on other two in the other house. Going to need to move your party. Have notified TJ, Marge and Jeni.'

'Weapons?'

'Equipment, saw no weapons. Assume have weapons and are not friendlies.'

When Jake came out of the bathroom, he saw TJ on the phone, he was staring at Jake. He heard TJ say, "That will probably make our friend happy. Guess I could go for a bite to eat myself."

Mark looked from Jake to TJ, he saw the nod and the silent message which passed between them. Partners who worked together like these two were like married people—they could finish the others' sentences. He had never had, nor felt the need for, either a marriage or a partner in the life. He heard TJ say something about his happiness, must be code for moving him, most likely some place to give him a more intense interrogation. He had anticipated this happening. He told Lisa he would check with her the next morning—no contact set up if he didn't. Couldn't risk her cover getting blown. Had to play along, find out what they know.

"The ladies couldn't find any place to buy alcohol. They found an all-night lounge not too far away. Let's go."

They pulled away from the curb, made a sharp left at the next corner, Jake floored the delivery van, slid into the next left bringing them parallel to the place they were staying one block over. He and TJ saw the lights of the other vehicle headed the direction they had taken. He took the next left, then another, pulled to the curb and stopped. This brought them back to their street. He managed the maneuver never turning on lights, using the emergency brake only.

"Nifty bit of driving Jake my man. Care to explain how you knew we were being watched? TJ, hope it is okay if I call you TJ--I believe you were told with the cell phone call, but Jake nothing was said to you, how is it you knew?"

"Had to assume. You should know," Jake replied.

Another vehicle followed shortly, looked like the one which followed them earlier, the one with Blakely and Thomas. They watched as both vehicles made the two lefts and the lights disappeared. A minute later, another vehicle slid to a stop next to them pointed in the opposite direction, their lights also not on. They piled out and jumped into the rear seat, Mark sandwiched between Jake and TJ. Marge floored it, took an immediate left, went two blocks before turning the lights on. They were headed out of El Centro.

'That was Carmichael and Devereaux in the second vehicle. Wonder who was in the first,' Jake memed TJ.

"Did you get a tag number for the first vehicle?" TJ asked the women.

"Already pulled it up," Jeni replied checking her tablet. "Company called Beacon Enterprises, listed as a British Internet Company, an affiliate of a Middle East investment group. The other…"

"Already know who the other party is," TJ interrupted.

"Thought we were going for drinks and food," Mark said.

"Looks like we'll be dining in after all," Marge replied. "Here's a liter of Tequila and some limes, best we could do." Marge held the bag up. Mark reached for it, Marge pulled it back.

"Give it to him, maybe it will shut him up," TJ said. He was hoping the opposite might happen. Otherwise, he and Jake would need to go extreme. Goina be a long night. At least this would help keep Jake's mind somewhat off Ariel. He would call Deane when he got a chance, let Jake talk with her. If everything about Ariel sounded positive.

'Wonder why Devereaux and Carmichael didn't come over and talk instead of watching? Their delay in coming after us seems to indicate they knew about the other watchers,' Jake memed.

'Have to assume others're hostiles. Friends possibly waiting to see what happened.'

'Then why not be watching them instead of us? If they thought they were hostiles, why not warn us? No, I believe they are more interested in Mark-- both parties want to know what he tells us. The ones you call hostiles, they could be DICE or some foreign group. If they aren't hostiles, maybe they are Mark's buddies. One way to find out. I say we go back and ask the two they left behind.'

'Pretty risky. Others goina return once figure out we lost therm.'

'We need to start taking players off the board which pose a threat. I say we start with these guys. Go in, taser their ass, be out and on our way.'

'Not much room left in here.'

'Have the trunk. We're wasting time.'

"Marge, turn the car around. Take us back. Hurry," Jake demanded.

"Not my orders."

"New orders. I'll notify operations. Meanwhile turn around and head back. Just do it."

Marge stiffened. Her neck and face flushed. She wanted to argue, hoped Hardy would override Jake. She slid to a stop, wheeled around, and floored the vehicle. These guys were risking everything. Beginning to piss her off. She would file a complaint.

TJ texted Hardy, 'Need to know who is who--start neutralizing hostiles. Get answers. Returning to house only two left. Give Jeni access to sats. Let Jake and I have eyes. Text the women, their feelings are hurt.'

Jake followed with a meme. 'TJ and I can be in and out. Need to know if these are hostiles.'

'Too risky,' Hardy memed back, 'Concentrate on Poponovich.'

'Everything is risky. Believe Poponovich is target. Need to know.'

There was a pause. 'In and out. No casualties. Captain Adams says abort, you abort. I'm busy, can't watch. Be careful. Other Gonzalez brother and gangs are out there. You two are prime target, now, more than ever.'

"You catch that TJ?"

"Got it.'

'Mission approved,' was texted to TJ and copied to the Captain and the Major.'

"Mission approved," TJ said.

"Received message," Marge replied, sounding pissed. "What's the plan?"

"Drop us off a block behind on parallel street. Jeni, you our eyes. Five minutes in, five out. Be on street behind house, trunk open when you see us," TJ replied. "If others return, tell us abort. We meet back here. Are stun weapons in trunk?"

"Yes." Jeni reached around her tablet, into the floorboard, pulled up three handguns, handed one to TJ then Jake, showed the other to Mark, handed it across the console putting it in Marge's lap.

Mark grinned, took a drink of the tequila, offered the bottle to each of the others, they all declined. "You guys are all party poopers. Cheers." He turned the bottle up, shook his head, saying , "yippee yi yo, yippee ki-yay, going to love watching the show with these two lovely fillies. Maybe I can teach you some roping tricks later, how about it?"

No one replied. The women shook their heads. TJ chuckled. Mark laughed.

Jake and TJ piled out before the car was completely stopped. 'Let's go have some kickass fun,' TJ memed. They cut the corner. A dog began barking.

Jeni's voice came in loud and clear. "Targets in kitchen, right hand side, lights on dim. No sign of weapons."

Without hesitation, TJ hit the door, shattering the jamb, Jake was right behind him. They each stunned the same guy. The other, a woman, was trying to stand, Jake tackled her, they hit the floor. She tried getting her fingers to his eyes, simultaneously, kneed him, missed hitting him in the groin. They rolled over and over, crashing into table, chairs, cabinets. Jake caught a glimpse of TJ—he had his phone out, aimed at them.

"Zap her damnit, Jake shouted.

"Hold her so I can get a good view."

"Do it damnit. Need to get out of here."

"Turn her over. Goina love the video." TJ stepped over them, when she ended up on top, he zapped her. She trembled like she was having an orgasm, then went limp. Jake rolled her off.

They did a quick search of the house, snappng pictures, taking what they thought would help identify them, aid in their questioning, including the chip from their monitoring equipment.

"Time to go," Jake grunted. "Let's take them, get the hell out of here."

They each grabbed their semi-conscious targets, threw them over shoulders in a fireman's carry, TJ snatched their targets' cells off the table--they ran back out the open doorway.

"Got targets. Get here now," TJ said in his mouthpiece, sounding completely normal. Jake hated it. His neck hurt with the weight, his breath erratic, despite the fact he was the one carrying the woman. He could smell the wine and cheese from her breath pushed out by his stiff hurrying steps, each one a reminder of the shot he took to his inner thigh; plus the pain from the scratches of her fingernails to his face. He was pissed at TJ's antics. The woman's eyes locked into his when he, not so gently, laid her into the trunk next to the man TJ had tossed in.

'Getting out of shape bro. That woman almost kicked your ass.'

'Just remember payback can be hell.'

Marge spun the tires on the sandy pavement. Mark was humming 'get along little doggees', the tequila bottle was half empty. TJ took it from him, took a swallow and passed it up front. Everyone took a hit.

"Time to party, Got any marijuana?" Mark shouted.

'Targets acquired, where to?' TJ memed Hardy.

'Major knows. Keep me updated.'

CHAPTER
21

Outside Cancun, near Tulum
Esmeralda Ochoa--Juarez Cartel and Pablo

Esmeralda Ochoa looked over at the peroxided-blonde older lady lying beside her. They had been enjoying the other's company after meeting at the bar of the hacienda the night before. She looked down at the woman's shaved pussy, red and swollen from having been introduced to Esmeralda's favorite toys, coupled with her long slender fingers, and pointed tongue. The woman pleaded for more and more, her voice muffled--tongue buried deep inside Esmeralda until they both lay spent. The woman named Suzie, had passed out.

Esmeralda eased out of the bed, tied the silk robe around her nakedness and stepped outside. She ran her hand across her close-cropped hair. The effects of the alcohol, drugs and sex lingered, the woman's scent overriding the night-blooming plants. She lit a cigarette, inhaled deeply, looked up at the stars. The cool breeze washed over her. She thought about the two Harper man's women. The one named Elena had been fun, but, as of yet, had not returned her favors. She had been looking forward to the other. Alperts had promised she could do with her as she pleased--once he used her to introduce him to the Cuban Ambassador.

Alperts should have arrived by now. He said give him forty-eight hours, then contact Pablo. She reached inside her robe pocket and pulled out her phone, sent the number. Pablo acknowledged. She texted David, 'Do what must be done.' Told: 'Keep Pablo guessing.'

She threw her cigarette butt in the plant bed. She need to be on her way by morning. The money in account, she checked, not trust Alperts' word that nothing happen to her, she get paid. She must tell Arturo there no Gaspard woman to play with, no Gaspard woman for him make suffer. Perhaps knowing about the meeting with Pablo, the Harper man's grandson's father, his hated nemesis, would make him less angry. As for herself, Arturo promise he had another target for her talents, a woman named Blakely.

She would enjoy the rest of the night with this puta. Perhaps she should be 'wakened by the taste of Esmeralda's wetness upon her face. Then she join her cousins, see what this Blakely woman like.

Suzie, the peroxided woman, watched as the cousin of her other targets, left the bed. Her firm, body glistened in the light of the moon. The vixen picked up a silk robe and stepped out through the sliding glass door. Sex with the Mexican had been better than some, she preferred men, but did as tasked. She had to find the two cousins and hopefully, their uncle, that was the assignment—find, call in for extraction of all three—eliminate only if no option. The uncle, stop him, was the mission. She would hate having to eliminate this one, but such was the life she chose. One she was good at. Few people suspected a nice, professional-looking woman to be in the business. This part was the best part.

She smiled to herself, laid back, fully exposed, pretended to be asleep, as the Mexican came back to the bed. She climbed on the bed, turned so her nice firm rear end was visible. The Mexican's legs straddled her upper body, her tongue travelled down from her belly button. Oh yes, very satisfying. She felt the Mexican's tongue sink deep into her wet folds. Then the woman lowered herself onto her face. They went at each other like there was no tomorrow.

Pablo walked down the cool marble-tiled floor barefooted. He stopped outside Gabriel's room, opened the door a fraction and looked in on his son. His back was to him. He appeared to be sleeping. The woman, Gabriel's nannie, and guard, was in the chair next to the bed, her eyes closed. The nannie cam had indicated she might be asleep. He wanted to test her. See how alert the woman would be had he been a predator. He would dress her down for her mistake in the morning. He closed the door. Made sure it made enough noise to wake her and not his son.

Elizabeth, his wife, Gabriel's mother had been an impostor. When they first met, she had captivated him with her elegance and intellect. Her parents' wealth and position enticingly suitable. His parents, hesitant at first, had decided an heir from this family would ensure the family name and improve their own family's secreted, forbidden wealth and coveted stature. They were delighted when Gabriel was born.

Then came the visit from Pierre Paul Alperts. He had proof Elizabeth's biological parents were common Americans. Pablo dared not tell his parents. An arrangement was made with Alperts' organization DICE to have them all disappear. This unexpected trip to Cancun, then Cuba provided an alibi for him and a means to keep his son far away from whatever Alperts' people did.

He had wired half the funds as directed to two separate accounts. The balance was to be paid when Alperts arrived in Cancun with proof. He was told to expect a call which would alert him of Alperts' arrival. Having received the call, he now must prepare to meet mid-morning at the designated location.

He had mixed feelings for what was done. He was convinced this was best for Gabriel. This would ensure Gabriel's inheritance from Elizabeth's stepparents—thirteen more years, the trust fund would be his.

CHAPTER
22

El Centro Cancun
Carmichael and Devereaux

Once more, Jake and company had given them the slip. Blakely and Devereaux had followed the other vehicle, trying to maintain the proper distance while maintaining visual contact amidst the congestion of other vehicles and pedestrians, going to, or returning from Hotel Row. By the time they realized the futility, returned to El Centro, they were at odds with each other as how to proceed. Devereaux wanted to stay in their quarters, hoping for their return. Blakely thought they should scour the area looking for their vehicle. They slowly circled the block, checking on the Israelis. They too had come back. Levon and another man, paced in and out onto the side porch, Blakely saw the side entry, it looked severely damaged. They went to their place—no sign of anyone else having been there.

"They knew they were being watched. The whole thing was a ruse to draw us out. Why would they have targeted the Israelis and not us?" Devereaux thought out loud.

Blakely shook her head. "Where were the other two Israelis, Yuri and the other one?"

"They probably took them. It's not likely they'll return—this is not good."

"No shit. We've got to locate them. Need to pack up and start looking. You need to report in."

While Blakely gathered their things, loaded them in the car, Devereaux texted their contact the news.

Harper's lady friend injured in blast, airlifted to Miami—Alperts dead. Harper man's illegit daughter has been reported missing, possibly kidnapped, last known sighting in Spain. FBI and told we, Interpol, conducting a search, investigating Alperts and DICE's possible involvement. The son, grandson reported here with father and grandparents. Arturo Gonzalez thought responsible for blast, in custody. Harper and company have Poponovich, plus two Israelis.

"Control is pissed we struck out, says we need to do a search in the area for Harper and company tonight. If unable to locate, we shift focus to the ambassador and family. Wants us to determine any possibility the father, named Pablo and/or his family, are involved in the woman's disappearance. The supervisor wants to know about the bug planted on the ambassador's wife. He believes the women in Harper's party will be nearby. Wants us to find them."

"Damn. Jake must be hurting. He'll be out for revenge. Nothing said about the other Gonzalez brother or any possibles who hired Alperts and DICE?"

"No."

"Jake and the other Gonzalez brother will be going after each other. We need to be watching out for the bangers. Be interesting to know what Jake will do regarding his grandson."

"Why so enthused? Probably hoping his lady friend doesn't make it."

"You're an asshole. Why have us concentrate on the woman's disappearance rather than figuring out who has the intelligence data?"

Devereaux thought, 'maybe because they have a good idea who the seller is and are closing in on that person.'

"Perhaps you should ask your old boyfriend. I've thought all along, we should be watching the Russian and Cuban ambassadors. Now we will. Plus, there's a good bet, your latest love interest will turn up. My immediate concern is getting some much-needed sleep. We'll have to take turns in the damn car."

"My biggest concern is, as it has been, why I got stuck with you."

CHAPTER
23

Control Center, Akumal
Jake, TJ and USec Hardy

Marge drove south toward Tulum. Less than an hour, near a resort community popular with expats called Akumal, she turned left onto a drive with heavy signs declaring *private, authorized vehicles only* in English and Spanish. She had been told they would be going to a hacienda-like complex on a secluded bay owned by Uncle Sam as an adjunct of the embassy, as such it was treated as sovereign territory, not subject to international law. The complex, with the nearby Tulum Naval Air Base, which allowed private jets, and the private secluded bay for watercraft access, was equipped with everything needed for clandestine operations. At times it was used for renditions and interrogations.

Two men sat inside a guard house fifty feet from where a barrier prevented any vehicle from approaching. Marge gave them the designated response given to her by Hardy. A scanner buzzed under the vehicle, a robot, infrared cameras for eyes and bomb sniffing equipment hummed as it circled the car, then they were instructed to approach the gate. Their weapons were handed over. The man and woman in the trunk treated as routine. The spiked tire buster was retracted, and they drove on.

When they reached the circular entrance four heavily-armed men took Poponovich and the two Israelis away, another lesser-armed man escorted them inside. The house looked like any other wealthy person's tropical retreat. They were led through a large open kitchen and living area onto a large, covered veranda and down some steps. The faint sound of waves in the distance could be heard from an upper terrace. They skirted the edge of a large oval swimming pool and went through a tiki hut looking bar into what appeared to be a storage room. It began to descend once they all squeezed in. The descent stopped; the elevator door opened onto a large hallway. Two armed Marines told them to follow them, led them through a series of doors, down corridors with some lit, others with dark, obscure-glass windows, beyond which Jake guessed were rooms, whose purpose he could only guess at. Everything was so sterile, like a hospital ward, and quiet--the only sounds their breathing and their footsteps. Not a word from their escorts.

Their prison guards, as Jake thought of them as being, stopped and opened two doors and ushered them into an enormous room where men and women seated, or standing were watching satellite feeds and colorful remote camera images on wall-to-wall monitors.

Relief, not a torture chamber, no inquisition tables or chairs waiting.

Hardy was standing, appeared to have been waiting to greet them.

"Welcome to our newest communications and command center, formerly located on the island of Puerto Rico, until Hurricane Maria rendered it obsolete. Our guests have been escorted to another area., Jake, TJ, and I will join them shortly. Major Duplantis and Captain Adams, you will be debriefed and brought up to speed on the latest intel by Colonel Helen Krantz, a senior intelligence officer and deputy commander of this facility." Colonel Krantz, a lovely stiff-backed lady stepped forward and introductions were made.

"We'll leave you to it. Jake, TJ, follow me."

They walked down one of the long curving corridors and through a series of doors which required visual recognition from Hardy. They came to a desk manned by two block-headed men. They were dressed casually. Their stiff-lipped demeanor and jackets with bulges the only indication they were anything but casual. The corridor branched off into two other hallways, like the hospital ward Jake feared. A woman got up from her stool, came around and led them down the right-hand hall. Inside one of the lit-glass enclosures sat Arturo. The lights were intensely bright, his eyelids taped open, the glass vibrated from the heavy metal music blasting away inside. Jake could hear and see everything via his implant and the monitor inside the room from where he stood outside in the hall. He wanted to go inside and do his own interrogation. Hardy told him he couldn't allow it. "Not yet."

"We have verified from other sources your belief the two other people were Carmichael and Devereaux. The FBI failed to inform HSI Blakely was not in WitSec as we were previously told. Apparently, they are both working for and with Interpol."

"Why spy on us?" TJ asked.

"Not sure. Supposedly, they are part of Interpol's investigation into the missing data. Interpol and the FBI are looking into Jake's daughter's disappearance. Trying to find any possible connections with Alperts and DICE, perhaps that is why they were surveilling you. They'll turn up again, hopefully we can persuade them to confide in us."

"What do you plan to do with the Israelis?" TJ asked.

Jake moved closer to the glass which suddenly became transparent. He wondered if Arturo could see them.

"We'll hold them until morning, then drop them at their embassy. I'm certain they are like all the other intelligence agencies, here trying to locate the data. Most likely they want to copy it, destroy it, deny they ever saw it."

'Mark said Arturo claims his people here to purchase from the Russians the ability to create mind-reading supermen--sound lot like the implant Jenkins and we have. He say anything about that to the interrogators?" TJ asked.

"No. That's interesting. Could change the whole nature of this operation. Why didn't you report this earlier?"

"Lot happening at the time, thought I told you." TJ nodded toward Jake, standing at the glass, staring intensely at Arturo. Hardy simply nodded.

"What else did he say?"

"Nothing of value. Claims he's a businessman, kidnapped by Arturo for ransom, ended up at airport where he found Alperts dead and Ariel in need of medical attention. Said Arturo insisted they be flown here to him. Claims he managed to overcome Arturo and his driver, went looking for Ariel, ended up with us."

Jake pulled back from the glass. "Listening to you two, praddle on and on, why are we here?"

"You know the mission…"

"Which mission? Isn't that what you said, and I quote, "this changes the whole nature of this operation?", end quote."

"Hold on Jake," Hardy said with authority.

"No you hold on. I'm tired of playing games. This shit is personal. It's time for you to level with me. We were coerced into having these damn implants. Why me? Why TJ? Why you? What good is the implant if all we're allowed to do is sit back and not take action?"

It came to Jake earlier, now again. It was like the implant was trying to tell him something. Was it telling TJ, Hardy and perhaps others his thoughts without him knowing it?

"This implant needs an on/off switch. I said this and was ignored before. You should know by now, we need to be able to turn this damn thing off-- have quiet time, have me time. Maybe it's because it is my nature to want to strike out when I am offended, attack when me or mine are threatened. You ever stop to think, my implant may think of me as a killer. Make me into a monster. These technologies could feed off our most devious thoughts, create its own "out-of-reality" world—the result, chaos, murder, and mayhem. Which brings me back to the basic question: "why me, why us? Why were we chosen? Who is the puppet-master? What is the real mission? Huh Bob? TJ do you know?"

Silence. He could see and feel their minds churning. "Who is man enough to talk about it, my mind is whirling, going off on its own, maybe pushing me to an unbridled extreme. Perhaps yours is also. Is this what *they*, whoever *they* are, is this what *they* wanted? Or are *they* clueless to what could go wrong with a person whose inner most demons take control? Perhaps that's what happened to Jenkins? What about this Hardy?"

Hardy replied: "No time to do anything about it now. We bring all perspectives, throw them into the blender, demand ourselves, our implants stay on track. It's up to us to discipline ourselves Jake, not let ourselves become monsters. Force ourselves to grab onto that anchor, our mission. We must trust we were chosen to form a team made up of disparate mindsets for a reason. We need to keep each other from going off the rails. It is our duty to put country first, follow orders, blindly perhaps, but always we must follow orders."

TJ was happy to know he wasn't the only one having to try to hold on.

"You right bro. Not easy having to adjust to this thing. The more you fight it, the more confused you goina get. All you gotta do is concentrate on a particular subject, thing's goina give you several options, gotta seek out that best solution. Just choose one, go with the flow. Problem is can't git all rebellious, give into your paranoid nature. You, the quintessential 'doubting Thomas'. Gotta git over it. Don't let it kick your ass."

"Jake, what brought this sudden stream of conscience on? This is a tool, another weapon in your arsenal, gives you an advantage, TJ's right, stop fighting it." Hardy tried his most beatific look.

"Okay. I asked this before, you didn't let Dr. Perkins answer, where is the advantage if what Arturo told Mark is correct? These so-called "supermen" are real, have the same or similar implant which negates the advantage. They can detect us—we can hack in, they can hack in. Everything's hackable This is a mind war. No, an implant war. Perhaps that is what was intended—see what strategies prove superior—survival of the tech fittest. *West World*, *Terminator* brought to fruition seems to me will be the end result."

"Jesus," Hardy said. Jake was getting too close to losing it. "You don't know this, shouldn't believe that gangbanger."

"Doesn't matter, shouldn't believe, what should I believe, huh? For me there is a much greater dilemma--how do you get the implant to know the difference between right and wrong? This is a battle I fight every day--has sent many soldiers and veterans over the edge--blindly told do our duty, follow orders some jackass military strategists, off in Washington or bung-fucking Moscow, North Korea, wherever--whoever comes up with the bullshit, often-times today with the aid of some supercomputer, which operates from algorithms created by people who never engaged in combat. These people and their machines created this implant, they are our puppet-master, we're just along for the ride, test pilot guinea pigs, tethered lambs. coerced, threatened by you Hardy and those mindless mothers you kiss up to."

"Damn bro. How about just enjoy the ride? We not here to change the whole screwed-up world. Like to think of myself as the good guy. I want to stop these mothers the same as you. Come on bro, get a grip on yourself. Don't go off the rails, keep it simple. Hardy's right. Concentrate on the mission--know this done become personal, makes you want to lash out, kill them all--understand that--feel the same way. Let's take it to 'em. We need to find out who and where they are, take them off the board, remember, that's what you said, *"take them off the board, one by one"*. Just concentrate on that for now—figure this other shit out later. How 'bout it?"

TJ saw Jake was hardly listening. "Come on bro, concentrate, focus your attention, treat it like all the other missions we've been in in hostile situations. Need you there, gotta cover each other's six. Think about Ariel, make it happen so's she can meet your other daughter, her son, your grandson, go back to your farm, then we have plenty of time to give the puppet-master bastards all the shit you wish them to eat."

Jake had been pacing. He stopped. Came back to where Hardy stood watching him.

"They own us. Isn't that what you said Hardy? No one owns me. For now, they own my services. I'll do my best not to go in there or out there and kill them all. You better hope they or you can stop me. Just remember I warned you. I'm here for my family's sake, then I'm through. The implant comes out, I go back to being me. Understood?"

Hardy simply nodded. He hoped he had successfully blocked Command from listening. "Okay Jake. TJ's right, the sooner we start the quicker we can make your wishes happen. Let's go talk to your CIA buddy Poponovich. It's time he opens up."

CHAPTER
24

Control Center
Mark Poponovich—CIA Clandestine Unit

"The party poopers finally get around to joining me, even brought the head party pooper, Homeland's own Robert Hardy. Hello Bob. Is it okay if I call you Bob? Doesn't matter, I'll call you what I wish. Hello Jake, where are the women, you and I we need women to really get the party going."

The room was bright, everything white except the metal table and chairs all bolted to the white-painted concrete floor. Jake and TJ sat down in the chairs across from Mark. The bandage on his arm showed blood stains. Hardy stopped at the end of the table, remained standing.

Hardy spoke first. "And what should we call you, Mark Castle, Mark Poponovich, or is there some other name you prefer?"

"Any will work, long as you're not announcing last call." Mark laughed. "What a sobering crowd we have here. Come to whittle away at corrupt flesh, dissect my organs until I sing? Who dareth bring forth the bones hidden in mere flesh? Why the somber look Jake, it's party time?"

TJ's chuckle sounded ominous. Mark laughed. His body shook and tears ran down his face.

"We need another bottle of tequila," Mark said in between gasps.

"Tell you what," Hardy said, "You come clean, answer our questions and we'll all celebrate. I'll buy."

"That 'I'll show you mine, if you show me yours' kinda thing is that it?"

"Something like that. I'll go first," Hardy replied. "No need to go over the Cuba episodes, we pretty much know all there is to know about that, including your desperate departure. Who wouldn't have panicked, no amount of CIA training could have prepared you for that one."

"You should know Bob."

Hardy ignored the interruption and the looks he received from Jake and TJ.

"It's a known fact about your connections to James Dean and crew. Don't understand why Devereaux would allow your people to outfit and use his boat. Had to be for the money." Mark didn't reply, just continued to smile.

"What puzzles me is your interests in Jake. Started before Cuba, not sure about the two years leading up to the present, we'll get to that in time. Recently, you show up again, first in the Carolinas, following Jake's lady friend. You follow her across Mexico to here. We all know the bullshit story of events you have told explaining the coincidence of being at the wrong place at the right time. We are grateful for your help in saving her. Who started this interest in Jake and his lady friend? Was it the Gonzalez brothers, or someone else?"

"Jake's a lady killer. Being a fellow connoisseur of the female flesh, I figured I needed to study the master." He saluted Jake. TJ chuckled. Jake just shook his head in amazement.

"Jake does seem to have his way with women. Nevertheless, I'm sure that is not your major reason. Most likely, the Gonzalez brothers, possibly, Major Jenkins. I believe you knew about Jake through your connection to them, care to explain the nature of your relationship? You have any idea where Jenkins is or your associate, David Gonzalez?"

Mark sat there, maintained a humorous surprised expression. The room grew quiet, the only sound was the air conditioning vents in the ceiling blowing cool, dry air. No one moved. No one said anything. Mark kept smiling.

After several minutes, Mark said, "Jake, he's got you barking up the wrong tree. Bob, why don't you tell us about the skeletons in your own closet. Bet these two would get a kick out of knowing how it is you became Undersecretary of Homeland so early in your career. Your interests in Jake started long before mine did."

Jake and TJ looked from Mark to Hardy.

'Jake memed, 'What's going on here?'

Hardy memed back, 'He's trying to deflect attention away from himself.'

"Try again Poponovich. Who else besides the CIA have you been working for? Your file is invisible, your work history nonexistent for the last twenty years. Intel places you in Spain and Portugal, possibly connected to a Columbian cartel. Next came Miami, had an office there, not registered with BBB, Chamber of Commerce, or any other organization. You closed shop, then showed up in Cuba. Simultaneously, a records search turned up a family member of the Gonzalez opened an office in Charlotte. She previously listed her employment at an address, records and interviews with others indicate, was the same as we discovered you had occupied in Miami and Charlotte. Mysteriously, she disappeared at the same time as the Gonzalez brothers, the offices in both cities were vacated. We also have your fingerprints from both locations, along with DNA collected from when you must have pulled out after screwing her or some other lady at those offices. Thought you boys were better at cleaning all traces of your presence than that. You testified before a Senate Select Committee concerning cartel money laundering. Care to explain yourself?"

"Please keep going. I'm intrigued, especially the part about my sex life. Can't deny I may have screwed some chicks in those two places. Want to hear about others. Perhaps Jake and I could compare notes. Give us some privacy, why don't you? How's that sound Jake?"

"Fine by me. What about it Bob, TJ?"

'Not sure that's such a good idea,' Hardy memed.

TJ, 'He may open up to Jake. I think it's worth a try.'

"Alright. Jake make sure this doesn't end up a bullshit session. We'll wait down the hall." 'And Jake keep your tendencies in check,' Hardy memed.

Mark watched them turn to leave. He could feel Jake's eyes on him. "No cameras, microphones, cell phones. No recording. Want an RF scanner in here, to make sure," Mark said before TJ opened the door.

Jake nodded in agreement. He memed them, 'I can record using this damn implant, right?'

'Right,' Hardy memed.

"I'll have to see if a scanner is available. Be right back." Hardy left.

TJ looked at Jake, returned the nod and walked out also.

Hardy returned shortly, handed the detector to Jake, Jake handed him his cell and he left. TJ and Hardy stood outside watching Jake do the sweep, then they disappeared.

"How you been Jake? Long time no see. Can't believe you've agreed to hold me hostage." Mark sounded almost sober.

"Figured you were putting on a drunk act."

"Takes a lot more than a bottle of tequila to get to me. Considering the circumstances."

"Thanks for saving Ariel."

Jake noticed Mark lightly touched the bandage on his arm and grimaced.

"Hope she makes it. I don't know how you manage to get these beautiful women. You aren't the best-looking guy. They must like the strong, silent type."

"Never thought about it. Anyway, what the hell did you have to say to me that you didn't want the others to hear? Have anything to do with what Devereaux was going to tell me?"

"Not sure. Devereaux refused to say. Man held out, despite my teams' best efforts. Now, we have his boat. Goes to show, you never can tell."

"Can we just get on with whatever it is you wish to say to me. I've got a daughter missing and a grandson I need to locate as well, you know anything about their whereabouts? Otherwise, I'm not sure I give a shit."

"Jake, Jake, Jake. Tell you what, you get me out of here and I swear I'll send Renai and Boyd to find your daughter. Dean and I will help you with your grandson. How about it?"

"Depends on what you tell me. Bullshit me, no deal."

"What if I told you your recruitment into Homeland was in the works long before it actually happened."

"So? Old news."

"What if I told you Thurmond Tindal was involved?" Jake rocked forward on his palms, leaned across the metal table. "Thought that might tickle your interests." Mark sat up straight. "Your buddy Robert Hardy, how well do you know him?"

"I warned you about bullshitting me. Keep it up and I'll leave you to whatever he has planned."

"Okay. Check it out for yourself. Before he joined Homeland, Hardy spent several years with Army Intelligence. He was stationed in Kuwait, guess who was CIA station chief in Kuwait at that time?"

Jake walked over to the glass partition, watching Mark's reflection in the glass. He kept twirling his ring. "What does that have to do with me?"

"I bet Hardy has never told you about his early connections to your father-in-law, Colonel Tindal or Major Jenkins, the cruelest of motherf'ers…" He paused. "There's good intel the then director considered bringing them up on charges. Tindal threatened to spill the beans, called on some politicians he knew, got transferred out, ended up at NSA. Left there after 9/11, started his own weapons-for-sale business. Same time Homeland was started. Hardy joined. Guess who recommended him?"

Jake shrugged.

"Some politicians Tindal was cronies with. Tindal came to North Carolina; the former secretary, also another Tindal acquaintance, promotes Hardy to Special Agent, has him assigned to the Charlotte Field Office. Then there's a Colonel Hunter, he's the man who performed all the inspections for DARPA approval, gave the green light for this weapon Jenkins supposedly stole the tech-shit for. This Colonel Hunter was Hardy's superior officer when he was with Army Intelligence. Fragmentary evidence—I don't think so, neither do others."

Jake's mind was already skimming the records to verify what Mark said.

"What's this got to do with my recruitment and the shit happening now?"

"Your first contact with Hardy was at a private billiards club, correct?"

"Dilworth Billiards, now closed, became a wine and cheese joint."

"Had a member named Billy Akers, went to Afghanistan to inform your ex-brothers-in-law their Uncle Walt died?"

Jake turned from the glass wall. "How do you know this?"

"Billy was a company man, served under your father-in-law and Tindal. Hardy was recommended for membership at Dilworth by Billy. Starting to connect the dots. The job just happened to open for you in the Bahamas and Hardy just so happened to recruit you to help Homeland at the same time all this shit was going down with Tindal. Get you out of the way, maybe something happens to you."

"As you said fragmentary evidence." Jake had verified some of what Mark said. "Where do you fit into this picture?"

"You got to promise you'll help me, if I help you."

Jake's priorities had changed since Ariel and their family entered his life. Hardy and Homeland used him, made promises--like the Army, promises they had not fulfilled. He didn't owe them anything, he had done more than his share. Putting his life at risk had been one thing, putting his family's life in jeopardy was too much to ask. Mark had opened another can of worms. Coupled with the implant threatening to rob him of who he was and what he wanted his future self to be, was asking too much, he had had enough.

He walked over to the end of the table, looked down at Mark, who stared up at him, tilted his head, flashed a grin.

"You best not be messing with me. My priorities are all about securing my family, everything else is no longer a major concern. However it turns out, I'm done with all this other bullshit."

"Wish I could say it was that simple. Tindal is determined to take you off the board. He won't stop. He hired Alperts to finish the job. Alperts and DICE had already kidnapped your daughter, prior to the meeting with Tindal. That means, there is someone else involved, DICE doesn't work cheaply. And, somebody other than Tindal is paying the bill It could be Pietr Okneyev. You saved us; his cargo ship bombing did not have the impact he wished. Blakely knows him better than anyone. She is a threat. He fears her; what she might have shared with you; that's why he wanted her dead; he thinks she betrayed him. Then there is the cartel. No telling what will happen when everyone involved knows Alperts is dead. David Gonzalez will not rest until you, your friend and families are finished. Now you have his brother. He'll be more determined than ever to get his hands on you two, make your families pay the price. Need to find who has your daughter, and why, before they have time to react. I have sources could provide answers."

"Why should I believe you?"

"Only one way to find out. Better think about it. Hardy has no intention to stand in Tindal's way once he has Jenkins and the tech-shit he stole. Unfortunately, I believe Jenkins is dead and the high-tech shit possibly already sold, which makes another set of problems for you. The Cuban Ambassadors' family with your grandson are here, as is everyone else that expects the sale and transfer are in the works, possibly a trade for that amphib, the subject of the other op, supposed to have taken place in Venezuela, then Cuba. Okneyev is out there. Anything can happen. I think because whoever took Jenkins, was or is, involved in the deal that's in the works. I believe they have whatever they wanted from him. They no longer need him alive. Of course, if it's you and your friend they're after, they wouldn't want anyone to know that. Something happened in between then and now, suddenly the deal is back on, or is it? Guess that's why we're all here. And what about you Jake?"

"What about me?"

"I checked, couldn't find any report concerning your last night with Blakely. Why is that? Does Hardy know?"

"What are you getting at?"

"Could be Blakely, you, whoever is involved, has taken advantage, and this is all a scam by them or other scammers. Common knowledge--scams are now a part of everyday life--just like the gala event set up by the staties and Homeland--good idea getting that space mining startup to sponsor it."

Jake was shocked. He thought the gala was his idea. Hardy planted the idea. Damn this freaking implant. How did Mark know?

"If there is a scam, you and your people are the ones most likely to pull the scam. Like I told you, I don't give a damn about this shit. I intend to find my daughter, get my grandson back to her, see if they want to join Ariel and me at the farm, or wherever. I'll deal with the bangers and Tindal in my own way after I get my family out of harm's way."

"To do that, you'll need help. The kind I can provide. Meaning, you need to convince Hardy to let me out of here."

"You haven't given me anything I can give him. He's definitely not going to do this if he feels threatened--the information you gave me, certainly does that."

"Okay. How about I give him information he can use against the Israelis."

"Not unless they know the answer to what this is all about. If you can prove it, he'll be interested, but I don't think that will buy your freedom."

"I know a helluva lot concerning the Juarez Cartel and Gonzalez brothers' finances. Good chance Arturo knows more than he'll say about the cartel's involvement in the impending deals and the threats to you and your friend's families. I can make him talk. I'll have to talk to my superior before I do this. I believe I can convince Arturo and my superior it is for the best."

"I do this and you renig on your promises, I'll make sure you regret it."

Jake went to the monitor station. TJ had his green tea, Hardy's coffee mug sat next to the monitor. His arms were crossed. Hardy stopped talking when Jake approached. They all moved down the hall away from the two attendants.

"He's willing to cooperate if you agree to certain conditions."

"And you believe him?" Hardy asked. He uncrossed his arms, then recrossed them. His face was red, his forehead furrowed with a frown as he shook his head back and forth.

Jake studied Hardy. Why the angry tone?

"Had some interesting points. I believe he could be useful."

"So Hardy was telling me bro. How…"

Jake turned to square off with Hardy. "The RF scan showed nothing. How'd you know what was being said? Wait a damn minute, you were listening through me, everything can be hacked, isn't that right? The gala event, you planted that in my head. Screw you, you bastard!"

Jake grabbed Hardy. He tried to pull away. Jake shoved him against the wall. TJ quickly stepped between them, faced Hardy.

"Is Jake right?" TJ asked Hardy.

"Calm down both of you." Hardy, brushed off what was his DHS emblazoned, pressed white shirt, and waved off the attendants who quickly stood and started their way. "Protocol demands any interrogation be monitored. That man in there doesn't get to call the shots."

Jake yelled, "Scheming motherfucker." He tried to step around TJ. TJ stuck his right hand out and grabbed him by his left arm.

"Hold on Jake. Not here. Not now. They'll throw you in one of these rooms."

"I had to hear what he had to say, that's why we're here, to find out what's going on. You intended for us to hear what he said. You should have realized that when you said you would record the conversation."

"TJ were you listening in also?"

"No." Hardy had been watching the monitor while they were talking. Hm?

"Didn't think so. Guess we don't have that ability, huh? So, you've been listening in on our conversations from the git go, planting ideas."

Hardy had a self-righteous, condescending tone. "That's not how it works."

"I was right, Hardy just admitted it, this "big brother" implant is hackable. How you feel about it now TJ?"

"Hold on Jake. What you mean that's not how it works?"

"Like any device, its storage is the vulnerable portion. When you said you would be able to record what was said, that means you were storing to allow sharing. That's not possible from outside these rooms. But I didn't need to do that. I simply opened my device's ability to share with the room monitor, which I turned back on after you did the sweep. Your devices could have informed you. If you had bothered to ask."

Jake jammed his palm against the wall next to Hardy. "Seems there were a lot of things we haven't been informed about." He looked from Hardy to TJ, then back to Hardy. "Seems our not-so-forthcoming-leader served overseas with General McDab, Colonel Tindal and Major Jenkins. Hardy was in Army Intelligence. Those two were with McDab, the CIA. Tindal is the one who recommended Hardy for Homeland, so Mark said, made sure he was moved to the Charlotte district. How about it, Bob, why weren't we told this?"

TJ locked eyes with Hardy. Hardy shifted his eyes to Jake.

"I knew nothing about his recommendation. My relationship with then Colonel Tindal was not so friendly. As you know, the military and the CIA seldom trust each other. Why he recommended me, I have no idea. My decision to come to Charlotte was mine. It meant a promotion. I took it. Tindal and I have never been friends. I didn't know he was in the area until he became a supplier of weapon technology to the armed forces. It's Homeland's job to vet these companies. When he bought a weapons manufacturing facility, we began paying serious attention to him and his organization. My association with him has been purely professional. I had no legal responsibility, no reason to share my background with you."

"That is bullshit. Teammates should trust and confide in teammates. Our lives depend upon each other. Mine, TJ's, and our families' lives have been put in jeopardy, so don't give me that bureaucratic crap. You had a moral responsibility to disclose the facts. What else have you not disclosed to us?"

Jake turned toward TJ. "Mark thinks Jenkins is dead, and this mission is a scam. I'm beginning to believe my earlier feelings that this has been an intelligence mind game. Hardy here could give a shit about us. He puts his career goals ahead of our personal ones." Jake turned back to stare at Hardy. "That ends right here, right now. Mark is on our side. He says he can and will help me get my family out of harm's way. That's reason enough to bring him and his team on board. Don't you agree TJ?"

"No reason not to trust your judgement."

"That's two, a majority. Are you going to make it unanimous Bob?"

Hardy's countenance grew even redder. He stood up straighter.

"This is not a democratic organization. I am your superior. Your votes mean nothing without my consent. When I want your opinions, I'll ask for them. Is that understood?"

Jake stepped in closer, saw the beads of sweat, smelled Hardy's aftershave.

"You'll get my opinions whether you ask for them or not. If you think you know me, you should know I'm done with the bullshit. As our teammate, not my superior, you, like the rest of us, must look at what's best for all of us. That's what I did in the Army, that's what I'm going to do now. My family's welfare should have been then, and will be now, a top priority. Either you agree and let Mark help, or you can kiss my ass. Understood?"

Hardy felt trapped, had no room to maneuver. He could see Jake was hoping he made a threatening move. He wasn't about to give him the pleasure.

"You are one insubordinate, cocky asshole. I could have you locked up and there isn't anything anyone could do to help you. I have looked out for your family. Ariel is getting the best medical attention, Interpol and the FBI are trying to locate your daughter. Your grandson is right here, not in any danger. Yet, you believe Mr. Poponovich's story about his superior's supposed accusations. This from the man whose superior denies his existence. And all this crap from he who claims he must get this superior's permission to cooperate with us. Yet, this man tells you *he* can pull members of his team away from their mission and help you? Get real Jake. CIA people are habitual liars and assassins, that's what they do. Homeland doesn't sanction killing. For all we know he and his people killed Jenkins. He'll say anything to get his ass out of here."

"Bob's right bro. Even if Mark says he will do this, it's not likely he can. You know as well as I do, spooks lie."

"Spooks lie. Friends shouldn't. Mark may not have volunteered to do this. We don't know what he or his team's mission is. For reasons I'm unsure of, they have been keeping tabs on me. He saved Ariel's life, I don't believe just for mine or her sake. I want to learn why I am his priority. He knows if he screws me over, I will destroy him. His life won't be worth a dime when I'm done. He has information you need about the Israelis and the cartels. I say we keep him on a short leash, see what happens." Jake turned to Hardy. "As for your threatening to lock me up, you think I'm helpless, think again. I have this implant. I can transmit and receive. Plus, I have TJ. We are a team."

"That's right bro."

Hardy shook his head. "The secretary warned me—field soldiers make lousy intel agents. I had my concerns regarding you two, especially you Jake. Unlike you, I do as I'm told. I've been given leeway regarding sharing with our sister agencies, told I would be held accountable. Poponovich will be put on a very short leash--everything goes through me."

Hardy felt it best to concede. For now. Let Jake and TJ feel empowered—he needed them to continue utilizing their implants. Jake and TJ were needed. The op must come first.

CHAPTER
25

South of Cancun
Carmichael and Devereaux

"We're not going to find them tonight," Devereaux said under his breath.

Blakely didn't respond. Her head rested on the window. She was staring out into the night, thinking of her last night with Jake.

She had sent Toby off in the car to determine if the skiff was waiting for them. If it was, he was to do what he had to do to insure Okneyev's man was neutralized, then return the next day to pick her up from the B&B in Cienfuegos.

She and Jake had dined out, they avoided talking about business or what the future might bring. Back in the room, they took a bath together by candlelight. It was one of the most romantic experiences ever.

Soaping and probing, Jake's hands were like magic. He teased her with his tongue. His lips and tongue kissed and probed hers. They dried each other with soft towels then lay on the bed, enjoying the humid-laden breeze blowing in through the French doors that were opened out onto a small, covered balcony. The streetlights twinkled, sounds of people and music ebbing and flowing from the city below, for her it was exactly right.

She couldn't remember who made the initial move, in her mind, they turned into each other simultaneously. The first deep kiss was tentative. Then his tongue fought hers. She felt his arousal growing between her thighs. She pushed into him. He paused, pulled loose from the embrace, and rolled her over onto her stomach. With his strong hands he began to knead and massage all the tension out of her muscles, starting with the base of her skull, moving downward. He squeezed and rubbed every joint and muscle downward to her feet.

Jake eased her back over and continued his massage upward. She tried to relax but his touch had her buzzing with anticipation. She rolled him over and eased him into her. She had experienced several small orgasms at other times. Never one like the one she experienced with him. This was lust and love combined with the feeling that she may never live to experience another one. The physical and emotional intensity frightened her.

She lay back spent. Jake rolled onto his side next to her. He reached out to touch her. She stopped him, the pleasure too painful, her nerve endings screamed. She drifted off to sleep.

Sometime in the morning, she woke, moved down, took him into her mouth, which brought him awake. She then moved up and onto him, leaned forward and sought his lips. Their kisses became hungry, bruising. She rode him to a mutual climax. He fell back asleep. She lay there listening to his breathing, trying to decide if she could or should trust him with her secrets. She wanted to. For reasons of uncertainty, she did not.

At daylight, they made love again and she finished him off while in, what he had told her, was his favorite position. For her, it was how she came to think of it, as their favorite position. The thought of him sharing himself with another woman, hurt and angered her. As much as she hated to admit to herself, Devereaux's comment about her hoping the Gaspard woman would die, had crossed her mind.

"You okay?" She heard Devereaux ask, his hand on her arm, close to her breast.

She knocked his hand away. "Must have dozed off. Having weird dreams." Her mouth felt dry, between her legs was damp. "We need to stop somewhere. I need something to drink and I need to use the restroom."

"Weird dreams huh? Sounded like you were having a helluva good dream, moaned, called out Jake's name a couple times. You really do have the hots for him."

"What if I do? It's none of your fucking business. Where in the hell are we?" It was dark out, no homes, nothing but tropical vegetation lit by the car's bright beams.

"South of a place called Tulum. Passed a few places looked like a Quick Stop back home. I started to pull in, figured I'd let you get some sleep. Glad I didn't. Would've missed the free show you put on."

"Devereaux you're such a pervert. Turn around. I'll drive, let you dream about some hard, sweaty body, probably doesn't matter which sex to you."

"Screw you."

"In your dreams. Get over it. Never gonna happen."

"Need to check the embassies again. Doubt they'll show up there. Think I'll call in, see if they found out where the Cuban Ambassador is staying. Hopefully, no one discovered the bug that tall gal placed in her purse. And maybe they can tell us who those two women were?"

"They already sent that information dildo brain. Both are US Air Force personnel. The taller one is a Major Marjorie Duplantis, USAir Intelligence. The other is Captain Jennifer Adams, has her wings, principally a drone jockey. Not sure what exactly their role is. Seems to be to keep tabs on the women, maybe Captain Adams is here for recceing?"

"Could be to provide the men with cover. Who knows, could get interesting, might really want to get to know each other."

"Not likely. Alvarez doesn't do that sort of thing. Could be Jake no longer does either. From what I witnessed the women are into each other."

"That's a shame. Too much of that going around for my liking."

"Going around? It's not a disease. Each to their own liking. Life's too short, do whatever makes you happy, is my way of thinking. Your sexual business is yours, not someone else's to judge. Knew lots of gay and bisexual women that worked at the club I managed in St. Louis. Most men never suspected-- course that seems to be most men's biggest fantasy, watching two women getting it on, thinking they might could handle a threesome. Rarely did any of those women come on to me once they knew I wasn't interested."

"Thought ever really seriously cross your mind?"

"No. Let's drop it. Thought we agreed not to go there." She pulled into a Tienda, convenience store. "Make your call. Want me to bring you anything?"

"Coffee, black. Any kind of chocolate bar. Would love a beer. Better not."

Blakely came back carrying a bag. She pulled out a coffee and a Snickers for him, a coffee for her and a six pack of bottled fizzy water and chips. "Thirty-eight dollars and change. How does anyone afford to live down here?"

"Expats don't unless they're into something illegal." He tasted his coffee. Not bad, even though it was ice cold. "Talked to your former boyfriend. The ambassador is at a hacienda south of here, few miles past where we turned around. Oh, by the way, we're being tracked—he wanted to know why we turned around. I told him we had not been given any information. Anyway, get this, the Americans moved their satellite and reconnaissance station from Puerto Rico to here after Hurricane Maria. Built it on a bay south of here, place called Akumal, not far from Tulum Air Base, close to where we turned around. Has a private drive with big signs saying private, authorized vehicles only in English and Spanish at the entrance. It's heavily guarded--he said he couldn't get us in there. Suggested we find somewhere nearby and keep watch to see which of the parties makes an appearance. Bet that's where our friends went."

"Wonder if the Israelis know about this? Better keep a lookout for them."

"Everybody has contracted paradise paranoia."

CHAPTER
26

Control Center
Jake and Mark Poponovich

"The crash and burn boys are back," Mark said, raising his head up from the table. "What's the haps Jake, ole buddy? We got a deal?"

One of the attendant guards walked into the room and disconnected the handcuffs and ankle chains. Mark stood up and kneed the guard in the groin, then rubbed the guards face in his crotch. TJ shoved Mark aside, lifted the groaning guard up and away out of Mark's reach. "That's for the rough treatment earlier asshole."

Hardy helped TJ take the guard out.

"Mark you're not helping yourself. Hardy is willing to listen. So, can the violence."

"I deplore violence Jake, but that guy doesn't know me. I never gave him a reason for what he and the other guy did. Stinks in here, smells like piss, right? Want to know why? I had to piss when we got here, instead of letting me, they punched me in my kidneys until I pissed myself. They should be brought up on charges."

"I'll talk to Hardy. See if he'll agree to let you shower. I bet someone around here has the same size clothes as you do. Might be a uniform. That be alright?"

"Thanks Jake. Could use another bottle, my arm's begging for it."

Hardy and TJ came back into the room. Jake told them the reason for Mark's behavior. "Why not let him shower. Doctor his arm, give him a painkiller, might help. I thought of something. Are the central casting people near here?"

"Not at the moment, why?"

"Look at Mark. He's the same size, roughly the same build as Jenkins, don't you think?"

Mark looked up. "Did I miss something here? Who is central casting? What's this about me and Jenkins?"

Everyone was staring at Mark.

"What the hell is going on here?"

"It was your idea, go ahead explain it to him."

Jake told him what he had in mind.

"Let me get this straight. You want me to pretend to be Jenkins so you can see who the people who submitted bids are, thinking they'll come forward. And what if Jenkins is dead?"

"Then whoever doesn't come to the table, or the scammers you mentioned, won't show. We'll know who they are—take them off the board, concentrate our efforts on the rest."

"Not if the deal has happened."

"The not-so-guilty people won't know that. Who do you think they'll believe has what they want?"

"The others will think or know this is a setup. You think I want to be the most wanted person since Osama bin Laden? Oh no."

Hardy said, "I'm liking the idea more and more. What about you TJ?"

"Seems to me Jake needs some relief being the most wanted."

"Come on Mark. We'll be right there with you. I can be made to look like a rich Irishman. TJ can stay out of sight, be the spotter and sniper."

"Whoa, no sniper," Hardy interjected, "innocent people could potentially be harmed which would create an international crisis. The border shit already has created major tensions. We can't afford to fan the flames. We can create a safe zone, manned by embassy personnel."

"You're talking as if I have agreed. Nothing could be further from the truth. No way."

"How about this? Jake replied, "We'll wrap you in the latest bulletproof material, have metal detectors, the works man. We set the meeting up where we can control the perimeter. Get these mothers where they have no way out. Make it a high roller gala event, roulette tables, baccarat, every game the high rollers love. You make an appearance, then disappear. Have some ladies circulate serving drinks. Let it be known they're accepting bids for you to decide. We get pictures, fingerprints, maybe some DNA, everything needed for the prosecutors. All you do is make one small appearance, very limited risk. Think about it, Mark. Be another shining moment in your career. We can test your makeover using Arturo."

Mark stared at each of them, spoke to Jake, "And you thought this shit up?"

"That's Jake. Never ceases to amaze." 'Bro, don't know what drug you're on, maybe you need to cut back on the dosage.'

"How about you get cleaned up, think about it."

"I believe you know something about the Israeli's and cartel finances? Before we continue, I need to hear it," Hardy said, blocking the door.

Jake doubted Hardy could stop Mark, but then again, Mark had to know he was at Hardy's mercy.

"What about the bottle, a shower, dress my wound, some clean clothes? I feel grungy, afterward, we can discuss terms of my cooperation."

"And, we need to discuss plans to find my daughter and grandson. That's the part of the deal I'm most interested in."

Mark was dressed in baggy shorts and a tropical shirt contributed by one of the techs in the control room. "Has any progress been made on who shot the two Russians in the bay in Miami?" No one said anything. "Didn't think so. Might want to ask those Israelis about what they know."

'Stop wasting time, if you know something, tell me."

"What do I get in return?"

"Out of here, depending upon if it's worth knowing."

"Got to be better than that. I tell you what I know, you do with it what you will, no conditions for my release. No having to play in the charade Jake proposed. And that bottle I asked for."

Hardy stood back up from the conference table. "I don't have to promise you anything. One way or the other, you'll tell us what you think you know." Hardy summoned the guards. "Get him out of here. Take those clothes off him, secure him in the cuffs and chains."

Mark quickly stood. He looked at the two guards, they had stun guns.

Jake and TJ, who had been sitting at the other end of the table had also jumped to their feet.

"Hold on guys. Mark tell him about the Israelis. Bob, if he gives us something useful, you need to give him something. Quid pro quo, that kind of thing," Jake said.

"No more deals. We already let him shower, get into clean clothes, he hasn't given us shit. Get him out of here."

Jake followed by TJ moved next to Mark.

"What is this?"

"Like you said, we need to stop wasting time. Mark stop with the teaser, tell us something. If it's useful, Hardy will agree to hear you out and release you. Otherwise, Bob you better be prepared to lock me up also. I need Mark's help. You screw that up and I'm through with this whole operation."

"Hey bro. Little drastic, but sorry Hardy, I'm with Jake."

Hardy turned red in the face. He stared at them. He waved the guards off. "Shut the door. Wait out in the hall."

They all sat back down.

"I saw the ballistics report on the bullet TJ turned over to the lab, it was a .338 Lapua Magnum cartridge, manufactured by IWI, Israeli Weapons Industries, fired from a IWI DAN .338 Bolt Action Sniper Rifle."

"That was not in the report I received," Hardy said.

"Someone in clandestine didn't want that known--the agency and FBI were told not to say anything by their respective former directors. HS directed the CIA to investigate in case the information was ever discovered. I discovered Tobias Tobolokov was a target, why I wanted to talk to him--one of the reasons I was there when we last saw each other in Cuba, Jake. Since then, he has disappeared without a trace. I suspect Miss Carmichael knows more than she has said. How about you Jake, did she say anything to you?"

"No. Last I saw of him, just like you, was when he jumped from Okneyev's freighter."

"The Israelis you have--the one named Yuri was in the states when the shootings occurred. I'd like to have a talk with him," Mark said. "Might help if TJ was with me. If Yuri was one of the shooting team members, he would most certainly know TJ was there when the Russians were shot. Be interesting to see how he would react to a big man, a fellow sniper. Maybe that is why he was spying on you guys."

"How about it Hardy?"

"Worth looking into. Okay, what about the Gonzalez brothers' and the cartel's finances?"

"Arturo is one of the key men in the Juarez Cartel. They have made millions, over a billion running drugs and people across the border. I was a part of an investigation to determine who was involved, where the money was and how it was being laundered, thus the offices in Miami and Charlotte. Surprised the hell out of me when I discovered TJ's undercover CI was David Gonzalez. Then you two ended up in the middle of my investigation. Not Jake so much, because of our previous acquaintance and Colonel Tindal's and

Major Jenkins' directed attempts to take his land. When your wife, Jake, was kidnapped, the op was in jeopardy."

"My money laundering investigation put me in the middle of a classified military weapon sale. Every agency had become involved. We all know how it supposedly ended; Jenkins took Jake's wife and escaped with the intel; the Gonzalez brothers fled back across the border; I had to close shop, got reassigned. The cartel thought I was involved in screwing their plans up and stole their money. I know where those funds are invested. They couldn't be touched without blowing my cover. I can't access them without codes which David Gonzalez possesses." He looked at Jake and TJ for a reaction. Was it possible one of them knew the codes as some suspected? Their faces said no. But?

"I thought David was the only one, besides me, with access to the accounts. Until my encounter with Arturo. He said those aren't their only funds. He planned on killing me because he thinks or possibly knows I'm involved with the feds. Which made me wonder why would he be willing to kill me and give up millions? What was it he knew? Had David hacked me or was it because he thought someone else had David's code information and the investments were no longer there?" He kept his eyes on Jake and TJ. Damn these guys are either good poker-faced mothers or they don't have the codes.

"My sources indicate Arturo is here to buy weapon technology to aid in the cartel's war with the US and the other cartels. Apparently, they have plans to meet with the Russians. Like you, the agency wants to finish out this op and stop this from happening."

"Lots of gaps in your story," Hardy said.

"Yeah, like your interest in me," Jake said.

"Your name kept cropping up Jake. We were monitoring the other agencies. No doubt they were doing the same thing. Hardy and Swanson were heading up the task force, sending reports. The agency heads briefed each other. Very brief from what I understand. My superior tasked my team with monitoring Hardy, while I continued my undercover work as an investor for the cartel, which included Andrei Bolstoy. He was a conduit for laundering huge amounts of illegal assets. When he was shot, I had to know where he deposited those funds. The Palmroy's and Tobolokov's names came up. I was warned off the Palmroys, then my team reported Tobolokov was on Great Exuma, seen with you and Miss Carmichael. Even before that, another source had reported other characters were interested in you. These, as you two later discovered, were, possibly Thurmond Tindal, and, we all know for damn sure, Major Jenkins."

"We received reports of you meeting with Agent Hardy. Therefore, you and Hardy became greater persons of interest to my team. I followed you to Cuba, couldn't get a handle on your connection with Hardy." He paused again, zeroed in on Jake. "There are some who believe you Jake and Miss Carmichael have a deal. The missing files, not just the ones Jenkins took, others the cartel possessed may be available. Someone is dealing. If Jenkins is dead, everyone has a theory about who and what. That's why we're all here. Isn't it?"

"I was back at my farm. I'm sure your sources knew I was no longer involved. Why were you snooping around, spying on me?"

"Your wife disappeared, turned up with Jenkins, leading many to believe you knew more than you let on about many things including the missing files. They especially became worried when I reported your latest hot-ass girlfriend met with DICE's Alperts. I knew Alperts had a meeting with Colonel Tindal. You came to Cancun. She left with Alperts. You know the rest."

"I get the feeling, there are those who think I'm a key player in Jenkins disappearance. That Blakely and I plotted to kill Okneyev and had or have the military weapon tech files he took from Jenkins which we helped him acquire. That she and I have these files and I also possess the cartel files TJ and I took from David. And that we are planning to pull off the biggest scam, the crime of the new millennium, then what? Seems you forgot a key element, I was on that freighter Okneyev sank with Blakely and others, including you--I saved your sorry ass. No wonder this op has been such a screwed-up mess. How does my daughter and my grandson figure into this purported scenario?"

"Maybe she's not missing. Maybe your girlfriend's, and your plan, was to get her son, your grandson, using Alperts and DICE's help, to make it look like a kidnapping, then disappear, leaving Blakely holding the bag."

"Why then would I need your help to locate my daughter?"

"Because with Alperts dead and your girlfriend in a coma, you have lost track of her, they have no way to contact you."

"What does Tindal have to do with this?"

"Alperts was playing both hands against each other. Very likely he planned to double-cross Tindal, probably, you and your girlfriend also. Tindal is all in—he wants what his money-maker Jenkins' possesses. Secured, have control of his property again. You out of the way."

"Really? How about you Bob, you buying this? I'm sure I don't have to ask you TJ."

"No way, bro. I know you. You'd never do anything like this shit. You not exactly a boy scout, but yo' mind don't work that way."

"Bob?"

Hardy began pacing, trying to think. He stopped several times to stare at Jake, then TJ. They were both dressed in camo cargo pants, V-necked tees, and black sneakers. Made them look like what they were, soldiers, not agents. He should have listened to Madame Secretary. Too late now.

Hardy memed Jake and TJ. 'I knew this guy couldn't be trusted. However, this could work to our advantage. Suppose we let people think this story could be true, we wouldn't need a Jenkins look-a-like. Sorry Jake, once more you become the tethered lamb. You hook back up with Miss Carmichael, we tweak and leak the story, see who does or doesn't make a move.'

"All of you stay put. I need to check on some things," Hardy said and left the room. He stopped and talked to the guards. Soon as he was out of sight, he memed Jake and TJ again. 'Listen up. Jake, tell TJ you're worried, say you're getting the hell out of there. The guards will take a fall, make it look real, but don't hurt them unnecessarily, take their keys, lock Poponovich in and run down the hall. I'll meet up with you at the exit. Don't have time to explain, just do it.'

Jake sucker-punched Mark in the gut. He fell onto the table. Jake leaned down and said, "That's for your lying bullshit and getting my hopes up about my daughter and grandson."

"I'm the last hope for finding your daughter," Mark huffed. "I have someone on the inside. Plans are underway." He grunted a laugh.

They went out the door, knocked down and handcuffed the guards, locked Poponovich in and continued down the hall to the exit, Hardy held the door open for them. He was out of breath. Marge and Jeni were waiting by a van in the furthest corner, nearest them. They got in, Hardy helped them into a compartment built into the bed, a panel operated by a hydraulic system slid over and locked into place. Jake's chest was pressed against the top, TJ was uncomfortable, hellaciously uncomfortable, his knees were pressed up against his chest. They struggled to breath the cool, pumped-in air.

"Don't you dare fart," Jake said.

TJ wished there was enough room so he could.

The van moved off, then stopped, muffled voices, doors opened, then closed, time creeped by, a bump, move, stop, move, the compartment slid open.

"Glad I'm not claustrophobic," TJ said, struggling to sit up and climb out. Jake followed. They sat on opposite edges of the compartment facing each other. A panel separating the front from the rear opened toward them. "What did Hardy tell you?" he asked Jeni who turned tired eyes to look at them.

"Marge is to take us to the department store where we'll sack out on cots. He said he would contact us mid-morning, which should give us about six hours of rest."

Marge spoke up, "We're being followed."

"Don't attempt outrunning them,' TJ said, "Drive onto Hotel Row, see if you can lose them that way."

When they reached the all-night partiers on well-lit Hotel Row, Marge said, "They know what they're doing. They dropped back, let a couple vehicles get between us. I got a glimpse, looked like the same rental the man and woman that were in the house across the street were driving."

"Go to the embassy. Let them drive past and park. Once they do, call Hardy, ask him to get a man or two to check them out. If it's the two from earlier, we'll pull back out and let them follow us. Keep an eye on them. Make sure they're not being followed."

"I don't really feel like talking to Blakely this morning," Jake said.

"Who's Blakely?" Jeni asked.

"An old girlfriend of Jake's."

"Never was a girlfriend."

"She may think otherwise, loverboy." TJ chuckled.

"Jeezum. I'm too tired for this shit. Used up the last of my energy back there."

"Blakely'll perk you up."

CHAPTER
27

Cancun Warehouse
Jake and Blakely

"Looks like they're headed to the embassy. Circle the block, see if it's them. I hope your hunch was correct."

"Who else would have left at this time of morning?"

They pulled over in the delivery drive of what they thought was an adjacent building. They were watching two Marines who stood on each side of the van and failed to notice another two other Marines until one of them tapped on the driver's window, startling them.

"Miss, you can't stop here," the one said when she put down the window. "ID please."

"We'll move on, okay?"

"ID please. Both of you." They had their hands on their sidearms.

Blakely and Devereaux saw no other option. Soon as they handed over their IDs, Jeni stepped out from behind the one holding their IDs.

"Thank you, Corporal. I'll take it from here."

He handed her their IDs. "Ma'am," they turned and went down the delivery drive.

"I'll hold on to these. Follow us. Make sure no one else follows you."

"They made us. At least we know they're friendlies," Blakely said.

"Just flunked tradecraft 101. Maybe see your lover, get some rest, wherever it is we're headed."

Blakely hoped Jake would be happy to see her again.

They twisted and turned until they were back on the outskirt of EL Centro. They drove into a garage door at the rear of a building of boutiques. The door closed behind them cutting off the outside light. The only light came from their headlights. Before the headlight timer, set to go off could extinguish the remaining light, a light came on from a side doorway. They watched the woman who took their IDs come to Devereaux' side, she handed him their IDs back.

"I recognize you, you're Captain Adams."

"Come inside. Someone wants to talk with you two."

Blakely had been anticipating this moment ever since she found out Jake was coming to Cancun. She now felt trepidation about how Jake would react to her unannounced appearance. Did she look different? People think they haven't changed until they compare photos of their then and now. Or they run into someone from their past who looks older and they suddenly realize they must look older to the other person also. She walked behind Devereaux.

"Thomas Devereaux. You still sneaking around peeking into bedroom windows? Should have come over and introduced yourself. Why don't we get that out of the way? This is my friend TJ Alvarez, some people confuse him for that movie idol The Rock. You met Captain Adams, this other lady is Major Duplantis. And this everyone is none other than Blakely Carmichael." Blakely hung back. They all nodded to each other.

"Hello Jake," she said, not sounding like herself, the intro catching in her throat.

Thomas looked at her and laughed. "Damn, Blakely Carmichael at a loss for words."

TJ chuckled. Blakely blushed. The room creaks became the only sound.

"Sure would like a beer," Devereaux said into the void.

"We came here to crash, not party," Marge said, "Been a couple long days and nights, as I'm sure you'll agree. You will remain here. We'll talk later."

Captain Adams went to a storage closet and pulled out four cots, sheets, and pillows.

"Looks like a couple people will have to sleep on the floor," she said. "There's plenty of stock on the shelves could be laid out for the guests."

"Think I'll sleep in the van," TJ said. He went over and grabbed a blanket and pillow from the closet.

"Carmichael and I should leave. We could catch up with you tomorrow. I mean later on today."

"Nonsense, TJ said, "Afraid we must insist you stay. My bro here would be extremely disappointed otherwise. Isn't that right Jake?"

"If you don't mind, might be better if I join you in the van," Devereaux said. I'm sure Carmichael and Harper have some catching up to do. Wouldn't want to be in the way." He looked at both their expressions and laughed. TJ asked if he was a noisy sleeper. He replied, "Haven't stayed awake to listen." He laughed some more, grabbed another blanket and pillow, tipped an imaginary hat to Jake, and followed TJ back into the garage. He checked his pocket. The extra key fob was there. He hoped TJ slept soundly and the garage door could be opened without much noise.

Blakely had given Devereaux a hard, eat-shit-and-die look. She refrained from saying what she wanted to say.

Blakely sensed Jake's discomfort. He said, "Guess I will grab some of the shelf items and crash out here."

"That's okay. I can sleep in the car and you can have the storage closet."

"No need. You take the closet. I'll be fine out here."

She heard the other two women saying something to each other. They stood up from the cots. The Captain went to the closet. The Major said, "The Captain and I have decided to sleep in the closet." They closed the door.

"Guess you know they're?" Blakely asked twisting her hand back and forth.

"Didn't ask, don't care," Jake replied.

"I'm sorry Jake."

"For what, spying on us?"

"Everything."

"What does that mean? Never mind, we can talk about it later."

"I've missed you, Jake. Never got to thank you for saving my life. Ever think about me?"

"Yes, of course I have. Right now, I'm too tired to get into it, okay?"

He went over to one of the cots and lay down.

He hated his thoughts. Blakely looked good; her attitude was totally different from the last time. Their parting and now meeting up again carried mixed emotions for him. She seemed to feel the same way. It had been a while, was she playing one of her many roles? What was her motive? No. There wasn't much doubt, the look in her eyes, no mistaking it, she had said she loved him that morning in bed. He had thought it was a natural reaction to the intensity of that moment. He had not said anything in reply, kept giving her, what she said later when they lay there spent, was the best sex and orgasm ever. He assumed she knew about his marriage, about finding the love of his life Ariel and discovering he had another daughter and a grandson? His newly discovered family members' welfare was now his top priority. No matter how good Blakely looked, or how much she still made the little head beg for a repeat performance. It could not and would not happen. He hoped she understood.

Blakely came over to the other cot, reluctantly laid down within reach of him. She wanted to join him, feel his arms around her.

He hadn't touched her. Not even a hug. What did she expect? That he would pick up where they left off. A great deal had happened in both their lives. Okneyev no longer controlled her life. The last time with Jake had been more intense because she felt vulnerable, like death was waiting. In some twisted way she felt liberated. She felt she could let go, enjoy the sensations, have an emotional bond with someone, not just anyone.

The freedom had not continued, not personally, not emotionally, she had to continue playing roles to allay suspicions, wait, let time move on, thinking eventually she could look Jake up, hopefully pick up where they left off. Only this time, she would open up, offer him everything in exchange for his love. Had she been, was she kidding herself? No, she saw something in his eyes, she could hear it in his voice, he was struggling to maintain control. Wasn't her imagination. Be patient. Give him time. Good things come to those who wait. She hoped, had to believe, that was true.

Her thoughts were interrupted by a squeak coming from the closet. She thought she imagined it. There it was again, muffled this time. She turned her face into her pillow to contain her laugh. She heard Jake chuckle. She reached across and squeezed his hand. He squeezed back then let go. She heard him roll over.

Jake lay there, his eyes closed pretending to be asleep. The women had come out of the closet and went into the small kitchenette. He smelled coffee and toasted French bread. He was tempted to join them. Blakely finally did after using the toilet. He heard her ask the women if they had encountered a mouse in the supply closet. He heard Marge snicker. Blakely quietly tried and failed to hide her laughter. He didn't hear anything from Jeni. They chit chatted, somehow the subject turned to sex and love.

Blakely was asked if she had ever been married. She said no. She asked them if they had. Marge said no, her career had come first. Jake was shocked to hear Jeni say she was married and had two children, a boy twelve and a daughter ten. Blakely said it was none of her business, but did her husband know about her relationship with the Major. Jeni tried to sidestep the question. Marge lowered her voice and said they had to be careful, they could be court marshaled. Not for being gay. Adultery was against the Military Code of Ethics. Especially between two fellow officers.

Blakely assured her she had no ulterior motive, that where she came from, sex was treated as a normal human function and monogamy was more rare than in the states.

"There's sex, then there's love," she said.

Jeni agreed, said her husband was a good man and good father, but she couldn't talk to him about her job. If it hadn't been for Marge, she would have imploded, that lots of her fellow joystick pilots burned out, marriages failed, more than a few committed suicides. Marge kept her sane, it helped save her marriage, she loved her family, and Marge.

Jeni asked about Jake. She had seen how they looked at each other. How nervous they both sounded. Blakely told them she wasn't sure how he felt, had been shocked when she found out he had married, that his wife had run off with Jenkins. And, that Jake had rediscovered an old flame from his early days who was in a coma and that their daughter was missing. To think he now had a grandson. From intel, she had discovered the father's parents were the reason for the daughter's disappearance. (This statement gave Jake a jolt. He hadn't thought of their daughter's disappearance possibly being connected to her in-laws.) Blakely went on to say, she wanted to be here for Jake, to be whatever he would let her be in his time of need.

Jeni said, "You sound like you're in love."

Blakely replied, "For the first time in my life, I think I might be, and it scares me."

Jake got up making noise to end their conversation. He hoped. He went to the restroom then walked into the kitchen.

"Good morning. You ladies save me any coffee?"

"Hope we didn't wake you?" Marge said.

"No. I was out like a light, then I smelled the coffee." He walked over, dug a cup out of a small overhead cabinet, poured the remains of the carafe into his cup. He was making another pot when he heard the outer door open. TJ joined them, Devereaux went to the bathroom first.

Hardy entered the kitchen behind TJ. "Morning sleepy heads. Ready to get down to business."

Jake looked at TJ.

"Heard a tap on the rear, the man door. In walks Hardy," TJ said in response to Jake's look.

"Didn't happen to bring any food with you?" Jake asked Hardy.

"I figured you would have eaten by now."

"Figured wrong. I need food and some clean clothes for after I shower in that rinky dink excuse for a bathroom. The damn thing is nothing more than an over-size porta-potty. Maybe then I'll feel like listening to what you came here to tell us."

"I see sleep didn't improve your attitude any, Jake. When I saw Miss Carmichael here, I figured your disposition would be better. Maybe you didn't get enough sleep?" Hardy looked from Jake to Blakely. "Guess I was wrong on both counts." Everyone smiled except Jake and Blakely. "Think I'll have a cup of coffee." Hardy walked over, retrieved a cup.

TJ reached around him and took two more cups out. He handed one to Devereaux who had come into the now crowded room. TJ looked in the other wall cabinet. "No tea bags?" Hardy tried to pour coffee in his cup. "None for me. I'm a tea man."

"Undersecretary Hardy, Jake isn't the only one needing to have clean clothes. A decent bathroom would be nice also. Jake's right that bathroom smells like a latrine and the water is brownish--good thing we had bottled water for the coffee," Marge said. Jeni agreed.

"What were you expecting the Marriot, or perhaps, the Hilton?"

Jake started to tell him where he could shove it.

"Just kidding. We're expected at the other warehouse," Hardy looked at his cell phone, even though with the implant he didn't need to, "in fifteen minutes. We can't all leave together. It's only a few blocks. Major, TJ, Jake, I sent directions to your phones. Miss Carmichael you can accompany Jake in my vehicle. Go now." He handed Jake the keys. "It's parked to the right on the other side of this row of buildings."

"Major, go with Devereaux in his car. TJ and I will lag behind in the van to make sure we haven't been spotted."

Blakely and Jake walked to Hardy's car in silence. At the car, Jake opened the door for her. She hesitated.

"Jake, I know you were listening. I remember what your breathing sounds like when you're asleep. I meant what I told them. I'm here for you. I'll be whatever you want me to be. You don't have to say anything right now, I understand." She leaned into him and kissed his cheek then sat down in her seat.

He closed her door, went around, and sat down. He waited a minute, started the car, turned the AC up, the radio on, volume up. He leaned over and whispered in her ear, "This car is probably bugged." He kissed her on the cheek. "I'm glad you're here," he said out loud.

"I'm glad to be here. I'm hungry. If you see a fast-food place, pull in."

"Will do. So, what brings you to Cancun?"

"Much needed vacation. What about you?"

"Hoping to see my grandson. He's supposed to be here with his other family."

"Congratulations, grandpa? How does it feel?"

"Trying to get used to the idea. He's been living with his family in Europe, I've never met them or him. It may be awkward."

They continued talking about little things. He didn't see any convenience store or fast-food establishment. Blakely reached over and took his hand. He didn't resist. She had to let go so he could turn into another garage which opened as he pulled onto the ramp. Two armed men waited just inside the warehouse, one on each side. A woman Jake recognized from central casting stood at the back. Jake pulled up beside her. She opened Blakely's door, waited on her and Jake to exit the vehicle and told them to follow her. She led them into a kitchen/dining area where there was a long picnic table on which were an assortment of tiny squares of breads, crackers, cheeses, meats and assorted vegetables, fruits and condiments with glassware and carafes of beverages on the nearest end. On the other end was silverware, sandwich size plates and napkins.

"Help yourself. Afterwards, you can go upstairs, there are ladies' and men's shower and dressing areas with an assortment of toiletries available. My assistant and I have provided undergarments and robes for each of you. We will then fit you in the proper attire for the occasion."

"What occasion?" Blakely asked as Jeni arrived.

Jeni and Devereaux stopped at the door. The man that escorted her and Devereaux turned and left.

"What occasion might that be?" Devereaux repeated.

"Mr. Hardy will explain. Please help yourself. You all look famished. IF you would excuse me, I must attend to the preparations. Have Mr. Hardy summon me when he's ready," she said, then departed.

"What in the hell is going on?" Devereaux asked. He followed Jake to the kitchen sink and washed his hands. Jake shrugged.

TJ followed by Hardy came in.

"You can wash your hands in the kitchen sink," Jake said to TJ, plopping a grape into his mouth. "Miss Agnes, or whatever her name is, said you could summon her when you're ready," Jake said to Hardy.

"And you thought I was going to keep you from eating. Hope this will do? We'll talk after you've eaten and get cleaned up."

'Heard some interesting remarks from our guests. When you're ready we'll discuss them and our next move. Bon Appetit.'

After they finished eating, they were escorted upstairs, used the toilets, took showers, donned the undergarments and robes, and were led into a conference room which had several large monitors on two walls. After taking seats, Hardy tried to lighten the mood.

"I know you were all expecting massages. Perhaps I can arrange that for you afterwards."

"A briefing dressed in briefs and a robe? Had me worried this going to be an orgy, Deane would've taken heads off."

Everyone laughed.

"Here's what we know. There are a number of intelligence groups here in Cancun, representatives of two of them were asked to join us."

Blakely never flinched. Devereaux seemed to be uncomfortable.

"There also are numerous, what we call hostiles, here as well, not all of them from foreign countries. We initially arrived here thinking our former colleague, gone rogue, Major Bud Jenkins might have initiated bringing everyone together. Made no sense, but we couldn't ignore the possibility. No one at Homeland thought this was a possibility. Many, including myself, believe Jenkins would never put himself in jeopardy. Evidence indicates he used the dark web to solicit bids, perhaps decided on an offer, prior to his escape. He took Jake's wife with him. She claims he left the place they were staying in in the company of four individuals, three of which were definitely male. One she said was possibly female. Now, she is not sure." Hardy paused took a drink from a cup.

'First I've heard of this,' Jake memed.

'I received the report this morning. Elena was questioned yesterday,' Hardy memed back.

"Agent Harper suggested we use a look-a-like of Jenkins to weed out the bad actors from the real deal. Namely, those who know about Jenkins and/or the weapon tech material he stole. My superior gave the go-ahead. The option is still open. Based upon new information given to me, I am somewhat skeptical and genuinely concerned about this plan of action. There is credible evidence Jenkins is dead and the intelligence material he stole, has been or is being sold piecemeal, perhaps as part of a trade involving a Mexican Cartel. Could involve Russia and Cuba or any number of bidders. Our intel indicates they plan to demonstrate the weapon's capabilities. To coin a phrase, this demonstration could prove there is a clear and present danger to national security for the US and our allies. The plan, Jake proposed, and the reason we're sitting around dressed, or undressed, the way we are, has been modified." Hardy paused, drank, looked hard at Jake and Blakely. "We need to clear the air, discuss options.

"Miss Carmichael, numerous sources indicate you witnessed Pietr Okneyev's, the notorious Russian oligarch, former KGB/ SVR's meeting with two Cuban generals. You once claimed you were a double agent. You supposedly were placed in witness protection by the FBI, at the request of Mark Poponovich and your superiors at Interpol. Seems that was a ruse, care to explain?"

Blakely didn't seem fazed. "Fairly obvious, isn't it? I've been working undercover for years as an Interpol agent. Initially tasked with infiltrating Okneyev's operation, prove he was the head of a criminal enterprise. During my investigations, I became aware he was stealing and selling intelligence information and disinformation on the dark web. He didn't care from which countries or to whom he sold it to. That is how I became aware of and in the middle of Operation Pink Flamingo. Why I began collaborating with Agent Devereaux, how I met Agent Harper. I didn't know he was Agent Harper until much later. As for Pietr Okneyev's meeting with the Cuban generals, I saw them on the freighter. They left with Okneyev. I never saw the amphib. You know this. I told the same thing to the interrogators at Guantanamo. My superior and others in America felt Okneyev and the SVR knew I survived his attempt to kill me. I was given a choice resign from Interpol, enter WitSec permanently or take a temporary leave, spread the rumor I had entered WitSec and remain incognito until things cooled down., which I did. I voluntarily reentered the arena because Okneyev and the Russians won't rest until I'm dead."

"You didn't infiltrate Okneyev's organization," Hardy stated, "you were already a member. Interpol busted you, forced your cooperation. You did so rather than face prosecution for offenses committed as a double agent which would have forced you to testify or face a lengthy prison sentence., Is it not a fact one of your offenses was your involvement in the murder of your uncle, who sold you to Okneyev when you were just a teenager to be his sex slave? Don't look at me like that. Interpol released the information to Homeland per our request. We needed to know who we are getting into bed with, figuratively and literally." Hardy looked at Jake.

"Agent Harper was with you onboard the freighter when Okneyev tried to kill you. Agent Harper vouched for you. You also said Agent Poponovich and Agent Tobolokov would vouch for you. Agent Poponovich has added additional info to his earlier statement. He says you threatened him with poison in the presence of Agent Harper. Agent Harper told me about the incident. I reported the incident as an idle threat by you to determine the nature of Poponovich's employment. Others, including myself, would like to speak to Agent Tobolokov and get his side of the story. Seems he has disappeared. Do you know his whereabouts, Miss Carmichael? You, Agents Harper and Poponovich were the last people he was seen with."

"Agent Tobolokov secured the skiff from Okneyev's man, which waited in the harbor to take us back to the freighter. He and I decided it would be too dangerous to return. The last I saw or heard from him was before I was taken into custody by the Coast Guard, while onboard Devereaux' former boat. He left in the skiff. His life, like mine, was in danger. Okneyev had become suspicious of us. Once Okneyev gets suspicious your days are numbered. I knew this. Tobolokov knew this. We parted ways, not knowing or wanting to know what happened to each other."

"He sedated Agent Harper. According to your testimony, you and he took Poponovich with you onboard Okneyev's skiff. You said Okneyev's ordered you to kill Agent Harper and bring Poponovich back to him. Obviously, you didn't kill Jake. You did take Poponovich back to him. What about the case Okneyev gave you containing the sedative and poison, where is it?"

"At the bottom of the bay off the coast of Playa Giron is where Tobolokov said he disposed of it." I had already removed the poison, flushed it down the toilet at the B&B."

"No way to verify this is there?"

"Poponovich went with me willingly. His crew was there. I'm sure you know this. Blakely fought to contain her anger. "If you don't trust me, why am I here?"

"To decide if we should trust you. The Israelis believe you and Jake are complicit in a giant scam. There are those who believe you had Jenkins killed. They say Okneyev was the one Jenkins made a deal with, helped him escape, that you were the woman with the three men Jake's wife reported leaving with Jenkins."

"That's impossible and you know it," Jake exclaimed, "the freighter incident happened long after Elena was taken and Jenkins disappeared. What the hell is this? The Israelis and our, supposedly intelligent, services can't be that misinformed. Why you throwing this bullshit out there Hardy, when you know it's a lie?"

"You think just because Jake and I had a fling, we've become traitors?"

Hardy ignored their outbursts. "Did you or did you not double-cross Okneyev, have him killed? Perhaps you yourself did it with the poison you say Tobolokov disposed of. Evidence indicates Okneyev planned to sell the info, possibly developed some of the technology which he put up for bid. And, made plans for this demonstration. Instead, he and the Cuban generals were killed by you and an accomplice, perhaps Tobolokov, after he made the deal. You distanced yourself from Tobolokov to cover yourself. The Israelis were spying on you and my people. There are those who suspect you and an associate came here to follow through with the plan. The FBI, and Interpol believe this is all speculation, Devereaux says he's in that camp, I'm leaning that way, that's why you are here. These people here are your judge and jury, they must decide if you should be trusted."

"You and Jake can elect to answer any questions or not. If anyone has any reservations, now is the time to ask, then we shall vote."

Jake jumped in. "This is not some kind of freaking game show. I haven't seen nor heard from Blakely since Cuba. You know that. Why are you trying to create doubt in these other women's minds?"

"For TJ, me, all of us, it's not about you. Can't have any doubts in anyone's mind. Need to know if we have a team or not. Things are about to get rough, lives on the line."

"Why not just come out and say I told you Blakely admitted to me she put the poison in Okneyev's Scotch?"

"You heard her, she said she flushed it.'

"That proves nothing."

"Exactly. This is not about proof. It's about trust."

No one moved or said anything.

Jake was furious. He memed, 'Is this why you chose me for the implant? You and the puppet masters suspect me. Well, screw you.'

'If you suspect him, I suppose you suspect me also,' TJ added.

'I don't suspect either of you. I need to clear the air. See where everyone stands. We have a mission to accomplish. I need everyone onboard.'

Hardy went around the room asking each one if they were sure. All said yes. "Good. I don't want to hear any more accusations. We've got a job to fulfill. I need everyone's cooperation. Any more questions?"

Devereaux asked Hardy what happened to Poponovich and the Israelis?

"The Israeli embassy demanded their nationals be released. There was no proof they broke any laws. They were released this morning. I warned them to steer clear of us. Poponovich is still under evaluation."

TJ asked, "how 'bout the Palmroys, were they ever questioned?"

"Not under oath. Like I said, I was told to back off. What the Justice Department or others did I have no idea."

"Okay. Before you join the casting rew to get fitted for your formal wear, we need to discuss the op. Here's what the plan is: Jake and Miss Carmichael, may I call you Blakely?"

She hesitated, clearly upset, realized she had no choice if she wanted to be a part of the op, clear her name, reluctantly, she nodded.

"Good. Jake and Blakely are the prime tethered lambs. They will be seen in public, acting suspicious, sneaking around, briefly meeting, hopefully, drawing the attention of the bad actors. TJ, you, and Jeni will follow Blakely. Devereaux and Marge will follow Jake. I will remain at the command center."

"We'll give it a day or two. If no one tries anything, we'll rely on plan B, the grand, invitation-only, gala event. We are starting to put this together as of today. The ambassadors and their chosen guests are invited, along with various venture capitalists and high roller celebrities. Hard to imagine anyone turning the invitation down. Especially, since a multi-billion-dollar contract is to be presented for a new space mining venture by New Dawn Intergalactic Industries. They initially planned to make the announcement next month at an industry convention in hopes of attracting more investors. Top Mexican and American officials will be wining and dining potential investors to make this happen—it's an offer they dare not refuse."

Jake half-listened. He was pissed, wondered what Hardy was up to. He tried to work through what he should do. He now felt certain the gala had not been his idea; seemed highly likely it had been planted in his head. They then must know his motives. He had hoped the Cuban Ambassador and wife would come to the gala so he could meet his grandson's other grandparents. Perhaps the father Pablo would join them, leaving the grandson in the hands of a nanny. A perfect opportunity to allow him the opportunity to pull off a kidnapping. Bet the family would be willing to answer any questions concerning the daughter after that. He wanted to be with Ariel when she regained consciousness, surprise her, let her first sights be him with their daughter and grandson. First he had to find and rescue them. After that Hardy and company could go screw themselves. He hoped his thoughts went through, loud, and clear. Screw them. Screw all of you mind-fuckers.

He needed to contact the hospital for an update. If the nature of her injuries were anything like his had been, they may keep her under for a month or more. He hoped this was not the case. What if her injuries were permanent? How could he handle the issues presented by having a newly discovered family without her? His familial and legal troubles continued to mount.

'Earth to Jake. Hey bro, you awright?'

'Thinking I need to check on Ariel, that's all.'

He excused himself. Blakely said she needed to talk to him, she wanted to come along. He told her no, he needed to be by himself. She looked crestfallen, then smiled. "Talk to me after, please."

"Yeah. We'll talk. Just not now."

TJ followed. "I need to call Deane." He decided it might be best to meme Jake. He sensed Jake was going off on some tangent. He needed to know what he was thinking.

'Hey bro, Hardy had me wondering what he's up to. He almost fooled me. Earlier, he had us thinking he was ready to throw Blakely to the wolves.'

'He is. Along with you, me, and the others. Nothing has been said about David Gonzalez and the other cartel bangers. They're out there looking for Arturo and us. How are we to protect ourselves? I don't like it. This morning I lay there thinking about how I could locate Elizabeth and my grandson Gabriel--came to me the authorities do much of their searching with satellites and drones--where are the drones we were told would be available to us? Why shouldn't I do my own searching. After all, we have the implants, we used them earlier to save Ariel. I tried accessing the sites Jeni put us on. Kept saying, access denied--earlier footage is all I was given access to. Hardy could allow access, why doesn't he? Could help see who and what's around us.'

'Let Jeni handle the drones, bro. I know your priority's your family; with you on that. But you do what I think you goina do, you'll be putting our lives in danger. Won't do them any good you and me get killed. Deane never forgive you or me if you or I got killed. Neither would Ariel.'

'I can not do nothing. Ariel risked everything. She would expect no less from me. I don't believe the authorities give a shit about Elizabeth. For all we know, some crooked police or another group is involved in her kidnapping. Gabriel's family is a possibility. I can't stop thinking about what I can do to help. I wish I knew hacking.'

'Whoa bro, don't even go there.'

'With the implant I could access Hacking 101, the implant and I could learn all there is to know from the web.'

'Damnit Jake, don't do it. Talk to Hardy.'

'Screw Hardy. This op is all he gives a shit about. It's all he's ever given a shit about. Not once has he shown any sympathy for what Tindal and Jenkins did to us, my family, my dog. What about you and Deane? There's a great deal going on and Hardy knows more than he's saying.'

TJ shook his head, Jake was on the edge, he pondered how to reply, he memed , 'Don't go there bro...'

Jake's meme tumbled into his. 'Screw the mother, screw them all. I can't help but think on what asswipe Poponovich said about Hardy's and Tindal's connections. I intend to find out. I'll do whatever I have to until I've found my daughter and grandson and then I intend for all of us to be there when Ariel comes around. After that, I'm done with Hardy and this whole screwed up mess. I'll deal with Tindal later, that's a promise. And, company man Hardy better stay out of my way.

CHAPTER
28

Warehouse
Jake and TJ

Ariel was in Miami University Hospital's Intensive Care Unit. TJ's wife, Deane was allowed in her room because Ariel had no family members to protest and because she was a nurse. Also helped that she knew members of the staff, most importantly, the neurologist assigned to Ariel. Her phone vibrated. She saw it was TJ. She went into the hallway before answering. The two guards on each side of the door eyed her. She nodded to them then moved off down the hall.

"Hey babe," she said.

"Hey to you. Everything okay?"

"No change. How's Jake?"

"Trying to keep it together. That's one of the reasons I'm calling."

"Hope not the main one?'

"You know not. I love and miss you always. Listen, Jake's goina be calling, reassure him, tell him you're there watching over Ariel. Tell him his being there won't change anything. I'm worried he's goina go off the tracks, do something that could put him in major jeopardy. You're the voice of reason, talk to him, help me with him, okay?"

"You know I will. There is one problem. They may say something to him about the medical bill. It's not good. Ariel's employer has denied any responsibility, they claim she voluntarily left the tv station where she worked. Their insurance company has a clause giving them the right to deny coverage for acts of terrorism, voluntarily travelling outside the country, putting herself in harm's way, etc. They are discussing moving her to Charity Hospital. I've talked to the VA administrator, they won't take her, she's not a vet. They may not tell Jake about this since they're not married, who knows? If they tell Jake, he'll definitely come unhinged. I'm looking into setting up a GoFundMe page, I'm working on other possibilities. Jake's buzzing me. I'll try you back."

"Jake, everything okay?"

"How's Ariel?"

"Her vitals are good. The neurologist thinks she'll be fine. He says they may be able to bring her out of the medically induced coma in a couple weeks if the swelling goes down. How are you holding up?"

"I feel guilty for not being there. Brings back not so good memories. I'll be there for her when she comes around. Soon as you know something, let me know, okay?"

"I will. I promise. Jake don't be mad, I spoke to TJ, he's worried about you. You know I can be a good listener, TJ isn't always the best sounding board, everything for him is pretty much black and white, got that macho Hood mentality. I know this is difficult for you, don't worry, I'm here for Ariel and for you also. You need to talk to someone, you call me, day or night."

"Thanks Deane. I appreciate what you're doing. But, what about your job?"

"I have accumulated lots of vacation time. TJ never wants to go anywhere for more than a long weekend. I also have sick days, don't you worry about me, I'll be right here. Besides, this gives me a chance to catch up with old friends and family down here. Don't tell TJ but I miss being here. This will always be home."

"Deane, I told the switchboard I was family. When I asked to talk to Ariel's doctor, she transferred me to the business office accounts receivable. They asked if I knew who to contact about the billing? I gave them the name of Ariel's employer. The woman said they had contacted them, the station told them she was no longer employed there. The woman at the hospital said her insurance company is denying the claim. She said she needed to know who was going to take responsibility for the bill. I told her I would see what could be done. She said they needed me, or whoever could answer them, to get back to them immediately. Sounded like a threat to me. I don't have a clue about Ariel's financial situation. I don't have any way to pay them. They have to treat her, don't they?"

"Don't worry Jake, I'll look into it and let you know what I find out."

"You didn't answer my question. The woman said something about transferring her to Charity Hospital. Deane, be straight with me, can they kick her out or not?"

"I'm going to start a GoFundMe page. She is a hero in my book. This happened because she was trying to defend her family. I'm certain there are enough people, mothers, who will be sympathetic. If not, I talked to her doctors, they are on her side, her neurologist is willing to work for free. I'm not about to let them take her out of here. Don't you worry about that. Keep yourself and TJ safe. Leave Ariel's well-being up to me."

"TJ's lucky to have you. So am I. Thanks Deane. I love you."

"I love you too Jake, please don't do anything rash. Call me anytime."

"I will."

Blakely had slipped up behind Jake. "Was that Ariel you were talking to?"

Jake looked over his shoulder, he turned around. She looked up at him, a concerned expression on her face.

"I told you I needed privacy."

"Sounds like she's gotten better. That was fast."

"That wasn't her. She's in an induced coma. It's not something I want to talk about."

"Just asking. Forget about it. Let me know when you feel up to talking. Hardy asked if I knew where you went--I came to tell you, that's all." She walked away.

Jake stood there thinking about the money. He couldn't let them kick Ariel out. Charity, GoFundMe. Damn! Uncle Sam owed him. Hardy had promised she'd be taken care of. Yeah, just like he was gonna personally take care of the quarter-million he promised when he recruited him in the Bahamas. Didn't happen. Not likely Hardy ever intended to help Ariel or get the money Homeland owed him. His farm was mortgaged, selling it wouldn't give him enough. The bill could be hundreds of thousands. He doubted Ariel had that kind of money. Not many people did. Damnit, there had to be something he could do.

'Hey bro, Deane told me she talked to you. She said she was keeping an eye on Ariel. Trust her, she's good at those kinds of things. Hardy wants us to rejoin the others.'

'Screw Hardy. He said Ariel would receive the best of care. Deane tell you Ariel may be transferred to Charity Hospital. That can't happen—not gonna let it happen.'

'Deane's not goina let it happen. Gotta trust her bro.'

'It's Hardy and Homeland that can't be trusted.'

'Hang in there bro. Let's get this over with, find your daughter and grandson and go home. Awright?'

CHAPTER
29

Cancun Beach
Jake and Blakely

After getting fitted for their gala event attire, they split up into teams and went to their first designated location, the beach along Hotel Row.

Jake wore knee-length bathing trunks, a plain V-neck tee, a baseball cap with a Cancun emblem, sunglasses, and strap sandals, which didn't help much walking on the noonday, sun-scorched walkways or the hot powdery sand.

Blakely carried a beach bag, a flimsy scarf hanging over the side, covering a taser and miniature audio/ video recorder she could control from a dial in the strap handle of the bag. She wore a skimpy one-piece, slit down and across the back and sides, not doing much to confine or hide her ample breasts or ass. There were many younger, more curvaceous girls, wearing skimpier attire, but Blakely drew more than her share of stares--the whole reason Hardy had approved of her choice.

The Major and Captain were much more modestly attired, so not to draw unwanted attention. Only problem was TJ. He was with Jeni, wearing a mask over his face, but there was no disguising his physique. Many older girls and women noticed him, some men also. Unavoidable. Fortunately, the ones thought to be bangers weren't paying him much attention. Or so it seemed.

Devereaux and Marge walked along in the water's edge, carrying their footwear in another bag slung over her shoulder. Devereaux seemed to be enjoying himself, Marge not so much--another older tourist couple—husband gawking, the wife disengaged.

"Are you going to keep on ignoring me?" Blakely asked.

"You're getting plenty of attention."

"What is it, Jake? What did I do to piss you off? Is it something Hardy said?"

"Were you involved in Jenkins disappearance? You were there, weren't you?'

She stopped walking and turned toward Jake. Her near nakedness made him uncomfortable.

"Why would you believe that. I was questioned over and over, much of it done under extreme duress. I was cleared. Hardy and the others want to believe me, why can't you?'

"They never said they believe you. They are willing to allow you to be a part of the team, just as I am, despite what others accused us of. Hardy trusts no one. Trust but verify. Keep friends close, enemies closer. Two of his favorite maxims. Why do you think he paired us?"

"I thought you two were friends, isn't that what you told me when I asked about your connection to him?"

"That was based on a superficial relationship we had before everything else happened. We need to keep walking." She reached out her hand. He refused to take hers.

"You sound like you don't like or trust him now. Am I right?"

"I trust very few people, especially in this business."

"You can trust me. I will do anything for you Jake. How can I get you to understand that?"

"By not lying to me."

"What do you want to know? Was I there when Jenkins disappeared? No."

Jake stopped walking. This time he turned and faced Blakely. She reached out lightly touching his hand. Her touch, her look made the little man stir. He concentrated on her eyes.

"What are you hiding? What didn't you tell me before?"

"Before what? Before we made love? Everything happened after."

"What else haven't you told me? Was Okneyev really on the freighter with the Cubans? Did they leave or did they go down with the wreakage? What do you know about Jenkins disappearance?"

"Okneyev and the Cubans left. Mark and the staff manager verified it; you were there. Ask Hardy if you don't believe me. As for Jenkins, I don't know. I was told he was taken to a General Toraz' hacienda near Juarez, as had been arranged. Supposedly, the men boarded a plane with him and left the woman behind. I was told she stayed another day to make certain no one followed or that Toraz didn't try to double-cross us."

"Who is us?"

"You don't want to know."

"Tell me."

"We better keep moving." She took Jake's hand, squeezed then released it and started walking. When he caught up, she said, "The men were Dean, Boyd and Tobolokov. The woman was Renai."

Jake stopped, then caught up again.

"Where do you fit in? You attempted to poison Okneyev. He was Jenkin's contact. Is the Russian SVR part of this? Was Okneyev? Are you a double agent, like you said? What about Dean and crew?"

"I had to have a way out of Cuba. Boyd tracked Toby and me, took me on board. Toby wasn't with us. He left in Okneyev's runabout. Hardy had the Coast Guard commandeer us, took us to Guantanamo. We were interrogated, then brought to the US after it was once more safe to travel. I was told by my Interpol contact that Dean and crew were a renegade CIA group working with Poponovich. It is believed Dean learned Poponovich had been holding out on them. Supposedly, Poponovich was running two ops. They found out he had an inside with Jenkins, was the money man for a Mexican Cartel which was trying to buy the intel that the op, their op, had been tasked with investigating. When Mark or his superiors didn't come to their aide after we were picked up and taken to Guantanamo, they decided to go off the reservation."

"They went to Mexico. Toby was there. I guess that was where he was told to go by our control. Renai used her charms on Toby, he spilled the beans about everything, including my connection to Okneyev, my SVR background and Okneyev's connection to Jenkins. It was either go along or they would finger me for Okneyev's murder. They told me they would place the blame on me; say I bought the weapon's tech Jenkin's was offering. They threatened to make me disappear."

"They took Jenkins and left Mexico. Toby, Dean, and crew ended up back on Devereaux boat. No Jenkins. This is what I was told. I wasn't with them. I didn't know about your wife until I heard about her from news reports. Why did the government buy Devereaux' boat? Devereaux and Poponovich is who you need to talk to."

"What about Devereaux?"

"You need to ask him. All I know is he knew there was a connection to you, Tindal, and Jenkins. He's suspicious of me so he doesn't confide in me."

"What happened to Jenkins and the weapons' intel?"

"I don't know. They want to pin this on you and me. To free myself from them, I need to prove my innocence. They may be in this with Jenkins, with someone else, another intelligence group, or on their own. Hardy was at Guantanamo, ask him what they said."

"Why didn't you tell this in there? Why tell me?"

"You're the only one I trust Jake. I love you." She moved off, kicking, splashing the receding water.

Once more Jake found himself wondering who Blakely was. She had lied to him before. She lied today to the others. Did she really believe she loved him or was this part of her act? He tried not to look, couldn't stop. Damn, she had a fine body. Looking was all he would do. He had a huge capacity for love, felt love for many women, his only *being-in-love* was with Ariel. He would not betray her. No matter what the other head lusted after.

Jake started walking toward Blakely, his eyes on her nice round ass cheeks, the string running into the divide. There was a burst of noise coming from everywhere all at once. Weapon's fire. There was nowhere to take cover.

Later, as he played the scene over and over in his mind, it all blended in, pieces like a mad orchestra of discordant sounds competing for attention. Not unlike one of his first patrols in Fallujah, the sounds of everyday life going on as it had numerous other days, your senses on high alert, the sudden change, shots, an explosion, diving to the ground, running for cover, checking yourself, looking to see who fired, who's down, or dead, your men, your brothers always came first.

TJ had been dividing his attention between keeping an eye on the people around them, constantly checking on Jake and Blakely and guiding Jeni through the crowds, her eyes fixed on the images on her IWatch, zeroed in on the drone hovering high overhead. She stopped, which created a dam in the flow--grumbles, bumps from those navigating another course on their meandering march past shops and street merchants and hustlers.

"Two jet skis headed toward shore at a fast rate. Two men on each." She zoomed in. "The passengers on the back are armed with assault rifles. They are coming toward us. Swimmers are trying to get out of the way."

TJ went into motion, shoving people out of his way, shouting "move", running, bellowing out, "get down, everybody down, Jake, Blakely look out, get down" just as the first shots' sounding like fireworks resounded from the breaker line followed immediately by screams of fright and disbelief as the first victims on shore went down.

Then it became total chaos, people fell all over their belongings and each other, ran helter-skelter, reacting, not thinking. TJ saw Jake go down with the first shots, then he was up and running as the jet skis spun in a circle, dove down each time they turned, the shooter's aim interrupted, the firing momentarily stopping, then the bursts would resume, raking the shore. TJ went from being up, then running, then diving down, his face sprayed with sand, shouting warnings no one seemed to hear. He heard Jake's scream of "no-o-o-o", saw him begin to drop, then he bowled him over. Spits of sand kicked up inches from them. He held Jake down. He heard the jet skis sound dying amidst the outpouring of voices shouting and wailing, an outpouring of pain, grief, and horror.

He rolled off Jake, who quickly scrambled around, Blakely lay still, face down, Jake pulled her face up out of the sand, felt her neck, hoping it wasn't broken, turned her face, let it rest on his left arm immediately brushed the sand from around her nose, mouth and eyes, saw her exposed chest faintly rising and falling, touched her neck to check her pulse, it was elevated. TJ joined him in assessing the damage. She had three visible wounds: one in mid-thigh, TJ tore his shirt and tied a tourniquet a few inches above the wound; Jake saw and thought he heard a sucking chest wound, saw a golf ball ragged hole above her left exposed breast, he tore his shirt and applied pressure; glancing down he saw blood pooling at her waist.

"No immediate sign of a major organ or spinal injury," Jake said, "help me roll her over."

They gently rolled her onto her back. Jake quickly took the string from his bathing trunks, took another piece of his shirt, folded it, and asked TJ to help him.

"Raise her upper body we need to tie off these two bandages for her chest wound."

They worked quickly and as gently as possible, trying desperately to keep the sand off the bandages.

Blakely's breathing grew less shallow. TJ held her head in his lap. A slight tremor passed through her body to him. She moaned.

Jake was pressing one bandage on her thigh and one on her abdomen.

"Blakely can you hear me?" Nothing. "Don't try to move." He heard the moan, felt the trembling. Early signs she was going into shock.

All around was chaos. People trying to comfort or help the wounded, kneeling over others, crying, praying, begging for mercy. Sirens could be heard. Soon Devereaux and the Major appeared with a lounge chair.

"Is she…? Devereaux tried to ask.

"We could use this chair as a stretcher," Marge said.

"Better not to move her. No idea of internal injuries," TJ said. "Devereaux go get the responders, hurry them up. Major grab a beach blanket to cover her."

Jake looked up at TJ. TJ knew.

"This is f'ing war. No rules. You understand?"

"Yeah bro. I understand. First we need to know who we're at war with."

"I have a good idea. Blakely told me something. She better live is all I know."

An ambulance drove down, swung around, and stopped. Two medics unloaded a stretcher, TJ and Jake loaded her on it and put it in the back of the ambulance.

Jake grabbed one of the medics by the arm.

"Look at me. What's your name?"

"Lonzo Morales."

"Lonzo. She's very important person. She better not die. Understand?"

"Si senior." He jumped in the back. Jake slammed the door.

Hardy memed Jake and TJ, 'How is she?'

TJ: 'Bad. On way to hospital Better get chopper to hospital, plane on standby.'

'The ambulance is being routed to the embassy. The medvac chopper is there. You and the others need to work your way back to the safe house. Stay alert. And don't let the authorities get their hands on you. Jeni, guide them back.'

CHAPTER
30

Control Center
Jake, TJ and Hardy

Everyone made it back. Except Devereaux.

Jake wanted to go with Blakely. Thought he should be there for her and a chance to be with Ariel. Hardy ordered him not to, said it was too risky.

"You were most likely the target, Jake. And a coverup campaign by the government has already started. There's nothing you can do."

"First Ariel, now Blakely. I'm getting fed up with being told there's nothing I can do. Where's Devereaux?"

"He's at the hospital." Marge replied.

"You checked?"

"Saw him dropped off. No need to check. Why?"

"Hardy, I need you to put in a request to whomever you trust that can trace down an off-books-disbursements-of-funds to either Poponovich or Devereaux. Any disbursement related to a boat. Devereaux was possibly paid by Poponovich for the use of his boat. I need to know if that's true." Jake switched to meming, 'I tried. For some reason, I was denied access.'

"What's this all about?"

"Enough with the f'ing questions. Do you know anyone that can do this?"

"I can? Why?"

"Major, Captain, would you let TJ and me talk to Hardy alone?"

"We're a team. I would rather hear what it is you have to say. If it's about me or something you think me and Jeni, your team members shouldn't hear, I want to know why, so have the balls to say it to our face?"

"Don't worry Major, if it was about you, I wouldn't hesitate."

Hardy told them to wait outside.

They were not happy. After the door slammed, Hardy joined them at the table. Jake's and TJ's expressions told him they were ready to jump ship.

'Why have them leave the room?'

'Don't you think sitting here in silence while we meme looks strange?'

'Guess you haven't gotten use to multi-tasking? What's this about Devereaux and Poponovich and the boat?'

"Blakely believes our government bought Devereaux' boat. Dean and crew are back on Devereaux' boat. Blakely says they threatened to kill her. The attack today may have been someone they hired."

"Have you considered, in all your rebellious ramblings, it was most likely you that was the target? That these were cartel bangers?"

"We should look at all possibilities, shouldn't we, including the possibility Devereaux may be involved?"

"We need to be discussing this with the rest of the team."

"Two women close to me have been seriously injured, I think we need to reconsider our strategy. TJ and I are combat-tested veterans. As an Army Ranger platoon leader, I always put the welfare of my team ahead of my own. I no longer want that responsibility. TJ and I are a team. You need to let us operate as one. Arm us. This bullshit of tying our hands, not allowing us to defend ourselves is going to get us and/ or more people around us killed. Innocents, like what just happened. No more defenseless bullshit. Not for me."

"You agree TJ?"

"With all due respect, yessir."

Hardy turned his back to them, walked over to the one-way glass, the Major and Captain were huddled together. He could see they were looking at satellite images tracking the jet skis. Hardy had alerted the control room staff of the attack. They immediately began tracking the perpetrators. He had been doing the same using his implant. He had also started the record search Jake requested. The NSA computers were not always open to him. Unlike some, he had to go through channels. He chose another route, found it blocked, due to increased traffic. His implant would keep trying. Hardy didn't like Jake's attempts at going where he should not go. He needed to re-explain the situation to them.

"Jake, TJ, if I were to turn you loose as you wish, you wouldn't get very far--apparently, you weren't listening very carefully when Dr. Perkins and I explained the implant to you. Perhaps I need to go a little more in-depth."

"Screw this. I don't want any more of your long-winded bullshit."

"You are going to hear me out. Wouldn't want your family to be further victimized, would you? So, for once, shut up and hear me out."

"When this implant was given the green light for testing, there were many within the intelligence committees and NSA who were against allowing the experiment to proceed. They feared the implant could be a security risk. Despite all the firewalls and the use of supercomputer programs continuously trying to block and catch any breach of our top-level networks, hackers manage to get in. Our entire country's grids and networks have vulnerabilities, our enemies are looking for ways to penetrate our security, been a rash of Ransomware heists, as I'm sure you're aware. Our allies attempt to penetrate our security--their attempts are often asked for and encouraged by our agencies to check for any possible weakness. This could have been one such test. I think not, but it's not just the cartels that are attempting to stop us."

"The green light is tentative. We are an experiment. Safeguards had to be put in place, our implants are continuously monitored, and hacking attempts must be assumed. Big Brother *is* watching. Everywhere your implant seeks information, is recorded, scrutinized, given permission, denied permission, based upon your clearance level and risk assessment for national and corporate security."

"Jake, you were right, we *are* test animals, made possible because of a preliminary change to the Defense Acquisition Reform Act initiated in 1994, which was enacted to prevent the military from influencing defense contractor decisions, the prima facie six-hundred-dollar toilet seat prevention act. Too many military acquisition failures have resulted because of this act. The implant is a test case for relaxing the rules. The development of the implant has implications for the future of nonlethal weapon deployment and ultimately changing what it means to be a soldier. To this end it was given a green light."

"Others were involved in the initial human testing—Jenkins' was unauthorized--others supposedly shut down. Don't ask me what that means, I don't know. Before Jenkins could be shutdown, he jumped track. No one knows how he managed to do this. He had to have help. The people who were instrumental in developing and testing the implant worked for a small company. That company was purchased by Tindal Industries. That is how Jenkins was able to get involved. We don't know if Doctors Guthridge and Perkins or any members of her development team know anything about Jenkins' disappearance. They were put through the wringer and cleared. What we did learn was that he received an earlier version which lacks the safeguards, which are part of mine and your versions."

"Jenkins is and has been the main priority. There has been growing belief Jenkins is dead and never delivered the weapons technology to anyone—it is believed we would have seen The Hive, had he done so. As for the implant technology, the rumor about Russian superspies may be more than a laughable rumor. This has fueled the ongoing debate taking place in those self-aggrandizing marble halls about ending the program. Those against argue it is attempting to play God, creating a modern-day Tower of Babel. They are the ones who laugh at Russian rumors. They think this is an attempt by the NSA and DARPA to get additional funding to develop something which shouldn't be developed. Others know the threat is real--enemy, ally, does not matter. The genie is out, it can't be put back in the bottle. Jenkins' whereabouts and the intel's status must be determined. Our enemies cannot be allowed to procure or steal the technology. In addition, it must be determined if the Russians, or some other foreign power, are trying to make a trade, and if, the possibly nuclear or bio-dirty bomb, armed amphib is in play. That has been, and still is for me, the major mission. Everything rides on our performance. We must show the merits of the program, prove it can be effective and safe. No threat to mankind. No security-risk."

"The merits? This should never have happened. It's like the LSD experiments used by the intelligence agencies. An offshoot, trying for mind control, another threat to mankind, We're not ready for it, maybe never will be. They say LSD stays in your system, can cause flashbacks at any time. Who knows what the long term affects for this will be."

Jake started pacing. "And how about the power source for this device?" Jake looked at TJ. They both looked at Hardy. He squinted and started staring at his hands. "Nuclear. TJ, seems Dr. Perkins and Hardy failed to tell us the power for the device is a NDB, nano-diamond battery, a damn diamond-shielded nuclear powered battery. How do ya like them apples, huh? I don't know about you TJ, but I wish now more than ever that I hadn't given in to their damn threats."

"Yeah, I can see that bro. Beginning to wonder myself. This first we been told about these others. And this damn nuclear battery. How 'bout it Hardy, why weren't we told? Why us?"

"Why you and Jake? Once more, some of this will be repetitive, I hope for the last time."

"I rejected the idea of seasoned agents--too easily compromised. Young recruits would require extensive training. I figured we needed veteran soldiers, tested under fire, unknowns to the intelligence services, disciplined, not mavericks, team players, people that could be trusted to follow orders, potential trainers if we were successful, and, the program is given the green light. Hopefully, I have been told, join the Space Force as a Top-Secret Cyber Intel Strike Force Unit. I thought you both proved yourselves by the work you did with Operation Pink Flamingo. General McDab was impressed, had your names on a shortlist. Problem is this has become personal for you Jake, and looks like for you too, TJ. Seeking personal vengeance puts the whole operation at risk. It will play into the hands of the detractors. You risk the program being shut down. We're close. Jake don't let your hurt and anger cause me to have to remove you from the team. I repeat: the implant must be shown to be a nonlethal weapon. If you think I'm doing this for selfish reasons, you're right. And I did it knowing the risks. You were in the military, that's what we do."

"We were suckered TJ. They didn't tell us, didn't want us to know this device has a nuclear-waste-powered battery. Hey Hardy, did you know before you were implanted?" Jake and TJ stared at him. His face was set, a mask. "You didn't, did you? Did you know before *we* were coerced into this shit?"

Hardy felt the heat creeping up his neck into his face.

"Long and short answers, no and no. Wouldn't have mattered. There are risks with everything, risks vs. rewards, risk benefit analysis. I did not then and would not now hesitate to do it all over again."

"All about your career, huh?"

"Seems to me you chose the reward over the risk, both of you, huh? And I think you would have made the same decision even if you had asked and been told all the technical details, which like me you didn't. So, here it is, if you decide to continue, I will make certain Ariel is given the best care and protection. Also, I told our secretary, and she agreed, to put continued pressure on those seeking to locate your daughter."

"And here's something else you should know. A quarter-million-dollar reward has been offered by your daughter's adopted parents for her safe return, no questions asked. They have also contacted the State Department, asking them to put pressure on the Cuban government to return their grandson to his mother. Face it, Jake, there is not much more you can do to help your family if you go off on your own. You need to consider with Alperts dead and your lady friend Miss Gaspard incommunicado, DICE's extortion attempts will possibly include you, which means someone will attempt to contact you. This will give us a way to locate her. Try to go it alone, I will have to detain you. The government will not risk you falling into other's hands. The Mexican authorities will not allow you to leave. They launched an investigation. Their police captain has been told our op and team are off-limits. In exchange their government agreed to let our team remain here to aid in the investigation."

Jake didn't like hearing this. Made leaving problematic, not impossible. What to do? He needed answers. He would not stay any longer than necessary. He wanted to be at the hospital when Ariel was taken out of the medical coma. He needed to tell her good news about their family. News he must make happen.

He also worried about Blakely, his feelings torn, concern for her—not wanting to but the possibility of Ariel and her in the same hospital—what might be said—how to explain--something he wasn't good at.

His priority, free their daughter and grandson. And this DICE, would they try to contact him? Had their contact been Poponovich, Devereaux, possibly Blakely?

"Any word on Devereaux' location? What about Blakely?"

"Devereaux will be rejoining us shortly. We'll keep checking on him and the others. Miss Carmichael is on her way to Miami. The prognosis is not good."

Jake felt being around him was a curse. He needed action, put himself out there, keep himself from sinking in self-pity. It was time to know what was what and find out who could be trusted.

"Devereaux may be the key to locating Jenkins and the intel. You need to check those disbursements."

"I have. Devereaux no longer owns the boat. Blakely was right. Uncle Sam took possession of it."

He turned to Hardy. Man stood there frowning, always dressed like the proud company man he was. "We need to put eyes on that boat."

"Being done. Captain Adams will keep me posted. The jet skis didn't go there. They ditched them, boarded a boat, landed south of here. They disbursed using several vehicles, went separate ways, numerous directions. I have sent two teams to intercept them. Possibly, we'll find out who did this and who the target was. Assume it was you until we know otherwise. Jake, TJ, you two in or out?"

TJ: "Jake, not looking like we have much choice, bro."

Jake said nothing. He faced Hardy, "I don't like being defenseless while the others have weapons and intend to kill us. If we're so valuable to the government, then we have to be able to defend ourselves."

"Mexican law. You get caught with a weapon, at best, you will be locked up. Too many crooked cops and government officials, the cartels own them. You know how it is. You, in or out?"

"I'm no good to anyone dead is how I see it."

"No one wants any team member to come to harm, especially us. We go back to central casting for disguises. We see how everything plays out. Continue setting up the gala event. Watch, wait, listen, gather intel. My bet is someone will try to contact you. We have bits and pieces from Alperts' and Mrs. Gaspard's phones, we're chasing down leads. There's that other woman, Gonzalez family member that was on Alperts' plane. She's here somewhere. We're trying to run her down. This is the way ops work. There is always risk. You try to stay one step ahead. We have an advantage with the implant."

"What if the other side does also?" TJ asked.

"There is a blocking program in place."

"Which could be hacked," Jake added.

"Jake?"

"Here's the deal, I'm here to save my family. Any more attacks, I'm going to do my utmost to get my hands on any weapon to protect myself and those around me. Laws or no laws, op rules be damned, I won't stand idly by."

"I agree," TJ said.

"Defend only. We need the attackers alive, if possible. Agreed?"

They both agreed.

Jake didn't feel guilty for what he considered to be a necessary lie. Not all lies are the same. He would do what he had to to protect his family and friends and a line had been crossed. Someone must pay. And pay they will.

"Good. We'll assemble the team as soon as Devereaux arrives."

Jake said, "I believe we need to bring Dean and his friends in. Blakely believes they went rogue, pissed at Poponovich, think he held out on them. She said they are the ones who took Jenkins, went to a General Toraz's hacienda outside Juarez. The General was Okneyev's and Jenkin's contact, helped him escape. She was told Dean's men flew Jenkins out on a plane. Blakely said she didn't know where they flew to."

"Alperts and Miss Gaspard were tracked from the General's hacienda also. I'll see about getting a team to pay him a visit. Your wife will have to answer some questions, see if she recognizes any of them. We have to know if there may be a chance she is involved?"

"I don't think so. Her father and Tindal knew each other, as did you. You worked with her father? Anybody question him?"

"Not as far as I have heard. What about him?"

"Elena told me he stayed at Tindal's place just before the shit hit the fan. I would think he would have been a part of the investigation."

He leaned away from the glass, fixed Jake with squinting eyes.

"Not to my knowledge. Why haven't you said anything about this before now?"

"No one asked. I was part of your investigation, remember. TJ and I were running for our lives, we were questioned, no one asked--I wasn't the one doing the questioning."

Jake stared back. The room grew silent. "You knew about my wife, you had to know he's the one picked her up. She went to his house. She and I barely spoke. Hard to believe no one questioned his possible involvement. Too late now, he's dead, heart attack, so Elena said. But then again, she claimed he had cancer. Reason she told me she needed to go to Louisiana, which ended in her being with Jenkins at Tindal's place. Might want to check his autopsy."

"Jeezum. What else haven't you told us?"

"No one was too interested in what TJ and I had to say. Next thing I know, I was in the hospital, then drafted onto your team, given this damn inplant. Here we are. You the one held all the cards. Never told me anything about your background, your connection to Tindal and Jenkins. Accusing me of holding out on you? That's really the pot calling the kettle black."

"Anything else Blakely told you which might be of help?"

"She reminded me Devereaux wanted to talk to me back when he was in the Bahamian jail. I've never had the chance. Blakely said he refused to talk to her about it. They never trusted each other. I'd like to know what he has to say, seeing as how both Dean and Blakely claimed he said it was personal. You were at Gitmo. Blakely said you questioned her, Mark, and the others. Care to share with us, or is this all one-way shit?"

"I was not part of the interrogation team. I was briefed. The report is classified. Nothing useful was said. They're good, all had their stories coordinated."

"So you say."

"Yes. So I say. What about you TJ, anything you haven't told me you'd like to share?"

"I'm sure Carl gave you a full account, doubt he left anything out. I never saw his reports, no way for me to know. The FBI and CIA took away all the people I knew about. I have no idea what became of them or what intel they provided beyond what Carl reported. The only people I wish I could question are Toby Tobolokov and the Palmroys."

"Tobolokov," Jake said, "Blakely said he was working with Dean and crew, was the third man who took Jenkins. She said he's on Devereaux' boat."

"Damnit, damnit to hell," Hardy said, slapping his hands down on the table. He pulled out his cell, called the control room. "Get a Coast Guard boat out to Dev's Delight, or whatever that damn boat you were tracking is called, have it escorted to the dock. Put the occupants in separate rooms. I'll be there shortly to question them. Treat them as hostiles. No one is to say anything to them without me."

That boat was government property. How did it end up in their possession? The CIA. Why had he not been notified?

Jake was sent to apologize to Marge and Jeni.

"My intent was not to insult you. Blakely told me things I didn't feel you should hear until I ran it by Hardy."

"You could have said that," Marge replied. "You and your friend don't want us here, you've made that clear. Miss Carmichael was your friend, I get that, I'm sorry for what happened to her. But, that's no excuse for treating us like it was our fault."

"I never thought that. Yeah, you're right. Three people I care about have been caught up in this fiasco, two lie gravely wounded in hospitals and I don't like having you or anyone else out there in harm's way. Because of me--I'm the target--has nothing to do with you being women. I don't care about some socio-political bullshit. That's not how I think or operate."

"I took this assignment, as did Captain Adams, knowing we were stepping into the lion's den. From what I've seen, you and your friend are suffering from dick-eye, blind in one eye, see nothing but potential pussy with the other."

Jake was startled, couldn't help but smirk. "Guilty as charged."

She saw his expression.

"Most men are hopeless. World would be better off if their dick and balls were cut off. Jeni disagrees. She's willing to let most men keep their dicks. You mess with us again she may change her mind. You can be one to keep his if you keep it in your pants and out of your eyes. Don't treat us like this again."

"Right. I'll have to think on that. Shouldn't be hard."

She gave him a withering look. "I guess apologizing wasn't all Hardy sent you out here to say?"

"I'll let him explain. May be about another makeover."

CHAPTER
31

Juarez, Mexico
David Gonzalez--Juarez Cartel Underboss

David Gonzalez decided he had no choice. They had his brother. Men had been sacrificed, did not do as told. Told take targets, not kill. Instead, they hurt and kill innocents. Now police upset. This bad for business. Good that these shooters they not know him.

He talked to Esmeralda. Essie her childhood nickname. She did not like him call her this. She say she not happy Alperts dead. He knew she wanted the news lady Arturo promised her. News lady important, like woman their men shot. Arturo say it was Russians take Pablo's wife from DICE. Russians offer sell her to them. Arturo never say how this sale happen. He need to find the woman and make trade happen. Let Harper and Alvarez men know, use her to make trade for brother and property they steal.

Essie told him about Pablo. Maybe this become the possibility he hope for. Essie say she will try arrange meeting with Pablo to make deal. He tell her to take Pablo's son then tell Harper man Pablo wish see him to have talk about daughter and grandson. First Harper man must free brother. If not, they will have someone in Miami kill Harper and Alvarez men's women.

Get Harper man's daughter. Let Essie have her, make video, teach Harper man, and friend they should not have treated him so bad.

Get brother. Get thumb drives. Kill them all. Get big reward Tindal man offer. Have Pablo pay big money for return of son. Uncle upset Harper and

Alvarez men have the files. David worried without Arturo uncle may do him harm.

Their uncle blamed him. Uncle he talk to Arturo now Essie about the files. He worried. Tell them the files are threat to cartel business. Other cartels and authorities must not see the files. Need make Harper Alvarez men return their property. Free nephew. Find way to get files for Hive. He tell her once have Hive the American wall it come tumbling down. Become no more threat to their business. This war require weapons. Must have offensive weapon not play-toy drones.

Essie tell him what uncle said. David tell her he wish to make Arturo and uncle happy again. He tell her his plan to free brother, get files.

Esmeralda hated her cousin call her by the childish nickname. She was a grown woman. More woman than David. She laughed, thinking of his tiny dick, a big clitoris. He could not satisfy any woman or man with that thing. As children, they played around. She knew she was only female he dared show his thing to. No other girl would want to touch him.

She grew up to be an attractive female which she hid underneath young men clothing. They were much less expensive than woman clothes. She had no desire to attract men. Never did. She was a closet tortilla.

Her awakening came at the hands of an older girl while attending a church retreat. One night this older, plain-looking girl named Angelina caught Esmeralda in their shared room masturbating. Esmeralda felt ashamed; tried to cover herself; begged Angelina not to tell. Angelina promised not to say a word to the nuns or the villagers if Esmeralda did what the girl wanted. She was too scared not to agree. She knew what her family would do. The girl locked the door, removed her clothes, and came to Esmeralda's bed. She used tender touches, probes of fingers and her tongue to teach Esmeralda what she knew about how to please herself and other females. Esmeralda did not resist. Over the course of the two weeks of camp their play continued. Esmeralda soon became the instigator. The other girl became her willing sex slave. This ended when the retreat did. Arturo made sure she never heard from the other girl again.

Her initiation as a feminista began after Arturo somehow found out and threatened to expose her if she didn't help her uncle and him take over their village. To do this, they needed something on the mayor. Arturo told her to seduce the mayor's daughter. A girl he had the hots for and who continually resisted his crude advances. David used secreted cameras to film the deceptive seduction of her and the threesome rape which Arturo forced her to be complicit in. Their uncle used the video to blackmail the mayor.

Her uncle rewarded her by sending her to Cuba for her education. There, along with learning several languages and other needed lessons to be a proper revolutionary, she was taught self-defense, guerrilla warfare tactics and the art of seducing men and women. No man ever penetrated her. She told them she would kill any man who tried. Her Russian female instructor decided it was not necessary she do men. "Women know their man's secrets." She said Esmeralda's talented predilections would be useful for this.

Esmeralda did not consider herself a communist and told her uncle this. He said it did not matter. Her talents would be useful for business opportunities with Cuba, Russia, or China. He was angry that the US was making their business more difficult across the border. He feared the loss of the files the Harper and Alvarez men stole from David would make many problems for business. Her training was to be used helping them get this information back.

Seduction and blackmail were Esmeralda's trademarks. She found she enjoyed her work. It paid well. Her resentment for her uncle and Arturo never diminished. David remained her favorite. The Harper and Alvarez men hurt him, humiliated him, made their uncle more angry with him. He nearly died from his diabetes, was in coma, uncle not care. This changed her cousin. He was becoming cruel like his brother and uncle. For this she would make these men pay. Make their women hurt. Her plans were someday to take over control of the cartel. She needed David's expertise with computers and drones for now. She hoped he would join her when her time came. For now she needed to do what her uncle ordered.

David told her about the failed abduction. He laid out a change of plans over her cell. She listened while she weaved her motorbike in and out of traffic attempting to overtake the ambulance with the Carmichael woman in it. David figured the Harper man would be with her. David notified her the ambulance wasn't going to the hospital. The vehicle veered off and whisked the woman to the American Embassy where she was loaded into an awaiting helicopter. David tracked the helicopter via drone to a private airstrip. He watched as they put her on a private jet he learned was headed to Miami.

There was nothing she could do about the woman, so she followed the vehicle that met the ambulance. The man who got in the vehicle wasn't the Harper man as they hoped. The vehicle went to a warehouse in the El Centro district.

Several hours later, a service panel truck, a boutique logo painted on its sides, emerged from the rear garage door of the warehouse. She saw the man who had been with the woman in the ambulance and another woman passenger go past her in a truck. She followed. She couldn't go far. Soon she must meet Pablo. Maybe he would have his son with him.

CHAPTER
32

Control Center Akumal
Devereaux and Renai

James Dean, his CIA Clandestine Unit members Boyd and Renai, plus Tobolokov, were segregated from each other and Poponovich. Hardy thanked the Coasties and they left in their patrol boat. Dev'sDelight was left tied up at the Center's dock, virtual observervation and foot patrol guards were posted. It had been cleared earlier by the Mexican Navy.

Hardy and TJ went in to see Poponovich first. Jake stayed behind in the breakroom with Marge, Jeni and Devereaux. The two women were not enthused about being left behind by Hardy. Marge protested when Jake said he needed to talk to Devereaux privately.

"It's personal. Need to ask him about something that happened when he and I worked together on a resort construction project. If I think it has anything to do with what is happening now, I'll share it with everyone on the team."

Devereaux bought a bottled water and a bag of chips before joining Jake in the far corner away from the two women, who continued to stare in their direction. They turned their backs to them. Devereaux began eating the chips, offered the bag to Jake. He shook his head no.

"Thomas, I haven't had a chance to talk with you since I last saw you in the Bahamas," Jake began. "Why didn't you tell me you were still FBI, and were working with Interpol?"

Devereaux stopped chewing, swallowed and said, "Wouldn't have changed anything. Called working undercover, you should know. Why bring up old shit?"

"Dean told me, when you were in the jail that you had something to tell me, only me. Blakely reminded me, said you wouldn't tell her."

Devereaux looked over his shoulder at the women, then back. He clasped his hands, twisting a nonexistent wedding band, stopped and took a sip of water, replaced the cap. "They don't know what they're talking about."

"Bullshit Thomas."

This was a different Thomas from the jovial, carefree acting Thomas Jake remembered from back in the Bahamas. "I thought you and I got along fairly well. You wanted me to put in a good word for you with Hardy. You warned me about Blakely. You know I never talked to the authorities about you killing those Russian SVR agents. As you know, there is no statute of limitations on murder."

"Better think again. You'd be considered an accessory after the fact, Jake."

"Hardy knows. I'm not worried, but you seem to be." Devereaux' eyes flared when he looked up at Jake from the table. He started fiddling with the chips, twirling the water bottle. "You were working with Blakely and Tobolokov then, Dean told me, you were the one who tasered me, helped them escape. How well did you know Okneyev?" Jake saw he hit a weak point, showed in Devereaux' eyes. Devereaux didn't answer.

"Did Okneyev ask you to kill those Russians, to help Toby and Blakely get away?"

"You're crazy. I never met Okneyev. Had nothing to do with him. I did what I was told to do, namely watch your back. I told you this when I first met you in the Bahamas. The reason I helped Blakely and Toby escape was part of my orders also."

He crumpled the chip bag, some of the remaining chips flew from the bag onto the table. He brushed them onto the floor.

"Did you know Blakely was connected to him?"

"Yeah. From her file. The Bureau knew about her employer and their ties to him when she managed that strip club in St. Louis. Had no clue until after I received a report about the shit that happened in Miami. Was told to be on the lookout for Tobolokov, help him get away, that he was Interpol. He showed, then you sent me for the car, I checked in with my contact at Interpol for instructions, was told to follow Carmichael's lead. Pissed me off, no one had told me about her. Probably what I wanted to tell you when I was in jail. There was a lot going on at the time. The Bureau was furious that Interpol made me the fall guy. There was talk of putting everything on you. I didn't know who to trust. Knew if you talked, I could get royally screwed. Satisfied?" He took another drink of water. The other hand continued squeezing the bag.

Jake wanted to see Dean and Devereaux together see what their interaction was.

"Did anyone at Interpol talk to you about my daughter or grandson?"

He drank more water, re-screwed the cap, set it and the bag aside.

"No. I know now they are investigating her disappearance. Had nothing to do with my assignment."

"What about Blakely, do you think she knew?"

"Possibly. We didn't talk much. You are a sore topic for her."

"Why were you two spying on us?"

"Ask Hardy. I told him."

"Was that when you were at Gitmo?"

Devereaux flinched.

"Talk to Hardy." Devereaux wondered how much Hardy told Jake and the others.

Jake noticed he continued fidgeting with the bag. What wasn't Devereaux saying?

"You suspected Blakely and I had something to do with Jenkins' disappearance?"

"She told you that?"

"I heard about y'all's run in with the Israelis. They think that. Accused Blakely. You were there."

Devereaux looked sideways at him. "Jake there's a lot of he said, she said shit going around. I was told this was a possibility. To keep my eye on you two. I'm leaning toward believing you. Blakely, I've still got my doubts about her. May never know."

Devereaux hoped Jake believed him. He still had his doubts about Jake. Why else would DICE have gotten involved? The Israelis had one of the best intel networks. They wouldn't suspect Jake without good reason.

"Anything you want to tell me before we confront Dean and associates? Anything you haven't told anyone that might help with the questioning?"

"I'm impressed Jake. It's you that has come a long way since we first met. Were you playing me back then? If not, you sure you had me fooled."

Jake stood up. Devereaux walked over and threw his trash in the receptacle. He came back and joined him beside the women's table.

The Major mouthed dickeye at Jake. He winked and laughed.

As they went down the hall, Jake remembered the recorder was on.

TJ stood outside one of the maddening sterile rooms smiling.

"Hey Alvarez, something good happen?" Jeni asked.

Jake said, "Nah. He gets off on this. He's got the same dickeye all us men have."

He and TJ laughed. Devereaux tried not to. As did Marge and Jeni. Their holding it in didn't last long.

They were all laughing when Hardy appeared. "Glad you find this amusing. Is there something you'd like to share with me, I could use a good laugh?"

No one responded. TJ memed, 'The Major thinks we suffer from something she calls dickeye. Seems the women think we're leaving them out.'

'I picked up on that. Jake seems to be forgetting his implant. Not sure if that's good or bad? We need the women. Guess I need to change things up.'

He switched to verbal. "Seems we all need to unwind, first we have business to attend to. I figured we'd let the women have a chance, show us their interrogation techniques. Figured let them question the female Renai first. Jake, we haven't been able to locate Elena yet. Her mother refuses to divulge her whereabouts. Apparently, she's off with her daughter. Her daughter's roommate says she's at a musical event."

"Her daughter Jennifer's biological father, Dr. Teddy something or other, is in the states again. He's in a band. My guess is that's where they'll be. Elena never really got over him. Before the incident with the game warden, I found out he asked her to meet him in New Orleans. May have been where she was going when she was abducted. The band's called *The Diddly Doowops*," Jake used his implant to check online while they talked. He was informed the band was on a swing through Texas. This week they were booked in Austin. "You might want to check the band's itinerary." He memed the info to Hardy.

Major Duplantis and Captain Adams entered Renai's room. The guys watched to see what happened by way of a monitor mounted in the side one-way-glass panel. The Renai woman had been pacing the room, her arms wrapped tight, goose bumps visible. She stopped at the far end of the table. She was wearing a see-through coverlet over her what-was-visible, lots-of-skin-revealing, one-piece bathing suit.

"Like what you see?" Renai asked. "You must be the two lesbo lovers I heard about."

Hardy straightened up and checked Jake's and TJ's reactions. They shrugged. Devereaux grinned.

Marge reacted by saying, "Sit down." She and Jeni went to two chairs on one side of the table. Marge waved her hand at the chair on the other side. "If you sit, I'll send for something to drink. Or you can stand there like some prima donna gypsy bitch and get nothing."

Renai didn't move, stood like a statue, her crystal clear, blue-hazel eyes, barely blinked. They were fixed on the two women like a cat eyeing its prey. Marge and Jeni looked poised, ready to make a move. She hoped they did.

Jake spoke into his mic, "Watch her Marge, Jeni. She's young and fast, I know from personal experience. Maybe she needs to be put in restraints."

Marge shook her head. "If you attempt to attack us, we'll shackle you to the seat. I hear you're a trained interrogator. You know the drill."

Renai didn't flinch.

Marge opened a folder. "Reba Heloise Renai; go by your last name, very utilitarian, military, Israeli, family was gypsies." No response. "You and other team members are Jewish, East European. You, Romanian. Says here you were held prisoner by Saddam Hussein when you were still in puberty. Sexually abused. You a man-hater? Wouldn't blame you." She paused. No reaction. "No. Hate everyone don't you? An equal opportunity hater, trained assassin. Mossad? Perhaps CIA or Russian FSB? My bet, you're an independent contractor? Whoever foots the bill? You the one killed Major Jenkins after you and your friends took him hostage?"

Nothing.

"Hope you enjoy the accommodations. Where you're going won't be nearly this comfortable. The questioning not so pleasant. Guess you already got a taste of it. This time it'll be several full course meals. Been nice talking with you."

They left the room, joined the others.

"That is a predator--kept expecting her to leap over the table and attack us," Jeni said.

"Nice try," Hardy said. "We'll give her more time, turn the thermostat lower. Any votes on who should be next?"

"I think we should save James Dean for last," Jake said.

"Why's that?" Hardy asked.

"The others won't know as much as he does. Need to crack them one at a time, make sure he knows he's the omelet. Tobolokov gets my vote. I think he's the softest."

Marge had been quiet, standing off; you could feel her electricity. Jake took notice.

"You have someone else in mind major?'

Marge ignored Jake. She turned her flashing eyes to Hardy.

He stared back at her. Twenty years of marriage; the social climate of the day; he knew he had to tread carefully.

"Speak up Major. My men tell me I need to be more inclusive. You have a problem with Tobolokov?"

"No Sir. Renai was chosen to pacify us women members of this supposed team. That pisses me off. Worse is you have chosen to move on to the men, as if women are less important. What are the captain and I doing here? How do you know that woman in there isn't the ringleader of this pack? With all due respect sir, you have a severe case of dickeye." She smiled.

Jake laughed. Damn that woman has some balls.

"I apologize Major. Captain. We men owe you for pointing out what ails us. Perhaps, "I am who I am" needs a tune-up? I gave you the opportunity to show I accepted you two as team members. Never occurred to me you would see this any other way. This was your chance to display your abilities. You hit a tough adversary. It happens. Best to move on. Either agree with Jake 's choice or choose another, doesn't matter to me. Put up or shut up. With all due respect, Major."

'Pretty harsh reality, don't you think?' Jake memed Hardy and TJ.

'Uh oh. Here it comes,' TJ memed. He watched Marge's face. It was twisted into a frown. When Deane did that, she was getting ready to unload on somebody, just thinking about the best move to put his ass in place.

"Sir. Am I an equal member of this team?"

"No such thing as equality in service. Said the same thing to these men. I have the final say. I'm trying to be more inclusive, but the mission comes first. We fail my ass will be the first to get kicked and kicked the hardest. By a woman, HS's Madame Secretary. For this op or any op, that's the way it is, should be, and hopefully, always will be. Anything else Major? By the way, I don't object to you calling me Hardy."

"Hardy. Sir. I would like one more chance with Renai. She pisses me off. Never a better time to learn what she knows, teach her some respect. I realize she had some hard knocks in life, who hasn't? I believe I can make her talk.

All I need is a few minutes and your promise of no repercussions for me, or her, for what hopefully doesn't happen in those moments."

"Can't have no Abu Garib shit here. Not on my watch."

"Nothing like that, I promise. It'll be an all-fair-and-equal chance for both of us to get better acquainted. I bet a hundred she talks." She looked around and smiled at Jeni. Jeni looked concerned, forced herself to smile back.

"Be careful Marge."

"I intend to. Need to show these men how we women do things. Any takers on the bet?" No one spoke up. Marge slipped her jacket off. "Hardy sir, would you mind turning the thermostat back up? Might help change the atmosphere in there."

Marge reentered the room, closed the door, and stood there, waiting on the warmer air to take the chill away. She watched Renai continue her pacing, didn't even look her way. Several minutes passed, nothing but the sounds of the warmer air coming in from the overhead vents and the almost quiet steps of Renai's bare feet on the hard-concrete floor.

She cleared her throat. Renai stopped pacing. "A few simple questions and I'll leave you be. The men out there are looking forward to a physical contest, don't intend to give them the pleasure. Must be difficult for you also. Having all that male testosterone to contend with, stuck out there on that boat day in and day out. I've had to deal with that shit my whole career. Now I find myself caught up in the same old shit once more. I told them they suffer from an affliction called dickeye, can't see beyond their dicks."

Was that a nod, a smirk?

"I think you're the brains of your crew. You don't have to speak, simply nod your head if I'm right." Renai unwrapped her arms, moved to within striking distance of Marge. Marge met her eyes, hoping any attack would show soon enough to limit the damage. She could smell her womanly sweat, mixed with hints of coconut oil. Any other time she might have been aroused. This was not one of those times.

"Danger turns you on. You probably like it rough," Renai said. There it was, that flicker of self-doubt showing in the other woman's eyes, even as she attempted a smile. She tilted her head, woman has peter-envy. Her friend probably wetting herself watching. Renai knew she would never be allowed to leave, at best, she would be transferred to a far worse prison. Unless she could convince them Jenkins was alive, and she could trade intel for freedom. She and the others had rehearsed for this possibility over and over. Give hints, make them want more. Learn what they know.

"How about we do this, I give you something, you give me something in return," Marge said.

Renai thought, I know what you like me give you. Why this bitch? Where was Harper?

"You stayed behind at General Toraz's hacienda when Jenkins left with the other team members."

Renai simply nodded. (Someone talked. What else?)

Marge thought nonverbal responses were better than none.

"Your team was pissed Poponovich held out on you."

Rinai gave another nod. (Hope bastard rots in hell.)

"Jenkins didn't have the intel shit with him?"

No response. (Let them wonder.)

"You went back to the house where your team picked up Jenkins, you discovered signs someone else had been there with him."

Renai nodded. (Come on clever bitch say who you think. Dean figured it was the Harper man's wife. She allowed Dean his claim, said he saw Jenkins arrive alone.)

Marge thought, her response was too quick. "You left there, went back to General Toraz' place, left the next day, rejoined the other members of your team and Jenkins aboard one of the Russian Okneyev's freighters."

Another nod. (Give them something to think about.)

"Okneyev was upset with your team and Jenkins, thought he had been double-crossed?"

No nod. (Seems logical. Waste of time.)

"Jenkins told Okneyev something to save his ass, trying to up the ante."

A shrug. (And?)

"Miss Carmichael was there."

A nod. (Chew on that bitch.)

"Jenkins is dead. Miss Carmichael killed him."

Renai shrugged again. A slight shift in her eyes and stance. (No chance verify that without Carmichael woman. Good luck, Harper's whore no longer able to dispute anything. The Harper man, most likely the target. Poponovich right. The man must have a horseshoe up his ass.)

"Your team and Miss Carmichael work together, she kills Okneyev. You are here to sell what you know to the highest bidder."

Renai stepped back, signaling the end to the questioning. (This talk go nowhere. Dean say what Jenkins have worth more than great riches. Say this guarantee immortality. Renai grew tired of this guessing game. Get the hell away from me bitch. Keep guessing.)

Marge knew it was over. She turned to leave, stepped back so someone could open the door, nervous for turning her back on Renai. To her surprise, she felt Rinai's breath on her neck.

"You make mistake with us. Others watch you." She licked Marge's neck. "Girlfriend smell. It still on you."

Marge froze. She felt violated. The door swung inward. She walked out without looking back.

"That was interesting," Hardy said. "Care to tell us what that last bit was?"

The others were staring at Marge, except for Jeni. She had her eyes on Renai's grinning face looking up at the corner monitor. It felt like she knew Jeni would be looking at her.

"She said it was a mistake picking them up. Others were watching." She reached a hand up, wiped the invading moisture off. "I've been trained as a human lie-detector. Most of what she indicated is believable. Gives us something to go on when we talk to the others. Too bad Miss Carmichael isn't here to confirm or deny what she indicated."

Jake memed TJ and Hardy, 'Pure conjecture. I want to give it a try, ask what she knows about DICE, Alperts and my daughter's disappearance. As well as about Devereaux. He hasn't been forthcoming about his time on the boat.'

"Anything else before we visit the next one?" Hardy asked.

"Yeah. I need to ask her some questions. See if she knows anything about DICE and my daughter."

"Be quick about it," Hardy said.

The Major gave him a eat-shit-and-die look. She opened her mouth to protest, decided not to.

Jake stepped into the room. "Hello Renai. Remember me?"

She smiled. "Mr. Harper, of course I remember you. Been wondering when you show."

"Why's that?"

"Miss Carmichael, she speak highly of you. Not know what she saw. She say you have "it" factor. A true innocent. Have bravado. Maybe you show me?" She laughed. "Hard to believe one screwing do that to someone like her. Perhaps there other times for you and her, with the wife, or while reconnect with childhood flame? Many think so."

Was she fishing, or, just trying to get under his skin? "What about your connections? Did you know a man named Alperts? I'm sure you're familiar with the DICE organization?"

"Know he dead. Was with one of your girlfriends when she injured. Upsetting, no? Your wife, think maybe she know about her, this love-child daughter and grandson?"

"What do you know about my daughter's disappearance?"

"Mr. Harper. I not have connection to DICE. That why you ask, no? No secret your daughter disappear. All organizations hear. I wish you luck. What about wife and Major Jenkins? You ask her about this?"

"How about you? Have you talked to my wife?"

"Would like to interrogate her and you. Perhaps girlfriend and Miss Carmichael at same time. Maybe you show me this "it" factor."

"What about Thomas Devereaux?"

Devereaux was shocked hearing his name.

"What about him?"

"Suppose you tell me. He was with you on the boat. Was he there when Jenkins joined you?"

"Devereaux is Poponovich's, Miss Carmichael's and your associate, ask him yourself. I would rather talk about you. I believe you know more than you say." She gave a provocative smile, licked her lips, posed in a wide-open stance, she was toying with him. "Go. Rejoin your women. Perhaps you tell me about rumor another time."

"What rumor would that be?"

"Hear technology available, capable connect soldiers each other and internet via a chip implant. Perhaps this Russian announcement not fake news. Hear America develop it. Major Jenkins we hear he know about this. Told he think to sell; maybe he lose, perhaps already sell this information to Russians. Hear you know about this thing. Say this why you here. This what bring trouble to you."

"Sounds like a scam. Something from a Twilight Zone program," Jake said moving toward the door.

She tilted her head, gave him a sideways look.

He imitated the gesture. "Hope you enjoy your stay. You think of anything you want to share--more questions, useful answers--let us know." He gave her a brief smile. She continued to stare at him, like she was sizing him up. Jake paused at the door, "How about one more thing, for curiosity sake, why talk to me and not the women?"

"No like closet queens. Curious, make me wonder what women see." (He knows something.)

"Often wonder that myself."

CHAPTER
33

Quintana Roo / South of Cancun, Mexico
Jake's and Ariel's son-in-law Pablo

Pablo was dressed in tight-fitting chino slacks and a light-colored polo knit shirt which showed his lean, fit, swarthy body in what he felt was a most appealing manner. He joined his mother and the Russian Ambassador to Mexico's wife near the pool of the Cuban Ambassador's hacienda. His son was playing in the shallow end of the pool, splashing water on the nanny. All eyes turned upon his approach, the older Russian lady lingered, taking longer than necessary. His son smiled and called out to him. He waved. The nanny watched him, her dark eyes seeking his—a trace of apprehension, mingled with humility. He enjoyed giving the reprimand for her laxity the night before.

She had accepted her punishment, her ass bright red, begging for more. He relished the memory of her blissful curiosity turning to fear, when he began choking her, not releasing until they reached their orgasms following her near-death spasms which caused her vagina to constrict so very nicely. He noted she had used waterproof makeup to cover the bruising.

Before he administered the punishment, while everyone was asleep, he received a text from an anonymous source wanting to meet. This person claimed to have information concerning his contract with DICE.

The day before, when he received the news about Alperts' demise and Elizabeth's mother having been sent to Miami, perhaps dying from wounds, he wondered what this would mean. Now this? Who could it be, what did this person know?

The meeting was to take place in a public place, one where his bodyguards would need to discreetly secure the perimeter to make sure this wasn't a trap instigated by Elizabeth's biological father. Alperts had warned him the Harper man would be a formidable adversary. He was told not to worry. DICE's plan took into account the Harper man coming to Cancun where he and others would be eliminated. Alperts was gone. The Harper man would now be suspicious. Was this person who contacted him with DICE or the Harper man? Both posed problems—both were threats to his future well-being.

Pablo wondered where they had taken Elizabeth. The Alperts man had promised she would be treated well—never to suffer any harsh treatment or be subjected to pain or humiliation. Pablo had never done anything such as this--he knew nothing about making someone disappear.

A year before he commented to a man at a social gathering concerning his unhappiness with his marriage. He had made the statement half-heartedly, somewhat in jest. This was done soon after his life-changing discoveries: the existence of trust funds set up for her and Gabriel; and the fact she had been adopted. She had not told him about either. Alperts claimed she knew nothing about her adoption until the introduction to her biological mother prior to her being taken. His investigator's inquiry showed Gabriel would be entitled to both funds upon his mother's untimely death. For his reputation, for preservation of Gabriel's lineage in his parent's eyes, he decided Elizabeth, possibly knowing these things, should never be allowed to disclose the truth. The deception must continue. To this end he wrestled with how to accomplish the deed. He lacked the expertise, the willpower to physically do her harm.

The man, he met at the gathering, had laughingly said he knew someone who might help make his life more bearable. A week later, a comely young woman at a bar in Barcelona, where he often hooked up with casual sex partners, came on to him. They danced, drank, and ended the evening at her apartment. After they enjoyed their dalliance, while they were lying back stroking each other's egos, she asked about his marriage. He told her he was not so happy, that he feared losing his son if he decided to end it. She said she knew an organization who could help him with his problem. She gave him a number—the organization was DICE. Later reflection led him to conclude the seemingly casual meeting with the man and later the woman was no accident.

At his first sit down with the man calling himself Alperts, they talked more about her biological and adoptive parents and the financial arrangements, than about what was to happen to Elizabeth.

He no longer cared. Their marriage had become unbearable. He suspected she found another lover—this concerned him—the thought of a divorce—

another man in his son's life—his parent's old-world Catholic views. This could not happen.

A plan was made. He and Gabriel were to travel abroad with his parents. Gabriel would spend a holiday with him and his parents, get to enjoy time in Cancun, then see their native land, Cuba. Elizabeth was told this would be a trial separation, give them both a chance to decide what was best. She said no, Gabriel could not go. The day before they were to leave, they had another argument. She said she would take Gabriel, go back to her parent's home, and decide their future. He told her this was not to be. He had proof of her infidelity--Gabriel would be taken from her. She threw her wine in his face. DICE's man was watching and waiting. That was the last he saw of Elizabeth.

He told his mother he would not be joining them on their trip to the aquarium. He had business to attend to. Perhaps he could join them for lunch at La Isla Mall. He kissed her on both cheeks, bade the Russian Ambassador's wife farewell with air kisses to both her rosy cheeks. Both women smelled of the iced, spicy aperitifs they were served from the sweating pitcher on the glass-topped, brightly painted wrought-iron table. They were seated on cushioned wrought-iron lawn chairs, also brightly painted. The pitcher was half empty. He tasted the bitterness of the expensive, perfumed suntan lotion they had applied to their sun-deprived, aging skin. He waved bye to Gabriel and the nanny and left.

The Russian Ambassador's wife leaned over to refresh her drink and said to Pablo's mother, "Does he know anything?"

"No. Pablo, he my deviously innocent man/child. Years in military gave small, brief hope. University serve only to make us grandparents."

"And his wife?"

"Better suited for the purpose, so my husband believe--and, there is Gabriel. Soon we have brunch, take Gabriel to aquarium."

Gabriel's grandparents had not told Pablo the Americans had demanded his son's return to his mother. The request had been refused. His grandmother smiled. Her husband's plans were going to give a boost to his career. Poor Elizabeth, soon she will be in hands of these filthy Mexicans. She and her friend sat back watching Gabriel, and her personally picked nanny, play.

Esmeralda received the live feed from the drone. It hovered over the hacienda where the panel truck went. David could not keep the drone there for long, a warning buzz told him another drone was closing. He moved his drone along the coast to the hacienda occupied by the Cuban Ambassador's family.

The drone commandeered by David had audio/video, as well as radar and collision avoidance capability. He and Esmeralda watched and listened, intrigued by the comments about Pablo, his wife and son.

"Wife better suited for what purpose? What filthy Mexicans? Did Arturo and David make deal? Not tell her? Perhaps uncle? Why they not hear from him?" Esmeralda wondered out loud.

"Alperts man no say anything 'bout wife to you?"

"No. I hear him say to her mother, daughter be okay long as she cooperate, do as he say. Nothing more."

"Pablo must be made to think we now have wife. Tell him he must pay half-million in bit coin for wife and Harper man be made to disappear. Do not tell him how. Be quick with meeting, soon grandmother take son see aquarium. I keep watch, tell you when take boy. Other men take care of bodyguards, help take boy away. Pablo, his mother be made think Harper man do this. Now, go meet Pablo."

"David you not know what woman's comments mean. Perhaps the filthy Mexicans they speak of are our rivals. You should talk to uncle. Perhaps he knows."

"Uncle he busy. He meet with president. You say he tell us to fix. We fix. Now go."

CHAPTER
34

HS Control Center, Akumal
Tobias Tobolokov Interpol

TJ, Hardy, and the others waited for Jake to rejoin them. Devereaux had a fixed, angry expression trained on Jake when he exited Renai's room.

"What was that shit about me? I've told you, I never met with Jenkins."

"You were on the boat. You were there when Jenkins was brought onboard."

"I was taken to Guantanamo by the guard boys. Hardy knows."

"I'm talking about after you were released from Gitmo. This took place when they flew from General Toraz' hacienda and came onboard Okneyev's other cargo ship where he fled with the Cuban Generals."

Hardy interrupted. "I just received word, a drone was seen overhead near here, our guys sent up one of ours to intercept. The drone took off. Reconnaissance followed it to a hacienda not too distant. Our team observed, the drone was surveilling the occupants there, which turned out to be where the Cuban Ambassador's family was seen. Russia's Ambassador to Mexico's wife was there as well. We will continue to monitor the occupants and the other drone."

"Was Pablo and my grandson there?"

"Yes. Pablo left. We have a team following him. Your grandson was in the pool with a young woman. They are now on the lawn having a snack." Hardy said, then memed Jake, 'You may observe via the feed.'

"Thought the staties requested Gabriel be returned?"

"To his mother, Jake. As of now, she has not been located." Hardy pulled away from the waiting station counter, straightening, flexing his back, and started down the corridor. "Let's see what our other guests have to say. Boyd or Tobolokov, any preference?"

TJ spoke up, "Tobolokov, Agent Swanson and I wanted to talk to him. I'd like a go at him."

"As would I," Jake said.

Jake memed Hardy, 'Someone needs to keep their eyes on Devereaux when we question Toby. Be interesting to know his reaction when I tell Toby we know about him, Devereaux and Dean's crew's abduction of Jenkins.'

Jake was finding it easier to do simple multitasking using the implant. He stood with the others outside Tobolokov's room, giving TJ time alone inside, while simultaneously monitoring Pablo's entourage cruising inland in three SUVs to his business meeting. Another view showed his grandson seated in a pool, the two ambassador's wives sat nearby looking on.

A lovely Hispanic woman stepped out of the pool with Gabriel in tow. She put on a wraparound semi-transparent skirt over her one-piece swimsuit. Gabriel went over to a table.

His grandson was a handsome little fellow, looking so proper, laughing at something the young woman said, then nibbling at his snack. Jake wanted to be there with him. He soon would be he told himself. Hardy and company would just have to get over it. He would stick around, learn as much as he could about Jenkins and the potential threats, get with central casting for a disguise, then he was going after Pablo for questioning about his daughter Elizabeth and secure his grandson for the planned reunion with Ariel.

Toby Tobolokov was seated at the metal table. He jerked upright when he heard the door open. He was shocked when in walked someone he hoped never to see again. It was him, the large muscular Cubano. The one from the club in Miami. The sharpshooter who crashed the door in and shot the man holding a pistol on him--the bullet taking the man's trigger finger off. This was not the someone he expected to see. Hours standing, pacing, sitting, listening, waiting for anyone, anything to break the monotony of his sterile cold cell. But not this guy. The one he heard was Harper's friend TJ Alvarez sat down across from him, a smug grin creasing his swarthy face, saying nothing, just staring. Toby did not know what he should say. He felt no guilt for what he did. This guy, what should he tell him? The silence continued. Finally…

"Tobias Tobolokov. Okay if I call you Toby?" Toby shrugged. "Remember me?" Another shrug. "Slipped away from us back in Miami. Understand you were with Interpol. What about now?"

"Who are you?" Toby asked, his broad Slavic face maintaining a quizzical look, eyebrows raised.

"Who I am's not important. What's important is the information you can provide which will determine the here and now and any possible future you may have. Once more, you still Interpol? Give us a contact. We verify your bona fides, you go free."

Toby needed to know who this guy was. "Prove me I should trust you."

"Your colleague Blakely Carmichael she's in Miami hospital, in critical condition, someone wants her out of the way. She confided to friend of mine, Jake Harper, you once worked with her, said you both Interpol. Simple question, you Interpol? Verify this and who knows."

"Are you American intelligence?"

"Yes."

"Prove this."

TJ pulled his wallet out and showed his credentials, keeping his thumb over his name and numbers.

Toby smiled. "I give numbers, you call, they tell you nothing. What then?"

Hardy memed, 'Get numbers, we'll run them through NSA database, see what turns up.'

"Give us numbers, we'll decide. Otherwise, you stay here until other arrangements made to ensure cooperation."

"Show me proof of Carmichael in hospital, I give numbers."

TJ pulled up admittance records. Hardy and Jake did also. Hardy excused himself, went down the hall, texting the unit staff to take a picture and forward it with her admittance records. Within minutes he had them and returned, TJ stepped out and took them from him.

"Satisfied?" TJ asked plopping the pages down, spreading them out in front of Toby.

Toby couldn't believe it. Agent Carmichael in hospital bed, tubes and electrodes projecting from her hooked to bags and monitors. "What happen?" he asked letting out the breath he'd been holding.

"She was ambushed while walking along the shore. We weren't certain you and your boatmates weren't involved. She told someone you guys threatened her."

"Why? If these people wanted her dead, she would be. Had many opportunities."

"Let's talk about Miami. What was your connection to Colonel Bolstoy and his Captain Jakovski?"

"Jakovski, former SVR, same as Bolstoy, work as black marketeers. I get to know them, get information, learn about their connections. Many years I work undercover. You show at club, I think you with rival group, perhaps you work for Russians, maybe Mexicans. I fear my cover no longer good, go to Bolstoy tell him he and I in danger. He said he help me get away. He not worried for self. Have connections, good lawyers."

"I contacted controller, he arranged for me go to Bahamas, see Carmichael, told she and another agent were connected to another Russian Oligarch, former FSB. She had not been informed, had not expected me, had no warning. She think I there to attack her and Harper man, she stunned me, Harper man took me hostage. She then talked to our contact. He tell her she and other man, Devereaux, they are to help me escape. She arranged with her Russian. He told her she too must come with me. Devereaux decided to stay behind."

"What was the Palmroys connection to Bolstoy?"

"Help him invest money. Suspect, but could not prove, they help launder his money."

"Who assassinated Bolstoy and Jakovich?"

"Not sure. Hear rumors. He had many enemies."

Jake opened the door.

"Hello Toby, long time no see."

Toby twisted slightly. Jake entered the room. A cautious expression and slight smile passed over his face, then the I'm-sincere mask settled back in. His eyes followed Jake until he was seated. "I hear about Carmichael, must be difficult have two lovers' injured."

Toby's snide remark came with a concerned look. Jake decided not to respond to the comment; he simply nodded. He needed answers, impatience fueled by what he saw from the satellite and drone images concerning Pablo and Gabriel.

"Who decided Devereaux should be the one left behind in the Bahamas, Carmichael or you?"

"Our contact. This was his operation."

"Who is your contact? We would like some verification."

"I cannot give anyone such information."

"Last time I saw you, you said you were going to disappear, maybe get a place on the coast somewhere. How is it you decided to join Dean and his crew?"

Toby smirked. "Your people took them to Guantanamo. I went to Mexico. My control send me there. Dean contacted me through my control--he tell me I must work with them…"

Jake interrupted him, "Miss Carmichael said Renai convinced you to join them, used her feminine charms, was this before or after you went with them to General Toraz' hacienda and met with Major Jenkins?"

TJ stood. Toby jumped up and eased back from the table looking from Jake to TJ.

"You were already working for both sides, weren't you? Mark Poponovich was your other contact, or was it the Russian Pietr Okneyev? You were a double, maybe even a triple agent. That's it, isn't it?"

Toby was stunned, was it possible, how much did they know? From what had been said, someone was talking. None of the others dared say anything. Or had someone broke? He had not told anyone. Only Carmichael and their controller shared information. Was it Carmichael? No. He did not think this true, she not know. They were guessing. Give a little, learn a lot.

TJ saw the hardening. The guy had fallen back on the discipline instilled by his training. When Jake said the two names, Toby had not reacted. Interpol's training was not known to create such hardened discipline. TJ walked away toward the door, then slowly turned to face him, Toby's eyes followed, as he hoped. Jake was watching him also.

"You're Jewish. Dean's crew's Jewish. That's the connection. You were recruited and trained by the Israelis before you became an agent with Interpol, right?" TJ saw the very slight flicker in Toby's eyes. "This whole op was, is an Israeli op. Something went wrong. You let Jenkins get away." No. That wasn't it, TJ realized. He memed this to Jake and Hardy.

Jake had seen the same thing TJ did. Toby's attention shifted to him.

"Not exactly. Jenkins didn't have the intel with him. Renai didn't seduce you, it was mutual. You thought, or she told you, she discovered something when she stayed behind at Toraz' hacienda. She went back looking for my wife Elena, found she disappeared, had left with her father. Suspicion fell on Carmichael. You knew she intended to poison Okneyev. You and the others think she has or knows where the intel is—that she possibly shared with me. What happened to Jenkins?"

Toby shrugged. "You, your wife, your lover Carmichael, perhaps all of you know. Renai say she heard Poponovich say Jenkins have way to communicate through telepathy. That he has what Soviets say make "super soldiers". His source said your government have this capability and that others may have same ability. Carmichael believed this could be true. Not impossible she helped him escape, and she has the intel. Possible Poponovich and others, maybe Dean and crew, maybe it was the Russian Okneyev, who knows who, helped Jenkins off boat. Possible he still alive and has the intel, look to sell to Mexicans; maybe already have sold to or was taken by Russians. I was not on boat when Jenkins disappeared. Others all deny they know anything. This is all I know."

TJ walked back and forth watching, listening, thinking how much was true and what the possible repercussions could be. The one thing he had not heard, was not mentioned the financier.

"Who was financing your op? You went to Bolstoy to warn him, figuring he would try to escape, you knew the Israeli assassins were waiting. The Palmroys were the ones financing the op. They were the ones standing to benefit from Bolstoy's demise. Always follow the money, isn't that right?"

Toby smirked. "Follow the money? Yes. Maybe your government help the Palmroys. Or Okneyev? Perhaps the cartels and their man Poponovich do this, with or without the Palmroys? Perhaps your president's people do this? Perhaps you know and wish to know what we know?"

"Who is we? The paranoid, quick to jump Israelis?"

Toby made no move to reply. They *were* guessing. He felt relief. Put on a puzzled look.

'From my point of view, this is the one common denominator seeming to be in play. Which makes Poponovich, Carmichael and Devereaux the wildcards. All of them point the finger yet provide no proof of what Jenkins final fate was,' Jake memed.

'Dead men rarely leave messages,' TJ memed in reply.

They watched Toby. He was watching them, looking from Jake back and forth to TJ. He shook his head. He seemed to be enjoying himself.

"Better hope someone steps up to ask about you Tobolokov. Otherwise, you will rot in a less hospitable place than here. Maybe you wish to pay a visit to Guantanamo. We have worse places. Perhaps you will wish you had been more forthcoming?" TJ leaned back from the table. He followed Jake to the door and was let out.

Once they joined the others, Jake said, "Seems we need to have a forensics team check out Devereaux' boat. Be great if the same thing had been done on Okneyev's other freighter. I wonder if divers checked Okneyev's sunken freighter. How good is underwater forensic data?"

Hardy: "Already happening. Told them put a rush on. Should have results soon. Okneyev's freighter was previously searched by the Cubans with the Russians assisting. Not sure what they turned up."

TJ: "What about Bolstoy's yacht, the Palmroys' home and business?"

Hardy: "Yacht was gone over by the FBI, I haven't been given the results. As for the Palmroys, not going to happen. No judge would give a search warrant, be political suicide. Even if one did, they've had plenty of time to hide any incriminating evidence. Come on, time's awasting."

They started down the sterile hall which brought them to Boyd's room. Hardy stopped, they all gazed at the monitor. Boyd was staring up at the ceiling monitor, his dark eyes showed no emotion.

"Jake, so far our team hasn't been able to locate your wife, stepdaughter or the boyfriend. The band is supposed to play in Austin, but that's not for several days. The other members of the band weren't very forthcoming, claimed not to know where he went—said they know nothing about the two women."

Thinking about Elena and her old boyfriend remained bothersome for Jake. If only she hadn't been so duplicitous. He and TJ warned her. Despite their warnings, she left in what he now knew was a failed attempt to join up with the backstabbing Limey bugger. The man who fathered their lovechild. She claimed she needed to go to Texas for her father's so-called cancer therapy. The result, she was kidnapped. Jake's and TJ's involvement snowballed because she had not been truthful.

If she had listened, he might not have been coerced into being here. No implant, living his simple life on the farm, doing woodwork, historical restoration, enjoying the seasonal changes. This time of year, a warm, inviting fire in the fireplace, a cognac, glass of wine for her, snuggling, making love by the fire. None of this had to happen—then again, he might never have reunited with Ariel, learned of their love child and grandson.

Jake walked off, turned, came back, eyes forward, speaking his thoughts, "We are wasting time. Boyd's not going to enlighten us. In my opinion, all of them are renegade recruits of Dean's, and he's Poponovich's recruit. Why hasn't anyone called for their release? The Israelis called for the others' release, why not these guys? Either the Israelis are running them as deep undercover infiltrators, or some other group is. Either way my bet is they are on a fishing expedition. If they took Jenkins, he's dead, captive or he escaped. I don't believe he's dead."

Hardy stepped back. The others looked from Jake to him when he started speaking.

"Okay. Let's say your guess is correct. Where has he gone? How and why has he been able to remain invisible, incommunicado?"

"What about General Toraz?" Jake asked. His thoughts wandered--Elena, her father and Tindal—what was the connection to the Mexican Cartel and the Russian Okneyev? Why did Jenkins take Elena, why did she leave with him? Where was she now?

"He's being watched," Hardy said, "physically and technically—every move, every communication. He's being very careful. We're going through channels, asking for permission to talk with him. So far no agreement has been reached. The Mexican government is investigating the discovery of numerous bodies across their northern state, including Paul Alperts. They want to know who the other woman reported with him was, where she is now?"

Jake continued monitoring the video feeds following Pablo and Gabriel. Jake saw Pablo had stopped, he and three of his escorts entered a small open-air marketplace. Two of the men split off, one dropped back, trying unsuccessfully to blend in. Pablo began walking through the small crowd, not doing a very good job of pretending interest in the fruit and vegetables, the cheap souvenirs and clothing displays.

Before he reached the end of one row, a woman dressed in a native colorful long dress appeared. Pablo glanced at her, she seemed to say something, he immediately looked around, she handed him something and walked off. There was something familiar about her.

'TJ, quick check the feed following Pablo. He met with a woman. She handed him something. She's leaving. Did you see her?' The video feed was following Pablo. The woman disappeared.

'Only see Pablo and his men.'

Hardy: 'The satellite images are recorded.'

Jake: 'I captured her image after she handed whatever she handed to Pablo.' Jake shared the photo with TJ and Hardy. 'Doesn't she look familiar TJ?'

TJ: 'Wait a minute.' He zoomed in. Jake and Hardy did the same. 'Kinda looks familiar. At Tindal's, wasn't she down at the hangar talking to one of the Gonzalez brothers' bangers. Yeah, has to be where we saw her.'

Hardy: 'Could be the woman with Alperts and Ariel. The one we were talking about, the one we've been looking for.'

Hardy sent a message to the team following Pablo, 'Did you see the woman talking to Pablo? Is anyone following her?'

Hardy walked off from them. Devereaux, Marge and Jeni had been sent to check on Dean. TJ and Jake remained outside Boyd's room watching the satellite feeds.

Pablo got in the back of one of the vehicles. The windows were darkened. Two of the three vehicles pulled out of the parking area, headed back the way they came. The third vehicle with two men inside remained behind.

CHAPTER
35

Quintana Roo/ Southwest of Cancun, Mexico
Esmeralda and Pablo

Esmeralda was warned by David she was being watched. She wandered around the area of the market, spotted two native Cubans, called Yumas. They were not doing much other than walking around, earbuds in one ear, obviously waiting for someone. David let her know Pablo arrived, the Yumas somehow knew also. She waited until they moved off toward the parking area, then she hurried over to a booth where an Indian-looking woman sold plain guayaberas and colorfully stitched and dyed, full-length skirts. She didn't bother to bargain as was expected. Instead, she paid the amount the woman quoted for the one she chose. She slipped it on over her fashionable athletic blouse, and designer jeans, underneath which was her bathing suit—had to be prepared for whatever opportunity the boy called Gabriel's grandmother and escorts provided her.

She asked the Indian woman in Spanish for a writing utensil, took the pen and wrote on the back of the paper receipt a message to the man Pablo, "You are being watched. Go back to hacienda, will contact you there. Be prepared to transfer half-million US in bit coin for services we do or else." Esmeralda pulled her cap off, pushed her sunglasses up onto her shoulder-length auburn hair and started down the row, watching for anyone watching her. She had no choice, but to hand him the note. Giving it to someone else to deliver was too risky. She watched Pablo enter, his escorts split up. The Yuma's had their eyes on Pablo, trying to look inconspicuous, their attention now divided.

She checked for an easy exit then moved in, handed the note to Pablo, and quickly moved to blend in and escape. No one followed. She ducked behind the Indian woman's booth, slipped the dress off, threw it to the young Indian senorita working with the older woman, hurried back through the greenery to the waiting motorbike and took off to accomplish the next part. She felt pleased with herself. Maybe she go see the blonde foreign lady with her shaved pussy again tonight as promised. Made her wet thinking of this—danger and sex, what she lived for.

She pulled over to text David what she did and get directions to where the boy was headed. David texted to say, 'many friends at aquarium and mall Have jet skis in water. Women look like you, have same clothing, have boys like him with them. Let Yankees follow; let see you have boy."

Esmeralda thought taking the boy was too risky. She told David the Russian Ambassador may be one has boy's mother. We should take boy. Use him to get mother.

David say he think this good idea. The Russians who have daughter, we take boy; make trade; not have to pay them. With boy and mother captive, we send word to Harper man that we have them and he must do what we ask--free Arturo and return stolen files.

Esmeralda used Google Map and chose the shortest route. She took the sim card and battery out, broke the phone apart and tossed it in the underbrush. She made her way to Zona Hotelera, cruised down Boulevard Kulkulcan until she came to Quintana Roo's La Rueda Ferris Wheel at mall La Isla. Soon as she pulled over, one of David's men, who had been told she was near and was waiting, took the bike from her, handed her another phone, a case with a tranquilizer needle and a stun gun then moved off into the traffic. She hoped the supposedly nonlethal weapons do what David promise. Old woman or boy die, make complications, even friendly authorities no like.

She walked toward the Ferris wheel, chose a seat at a table with an umbrella. The temperature had risen, the heat radiated off the sand and concrete in waves. She and David figured the ambassador's wife and party would not spend any more time than necessary exposed to heat or potential threats. They were right.

One big black SUV vehicle came first. Two of Pablo's men got out, looked around, then walked around the area. Maybe they were looking for her? Two more vehicles came not long after, six men, three in each stepped out, looked around, then opened doors. The Ambassador wife and grandson exited a black Mercedes Sedan. Not very discreet. She watched the armed men take strategic spots along the intended route. How stupid of them, Esmeralda thought, all she need do was observe, then move ahead of where their maneuvers indicate. She saw they were headed straight to aquarium. She moved in, the place was not large, easy for her blend with others inside, also, easy cover for boy's people--dangerous, no way can be done here. She watch, wait, think--other woman had said she go to mall, no doubt boy's grandmother go too with boy when leave aquarium. Be best to make move once they exit aquarium. Pablo set trap want Harper man. Esmeralda think wait, use boy as bait—too dangerous making escape with both.

She moved to restroom, went in stall, texted David to go back over plan, make changes. Need men be ready to disable bodyguards. Have some men come in entry to aquarium, stay out of sight behind guards. Have six guards with woman and boy and two of Pablo's who follow me here. They spread out, easy to tell, have weapons. Tell men do not do anything until boy's grandmother and boy are out of aquarium. They must use stun weapons only, no noisy weapons. I will stun woman, take boy, use tranq if have to, then we leave by water. Have other female friends with boys wait out of sight until we stun, come to me, move fast, go in different directions, confuse watchers. She told him, "should wait, not take Harper man."

David say he want both.

She took her bike jacket off and put it in her fashionable backpack along with her boots. She now wore a silky blouse that hung over her jeans and a pair of designer tennis shoes that would help her blend in. She slung the pack over one shoulder, checked herself in the mirror and slipped back out into the growing crowd.

CHAPTER
36

Off Cancun Coast
Coast Guard Captain Conroy

Hardy directed the Major and Devereaux to question Dean. "Have him start from early recruitment. Who, why, where--beginning until now. His role as team leader, his controller, everything about Jenkins. And Devereaux, I expect you to listen to all parts you were involved in. We shall be comparing his version to what you and the others have told us. Harper, Alvarez, and I have other urgent business to attend to. Captain Adams, you need to join the others in the control room helping man the drones. We will all get together and brief each other later."

Hardy hurried back to join Jake and TJ. He had informed the American Ambassador of the situation unfolding at the aquarium, promising to keep him informed. The ambassador suggested sending some marine staff from their nearby embassy, but Hardy said it would be too risky. They both agreed they couldn't take a chance of another bloodbath creating a diplomatic fallout.

He told the ambassador it might be best to have them on standby, just in case. We need to keep this in house sir. We don't need the local authorities or Russians involved." The ambassador didn't like it, but he agreed.

Hardy had been informed by the control room they had located the other satellite which vanished earlier. He instructed them to have Captain Adams take the damn thing out anyway she could.

Jake continued watching the split images. One followed Pablo and two of the three vehicles returned to the hacienda. The other satellite image showed the woman and his grandson on their way, then arriving at the aquarium. The other vehicle which had been with Pablo appeared shortly before the woman's arrival. Two men exited the vehicle and wandered around, trying to seem inconspicuous.

Jake memed TJ, 'I need to find a way out of the compound and get to the aquarium.'

'No way Hardy's goina let you go there. Besides, by the time you got there, they'll most likely be gone.'

Hardy joined them. Jake told Hardy he needed to get there fast.

Hardy picked up on the tail-end of their discussion. "TJ is right Jake, you could never get there in time. Even if you got there, you'd most likely get yourself killed, or, unfortunately, cause your grandson to possibly get caught in the line of fire."

"He's in danger of something happening to him without my being there. I won't stand by and do nothing. I did the analytics. The quickest route is by water. I can be there in under thirty minutes."

"Then what?" Hardy asked. He panned out to get views along the seaboard. After talking to the ambassador, he alerted the Coast Guard; instructed them to wait just offshore. They were on their way. They weren't visible, but he noticed numerous small amphibious craft hovering just offshore. He zoomed in, looked like bangers on jet-skis, same as the ones from the earlier attack.

Jake said, "I can evaluate the situation like I've been trained to do, assess the possibilities and take the best course of action. I cannot just f'ing stand here and do nothing." He started toward the exit they had taken the previous time they had been here. He heard TJ behind him, hurrying to catch up. Hardy shouted out, "hold on."

Hardy sent an order to the Coast Guard to get a boat dispatched to the dock at the Center ASAP. "A boat will be here to pick us up within fifteen minutes. They will have vests and nonlethal tranq weapons, I say again, nonlethal, we cannot create more international diplomatic problems on already strained relations; there are those here in Mexico who want us out. Any lethal action will mean they'll have their way. That won't help us, or, your cause Jake."

"If they take my grandson, they'll have the upper hand. I can't let that happen. I don't intend on turning this into a shootout or a hostage situation. Several things need to happen to prevent this: neutralize her banger friends; isolate and contain her, cut off means of escape. Neutralize her before she does anything to Gabriel."

Jake continued, "We need to have some help on land to contain the inland escape route. We use the boat to cut off any water escape and to eliminate the jet skis. If they have lethal weapons, getting in range with nonlethal weapons is putting us at risk, have you thought about that?"

"The boat is shielded and has a water cannon, shoots a steady stream, or can shoot water balloon-like balls from a pressurized system. The jet skis might be able to outmaneuver us, but that limits their accuracy. We can move in close to shore and use the cannon on the jet skiers and their friends on shore. I will notify the ambassador to send marines in two vehicles to seal off the roadside exit points near the aquarium. Captain Adams and our drone jockeys are authorized to take out any perceived hostile drones in the area. One major problem is the innocents. That bitch banger leader and her people can and probably will use them as shields. If she gets to the mall, things could get out of hand."

TJ had been listening to Hardy and Jake. They were walking down the corridor. He followed them out through the exit and down to the dock. He had been thinking about the distance, the accuracy of the tranq weapons. He knew it wasn't very far which meant he would have to be in a vulnerable area. Meaning he would have to be too close to the bangers' lethal weapons to make the shot to drop the woman with a tranq. If they could somehow pin the bangers down or distract them, maybe he could slip in behind her. Hardy's comment about the drone reminded him of when the drone appeared outside the bathhouse in the Sumter National Forest, where he had taken David Gonzalez when he and Jake had been on the run. That damn sure created a sense of panic—scared the shit out of him.

They stopped when he spoke up, "Hardy how many drones of ours are in the area?"

"Two are in the air, three are on standby at all times. Why?"

"They could be used for diversion, draw their attention to one side or the other. If I could get onshore without being seen, we use the drones as diversions, I might could get in behind her and take her out. Take out the queen, the pawns will be less effective."

"Or they could be like bees and move in to shield the queen," Hardy replied.

"Makes them easy targets if they do," TJ added. "We've got to do like Jake said, isolate and immobilize her."

The dock was made of concrete. Jake felt the vibration of the gentle waves rolling off to the sides, heard the gentle splash against the spotted-algae-slick hull of the small motor-yacht that had once been Thomas Devereaux, which now supposedly belonged to the CIA Counterterrorism Command, which neither confirmed nor denied Mark Poponovich's or the others' membership as agents of the agency.

Jake wanted to go onboard, memories of having been caught napping by Renai back on the Bahamas still resonated. He was denied the privilege. An armed guard sat under its aft awning, trying to keep from nodding off in the gentle sway, the approaching afternoon heat, and the tedium of staring at the same scenery hours on end. Hardy was allowed onboard, went as far as the aft deck while Jake and TJ waited on the dock, each tuned into the video feeds coming from the drones, high overhead at the aquarium.

'Not to worry bro, nothing goina happen to your grandson.'

'There's no way you can guarantee anything. Despite what Hardy or anyone else thinks, I'm going to do whatever I have to. It's time to put an end to the Gonzalez brothers. We should have done this when we had them in our sights back at Tindal's place way back when.'

'I've been reccein' the area. Looks like just south of the park's an inlet. You guys can drop me off there. I'll make my way inland, come out on the other side of the aquarium, slip around through the park where the Ferris wheel is. I can cover both entrances that way. Hopefully put some of the bangers down before they know what hit them.'

'Not you, we. I'm coming with you. No need on me staying on the boat. All I'd be doing is watching and worrying. Not my way of doing things. The guard boys can handle the jet skiers; they don't need me.'

'The J Bros strike again. Soon you goina be with your grandson.'

'Scares the crap out of me. Not the way I'd pick for us to meet.'

Hardy came back off the boat. He had been talking to a man wearing apron, gown, footies, gloves, and a facemask which he removed while they talked.

"Jenkins was definitely onboard at one point. Lots of hair and fiber containing his DNA found onboard. Seems our friends have all been lying to us."

"No big surprise that," TJ said.

"Everyone we've talked to has DNA on there, including you Jake."

"Ditto what TJ said, no surprise."

"Really. All this time, you'd think they'd have gone over that boat making sure it was clean. Don't make sense."

"How you going to make a case from just DNA," Jake said.

"Gives us probable cause. Under the Patriot Act, we can hold them indefinitely," Hardy replied.

They heard the roar of the Coast Guard patrol boat coming into the bay. Captain Conroy was on deck to greet them. TJ was surprised and glad to see him. Hardy and Jake wanted to know how it was they knew each other.

Captain Conroy explained. After he did, he followed with some interesting news.

"Agent Alvarez, you might be interested to know the *BolsToy* has been recommissioned, now called *SwaleMaiden*, flying Swedish colors. Seems an investment group had a controlling interest and took possession of her."

"Let me guess. Investment group's owned by none other than our old friends the Palmroys?"

"Exactomondo. That is why I'm in these waters. I convinced my Commander, by laying out the facts, and with a great deal of help from Agent Swanson before he retired, that the Palmroys were knee deep in what happened earlier on the BolsToy. Among my other duties on my patrols around the Caribbean, I am allowed to keep eyes and ears only on the *BolsToy*; I mean *SwaleMaiden*."

"Another thing, on the way with the Devereaux crew to Guantanamo, I had the fortune to remember you and Agent Swanson were pursuing a Tobias Tobolokov, who, as it so happened was onboard the Devereaux boat. He insinuated the Palmroys may have been responsible for Colonel Bolstoy's and Captain Jokovski's demise. He later denied this, but Agent Swanson used his earlier statement to leverage my continued investigation." He saw the shocked look on TJ's face, the quizzical look on Jake's and the sudden turning of Hardy's head. "I'm surprised no one told you this. I thought that was why I was summoned. The *SwaleMaiden* is lying offshore."

"Not as surprised as I am," TJ replied.

Hardy shook his head. 'Not now,' he memed. Turning to Captain Conroy, who was observing with a questioning look.

Hardy said, "Captain Conroy, I need you to outfit us with armored vests, tranquilizer side arms and stun guns. Your water cannon is in operating condition, am I correct?" Conroy replied in the affirmative. "We're going to the vicinity of the Interactive Aquarium. There are a group of cartel members on jet skis in the water. They are thought to be some of the same group who shot one of our team and a lot of innocent bystanders a couple days ago. I'm sure you heard about that." Again, Conroy responded affirmative. "How long before we can get there?"

Captain Conroy spoke into his collar mic. "Less than twenty minutes. Come on gentlemen, let's get you geared up."

TJ memed Hardy, 'What the fuck? Why haven't you told us about the Palmroys?'

'You had returned to your SWAT team. I figured Swanson told you.'

'Swanson didn't. You would know he didn't. You should've told the team. This is important to the investigation. Here we go again, what else you keeping from us?'

'We'll discuss the reasons once again later. For now, we need to concentrate on this mission.'

Jake memed Hardy telling him his and TJ's plan on conducting the mission. Hardy already knew, started to argue, but since it was Jake's grandson, and he couldn't find fault with their decision he relinquished. He told Captain Conroy the plan.

TJ memed Hardy, 'Didn't tell the Captain, there's to be no lethal action. Guess that applies to only Jake and me?'

Hardy told Captain Conroy there was to be no lethal weapons used against the cartel.

"If we can capture one or two all the better. Our target is a woman onshore, thought to be the ringleader. We believe she is here to kidnap a young boy who is with his grandmother, the Cuban Ambassador to Spain's wife."

"Jake's grandson," TJ added.

Captain Conroy looked at Jake quizzically. He looked like he was in an emotional tornado—anger, determination and fear seemed to be written there. Understandably. Conroy dared not ask how this relationship was possible.

"Don't worry Agent Harper, I have a well-trained crew. We'll do our part."

TJ pulled Captain Conroy aside once they were out of sight of Hardy.

"We going into a maze of shops and shoppers, goina be a big disadvantage armed with nonlethal weapons when the bogies most certainly are not. Do you have any flash charges? We could sure use the diversion."

"Our boat has LRAD, long range acoustical device used to ward off unknowns, but we couldn't use that here, might deafen people, break glass. We do happen to have ultrasonic sound guns, they cause disorientation, nausea; too long exposure can do permanent damage to hearing, even brain damage or death. Their existence is a military secret, developed in response to the attacks made on embassy personnel in Cuba and China not long ago, thought to be by similar weapons. I'm afraid I can't issue those to unauthorized personnel—told to keep them under wraps—emergency use only."

"Whose authorization you need? What 'bout Undersecretary Hardy, could he give the authorization?"

"No time. Would have to go through channels—that takes time," Captain Conroy said. "Sorry Agent Alvarez, after what happened in Miami with Homeland's Agent Swanson having gone over his head, not once but twice, including continued Palmroy surveillance, my commander would make it impossible for any request regarding this mission. Wish I could do more. Afraid I can't."

Jake listened to TJ's and Conroy's conversation with interest. Seemed the mission was weighing on TJ's mind as much as it was on his. Their success depended on surprise and a lot of luck.

"We lose the element of surprise if we put the armored vests over our touristy-looking clothes—makes us stand out, might as well be wearing a sign saying *hey look at me*," Jake said to TJ and the captain.

"I should be able to help with that," Captain Conroy said. He spoke into his mic, a couple clicks later, he nodded his head. "Couple of my men about your size Agent Alvarez have agreed to lend you some of their civvies. Might be a little tight on you on top of the vest, should fit you fine Agent Harper."

He was right about TJ. TJ almost ripped the Parrot head tee when he pulled out on it so the vest seams were less conspicuous. Jake took TJ's button-up flowery shirt he had been wearing instead of the other guardsman's too loud tee.

They were given comm-sets as part of their gear. They didn't need them but couldn't say anything without raising suspicions when they communicated, if need be, with Hardy and the boat. The sets looked like the ones cell phone users wore, so wearing them didn't seem to create an image issue. He heard the hum of the motors change, the boat began to slow, then came to a halt.

They were a quarter mile or so offshore. High-towering condos stood just in from the water. The beachfront was a mosaic of colors and sun lovers in motion. Jake and TJ stood on deck, a rubber dinghy waited their entry, a guardsman seated in the prowl.

"Ensign Kale will take you into shore. A little further away than you asked, better to keep unwanted eyes from seeing you coming. The jet skis are all over, they rent them at several locations, one of which you'll be dropped off at. Undersecretary Hardy and I figured this to be the safest bet. We'll be waiting offshore, trying to pick off perceived targets and waiting to pick you up. Need to get your grandson into international waters as soon as possible. Otherwise, if land is your best escape, the embassy is not far north from the mall. Good luck gentlemen," Captain Conroy saluted them.

Hardy stood grim-faced beside the captain. "Take no unnecessary chances. Better to be safe than put you and Jake's grandson's lives in jeopardy. I'm putting my ass on the line doing this. Don't screw up."

CHAPTER
37

La Isla Amusement Park, Cancun
Gabriel—Jake's grandson

They made it to shore, rented two jet skis, then continued to their planned landing spot without incident. They pulled the machines up onto the dunes, pocketed the keys and went off to their designated locations, each following the other's movements as well as the other parties' positions via Jeni's and fellow joystick pilots' drone cameras and vocal cues. She informed them the opposition's two drones had been forced out of range. "One nosedived into the drink," was gleefully declared. "Good job ace," Jake said, followed by TJ's seconding it.

Once Jake thought he was where he needed to cut in, he found a maze of sorts, provided by the condo's proprietary fencing and keyed entries blocking him, forcing him to retreat to the beach and follow Jeni's directions around and through. At last, he came to a bridge over a mote, apparently, part of the aquarium complex. There were miniature gondoliers in the narrow stream. On each side the curved space was lined with shop signs prominently declaring what could be found beyond the pastel-painted walls. There were people everywhere, moving in, out and through the whole area.

TJ was finding his trek similarly daunting. One thing studying aerial and map views, entirely another when on the ground trying to find your way while dodging other objects and people who were milling around with no set destination in mind. The Ferris wheel was lost from view by the tall buildings, shops, umbrellaed seating areas. The directions he received were about as useful as the views and maps he pulled up in his head. No wonder people got lost or died using these damn software programs. He was keeping time, watching Jake's and his progress, listening to the dronies talk about the whole scene unfolding and trying to keep his implant and physical eyes out for the bangers and their target. Good thing he and Jake were locked and loaded and were veterans at picking out and taking down targets. Been a while for Jake, good thing Gunny at Fort Polk had run them through the refresher course. This was Fallujah in the tropics, just like the Philippines.

'How's it feel being back in action?' he memed Jake.

'Wish I was armed with something more than these things. Going to be tough, I don't know about you outside the Army and all, but, most of my tours were spent covering ass and looking to take out the bad guys permanent like. Course there was that raid we pulled on David Gonzalez' place in NoDa.' There was a pause. 'Too many f'ing people out here. Haven't seen anyone suspicious on my end, how about you?'

TJ saw a non-touristy-looking man leaving the north exit of the aquarium, his head moving slow, eyes sweeping from side to side. He pulled back, scrunching down behind a wave of people. 'Got one, bro. Definitely not dressed for the area, coming out of the north aquarium exit, headed your way. Here comes another. Be ready.'

Events unfolded fast at this point. Two men dressed like locals stepped out from a shop, walking fast toward the aquarium exit. An elegant, elderly lady holding a boy's hand came out with two more guards on each side and two more right behind. The ambassador's wife and Gabriel.

'Got eyes on target. Heavily armed personnel have taken up positions.'

Seemingly out of nowhere three young men and three young girls, who had been laughing and walking nonchalantly along, burst into action. The first two guards were zapped by the first two men TJ saw coming from the shop. The other four guards were reaching for their weapons when the air sizzled with the pulses coming from the other men and girls' stun guns.

TJ next saw their other target exit the aquarium, the Gonzalez' gangbanger bitch. She moved in on the ambassador's wife whose face contorted, attempting to scream, her attempt cut short as her spasming body collapsed to the street. The other woman grabbed the boy and began running away from Jake, who was coming fast. TJ pushed through awestruck by-standers to cut her off. He had his stun gun in one hand and the tranq gun in the other. He fired two pellets, stunning two of the women running behind her. The other girl broke off, two of the men stopped and turned toward TJ. He had to slow down to tranq them. Two more pellets left. He hoped that would be enough.

Jake caught up and stunned the other girl. The woman with Gabriel over her shoulder darted into the crowded mall.

By the time Jake and TJ entered, she seemingly disappeared. They stopped and looked around. "There she is," TJ shouted. They started moving fast pushing their way through the protesting crowd, keeping their eye on her, struggling to get through ahead of them. TJ memed Hardy informing him of their plight. He replied he would notify the marine detachment to move to intercept from the other end.

When they caught up with the other woman and the protesting child, they were shocked. It wasn't them. They were dressed like the banger and Gabriel. They had been led astray. TJ threw quick demanding questions in Spanish to the woman who acted hostile and indifferent. Jake memed Hardy, telling him what happened. Suddenly, Jake caught sight of two other women with boys in their arms going in opposite directions. He grabbed TJ by the arm. 'There and there. Two more.' He pointed them out.

"Go after that one headed toward the beach," he yelled and took off after the other pair headed toward the Ferris wheel. The pair he was chasing seemed not to be in any hurry. He started searching for reasons, checking the crowd surrounding him for potential threats. The woman was headed at an angle away from where she had taken Gabriel and the crowd gathered to gawk at the numerous people sprawled on the sun-dappled hot concrete between the aquarium and the entrance to the mall. Off in the distance, came the sound of approaching sirens, signaling emergency vehicles. No one was paying attention to the woman cradling a child pushing against the gathering throng, nor the American bouncing up and down to keep her in sight.

Jake asked Jeni to get eyes on the woman he was after. "She's veering south of the Ferris wheel, headed toward the highway."

She replied, "We've got eyes on the CG vessel and the attacks by the jet-skiers. Alvarez has requested eyes on the beach area…"

He cut her off, "Get eyes on the two women, TJ's and mine, these are the targets."

Hardy told Jeni to comply with Jake's and TJ's requests. "The guard men have these skiers at bay, acquire and stay with targets."

In less than a minute, Jeni came back saying she was overhead and had both targets in view. Jake turned his efforts to the drone images. Movement to his rear caught his attention, two Hispanic men were closing in on him. He crouched lower and cut to his right to take an oblique angle in the direction his target seemed to be heading. This tactic slowed the pursuers. He zoomed the image out, hoping the woman was headed in the direction of the

Marines—where were they? He memed Hardy asking about the Marines' location.

Hardy memed back, 'The Mexican authorities are on the way, the Ambassador pulled the Marines back to the embassy. Sorry Jake, I've been told we need to disengage. The CG vessel is to pull out as well. Will keep eyes-in-the-sky watching, best I can do. You and TJ must disengage.'

TJ memed, 'Have closed on target. Wasn't them. Jake, headed your way.'

'Got two on my back. Do you see them?'

'Got'em. Will be there quick as I can.'

'Looks like she's headed for the highway. I don't see any vehicles, what could be her plan?'

Jeni brought the other drone into the area up higher to give a broader view, per Hardy's request. "The jet-skiers broke off and the CG patrol boat is headed out to sea," she informed them. "I see no vehicles other than the emergency vehicles making any abnormal moves. Could be any one of the others, but traffic is crawling, wait a minute. On the other side of the highway, in the lagoon—could be that's where she's headed."

Hardy memed, 'Disengage. That's an order.' They ignored him.

"Has to be her," Jake took off staying low, trying not to be too obvious as he pushed his way in, around and through the people. He needed to cut her off.

TJ memed, 'Jake your pursuers are moving toward your target. No way of knowing if they're the Gonzalez' boys or some other hostiles after her and your grandson.'

Jeni's voice sounded in their ears, "warning signal from upper drone, bogey has returned. How should I proceed?"

Hardy ordered her to take out the other drone as quickly as possible.

The higher view disappeared. The other drone images showed the two men closing in on their target. Jake hurried to intercept. The woman was crossing Kulkulcan Boulevard. Jake reached it further up. There was no way he would get to her before they did. TJ was several minutes distant.

The other drone view returned. There was a small motorboat and two jet skis on shore, two other men headed toward her. One took the boy, they were joined by the other two and they hurried, but not too fast to the boats. The only course of action was to pursue them by water. Jake saw there were several other jet skis on shore near him. He ran to the nearest one. When the people gathered on shore saw the stun gun pointed at them, followed by his demand in English and gestures, one of them nodded and threw him a key and pointed to a large newer model. It fired right up. The tank level on the panel registered half, he hoped that would be enough. He backed out, swung around, and began the pursuit.

TJ memed, 'Hey bro, this is a bad idea, five against one, they don't stand a chance.'

Hardy ordered him to break off. 'We can follow them via aerial recon.'

Jake didn't reply. The boat and two skis seemed not to be in a big hurry. He felt certain they knew he was behind them—an ambush. No matter, they had his grandson, aerial views had their limitations, if taking him was their intention, at least TJ and Hardy would know where he was and what they were up to—saving Gabriel was why he was here, even if it was the last thing he ever did.

CHAPTER
38

Laguna Nicupte, Cancun
Jake's grandson Gabriel

Esmeralda heard the excitement in cousin David's voice when she told him the Harper man was following them across Laguna Nichupte. He told her his men waited at the El Centro Park area. They decided to let the Harper man follow; come to them. An appropriated taxi waited with more men on shore.

Jake memed TJ asking if he thought he could get to the other side of the lagoon to intercept them?

'Have to follow by water bro. Traffic too slow. Emergency vehicles and the authorities sealed the place off. Am a few minutes behind you. You know, this probably a trap. Hardy's not happy.'

'Tough shit. You don't have to do this, lag back. Jeni can track me and them. You can be the cavalry.'

'With what bro? Stun guns and tranqs against armed overwhelming numbers of bangers? This a suicide mission.'

'I have to do this, you don't.'

"Screw you, bro. Deane would kill me, that's if the bangers don't. Best plan, don't let them take you in the first place.'

'They know I'm here. She's not in any hurry. Which means she's calling the shots or following someone else's orders. Either way, I have to play the hand I'm dealt.'

TJ was quiet. He began calculating using the images, time, distance—good thing he conquered his fear of water—his SEAL buddy had been harsh—put him through it. He opened the jet ski full throttle.

'I did the analytics bro. Go all out—we can overtake them before they reach shore. These jet skis are faster than her boat. We take out the two banger escorts and cut her off. If you let her reach shore, they have control—that banger puke Gonzalez knows we're watching—doesn't make sense—has to be a trick. Think about it.'

'She has my grandson. No telling what that crazy bitch might do.'

TJ was gaining on them. Jake was thinking with emotion, not logistically. 'They need him alive, otherwise he'd be dead. Think Jake. He's bait—bait for who? –You--Damnit. Don't make me have to do the op without you.'

Jake saw the overhead visual. Maybe TJ was right. He opened his throttle--full tilt boogie. God, I hope this works. He had cut the distance in half before the bangers reacted. He saw her waving to the other bangers, pointing back. The boat picked up speed; TJ was closer; the other jet skiers were swinging around.

'I'll take the one on the left,' Jake memed . He remained steady on his course. Let the banger come to TJ. The boat was his concern. He was slowly gaining on it.

TJ decided the tranq was the safest bet out here on the water. He memed Jake even though he felt Jake would know this. His intended target was coming straight at him. Come on mother. Wanta play chicken. Two hundred yards, closing fast, he saw the gun, he began zig zagging erratically. One hundred—the banger fired; he heard the ping somewhere on his ski. He ducked down, hugging the ski, his body and head off to the right side, his right hand holding the throttle, his left hand cradling the tranq against his thigh. The banger began opening fire—the windscreen exploded, TJ felt the tug on the back of his vest as the rounds stitched a path, ripping the borrowed shirt which began flapping in the breeze. Ten yards, he swung the jet ski sharply to the right, then hard left bringing him around directly in line with the side of the banger's ski. His tranq caught the banger in the thigh, which caused the banger's shots to fly wide. TJ veered right just missing colliding into the side of the banger's ski. He swung back onto course, staying low, hoping the tranquilizer worked its magic fast. He watched Jake. Jeni had zoomed in on the action.

Jake saw the banger raise his weapon. He ducked down as the shots tracked toward him. He veered right, then cut back sharp left, raising his tranq gun so the banger could see it. The banger reacted the way Jake hoped by swinging off course, throwing his ski into an uncontrollable slide, causing him to have to throttle back to keep from going over, giving Jake the chance to close in. The banger realized his mistake too late. He was swinging around with his weapon, his round, dark face's snarl turned to shock when Jake shot him in the neck. He reached for the dart, Jake banged into him, wrenched the gun from his grasp pulling him off-balance into the water as he throttled onward. TJ was close enough for Jake to hear him shout, "Alright. Let's go git the bitch.'

'We've got to cut her off,' TJ memed, 'it's going to be close.'

Jake: 'The other two bangers with her have weapons. Come alongside, get the one I took. You're a better shot.'

Jake slowed slightly. TJ came close enough for the handoff.

TJ memed, 'I know. You want me to be the one gets in the shits with Hardy. He's already pissed.'

'So, what's new? We told him if we had to, we'd defend ourselves. This is a had to in my book. You got a problem, give me the damn thing back.'

TJ shot him the bird.

'I'll go left to draw their attention. If we're right, they want me alive— hopefully. See if you can go around, get in front of them without getting shot, take out the female if you can.'

Jake planned to divide the two male bangers' attention. Give TJ a chance to get a shot. He swung out left, far enough to make hitting him with their handguns problematic.

Jeni had the aerial view locked in on them. Jake was startled when out of nowhere another drone appeared coming toward the front of the boat on a collision course. The female banger had been looking from side to side trying to keep an eye on them, her head whipped to the front, the boat veered right. For one horrifying moment Jake thought the drone intended to pull a kamikaze. It swooped skyward at the last possible second. This gave Jake and TJ the cover they needed. Jake steered in from the left just as TJ seized the opportunity to close in and tranq the female. The two male bangers, who had thrown themselves down were rising to their feet when the boat swerved sideways as the female collapsed onto the steering wheel. They were thrown off-balance--one went overboard, Jake shot the other with a tranq. He maneuvered in close, jumped onboard, his jet ski slammed into the side of the spinning boat. Jake rolled on the bottom, grabbed a seat, crawled forward, and pulled the throttle lever back to idle.

Jake engaged his mic. "Thanks Jeni. I owe you big time."

"Better believe it hotshot. Hardy says wait out there while the Mexican authorities round up the bangers. He's called for a chopper to get you guys out of there. Hang tight."

"Roger that."

Gabriel was nowhere to be seen. TJ pulled next to the banger who went overboard, tranqed him, held him by his collar, came alongside the boat, where Jake helped him pull the banger onboard. He tied the jet ski off and joined Jake in a search for his grandson. TJ found him in a compartment huddled beneath life preservers. He stared at them wide-eyed like they were monsters from another dimension. TJ pulled him to his feet and began speaking to him in Spanish, saying words of comfort, telling him they were the good guys. Jake caught the gist of it. He could see Gabriel was not convinced.

"Tell him I'm his mother's real father. That we will take him to her."

To their astonishment, Gabriel knew English. He looked at Jake and shook his head. "You not my poppie. I want my papa."

'Any ideas poppie?' TJ memed.

"Gabriel, I know you have no reason to believe me. Your mother will explain when you see her. Soon a helicopter will come to get us. You ever been in a helicopter?"

Gabriel started looking around. He fixed his eyes on the female who had attempted to kidnap him. "She hurt my mamere. She stick me, make me sleep." He watched TJ drag her back to the male banger. "Is she dead?"

"No. They asleep like you were. Soon they wake up. We take them to jail."

"Are you police?"

"Something like that," Jake replied. He squatted down so he was more on Gabriel's level. Gabriel looked a lot like his father. He could see some traits of Elizabeth and Ariel, nothing resembling his immediate side of the family tree, other than hazel blue eyes, picking up the color of the lagoon. But, nothing definitive there, Ariel's eyes were the same color. He wished she was here. God, he missed her. Soon he hoped they would all be together. He needed to find Elizabeth. Why had no one contacted him? Using Gabriel against Pablo was not something he liked to think about, but it seemed to be the only available option. First, he had to get him somewhere safe, keep him away from the ambassadors—Cuban, Russian and, went without saying, the American Ambassador. Hardy was not going to want this. Too bad.

"Want to drive the boat?" Jake asked him.

Gabriel nodded.

"You can sit on my lap. We'll ride around and get the other bad guys. You can be our deputy."

He memed Hardy. They argued about the legalities and repercussions of keeping Gabriel away from his father and ambassador grandparents.

JT, Jake, Gabriel, and Esmeralda were taken onboard the helicopter. The banger men were left in the boat. TJ disabled it. The one Jake took the revolver from had drowned, the other three were alive, left for the authorities which were notified through channels, to avoid any direct connection to the Americans. They landed at Tulum Naval Air Base and were whisked away in a nondescript van to the Control Center where an angry Hardy waited.

CHAPTER
39

Quintana Roo
David Gonzalez

David Gonzalez' failed attempts to reach Essie infuriated him. His men on shore notified him she was taken away in a helicopter, along with the boy, the Harper man, and the Alvarez man. His uncle to come to Cancun with president to attend gala. Uncle expect him have problems taken care of before he come.

David quivered, thinking what happen when uncle find out Essie also in American hands.

Essie tell him about woman she meet at beach bar. She think woman know DICE man. Arturo told him about DICE man. He was to contact this man. David forgot when everything happened. David had to look, finally found phone number.

Suzie, the bleach blonde agent, did not recognize the number. She had given her number to her contact who said he gave it to Esmeralda's cousin. Suzie wasn't surprised when Esmeralda showed up at the Tiki bar. She recognized her from the online bio photo. Suzie wondered if Esmeralda knew about her and traced her from her phone. No matter. The evening was enjoyable. They traded phone numbers. Suzie had not expected her to call. She connected and didn't say anything. A Hispanic man hesitated then said he need talk to Gerald. She thought this must be Esmeralda's cousin. She told him, "You must have wrong number." She waited for him to repeat the name and number that he was supposed to recite.

David paused. He saw a name and number written at the bottom of the note his brother gave him. He asked if this was Jackie 8882252200?

She disconnected and called him back on another phone.

"You must be Esmeralda's other cousin David?"

"Yes. We wish to make deal. We want Pablo's wife. Uncle say you know who have her."

Tomorrow night, you name time and place."

"Ten. He gave her coordinates for the meeting."

"If agreeable, I call you back. You have scrambler?"

"Yes."

"You say Romeo, if all clear, we talk terms."

"Suzie" punched the speed dial number for Terrence the agent Alperts left behind in South Carolina. "He called her back. Have you been able to locate her?" she asked him.

"Not certain. Our man thought they were Russian. Street surveillance cameras had a picture of the license plate. Rented to a shell company, other surveillance showed it went to a boat, reported somewhere in the Caribbean, been moving around is what was said. Last location, somewhere off the Bay of Campeche. There's a tropical storm forming, makes pinpointing difficult. Tindal is getting restless. He may have found out about Alperts' demise. Any word on Jenkins?"

"No. Homeland has most of the players under wraps. This woman Elizabeth is our best hope."

"Don't see anything can be done until I can get a fix on her. Even then, could be a bust. Depends on who has her."

"I heard something about a gala event to take place down here, being sponsored by some big off-planet mining startup, New Dawn Intergalactic Industries something or other. Lots of movers and shakers supposed to be attending. You heard anything about this?"

"Tindal, Colonel Hunter and his new COO were invited, plan to attend. Thought I should head that way. No telling what it's all about. Could be useful. What you going to tell the Gonzalez man?"

"I'll use the storm as an excuse. He wouldn't have come to me if he had an alternative. The whore-dyke said something about her uncle, my target, coming here. We need to see what we can pick up about that. Could be he's going to be attending this gala. Need to get our hands on the guest list."

"I'll see what I can find out. I'll let you know my itinerary."

David Gonzalez was worried. He received call from the woman. She talk quick say no meeting due to big storm coming. What storm have to do with meeting. She not say. Not answer questions. Say she call back. Disconnect call. To him, he think this mean Pablo's woman on boat. He looked at screen, saw storm, saw many boats head to safety. She say nothing be done--maybe this not so. Must stay with plan, tell Pablo have wife and son, have him pay, then hold him, let uncle decide what to do with him. David wondered why uncle not ask about Arturo or Essie. This worry him.

CHAPTER
40

HS Control Center, Akumal
Jake, TJ and Hardy

Hardy tried hard to control his anger. Jake had come close to jeopardizing the whole operation. He had to admit Jake and TJ had performed admirably, adapting using nonlethal actions--with the exception of one casualty. The secretary had been informed. His ears stung from having been dressed down. He was told the committee toyed with the idea of shutting Jake down. Had either Jake or TJ fallen into the cartel's hands, they certainly would have been in favor of taking drastic measures—the whole experiment would have been shelved.

Not until the op is over. Or would they? he asked his implant. No reply.

He needed to push these two to explore all the capabilities of the implant, but they must follow orders, prove to the naysayers how valuable the hardware was. It was now, or possibly never.

The Major and Devereaux went with control's security to lock down the burr-headed female banger, looked like traces of Indian bloodline in her facial features. Even though she was still under the influence of the tranquilizer, her half-shut eyes flashed raw, aggressive hatred toward them.

Hardy tasked Jeni with being responsible for Jake's grandson—after all, she was a mother. The boy seemed to be in shock, Jake seemed to be ignoring the signs—his new-found, overly-protective grandfatherly reactions not quite up to the instinctive parental level. Hardy recalled Jake's lack of parental skills. He had been an absentee parent who struggled with the guilt of never having a close relationship with his children. He hated that Jake might not make his son's wedding—another layer of remorse added to Jake's burden.

Jake resisted Hardy's request. He didn't believe he should trust anyone. This was reinforced by the earlier admonition to Jake. The ambassador was adamant, the boy must be returned to his father.

TJ was siding with Jake. This posed a greater dilemma, would he once more put duty ahead of his personal friendship with Jake?

Hardy was sympathetic. On a personal level, he felt Jake's pain. Personal had little to do with this. They all had to follow orders.

Jake argued that having his grandson was the best way to get the boy's father to admit his complicity in his wife's disappearance which increased the odds of finding her.

Madame Secretary had been blunt with Hardy—"Homeland and the State Department are no longer looking into her disappearance. You must keep this op on track. The gala event is the top priority. Sec Def and The Secretary of State are scheduled to attend, even though I tried to dissuade them. Their security and the security of other dignitaries and celebrities were to be ensured--there can be no distractions—no foul-ups, are we clear on this?"

"Yes Ma'am." Hardy wondered why she never asked or mentioned anything about Poponovich's CIA team. Did she know? If not, why not? Why would the task force wish to keep them separate? Seemed counterproductive.

This news from Madame Secretary created a logistical nightmare—threatened the op. He would need Jake and TJ, along with the rest of their team to concentrate on the mission, namely, counter-threat management. Their adversaries, the targets, would be in attendance along with other possibles. There was no room for Jake's personal mission—no distractions would be allowed. DHS's Secretary said, the daughter/mother/wife was thought to be like Jenkins, dead or in the hands of some very bad actors. Her orders were, "there will be no diverting resources, op time away from Jenkins and the national security threat. Period."

Time to push the envelope, get them up to speed using the implant's capabilities—explore the boundaries—take it to its limits—stay non-lethal. He ran through his implant-aided memory bank protocols. This was the put up or shut up operational command time. He knew Jake and TJ would resent the fact all lethal weapons would be in the hands of the joint US Marshals, Secret Service and Mexican Federal Police, Navy and National Guard elements.

"**T**his is bullshit," Jake said, jerking around to face Hardy. He and TJ had entered a small office situated next to the control room. Jeni had taken his grandson to tour the room at Hardy's behest.

"I'm not letting my grandson's asshole father, or his family, take Gabriel anywhere? You heard, you know, that mother is complicit in his mother Elizabeth's disappearance. Little doubt, the ambassador and his wife knew all about this. I don't like using Gabriel as a pawn, but he wants his mother, needs his mother, and by god, I will do whatever I have to to make that happen. So, screw you and Madame Secretary and all the other bureaucratic mothers. Best you don't try to stand in my way."

"They'll shut you down. I can't do anything to stop this from happening if you don't comply."

"Hardy, sir" TJ cut in, "Don't see why you can't stall them until the gala. Tell the ambassador Jake will bring him to them afterwards." Jake started to interrupt. TJ held up his hand to halt the interruption. "This buy us time to do our own investigating." Hardy had memed TJ about the upgrades to the implant and his demand they explore all its capabilities. "Tell Jake what you told me," TJ said. "Hear him out Jake before you go off the rails any further?"

"No, TJ, open your eyes. Did you not hear what he said, they will shut me down. *They* TJ. Our fearless leader here is not in charge, *they* are. Now Hardy, care to explain who *they* really are? And, don't go into that let me explain how this shit works and why we were chosen bullshit again. I don't give a damn. If anything happens to my family, I will find out who *they* are. Let them try to stop me."

Hardy looked quizzically at Jake. Shook his head.

"Those faceless mothers only care about the op. *They* could give a damn about me or my family. I'm an experiment, an investment. We all are. I got hooked-in for fear of losing my farm. The farm. My security blanket, my refuge, for what? An injury I received doing my duty which *they* refused to pay for, so they could keep me under their thumb. Was my service career and, that farm worth the price of two failed marriages, children who hardly know or give a shit about me, and, the love of my life lying at death's door, our daughter missing perhaps dead. Yeah, I read your mind. Now, *they* want me to turn my grandson back over to those responsible for my personal problems. Enough is enough. Shut me down then damnit, go ahead mothers if you're listening, do it."

TJ and Hardy stood motionless, staring at Jake's rage-infused face.

"Guess they're not so powerful after all. Here's what I'm going to do. I'm going to go in there with that banger bitch, she is going to tell me what she knows about where Elizabeth is. I want drugs. If that doesn't work, I'm going to do whatever I have to. She's going to talk." Jake looked hard at Hardy. "The only way you're going to stop me is kill me. Do anything else and I will come after you and those faceless mothers from now until I *am* dead. In case you think I'm bluffing, you and they will find out how wrong you are. My implant recorded everything. It has been downloaded to an encrypted file on the dark web, in an infinite flux. Anything happens to me or my implant, any attempt to recover it will result in its release to every major news organization the world over. I gave my all for duty, honor, and country. Seems the ones calling the shots have their own personal agendas—rules don't apply to them. I'm through being screwed over. This time my family comes first."

Hardy had summoned two security personnel in case Jake grew violent. They were approaching the office door. He motioned for them to wait. Jake and TJ followed his attention. He saw them both tense up, he had to keep this from getting out of hand.

"I'm needed elsewhere. We'll continue this conversation when I return. Jake. On one point I agree, we will interrogate the female. You two talk about the interrogation. I shouldn't be long."

Hardy had not expected this. Jake had been listening to what he said about the implant's recording ability. Pushing him to explore the implant's possibilities seemed to be unnecessary. Could the implant's primary directive be overridden, compromised?

Hardy recalled what Dr. Perkins said about the implant: the implant/brain interface was often at odds with itself. The implant used deductive logic, whereas the subject brain often used inductive or abductive reasoning, leading to emotional responses, which the implant might struggle to understand. The result of the subject being at odds with his implant, would delay the implant's ability to bond, nevertheless, the implant would perform subject's commands, while continuing its deductive programming algorithms, which included performing its function of informing the subject of all possibilities.

Jake's implant had known of the recording function and responded to Jake's curiosity after hearing him tell Jake of the possibility. Jake's actions would be considered treasonous. The penalty…Jake knew the penalty, they all did. Hardy asked his implant, *have all our actions and thoughts been recorded and stored from the beginning?* The answer was yes. Damn. *Does the newest upgrade allow privacy, prevent hacking?* No response. *Can you be turned off?* No response. He told his implant to contact Dr. Perkins.

Hardy memed TJ, 'Talk to Jake, try to reason with him, he's putting himself in danger. Keep him there until I return.' He hoped if Jake intercepted the meme that TJ could handle him.

Hardy posted the security men at the command control door out of the monitor's, Jake's, and TJ's sight, directing them to contact him if Jake or TJ left the office. He turned to go down the corridor to have privacy for talking to Dr. Perkins. An aide approached from the control command center with a memo—a major overhaul had taken place in Washington. Secretaries of Defense and Homeland Security had been ousted. Homeland's Acting Secretary was former CIA Director, General James McDab. Uh oh, this could be a problem for this team, McDab had been former head of the Clandestine Unit of the CIA, Poponovich's probable former boss. If what he surmised about Poponovich was correct, this could spell problems for the op and the upcoming gala event. This would not help with Jake's situation either. He thanked the aide. Perkins came online and gave him a number where he could be reached.

"I guess you heard about the change in command," Hardy said once greetings were exchanged."

"I'm afraid so. At the same time, I was informed by Colonel Hunter that my former boss and colleague Dr. Lisa Guthridge, the new COO of Tindal Industries, is once more in the driver's seat on your end. Thurmond Tindal, successfully wielded his political muscle and has once more been awarded control of his projects, pending future legal and departmental hearings."

"The upgrades you promised have not been received. Does this change have anything to do with this?"

"I am not able to answer any questions at this time, all inquiries are to be directed to Homeland's General McDab. You can check with Dr. Guthridge she may be able to tell you more."

"Give me the number where I can reach her."

CHAPTER
41

York County, SC, USA
Dr. Lisa Guthridge Neuroscientist, CIA

Dr. Lisa Guthridge stood on the landing of Tindal's estate. She stared at the ghastly demolition taking place across the river. The last rays of sunlight, like fiery daggers, pierced the remaining trees, as if a mythic creature threw them from the clouds on the horizon down across the murky brackish Broad River, ripping and tearing, leaving a swath of destruction behind. The sounds were dying. Day after day, these manmade creatures, with their droning roar, brought trees crashing, the noisy last breaths of the once verdant hillside. The earth being shaved and shaped to make way for the foundation of Colonel Tindal's manufacturing facility. The new Pinckneyville, once a historic colonial county seat--no more. Tindal's wannabe namesake was rising up from the ruins. A monument to his hoped-for, modern-day empire. It was Dr. Perkins and her research and development which made it possible. Like the hillside destruction, she too was a victim of their creations' successes.

The headaches, created by Dr. Perkins' implant activation would soon pass. What the implant meant for her future was no longer certain.

She watched the two Colonels, Tindal and Hunter as their plane taxied for takeoff, headed to Washington to join a team of attorneys in a meeting with a committee and the newly appointed heads of the agencies and their micromanaging leader, and a select group of investors whose interests coincided with their own.

Thurmond Tindal had persuaded DARPA's Colonel Hunter to come onboard after these same attorneys successfully argued their case before a sympathetic federal judge. Due to observation and what she read between the lines from thumb drives containing notes Jenkins failed to take with him, and the FBI failed to discover, and left behind after Tindal's arrest and Jenkins' disappearance, leading her to believe under-the-table deposits to unadvertised board members' personal offshore accounts and continued campaign donations to influential government officials, had gone a long way toward making this possible. Colonel Hunter's change of heart was blackmail. She had seen copies of the recorded spyware evidence after Jenkin's flight, which had been most certainly shared with Colonel Tindal, detailing prearranged extramarital affairs which, no doubt, Tindal used to persuade him to come on board. Hunter looked at her in ways which made her skin crawl. Her rebuffs had amused, then angered him. Not a wholesome environment to work within. On this they agreed.

Colonel Hunter informed her that he and Tindal knew she placed the implant in Major Jenkins' head, and, that she and Perkins had done the same for the Homeland Security team members, including Jake Harper. This put her and Dr. Perkins in the precarious situation of being included in Colonel Tindal's impending lawsuit against the government for illegal seizure and use of property without due process. Dr. Perkins was given the choice, work as part of Tindal's team or be sued. Lisa was given the choice to sign a long-term contract with an extensive non-compete clause and submit to having the implant placed in her own head.

Made her feel dirty. She was a scientist. Her father had been a noncom, killed in the first Gulf War. She remembered him as a good man, a good husband, a good father, a good citizen soldier. He had joined the National Guard to pay for her education—it cost him his life. The implants, the Hive and Bumblebees were developed in hopes of making warfare more civilized, help secure the borders without a damn wall. She had been naïve. After Tindal bought the company and her services, she questioned her own motives. The shooting of the Harper man's dog and the subsequent cover-up woke her up, she realized Tindal and Jenkins were evil, self-serving jerks that had to be stopped. Along came Mark, she thought of him as her savior. Now, she wasn't so sure. She had to do something to get her feel-good back. She was making changes to the device. Changes only she and her team knew anything about.

She dreaded the upcoming gala event she would be attending along with Tindal, perhaps Colonel Hunter, and the newly appointed Homeland Security Acting Secretary, once her former boss at the CIA, General McDab. The Secretary of State and many political and social celebrities would be there, potential investors in the start-up New Dawn Intergalactic Industries, many of them backers of the former president's newly-formed Space Force. Some had preferred it to be a separate military entity, not part of the USAF. The former Secretary of Homeland Security had proposed Undersecretary of HSI, Robert Hardy become the leader of a Space Force Cyber Intelligence Strike Force Unit. Tindal and Colonel Hunter needed to know if he could be trusted. Talking to him was a priority; why her implant was activated; why they were sending her to Cancun.

Lisa's implant would serve as a way of penetrating Hardy's team's thoughts—a form of interrogation never used before. She would not only be checking Hardy out, but she would also be doing scientific research: observing the other implant recipients, interviewing them, finding out how well the implant performed, checking for any deficiencies, see if it was doing what was intended. Information she had regrettably been deprived of before becoming her own altered-version recipient. Personally, she hoped to learn of where Mark Poponovich was; that is, if he was still alive.

Her thoughts went back to an earlier conversation with the new DHS Acting Secretary, General McDab. Their conversation had been brief. He needed to know who knew what concerning Operation Pink Flamingo. Strangely, he was not willing to talk about Mark and his crew, no mention of the implant. Made her wonder how much he knew about her relationship with his former agency and Mark? Why did he ask her to gather information about an op she had peripherally been involved with? She was a scientist, not an undercover investigator.

Her phone vibrated. It was Hardy. Dr. Perkins told her to expect the call.

"Hello Director Hardy."

"Undersecretary, unless you know something I don't. I'd rather dispense with formalities, call me Bob or Hardy, Dr. Guthridge."

"How about you call me Lisa, Bob. Sorry about my confusion. Anyway, I'm guessing your call has something to do with the recent changes in Washington. I'm afraid there has been another. The Head of Border Security and Protection has resigned over the border issues."

"Not why I called Lisa. Congratulations, by the way, I'm sure you are happy to have your pet projects back. I have questions about the NM0099."

"I have been working with Dr. Perkins on the implant, surreptitiously, few people know, so please do not mention this to anyone, might not go over very well with certain parties."

"Your boss Thurmond Tindal, does he know?"

"Not that he has said. Colonel Hunter knows. He is now the Project Director for Tindal Industries. I would not be surprised if he hasn't discussed his knowledge with Colonel Tindal."

Hardy wondered if Dr. Guthridge was in the loop, if not, why not?

"Then perhaps you can tell me what happened to the on/off command for the implant? Does the changeover have anything to do with this?"

"Yes and no," she lied--not sure why she did. "I'm afraid Dr. Perkins and I were premature with our announcement. Colonel Hunter's departure from DARPA and Tindal Industries reacquiring control of their property has caused a delay in the government approval. Since you and the other recipients are government employees, you are part and parcel of the approval process. Which means, you are to be subjected to a scientific review process conducted by Dr. Perkins and myself. Colonel Tindal, Colonel Hunter and a group of attorneys are on their way to Washington to meet with the oversight committee. They will decide how this quasi-public-private venture will continue. I have been given the go-ahead to investigate and review the implant's impact. To that end Dr. Perkins and I will be coming to Cancun. Our flight is scheduled for tomorrow. We will be there midmorning."

"There is a gala event planned to take place this coming weekend. We will be terribly busy setting up security. I'm not sure how much time we will have for a sit-down with you. Perhaps it would be better for this review to be conducted next week."

"Your new secretary set the schedule, not me. Like you, I do as I'm told." Lisa decided not to tell him she was coming there to check on Mark and help with cleaning up after Operation Pink Flamingo.

"This is a logistical nightmare for us. I hope you will not make it worse." Hardy's dealing with Jake just became even more of a major problem.

"I'll try not to get in your way. This will give me a chance to evaluate the implant's use in a real-time situation. See you tomorrow." She cut the call.

Should she have disclosed her having the implant to him? She wasn't sure whom she could trust. She wasn't sure what affect her withholding her implant's involvement in the investigation would have? There was one other nagging thought, where was Mark?

CHAPTER

42

HS Control Center, Akumal
Jake

His grandson reminded Jake of Ariel. How beautiful she had been and still was despite the years, seeing how much of her was in his and her missing daughter; the product of their youthful lovemaking--the secret she had lived with all these years. The longing feelings were achingly real. Thinking of her lying in a hospital, far from him, needing her, needing to be there, for her, for him, for a chance at being a part of a family. He owed her, them, not anyone or anything else.

His implant was directed to do a search based upon all possibilities, correlating the bits and pieces from all sources, looking for Elizabeth. Suddenly, a strange mechanical voice echoed in his head: *Searching.*

What the f'?

I am It, verbalizing communication.

Jake clutched his head. His head hurt. The voice was in his head. What's going on. Stop. Get out of my head. The walls started closing in on him. Was this device causing him to hallucinate? Was it retriggering trips from his youthful experiments with LSD and mushrooms? He had laughed at those. This wasn't funny. TJ reached out to grab Jake's arms. This startled him. He threw up his hands, deflecting his attempt. "To hell with this," he yelled.

TJ saw the far-off look in his eyes, battle fatigue. He was zoning out.

"Whoa bro, you losing it, get ahold of yourself. Don't go there. You will be brought up on charges. They'll lock you up and throw away the key."

"And I'll do what I threatened," Jake said more forcefully than he intended. He shook his head. The voice was no longer there. The pain subsided. He still felt panicked, worried the voice might invade his thoughts once more. Had it drug up tripping memories? Was that what caused this voice inside his head? Or was it them? Was this the beginning of reprogramming him? Shutting him down like Hardy threatened. Is this how it started? He stood up and began pacing.

"Here we go again. You heard Hardy. They'll shut you down. You can't win. They'll do what they threatened to do with your grandson, you'll never meet your daughter or see Ariel again. Think what might happen to Ariel if they stop funding her recovery. You would lose everything. Your farm, I know you didn't mean it when you said you didn't care. And me, I might never see you again. Maybe that's no big loss for you, but it damn sure would be bad news for me, and Deane. All eyes would be on me, I'd have no one to point my finger at. Three hots and a cot, that what you want? Think bro, no pussy. You wouldn't be able to survive." TJ thinking, he's getting' worse. Does the implant have anything to do with it? He hoped not. Hardy better wizen up.

"Just shut the hell up, TJ. Okay?"

"Come on, bro. You got to lighten up. Hardy's following orders. Like you said there is the "they". Whoever the hell "they" are, they own us. No different from the military. Stick with it. I don't want to do this without you. We'll find your daughter, then you'll feel better. Don't throw your life away. I don't know what else to say."

"I do," Hardy said coming back into the room, hearing TJ's last plea.

Jake shook his head, pushed by TJ, then Hardy. "Screw this, I got to get out of here, I need fresh air." He went charging down the corridor toward the exit. They followed him, the security people in tow.

Hardy called out, "the doors are all locked Jake."

Jake hit the burglar-bar on the door to the dock area. Locked. He hurried on by to the parking lot exit. Locked. He was trapped, outnumbered. They stopped several feet away. The security people had tasers drawn, tried to go past TJ and Hardy. Hardy held up his hand, ordered them to stand down.

TJ took a step forward, hands spread in a beseeching manner. He had never seen Jake have a panic attack. The look in Jake's eyes was that of a caged animal. He turned back to Hardy and the security people. "He needs fresh air."

Hardy nodded. "We'll go out back, down to the dock. How about that Jake?" Hardy turned to the security guys, "Follow me."

They went back up the hall, Hardy had the security men deactivate the lock. They stepped outside. Hardy told the men to move off and wait for his directions.

"Give us space. Don't act threatening."

"Come on bro, let's go down to the dock. I got your back, nobody's going to screw with us, we're the J'bros."

Jake didn't know what to think. This had never happened to him, not in combat, not when Joanna took the kids, not even Ariel's or Blakely's near-death events. The visitations of ghosts never shocked him, but that voice, this was different. Was this really the implant, had this implant somehow retriggered a forgotten schizophrenic bad trip? Had Elena been right about him having PTSD? What else could this possibly be?

He followed TJ up the corridor, out the exit and down to the dock. A tropical storm approached; the smell of humid tropical air made for instant discomfort. The guards caught the wind-swept door, keeping it from smashing back into them. Hardy stayed several paces back. Jake and TJ went out onto the dock and sat down. Jake slipped off his shoes.

The water was warm, almost hot. The wind gusted, pushed clusters of the red tide, the mass, looking like vomited Aruga, swirled back and forth. A distant memory of news reports of a growing mass of red tide reaching across the Atlantic, once sensational, now... He needed to keep his thoughts neutral, hoping the voice was no longer there. Jake looked at *Dev'sDelight*. The guard was no longer in sight. He thought about stealing the boat and go, get away from it all. He wouldn't go without Gabriel. What was happening to him? He focused his attention across the bay out to the open water--jet skis, a distant hum, sounds echoing. A few sailboats, mini-catamarans, fading figures, bouncing across the wind-roughened water, the colors darkening as a storm-induced twilight settled over the scene across the bay out toward Cozumel. Was this the onset of schizophrenia? Hearing voices, was that what this was? He didn't think so. He hoped not. He was afraid to ask *It*.

"Feel better bro?" TJ asked after a long pause. He could see the panic had left Jake's eyes.

Jake hesitated. "Has your implant talked to you?"

"It answers my questions, same as yours."

"That's not what I mean. "Did you ever do hallucinogens, LSD, mushrooms?"

"No. Is that what you thinking, what causin' this panickin'?"

"No. I don't know. This almost mechanical-sounding voice talked to me. My implant *It* said it could communicate verbally. You experienced anything like that?"

"You sure about this? Maybe yo' implant bringing back yo' trippin'. Causin' flashbacks?"

Obviously, TJ had not experienced anything like this. "Do something for me. Ask your implant if it can answer with a voice?"

"Seriously bro?" Jake nodded.

TJ felt foolish, thought what the heck.

Communication activated, came a reply.

Jake saw TJ's eyes open wide. A twisted grin infused his face.

"Kool. Damn bro." Then he started laughing. "Did you shit yo' britches? I bet you did. You the ghost man, the Voodoo man. You got freaked out by a voice juju." TJ laughed.

Hardy walked up. His dark hair ruffled by the wind. "Feeling better Jake?"

Jake and TJ looked up at him. TJ said, "My man here just turned me on to the fact our implants have a voice. Is this somethin' else we should've known?"

Hardy glanced back at the security guys, looked to make sure the Coastie wasn't on the deck of the seized boat. Then he checked the bay for any other boats close by. "Need to keep your voices down. Sound carries out here." TJ and Jake glared up at him. "This is part of the upgrade, uses JUDI, Joint Understanding and Dialogue Interface software--can mimic any sound, any voice you wish it to copy. Beats reading mental script. Is that what freaked you out in there Jake?"

"Everything about this implant freaks me out. This *is* mind control, Big Brother bullshit to the Nth degree. If I had known it was gonna be like this, I wouldn't have allowed myself to be a f'ing test dummy."

"Dr. Guthridge and Dr. Perkins will be here tomorrow to evaluate us. This will be your opportunity to join forces with those wishing to scuttle the program. Might want to keep in mind what that will mean for you and those near and dear to you. Not a threat. A fair warning." Hardy turned and started back to the center. He memed TJ, 'You need to do a better job with our friend. I'm giving you ten minutes. I'll be waiting inside. Our newest arrival has been taken to a room, maybe she knows something about Jake's missing daughter.'

'This is screwed up TJ. What else are they going to spring on us?'

'Come on, bro. Hardy wants us inside. You want to talk to that banger bitch. Now's the chance.'

'I picked up on it. I don't need this. Why now? Why me?'

'I don't know. Guess *It*'s been checking you out. Maybe learned the shit you used to talk about way back when I wondered about whether I really wanted to git to know your cracker jive ass. Damn sure gave me pause. You was one of the most far out people I ever knew. Now your implant done gone and learned how to play you. Maybe Elena was right about yo' PTSD and *It* done gone and got it, done caught the hebegebe crazies.' TJ laughed, saw the eat-shit-and-die look Jake gave him and let the laugh die away.

'You gots to lighten up bro. Git back your ole self. The man I once knew who laughed at himself. Git that ole why-give-a-shit-jes-go-with-the-flow attitude again. Now git your ass up and let's git this shit over with, so you can git your ass back to playin' farmer John, family man.'

CHAPTER
43

Beach near Akumal
Suzie--CIA and Terrence Lee--DICE operative

Dice's man Terrence Lee arrived aboard a privately chartered jet mid-afternoon. Suzie had arranged an Uber driver to pick him up and deliver him to the same condo complex she and Esmeralda were booked into. She left a message telling him to meet her at the beach out front.

"How were you able to track Esmeralda?" he asked, taking a sip from his Mojito, eyes straying from the bikini clad young nymphs on the beach back to the older, curvaceous woman, calling herself Suzie.

"Not anything you need to know." She watched his wandering looks. He wasn't her type, had a mean, squinty-eyed oriental look; made keeping it strictly business easier. "The more relevant question is, how did your people allow the young woman to get away?"

"Incompetence. The frog Jew Alperts, may he rot in hell, hired a young operative. Perhaps the freakin' punk was bribed or, as he claimed, rendered helpless. Either way, she's no longer in our hands. Unfortunate for us; more unfortunate for him." He held up his hand, shaking his empty glass until a waiter arrived to pour him another.

Suzie thought how lazy and arrogant. She wasn't impressed.

"Have you been able to ascertain her whereabouts with any certainty?" He asked when the waiter left.

"Who, the Harper man's daughter or the gangbanger slut? I know where the banger is. She's not far from here in Homeland's custody. Have a man inside. Haven't heard from him since they took him and the others there. As for Harper's daughter, I believe she's on a boat in the waters out there." She nodded her chin toward the bay, then turned to face him. "Were you able to get any info on the gala event guest list? Would help if we knew who was invited. Perhaps whoever has the Harper woman will be in attendance. Could be someone the cartel hired. The Gonzalez uncle who thinks he runs the Juarez Cartel could be coming with the Mexican President's group. I know their President's coming, been on the news. We could spread disinformation, shake the tree, see who falls out."

He drank a third of the refreshed drink. His mind was on the reward Thurmond Tindal offered for separating the Harper man from his property. He told Alperts he didn't care how it happened. He had a bigger target in mind. The daughter could be the key.

"We need something or someone to use for bartering."

"David Gonzalez maybe? Another possibility is the Cuban Ambassador's son Pablo? I believe I could arrange to get our hands on both. This will require careful planning and money to make this happen in the little time frame we have left."

She saw the twisted smirk on his face. Come on mother go for it.

"You're worth more than they are to Uncle Sam. I believe your people owe me. I do this, I expect double for each, triple for the daughter, same for the Juarez Cartel boss."

The biggest prize would be his for the taking—no need in going into that with her.

"What's in it for me?" His eyes were squinting even further. No way to trust anything he offered.

"We split seventy thirty."

"Fifty fifty, my boss finds out, I won't live to spend it, neither will you."

"Forty sixty. I'm going to be on the cartel's most wanted list. I could do this without you. Safer for me."

Not that this bartering meant anything, Suzie thought, neither one would ever see the money. Her goal was to learn the source.

He looked her up and down, a snarly smile on his round, yellow-bronze face. "Who else is going to pay the kind of money we're talking about? Who else can deliver? I don't think either one of our lives will be worth anything if we pull this off. I'll see about the money. You see about the muscle. Fifty fifty. We pull this off, split the money, go our separate ways." He held out his glass, she touched her empty one to his.

Mark, I hope I hear from you real soon. Suzie felt a chill, what if she didn't? She needed to check on Devereaux's confiscated boat. She rolled over and out of the umbrella-covered lounge chair.

"Let me know when I can verify the funds. I'll meet you in the lounge, let's say the day before the gala, at ten o'clock. Think you can have the money transferred by then?"

"Let you know when we meet." He hoped she brought the muscle he hoped for; his people will be waiting. He turned his attention back to the young women on the beach.

CHAPTER

44

HS Control Center, Akumal
Undersecretary Hardy

Jake hadn't moved. He kept staring out across the bay, watching the storm rolling in.

"What you goina do bro?"

Something with big eyes stirred the water. It was coming their direction. TJ stood up. "Better get your ass up and your feet out of the water, think that gator likes what he sees."

Jake raised his feet up, TJ reached down to give him a hand and pulled him to his feet. Jake slipped his feet into his sneakers.

"You need to stop asking me if I'm going to do what I said--I'll stay until I know something about Elizabeth. I *will* be there when Ariel is brought out of her coma. Gabrielle *will* be with me. Hopefully, his mother also. Then I'm going to do what I can to be *me* again."

Hardy's implant, he decided should be named Harlee, signaled an incoming call from Dr. Guthridge. He hurried to his office and shut the door.

"Yes Lisa," he said into his cell.

"Have you received a call or directive from General McDab since we last talked?"

Hardy checked his printer to make sure he hadn't missed anything. Any call, Harlee would have notified him. There were two pages in the tray.

"Give me a minute while I read over this."

"Oh shit. Blakely Carmichael is pregnant. The fetus DNA confirms the father is Special Agent Jackson Harper's."

"Read on. The committee is convinced there is a high probability Jake and the women in his life, Ariel Gaspard, his wife Elena, or Blakely Carmichael, know more about Major Jenkins and the data he stole than has been disclosed. His wife Elena disappeared again. Ariel Gaspard is being kept in a coma, Blakely Carmichael is on life support and preliminary tests reveal the fetus received cerebral trauma resulting in permanent disability, that is if it survives, which it won't if the Carmichael woman is taken off life support."

"Dear God… Jake… this could be the last straw."

"There is more troubling news. Dr. Perkins and I will be doing extensive evaluation of Agent Harper. General McDab informed me, and I'm sure Dr. Perkins also, that certain parties believe removing Jake's implant is necessary. I told him this would not work, most likely would be fatal. If our evaluation is not satisfactory, meaning Jenkins or the data are not located, he says further, more drastic measures will be taken."

Hardy plopped down in his chair. He warned Jake. The op had become critical, Jenkins had to be found.

"Bob, you there?"

"Yes Lisa. They are wrong, Jake has put his life on the line. No way is he holding anything back. The command monitors know this."

"That is not all. Have you heard of iPSCs, induced pluripotent stem cells?"

"What does this have to do with what we're talking about?"

"Some researchers have been able to take stem cells and grow organs, including a brain. This is real, was done on the International Space Station. Under a study with Harvard Med. This is troubling, the Russians, Chinese and others onboard the station could know. If the Russians or a hostile has Jenkins, General McDab is worried, our national security could be doubly at risk. No one is sure human tests haven't been performed. No published reports have been reported to the medical community. I believe Agent Harper received this treatment. Are you aware of this?"

Hardy didn't answer immediately. "Have you asked Dr. Perkins about this?"

No. But I will. And the NM0099 implant…I've been doing research. There were earlier recipients of the implant. Dr. Perkins was involved. This was done at the Air Force Base, the notorious Area 51. Dr. Perkins refuses to discuss his involvement or who else was involved. There may be others out there. This is troubling. Sorry, I digress. Getting back to the iPSCs and Jake.

If the op doesn't produce the desired results by the time the gala event is over, Dr. Perkins and I have been told we will be taking brain cells from Miss Carmichael and will insert them into the fetus. We will also perform operations to place implants in Ms. Gaspard, Miss Carmichael and the fetus."

"This is diabolical. They can't be serious."

"This is what I said. General McDab's people used the national security catchall. I quote,"the future is now, we are building a cyber security force, a special unit like no other before it. There will be many who oppose us, here and beyond. This will require doing the unthinkable. We must maintain an advantage. We cannot let our competition compromise our mission to lead the world forward. The president has issued the order." End quote. General McDab, the Secretary of State and Tindal plan to talk to you before the gala event."

Cyber Security Force. And what about his agents, the op, find Jenkins, the data, make sure no one else has it? More cutthroat bureaucratic bullshit. He should have been in the loop. Not getting info secondhand from Dr. Guthridge. What else had he not been told?

"I'm puzzled, why would Agent Harper and his women have anything to do with hiding the files? Be difficult with the implant for Jake to withhold this information. Same with Agent Alvarez, his best friend? I can think of any number of more reasonable suspects, including you. After all you worked hand in hand, you were one of the last people to see Jenkins before he took off. Why not you?"

The thought had occurred to her, perhaps insisting she receive the implant meant putting her in a compromising position. Was this because they suspected her? Did they plan to take the implant from her head, fearing what she knew? Did all of this have something to do with her future—why tell her about the cyber security force?

"I don't believe anyone's above suspicion. But you do raise an interesting question, why Agent Harper? Seems personal, doesn't it?" She let the question hang. Wasn't much doubt who was pushing Agent Harper as the lead suspect. Who stands to gain the most by taking him off the board?

"We're going to need all the help we can muster. You have, we have three days to get results, or it will be out of our hands. I was originally, scheduled to land midmorning, had to change flight plans due to the tropical front building offshore. Dr. Perkins and I will be arriving around nightfall at Tulum Naval Air Base. We will be at the center early tomorrow.

Hardy laid his phone down. Why had Dr. Guthridge called and not General McDab? One of many questions, not enough answers. The op had become surreal to him. All too real for Jake. He was left with little choice. The people in their custody, their cooperation was critical. He memed TJ, told him to come to his office. He memed Jake told him to meet Major Adams at the banger bitch's room.

TJ was dumbfounded. "Can't be right sir? You and I know Jake hasn't been alone with Miss Carmichael since Cuba. If she's pregnant, it can't be Jake's."

"The DNA confirmed Jake's the father."

"I need to call my wife. Deane can investigate."

TJ called Deane. Hardy called the hospital administrator.

They received calls back within minutes. The charts had been entered erroneously. Ariel was pregnant, not Blakely.

"Jake is not to be told." Hardy began pacing.

"Bullshit Hardy. He will find out. If he learns you and I knew… You don't know Jake like I do. You don't know what he is capable of. I have to tell him."

Hardy knew Jake well enough. Should he have him detained? TJ was right, Jake could find out.

"Ok. Wait until we've interrogated the banger bitch. Perhaps, she knows where his daughter is. Hopefully, she is where we can get to her. This means Jake will have his daughter's fate and the news of Ariel's pregnancy to deal with. This complicates the hell out of everything. If Pablo, this daughter's husband is implicated, we'll make the case for retaining his grandson. That might help." Hardy leaned forward in his chair. "We're running out of time. Tomorrow, we'll be tied up dealing with the implant evaluations. Dr. Perkins and Dr. Guthridge will need all of us, including Jake, here for the evaluations. I can't let him leave." Hardy ran his hand through his hair.

TJ stood. He wasn't smiling. "This shit getting' too screwed up."

Hardy came around the desk. "Agreed. We got to put this investigation into high gear. Come on. Let's go see how Jake and Marge are doing with the Gonzalez woman."

If you only knew, what I know, TJ. And Jake. The shit was hitting the fan. What wasn't said in the report was the rising rate of the Delta and other variants and lack of beds in Florida. God, he hoped neither of these women became infected or were released for lack of beds. The VA Hospital was not an option. He would see if he could have them moved to HS's new clinic in the Carolinas. McDab would have to approve the move. The question was would he?

CHAPTER
45

Control Center
Esmeralda, Jake and CT

Marge stared at the dark-skinned woman sitting across from her. Esmeralda Gonzalez had a rumpled cotton shirt over a one-piece bathing suit which hid any feminine qualities she might have. Her squinty-eyed hate-filled face and militaristic posture didn't help.

"Miss Gonzalez, we have your cousin Arturo. Soon we will have the rest of your family. You failed in your attempt to kidnap this man's grandson. If you don't tell me what you know concerning his daughter, I will leave the room. The Harper man is not going to ask you nicely. One last time, did Pablo have anything to do with her disappearance? Where is she?"

Esmeralda kept her head down. Said nothing.

"Okay if that's the way you want it. She's all yours Jake. She is English literate."

Marge left the room. Devereaux had been joined by Hardy and TJ.

"She's tough. I don't believe she'll talk. Where's the incentive. She knows we'll not let her go."

TJ said, "where she comes from, the cartel, her family, they her future. The way she sees it she talks there is nothing to look forward to. Jake's daughter, what she may or may not know, was and is her only hope. She talks, all hope's lost; they'll know; her life will be over; she knows this. Female bangers can be the toughest to break. Their initiation is brutal, mentally and physically."

"You think we're wasting our time?"

"Unless you willing to let us use extreme interrogation methods?"

Jake stood on the other side of the table from Esmeralda. She had not moved since he entered the room.

"Your cousin David, did he tell you what we did to him?" He saw rapid eye movement, the intake of breath. Her breasts rose slightly inside her skimpy top. Her skin tone grew darker. "Be a shame to disfigure you. I wouldn't want to do that. Your family should not have bothered my family; attacked us. Your cousins and their banger crew started this. I intend to finish it." Jake went around the table, took her chin in both his hands, pulled her head back. Her brown eyes locked with his. He knew his eyes were stabbing into hers; hers stabbed back.

"You will talk. I'm sure you've heard of waterboarding. Everyone talks eventually."

He pulled harder on her neck, a little more and it would break. She was strapped to the chair. She began to struggle. Jake knelt so his eyes was all she could see. He saw panic in her eyes. "A little more and you'll be a paraplegic. See how easy it can be. Waterboarding can be worse. You could drown. Tell me where my daughter is? Is her husband Pablo responsible?" He let go of her chin. She jerked forward, gasping. He saw tears bounce on the metal table. She shuddered. Said nothing.

"Think you can hold out. Think again." Jake went to the door. They let him out. All stood there watching him. Jake trembled, his face a mask of intensity, his eyes flashing.

Devereaux broke the silence. "I thought you were going to kill her."

Jake turned to Hardy. "She'll talk. Everyone does eventually."

Marge was shaking her head. Hardy told Devereaux and her to leave. They started to protest. "Go. Better you don't know what I decide." Dr. Guthridge was right. Time was running out.

"Do it. I don't see an alternative. I'll be in my office. Jake once you cross that line, there is no turning back. TJ, same for you."

TJ: "they dealt it. I say, after her, we put Mark Poponovich and Arturo Gonzalez in a room together. Sit them down across from each other. Be interesting to witness their interaction."

"Agreed. I'll have the guards arrange this. Give Major Adams and Devereaux something to do. Make them feel useful."

"Might want to tape Devereaux. Interesting to see his reaction," Jake added.

Hardy arched his eyebrows. "Use the ladies' locker room in the gym. Lock the door. There is no camera in the shower area." Hardy left.

Esmeralda fought them every inch of the way down the corridor. Opening doors meant a hand was no longer holding one of her booted feet. The Alvarez man avoided her attempt to kick him. He moved to the side and wrapped one arm around her calf. She twisted and squirmed. The Harper man dropped her onto the floor when she tried to bite him. They stretched her out, each took an arm, zip-tied her hands and feet and drug her, thrashing to the point of exhaustion, into the shower. They strapped her with difficulty to a weight room work out bench, tilted downward, her head at the lower end. A towel was placed over her face. Over and over, they poured water down her throat, her mouth squeezed open by one of them. Each time they continued until she went limp. She finally had to inhale, cough, sucking the water down her nose and throat into her lungs. She knew they saw the hate turn to fear in her eyes each time she came close to drowning. Urine ran out of her, tears leaked out. They raised her up each time, hands turned her head, pushed down on her chest, the water exploded out. She couldn't help it, she sobbed. Her resistance was strong, grew weaker.

It hurt to swallow, to talk, her voice was hoarse. She wanted to say, "You hurt my cousin. Changed him." She spat at them. She slumped. She wanted to die. She feared drowning more than anything.

When they covered her face with the towel again, she screamed "No."

She started cursing, talking haltingly in Spanish. Jake told her to speak English. She glared at them. When Jake made a menacing move, she resumed in English.

She cursed them, told them what she had wanted to say about David.

"What about Arturo? My daughter?"

"Arturo he hear Alperts tell Jenkins Pablo bargain with Alperts man. He decided we must take daughter, Pablo's wife. Arturo tell me find Alperts man and arrange punishment for what you did to David. And, for interfering in business. Alperts say he have yours and news woman's daughter and plans to use her to get much money and bring you out in open."

She took a trembling breath. "Arturo see this give us opportunity to punish you, make money, then kill you, your family and your friend. He tell me go with Alperts. We fly to El Paso. Alperts man tell me go with plane to Cancun wait there for them. I talk to Arturo he say he have other men they follow Alperts. They fucked up, kill Alperts man, injure news lady. Cousins they angry, want news woman unharmed, say they need her to punish you."

"Plans were changed after you take Arturo prisoner. This make David angry. David tell me take Pablo son and use to bring you to him. Cousin hate you Harper man, you Alvarez man, he want to punish, kill you. He say he hear Pablo wife she on boat. This all I know."

They watched her struggle to get her story out. Jake got in her face.

"That's not all you know. We saw you at Thurmond Tindal's place in Carolinas with your cousins and Jenkins. What were you doing there? What do you know about my wife?"

She didn't answer.

"Looks like she needs more encouragement," TJ said. He placed the towel back across her face.

"No. I tell you." She would say what they know, nothing more.

"Better start talking," TJ said. "The smell of you is getting to me. And not in a good way."

"Arturo told David to track you and your women. Jenkins he helped. Arturo told David to find Harper woman; send men to bring her to Tindal home; Jenkins agreed to hide her. Arturo told me to watch her. When David disappeared, Arturo he get very angry; wanted to hurt your wife." She paused, a wicked smile crossed her lips," I told him I know a better way. Jenkins he watched and taped me. I make your woman happy."

Jake turned red. TJ stepped in. "Save us the details about your assault."

"Was no assault, she liked what I do." TJ took a step closer. She gave another smirky smile, shrugged as best she could, then nodded. Jake grabbed the bucket and towel; panic creased her face.

"No."

"Better not screw with me. Tell us what we want to hear, or I'll drown your worthless ass," Jake said standing next to her. Her features vacillated between hate and fear.

Esmeralda wasn't sure what they accept. She feared she'd said too much. She tried to spit again. Her mouth was too dry. She tried to swallow. There was nothing she could do. What more is safe for her to say?

"Arturo, he didn't believe your offer of trade. David he bugged Jenkins office. Arturo listened to Jenkins make deal with Poponovich, know they plan to cheat him. Then police come. He tell me run. I get away. I see Jenkins launch Hive, stun Arturo's men; take Harper woman and put her on plane."

Jake studied her. No way she could have gotten away.

"How'd you get away?"

"Through orchard."

Jake's bullshit detector rang loud and clear.

"That's a lie. You were on that plane, weren't you? How is it Jenkins didn't find you?"

They saw the look. Jake and TJ knew he was right.

"You followed them to Texas. You were the other woman at General Toraz' hacienda."

Esmeralda stopped talking. Arturo, their uncle, they kill her if they know she talk.

"Where's my wife, her boyfriend and daughter?" Jake asked straddling her, his rage threatening to consume him. TJ struggled to pull him back.

"Not now bro." He memed Jake, 'we may need her. We should take her in to see Renai. Might get some answers.'

Jake glared at her, walked around stood next to her head. The light had gone out in her eyes. "Where's Jenkins?" His voice harsh, dripping with venom. She closed her eyes.

"You better not have lied about Pablo's wife, my daughter."

TJ led Jake out of the shower area. He needed to try to calm him down.

"She's tougher than her cousin. Thought we lost her coupla times," TJ said.

Jake began pacing. "Sounds to me like Elizabeth is on a boat." He felt disembodied. It was all he could do to bring himself down. And, try to think through what was said. In a combat zone, finding a way to take out your frustration always presented itself. Those who didn't brought their angst home, reenacted it in ways which harmed themselves as much or more than those who were in contact with them. Jake tried not to let his anger get the best of him, but this was combat with his hands tied behind his back.

"We'll find her bro. Got that tropical storm coming. Boats'll be heading out to sea, or a safe port."

"Need to tell dickhead Hardy. Maybe he will alert Captain Conroy. Get the tech geeks to monitor boat communications."

"My bet is Bolstoy's ole yacht. Love to check that one personally. Make me happy to get another chance to talk to the Palmroys. They're tied into the Russian assassin shit that went down, no doubt in my mind."

Jake didn't reply. TJ saw his face. Uh oh.

"Guess we better get the Major to help us with the banger bitch. I'll go find her and talk to Hardy, relay your requests. Hang tight. We know she'll talk. Not the time to take her over the edge. Okay?" Jake didn't answer. "Don't do it bro. We may need her."

TJ went to the juice bar refrigerator, grabbed two bottled waters. Handed one to Jake.

"Calm down bro. Sit down, cool off. Need to get it together. I'll be right back."

As TJ hurried off, Earl, his implant reminded him he forgot to tell Jake about Ariel's pregnancy.

Jake sat down drank the water. He needed to think through everything that bitch said. She deliberately provoked him. He needed access. *Okay It, you got me, I got you. In your search for Elizabeth include ship to shore communications from Russian, Chinese, Israeli, and Cuban vessels, especially the SwaleMaiden. IT?*

On it. Do you wish text or verbal communication?

Jake wasn't sure he wanted another voice inside his head. The implant was there. Nothing to do but use it. *You're no longer IT You're now CT. CT was my father. This is how you will be addressed.*

You mean I'm no longer the horrible, threatening It?

Just get on with what I told you to do.

Your father asked you to define "it". You said "it" is in and of itself, whatever "it" wants to be. Is this why you wish me to be CT? Should I announce my presence by calling you son?

Now you're being invasive again. Yours is not to reason why. Got it, CT? Now get on with it.

God, I hate feeling like I'm arguing with myself. I need that off switch.

Don't get your panties in a wad son. Okay. Okay. Not good news. According to hospital records, Ariel Gaspard is pregnant with your child. The fetus suffered temporal damage, feared permanent. Mother and child are being closely monitored. Tests are being run. Surgery may be required. Variants of coronavirus are a major concern. Visitors are not allowed. No record of Elizabeth leaving Spain. No communication mentioning her name.

Jake jumped to his feet, stunned by the news—Ariel pregnant, fetus brain damaged. And the coronavirus variants. Ariel was vaccinated, was that enough? Oh shit, what should he do? What could he do? Find Elizabeth. Be there with their daughter and Gabriel when Ariel is brought out of the coma. They would have to let them see her. If not, he would move her. The Gonzalez threat had to be neutralized, eliminated, no—exterminated. And fast. Then, once those bangers were no longer in the picture, no threat to him, TJ or their families, and did not have Elizabeth—take them off the board--then go after the other threats. Jenkins, Tindal, McDab and anyone else responsible for what was happening to his family.

The GPS chips, CT reminded him, *David Gonzalez had one. Probably has another. David insinuated Arturo had one. This woman could have one. She's playing you.*

He went back into the shower area. Esmeralda remained motionless, her eyes closed. Her eyes popped open when his hands began massaging hers. She hissed, the gag muffled what he was certain were curses when he ran his hands under her arms and over her body. She squirmed and fought, tried to pull her arms loose from the strap that bound her to the bench. Then when he ran his hands up her muscular thighs, the backs of his hands brushed against her pubic area, couldn't be helped due to the strap binding her legs, and her squeezing her legs tight, along with her twisting and squirming motions, He didn't feel or see any abnormality.

CT's voice said, *you should mess her up, she assaulted your wife. The ultimate humiliation would be to have sex with her.*

Don't go there. I have not nor will I ever force myself on anyone, not even her. You didn't get this from my conscious or subconscious mind. Where did you come up with these thoughts?

Your memory includes many instances of personal promiscuity, immoral thoughts, and unwanted advances toward women.

Never raped anyone. Rape is sexual violence. Past behavior is no longer indicative of current or future behavior for me in the sexual realm. Okay?

Your looks and thoughts say otherwise. You are touching her without permission son.

CT you're beginning to annoy me. Go monitor the people you should be monitoring.

Because of his internal dialogue, he had not heard Jake and Marge enter. It shocked him when his attempts at feeling a chip were interrupted by TJ clearing his throat and Marge demanding to know what the f' he was doing? Jake jerked up, glanced back saw the puzzled look on TJ's face, the remonstrative look on Marge's.

Despite the gag, Jake was certain the "he threatened to rape me," the wide-eyed Esmeralda struggled to say, was understood.

Jake glanced over his shoulder, saw Marge's outrage. He said to her, "Not that. I was searching for a GPS chip. TJ you need to get an RF scanner. Remember David's chip. We need to run a check on her and her brother."

"What are you talking about?" Marge sounded incredulous. "Unstrap her. Take that gag off. You've got some explaining to do."

TJ turned to Marge. "Hold on. Jake's right. Her cousin David had a GPS chip under his skin. His brother and Jenkins tracked us once when we captured David. David said Arturo had one. Stands to reason she has one also."

"What good will that do?" Marge asked. "Doesn't matter. Still doesn't excuse this kind of behavior."

"I'm sorry this offends your sensibilities. Guess you forgot what her and her banger buddies do, what they did to Ariel and Blakely. She had my grandson, may have my daughter. I tell you what Major if this bothers you so much then go file your complaint. I'm not going to listen to it." Jake turned to TJ. "We can use her or her cousin Arturo as bait. Bring David to us,"

"Good thinking bro." TJ memed Hardy, asked for a scanner. Told him the plan. Hardy said he would send a guard with one.

The Major stayed. She was upset with Jake. And herself. She felt she should say more, do as she threatened, but a part of her sympathized with Jake. She hoped he was right.

Esmeralda had the chip inserted on the inside of her upper thigh, higher than Jake had earlier ventured. He looked back at the Major. She didn't say anything. Her face lost its angry expression. TJ said they should remove it.

"No, we need to leave it, for now. We can use her as a decoy to draw the bangers." Jake memed TJ, 'my bet is all the Gonzalez are connected using the same chip device. We should check Arturo. If I'm correct, there is a good chance we can locate David on the same frequency.' Jake memed Hardy, 'did TJ tell you this one told us Elizabeth was on a boat? Need you to contact Captain Conroy, let him know.'

'The Coast Guard is monitoring *SwaleMaiden*. Captain Conroy's vessel is following the *SwaleMaiden*. Both are headed out, away from the path of the tropical storm. There has been no mention of Elizabeth.'

Hardy sent a guard to tell Marge to find her some clothes, then have the Gonzalez woman shower.

The guard said he would remain posted outside if she needed him. He handed Marge a taser.

"Just in case she needs persuading. Careful, that thing and water can be lethal." Marge gave him an eat shit look. "Undersecretary Hardy wants us to bring her to him when she's more presentable."

TJ pulled Jake aside, told him he needed to talk to him. 'There's something come up about Ariel I think you should know.'

'I know about the pregnancy, the fetus' brain injury. Is that what you needed to tell me?'

'I'm sorry bro. Deane informed me. How did you know?'

'My implant is monitoring the hospital. I will be there when they bring Ariel out of the coma. As I have said numerous times, I plan for Elizabeth and Gabriel to be accompanying me.'

Jake felt like he had overreacted, shouldn't have jumped on the Major the way he did. She had caught him offguard, and it had come after he had berated CT. He would apologize later.

He told TJ. "My implant has autonomous thoughts. Dangerous thoughts. He suggested sexual assault of the banger bitch. Sexual assault or rape are and always have been repulsive to me. He interpreted my past sexual history as a green light for sexual assault. Rape, sexual assault are not due to sexual attraction, they are acts of violence. Something's not right. Don't you agree?"

"Yeah bro. You need to take this up with Dr. Guthridge. Independent analysis like this is dangerous. You sure this wasn't "a failure to communicate? Loved that movie *Cool Hand Luke*."

"Come on TJ. No. And, I'm worried the damn thing is hearing this."

"You stressed out about the implant and all this personal shit bro. Maybe that's what caused your, I mean CT's, reaction. Best not say anything to Hardy. Hopefully, you're wrong; 'cause, if Hardy or those other mothers monitoring us pick up on this, they'll damn sure shut you down."

"No more CT. You listening CT?'

No response.

'What if it's someone else sending garbage to my implant. If they can monitor, perhaps they can transmit directly to our implant. The gala wasn't my idea. CT did a search, the event has been in the works for quite some time. Hardy had to have known. We're being played.'

'Watch it bro. You're making me get paranoid. We need to rejoin Hardy. Get this shit over with.'

CHAPTER

46

Control Center
Jake, Hardy and Dr. Guthridge

Jake and TJ went with Hardy to join Devereaux outside the room where Arturo and Mark were shackled to seats across the table from each other.

"They cursed each other, then it became a staring contest. If looks could kill, they'd both be dead. Didn't last long. For the last ten minutes they've been conversing in Spanish, mostly it has been Arturo. My Spanish is not good enough to keep up with what was said." Devereaux felt Jake's eyes on him. "What's your problem Jake?"

"Arturo's cousin should be joining us shortly. Ever meet her, say down in Mexico? Maybe out on your boat?"

"I was never in Mexico. She was never on the boat. Ask Hardy, he was at Gitmo when we were taken there? What's with you Jake? Why the hard-on for me?"

Jake turned back to watch Arturo and Mark. He chose to wait, see who blinked when Esmeralda was brought into the equation. Mark and Arturo stopped talking. Jake, like Hardy and TJ, scanned the recording. Arturo accused Mark of being a Yankee traitor. Mark defended himself. Not any useable intel came from their confrontation.

TJ said, "We need to scan everyone for any hidden devices. Including you Devereaux." TJ pulled out the scanner. Devereaux tried to back away. Jake grabbed him. Hardy ordered him to allow the scan.

Jake held Devereaux. TJ scanned him from his feet upward. The scanner picked up a signal on his head. Devereaux began struggling. TJ handed the scanner to Hardy. Jake pinned his arms behind his back. TJ sat on his legs and held his head. The scanner's meter posited there was something in the ear area. Nothing was visible.

"Son of a bitch," Hardy exclaimed. "Explain this Devereaux or I'll have our medical staff find it. What device do you have? What is its purpose?"

"You will need to talk to my director."

"You are assigned to me as a member of the joint task force. I will sequester you. You will have no outside communication. We will conduct a cat scan. If it poses a threat, the device will be removed. Put him in room 8."

Jake and TJ led Devereaux away. He didn't resist.

Turned out only two of the detainee's scans provided anomalies which might be an implant, James Dean and Boyd. Devereaux had a metal plate with screws; a repair from an injury which should have kept him out of the field. Arturo had two, a GPS and an RFID chip. Mark Poponovich, Renai and Tobolokov did not have anything detected inside their heads. But they did have GPS chips elsewhere. Dean like Boyd refused to provide enlightenment.

'We're dead in the water until Dr. Perkins and Dr. Guthridge get here. They arrive tonight. We were supposed to be evaluated by them tomorrow. This can't wait. We've got four hours until they touchdown. I've got some calls to make.'

'I'm going to spend some time with Gabriel,' Jake memed.

'Believe I'll talk to Deane. Then take a closer look at the *SwaleMaiden*,' TJ replied.

'Gabriel and I will join you in the rec room.'

Hardy was angry. Who knew about Dean and Boyd? Why had he not been informed? He learned General McDab was unavailable. He left a message for the General to call him. He called Dr. Guthridge. She was boarding a cargo plane.

"Dr. Guthridge are there any other implant recipients currently active that you are aware of?"

"None Bob. This is Tindal Industries proprietary product. To my knowledge, there are no other active recipients."

"Would you ask Dr. Perkins?"

"Dr. Perkins is not coming with me. He rescheduled. He will be coming with Colonel Tindal day after tomorrow, weather permitting. Why would you be asking about other recipients?"

Hardy told her of their discovery. She was quiet. He thought the call had been disconnected. "Dr. Guthridge, can you hear me?"

"Bob, I need to make some calls, I'll call you back." Lisa was flabbergasted. This was unexpected. Dr. Perkins had said nothing to her about any current recipients. There were reports from early test recipients having received the implant before she joined him at Marberry. He claimed the results were unsatisfactory. They were quarantined. One died when the implant removal operation failed. The other two were in a secure facility, their device not active. So, he said. When he was with DoD, he had control of the programs. Dean and Boyd, did they have this implant, were they the other inactive two she had been informed of? Had they received this or some other implant later at the behest of DoD or another agency? How could this be? Did Tindal know?

She attempted to reach Tindal. No answer. She left a message. Dr. Perkins left that morning for Miami. Said he needed to do the preop meeting with the staff for the upcoming operations. She was to assist in the operation. Was it moved up? General McDab and Tindal insisted she go on ahead to Cancun. Dr. Perkins told her evaluations were all that were to be made. He could handle the preop meeting without her.

Now this. She was worried—how many other possible past implant recipients were there? She had argued against the almost certain fatal future implant operations planned in Miami. Had Dr. Perkins, Tindal and McDab decided to keep her in the dark? Had they gone ahead with the operation on the Carmichael woman and the Gaspard woman and her fetus? What did they know about Dean and Boyd? This was troubling. Had she become a liability?

She had no answers. She wasn't sure whom she could trust. Should she tell Hardy, she had the implant?

"Bob, I cannot get in touch with anyone. General McDab and Colonel Tindal are in Washington. Dr. Perkins is in Miami. He is in a meeting."

"Does Dr. Perkins meeting have anything to do with the proposed operation you told me about earlier?"

"I don't know. I would not be surprised if it does."

"There will be a vehicle waiting at the airport. As soon as you land, I need you to come to the center. Hopefully, you or I will know more by then."

Hardy found Jake and TJ in the rec room. Jake had Gabriel on his lap. They were engaged in a game of drone combat with TJ on a simulator. It was obvious neither Jake nor TJ were using their implants. Gabriel was doing an admirable job for a child. Pretty sharp, had picked up some nifty moves. Probably Captain Adams doing. He hated to interrupt. Didn't have to.

TJ memed, 'I talked to Deane. Dr. Perkins arrived. He's in a meeting with a preop team. Seems the operation is scheduled for tomorrow on Blakely. No news about Ariel or the fetus. Jake knows. Can you stop them?'

'Doubtful. Dr. Guthridge is on her way. Be here in a few hours. There may be something she can do. I've requested the women be moved to the Carolinas. McDab will have to approve.'

'Deane would like that. She has asked for extended leave. May not be granted. What does Dr. Guthridge know about Dean and Boyd?'

"She said she was not aware of their implants. We're looking into it. Hopefully, we'll know more when she gets here.'

'Jake and I checked with Captain Conroy. Looks like *SwaleMaiden* decided to go to Hemingway Marina in Cuba. Jake contacted someone he knew who lives near there. This person agreed to have someone watch the boat. Jake asked him to board the vessel, do a search. Not certain this will happen.'

Jake's attention was split, captured by the simulator machine bursts which brought squeals of delight from his grandson and the muted sounds of the wind-driven rain lashing out, crashing into the bomb-resistant glass facing the bay. He did not react to Hardy's and TJ's meme conversation. He was enjoying his time with Gabriel. CT was monitoring them while doing assigned tasks.

One thing CT had learned from checking Mark's contacts was how to get in touch with his friends in Cuba. Jake had excused himself and stepped aside to call Koko. He was surprised to hear from Jake. They chatted briefly about inconsequential, personal matters. Then Jake asked Koko if he could possibly arrange a search of the *SwaleMaiden*. This had been Jake's heads-up to Koko at his daughter's fifteenth birthday celebration concerning the rogue generals meeting with Okneyev when Jake had been in Cuba with Hardy. This had earned him major brownie points with Koko. This was their secret--the Cuban authorities nor Hardy knew he told Koko about them.

"Problem is," Koko said, "the ambassadors' presence in Cancun means resources are stretched thin. Perhaps Tomas can watch the vessel." Jake heard Koko talking to someone. "Tomas says he can watch the boat for a small favor. A little money and a care package of American goodies. We would like you deliver these personally." Jake told Koko he would see to it.

When Jake told Hardy about his request, Hardy memed, 'General McDab sent me a memo, in it he said he and Tindal would be joining other government personnel onboard the *SwaleMaiden* before the gala. I find it highly unlikely the Palmroys would have that meeting with your daughter Elizabeth onboard.'

'If the banger bitch is correct, and we have to assume she is, Elizabeth is on a boat. My bet is she is being held on the *SwaleMaiden*,' Jake replied. 'That meeting means they will stow her or get her off the boat beforehand. Remember they have a powerboat and a helipad. Taking her off is simple. They may do this while in Cuba. I hope my associate is watching and Koko is able to pull a raid before they disembark.'

'Captain Conroy's crew is monitoring the vessel. There has been no mention of Elizabeth. I hate to say this, but, also in the memo, I was instructed to finish all our inquiries of the detainees before their arrival. McDab will review our results and determine their fate. Poponovich and his crew will undoubtably be released unless we provide irrefutable reasons for holding them. We have twenty-four hours. And I'm afraid he will most likely order me to turn Gabriel over to the Ambassador for return to his father.

'Not going to happen,' Jake replied, 'I hope he doesn't order this. I'm hard-wired for action and a CIA mother, general or not, would help satisfy my primal urge. It's a good thing my grandson is with me. They better not try to change that.' Jake's look was that of a combat-crazed automaton. It was like a switch was thrown, then Gabriel squealed with delight and Jake took his eyes off Hardy.

Hardy knew there was no use trying to reason through this again. He needed the on/off switch he hoped Dr. Guthridge would provide. Otherwise, this would be the end of his team.

"We have work to do. Jake, you need to return your grandson to Jeni's care. Your grandson seems to have the hang of it. Jeni may have him certifiable as a drone pilot before we're done here." Hardy spoke in a soft tone. He was trying to contain his inner turmoil. Jake needed more downtime. Time, something that was in short supply. Jesus, if Dr. Perkins did what General McDab proposed, or if they try to take Jake's grandson, there was no doubt, there will be bloodshed. Dr. Guthridge better have some answers.

"Okay sport. Enough practice, time to go back and show Jeni how much better you are. Don't tell her you beat the socks off TJ and me, okay?" He set Gabriel down next to the simulator. Gabriel looked up at him and grinned. Damn, Jake thought, he has my grin, better looking, going to be a lady-killer. Wasn't difficult to push his anger momentarily aside after seeing that. *He's happy with you because he gets to play instead of taking a nap*, CT interjected. Gabriel put his hand up, they high fived. He took his little hand and they started to leave. TJ stepped forward and Gabriel slapped palms with him. TJ was all grin.

Jake asked Jeni about kids taking naps. She told Jake not to worry, she was due a break soon.

The Major brought Esmeralda to outside Hardy's office. Hardy instructed TJ to go with the Major to put her in with the Gonzalez banger bitch. "We need to observe the interaction, see if there is anything there to follow up on."

"Jake, you need to confront Dean and Boyd. Dr. Guthridge has given me reasons to believe they were early recipients of the NM0099 implant. We need to know what implant they received, when and where it was done for starters. They know you. Maybe you can get them to talk. Please try to control your impulses."

"They are Poponovich's men. I need to talk to him first see if he's willing to play ball. Having him talk to them with me might help. I could be wrong, but I don't think Poponovich had anything to do with Jenkins' disappearance. I think someone else was pulling the strings. If we propose to let him loose again in return for his cooperation, he might go for it, especially since his friend Dr. Guthridge is on her way. And, as you said, dickhead McDab will most likely order his release anyway."

CHAPTER
47

Control Center
Renai and Dr. Guthridge

The room smelled of suntan lotion and urine. They looked tense; reminded TJ of two caged feral cats.

The sound of the closing door startled them. Renai turned her head. Her eyes strayed across the Major and settled on him. Esmeralda blinked, gave the Major a hard stare. Her anger was palpable.

"No need for introductions. Our intel has been confirmed. Who wants to go first?" TJ said grinning.

Neither spoke. The room was chilled. Renai hugged herself.

"Okay, guess you need more persuading. Gonzalez. Come on Major let's take her back to the shower." TJ walked over and fastened his big hand on her arm. She tried to shrug it off.

"This puta, she say I steal something. Try make me talk."

"Puta. Ha. You the one who bitch-fucked anything. Whore too nice word for you." Renai looked at the Major. "Maybe you like." She turned to TJ. "You waste your time. This bitch know only lies. Ask Dean and Boyd. She offer do everyone. Give me five minutes, she tell everything she know. I do favor to world, put her out of misery."

Esmeralda tried to pull free. TJ held firm. The Major had lost her grip and Esmeralda tried to stab the loose arm's fingers into his eye. He deflected it, grabbed the wrist, and brought her to her knees with a twist into a wrist lock, his other hand pressing down on the elbow. "Keep on. You'll never use this arm again." The Major pressed a taser into her neck. TJ shook his head no.

She stopped struggling. TJ heard Renai laughing, her cold dark eyes mocked them.

"Perhaps we should take you to the shower," TJ said to her. She continued to laugh, but it seemed more forced. If she wasn't insane before, TJ was certain she was getting there fast. TJ memed, Hardy and Jake what he learned. Told Hardy he thought they should take Renai, Boyd and Dean to the showers. 'I feel certain they know about Jenkins' whereabouts. Jake, could be Elena, your wife, and her daughter are in danger. I believe Jenkins gave her the info he stole.'

Jake stood across the table from Mark Poponovich. Mark sat back. "How you like the au de urine cologne? Could be a winner, what you think?"

"Glad to see you haven't lost your sense of humor."

"I believe it was you told me, if you can make them laugh, you can screw them."

"Hasn't worked for you, has it?"

"Did you miss me is that why you're here? No. Let me guess. Someone whispered in your ear and told you let me go. I hold the keys to the cartel treasure chest and you guys are ready to bargain. Am I close?"

"What makes you so certain you're the only one with the key? As I recall, you said anything can be hacked. Your partner David Gonzalez is a master hacker." Jake paused. Mark leaned forward. "Seems your teammates have been running an end around on you. Making their own deals. Goes to show, never trust agency mothers."

Mark smiled.

"You think I didn't expect this. They tell you anything noteworthy? Didn't think so. That's why you're here."

Now Jake smiled. "Want to keep playing guessing games or do you want to get back in the game?"

Mark liked the sound of this. Something happened. He was tired of sitting here. He couldn't run the op from in here. General McDab was coming. His contact Suzie was sent word to notify McDab of his location. McDab wanted those funds for off the books' operations. Jake was thought to be in possession of the codes. Mark wasn't so sure. Only he and David were to know. If David discovered a back way in, could override his part of the code, this would pose a problem. Was that why Arturo was so cocky? His team had they talked? Wasn't much they could disclose that meant diddly squat as far as causing him a personal catastrophe.

"Okay. What's the deal ole buddy, ole pal?"

"You agree to cooperate, tell us everything you know about Jenkins, anything which has anything to do with our op. And, you agree to help me locate and free my daughter. In return we will help you bust the cartel and give you the opportunity to see your girlfriend Dr. Lisa Guthridge."

Mark arched his eyebrows. "What makes you think I have any interest in this Dr. Guthridge?"

"She is on *our* team. We know all about yours and her relationship." Jake stood back. He was enjoying the theater play in Mark's eyes. "You've got all the time in the world, that is until I walk out that door, then the game is over for you." Jake started toward the door. Mark started laughing.

"Badass Jake, the tough negotiator. What about my team?"

"You'll get a chance to see and talk to them. Might find this interesting." Jake stopped at the door. "In or out?" The door began to open.

"Okay. I'm in on one condition."

"I gave you the conditions."

"Damnit Jake. I took an oath just like you did. I must run this up the ladder. One call, that's all I'm asking."

"Hardy will decide." Jake went out into the corridor. Hardy and TJ stood by the monitor.

"Good work," Hardy said. "As you heard, TJ thinks members of his team know where Jenkins is and possibly your wife and stepdaughter. You want to trust him?"

"Where's he going to go where we don't have eyes and ears on him? You okay with him calling his superior. My guess is that is McDab. Is he still head of Clandestine Operations?"

"I'm not sure. Poponovich wouldn't know about the changes in command, so stands to reason it will be General McDab. Poponovich knows we'll be monitoring the call. Even if he demands privacy, like you said, there is no such thing. Be interesting to know who he calls as much as it will about what that person tells him to do. Guess we'll know how far we can trust his cooperation. What do you think TJ?"

"My bro, never cease to amaze. I agree. Give him enough rope and let's see he hangs himself. Before we turn him loose, I'd like a go at Renai, Boyd and Dean in the shower. How 'bout it Jake?"

"Absolutely. Like you said Hardy, we're short on time."

"Just so we're clear, I know nothing about this. Don't screw up and go too far, whatever it is you plan to do."

They stepped into Renai's room. She watched Jake, her eyes those of a predator tracking their quarry. She saw the look in Jake's eyes, knew this was to be a contest of wills.

"Once again Agent Harper, bring your muscle with you. Scared to be alone with me? I don't bite, nibble if it help. Man like you he cannot go too long without woman."

Jake plopped both hands down on the table, leaned forward locking eyes with her. "Came to give you a chance to explain yourself. I know a little more since last time we talked." She tilted her head, reminded Jake of a cat. "No more games. You're going to answer our questions one way or another. I'm sure you know what this means. If you do it peacefully, you will be allowed to get cleaned up and join your fellow agency mothers. If what you tell us is true and believable, you could go back to playing super sleuth. We know you were part of the team who took Jenkins away. Where did you take him?"

"Why ask what you know?"

TJ moved over behind her.

"Last time, where you take him?"

TJ placed his large hands onto her shoulders, dug his fingers into her muscles. Jake reached across and clamped his hands down onto her arms. She was trapped. She let her mind go blank the way she learned in training. To her surprise she heard her restraints being released. Did they intend to do her bodily harm, sexually assault her. She had learned how to deal with this in her training. It was useless to resist. Would never have thought Harper and his fellow agent the kind to use these techniques. She was lifted out of her seat.

"Any resistance and the guards will tase you. Ever been tasered? Hurts like hell, feels like you might explode."

Renai was led down the hall, blindfolded, her hands zip-tied behind her back. She had to take short choppy steps due to the tethers on her ankles. They took her through the weight room to the shower area. Laid her on the decline bench, strapped her down, removed the blindfold. She saw Jake standing over her with a towel and a bucket, water dripping from its edge. She had been water-boarded in training, witnessed a Palestinian undergo an extreme measure of the torture. She knew her instructor was correct, everyone talked eventually. She felt the towel as it covered her face.

"No. Okay. Jenkins, he was taken to General Toraz' hacienda. He did not have the data chips with him. General Toraz said he not want him questioned at his place."

"That's not all. You went back to the place where Jenkins waited for y'all. Was my wife there? Who was with you?"

She shook her head trying to get the towel off her face. Jake poured some water onto the towel. She struggled against the restraints. Jake poured more water. She coughed and sputtered.

"Boyd went with me," she croaked. She coughed and coughed. Jake waited.

"We found signs someone had been in other bedroom. We check area. Boyd, he called to report suspicion and ask for more people who know area. He talked to people who own house. They say woman come with Jenkins, say other woman come too. We find Mexican whore, think she the woman. General Toraz, he say she was cartel boss' family. Spic whore tell him she hide on plane, say your wife was on plane, say she see us, follow to hacienda, she go back look for your wife. We learn your wife she already leave, go with father and daughter. We decide best to go to boat. Boyd he try to locate them. Now we here."

"Still haven't answered the question, where is Jenkins?"

"We left him with General Toraz. No good to us. Our job is get stolen data. Jenkins he had nothing on him; tell us information in his head; offer to sell to us. We did not believe his story; why we left him. Poponovich angry we left Jenkins, say he need him. Poponovich told us he go alone to see General Toraz and cartel boss; find Jenkins. Tell us stay on boat, have Boyd continue search for your wife; continue to try to track Jenkins, the DICE man Alperts, and news woman."

"Any questions TJ?"

TJ was leaning against the shower wall. He walked over, stood next to her head.

"Did Boyd learn where Jenkins or Jake's wife were?" No reply. "You a gypsy, gypsy's take pride in being liars, especially to *gadjos*, right? Do not lie. No one knows you're here. Saw some hungry gators out there in the bay."

Renai wasn't a good swimmer, never spent much time in the water. They think this a joke. Not to her. She knows they have answers, no harm telling what she think they know.

"Boyd say he find notice on dark web for intel, for sale to highest bidder. Boyd trace post address show post come from Texas. Could be a false trail, Boyd think not, think this is Harper woman, wonder who else knows, maybe you Agent Harper? Post say exchange take place in Cancun. Not know who make exchange, what intel to be exchanged. This why everyone here."

"Who you workin' for, CIA or Mossad?"

Renai smiled. "Whoever pays."

"Thought you not a whore?" TJ snarled.

The smile vanished. "Everyone whore, depends on who pay, how much willing to give in return."

Jake felt her statement like a punch upside his head. This was exactly how this whole op had made him feel--dirty, used, violated, a whore.

Hardy memed, 'Let her get cleaned up. Poponovich has agreed to our terms. I told him I was going to keep his crew separated until he makes his call. First, we need to talk to Dr. Guthridge. Be good to know if she can be trusted. The Major and the two guards are on their way.'

Jake took the towel off her face. He leaned down, his face upside down from hers, "so you know, I have my scruples; I never cared for dangerous, emotionless whores like you."

Dr. Lisa Guthridge looked nothing like her photos. Hardy was struck by her height, the way she carried herself. She wore jeans, a cotton blouse, flats on her feet, no jewelry, little or no makeup, her hair pinned up in a bun; seemed she was attempting to hide her physical attributes—her demeanor and bearing were very professional, nevertheless, there was a certain appeal about her. Her handshake was firm, her eyes locked onto his.

Lisa read Hardy's seemingly flattering thoughts. His implant was open, intending to record their conversation. In a strong feminine voice, she came straight to the point. "General McDab has not been completely honest with you or me."

"About you and Dr. Perkins? I take it you're referring to past recipients of the implant."

"I did some investigating. The NM0099 Implant Program is and always has been a covert military weapon's project. Dr. Perkins did the research and developed the implant at Nellis Air Base's research facility, the Nevada Training and Test Facility, Homey, popularly called Area 51. Mine and his former employer, Marberry Industries, was a cover company. Thurmond Tindal is a frontman, his purchase of Marberry, his lab and future manufacturing facility and my hire to develop the implant for peaceful purposes, are all a part of the plan. I'm not certain Colonel Tindal knew at the time. Certain politicians, former agency and military ranking officers are on a mission to enrich themselves now and in the future. There is no way out for any of us. We either agree to their terms or suffer the consequences."

Hardy was stunned, was this woman delusional? Was this a test?

"How did you arrive at this conclusion?"

Lisa smiled. Hardy was alarmed. His implant was running a further background check.

"Come now Undersecretary Hardy you ran background checks on the program, everyone connected to it prior to receiving the implant. Like me, you bought into the propaganda. Neither of us had any reason to question this elaborate scheme. Go ahead, you know more insiders than I do, do your own search. No need looking online, the info is either not there or DoD's database is blocked. Makes you and your implant wonder, doesn't it?"

Hardy's implant Harlee told him it could neither confirm nor dispute her assertions. What else did she know? This was dangerous.

"Your implant has been programed to accept their story. The upgrade you were promised, the on/off algorithm, has been placed on hold by General McDab. Dr. Perkins is placing the implant in Miss Carmichael's brain along with the iPSCs which they believe will repair her damaged system. The implant will be placed in Ariel Gaspard and her baby. Of this I am certain. Colonel Tindal, General McDab and the rest of their team are meeting with potential investors, after which, as the mob boss would say, you and others will receive an offer you cannot refuse."

Oh shit. Jake. Hardy knew these actions promised disaster. Was this why they kept threatening to shut Jake down? Had he been misled?

"Agent Harper? Is this why they threaten to shut him down, is that why you're here?"

Lisa read Hardy's face and thoughts. "General McDab is the only one to answer that question."

"How do you fit into all this?" Hardy asked. Harlee was silent. How was this possible?

Lizzie, Lisa's implant shut Harlee off. She saw the puzzlement in Hardy's eyes.

"The gala event, the planned space mining venture, the President's Space Force, my presence here, Jenkins' disappearance and the op to find him, Poponovich's supposed recruitment of me, your implant placement, how far back, how many threads do you want to pursue? You knew about this event, yet you let Agent Harper believe it was his idea. Why?"

"Need to know. It was decided the time was right for the team to know. I was surprised they chose Jake to disclose the news."

"And I assume you know you are the covert team sent here to protect their investments."

She saw the puzzled look cross Undersecretary Hardy's face, then quickly disappear. How open should she be? How much did he know? She tasked Lizzie to check all communications with his implant; one way, his to her only.

"General McDab was tasked with putting this team together, to be its overall director. Me, you, Harper, and Alvarez have been selected. There will be others. Dean, Boyd; there may already be others. I know of two more."

Mark Poponovich may be able to shed some light on this. Lizzie told her. *He has agreed to allow Mark to make a call to his superior. I can monitor the call.*

Lisa unlocked Hardy's implant.

"You have one of General McDab's CIA covert groups here. Don't look surprised. You know damn well Poponovich has communicated with me. I knew he was following DICE's Alperts and Ariel Gaspard. Haven't heard from him since he was taken captive by a cartel gang. He texted me, then disappeared. I need to talk to him and his people. They are here, aren't they?" Lizzie had confirmed her suspicion. She saw wariness in Hardy's expression.

"I assure you, Jenkins, you, the Harper and Alvarez men are the only ones I personally assisted or performed the placement procedure on. I know others received the implant prior to my recruitment. I read the reports provided by Dr. Perkins and his team. There were no subject names included in the reports. I am not here to seek the others' release or evaluate Dean and Boyd per se; although this might prove helpful for the simple fact, you never suspected them having an implant. Something you and I should know, how is this possible? General McDab nor Dr. Perkins are aware you and I know the real story. I'm not certain who knows, nor do I have any knowledge their implant is the NM0099."

Lisa debated telling him about the cargo she brought on the transport, accompanied, now guarded, by a SEAL Team. He had not mentioned this or questioned her about it. Had General McDab failed to inform him? Lizzie informed her this was the case. The SEAL Team leader and the two agents, she guessed were covert CIA operatives, kept her isolated, refused to disclose their orders. Apparently General McDab's instructions to them that she was in charge were not given to them. Why? And why had Undersecretary Hardy not been informed? What were their orders?

Hardy wanted to believe her. Had he been duped by General McDab and the others? He had to be careful Harlee told him. Harlee detected Lisa's Lizzie, couldn't block her, couldn't read her. He needed to know what she knew.

"Is there a way to detect the implant, such as a cat scan?"

"The implant is able to talk to any scanner and erase its presence from the scan memory. An RF scanner can detect the presence. But looking at or verifying what the RF scan detected as the NM0099 Implant is not possible. Your implant should be able to communicate with any other NM0099 implant if the other party's implant doesn't block you." Lisa decided to delay telling Hardy her version's upgrade provided the capability to block or unlock another recipient's upgrade. DoD had requested this. They wanted variants on this ability. This would give higher ranks a way to control lower ranking members and allow shutting down a threat, due to enemy capture or death."

Hardy didn't like what he was hearing. General McDab was keeping him, and perhaps Lisa and others in the dark, why him? What did she know about Dean, Boyd, and another implant team?

"In your opinion, is General McDab putting together a backup team? Could Boyd and Dean be part of this other unit?"

"I am not aware of any contingency plan. Is it possible? Yes, in almost every military or political situation, as you know, there is more than one plan. I believe your team is plan A and I am more than certain you are the number one choice to lead the unit. As for Agent Harper, he has been on their radar for a long time. Pretty certain, Colonel Tindal would prefer not to have to deal with Agent Harper. General McDab may agree. The question is can Agent Harper be controlled?"

Hardy's mind was whirling. For Jake, this had been a nightmare, too personal, why? Devereaux, Boyd, Dean and Poponovich had they been sent to test Jake? Was Tindal the only reason? Colonel Tindal, she said. Was he still an active CIA asset? Were Dean and Boyd Jake's and TJ's possible replacements? Could he accept General McDab and company's offer without Jake or TJ? Did he trust Lisa? Too many unknowns. He didn't like being kept in the dark.

Lisa saw, read, and felt his turmoil.

"If what you say is true, there will be no controlling Agent Harper. I'm afraid Agent Alvarez will join him. I'm not sure about myself. This makes me question how far they are willing to go. In general, I agree, the ends justify the means when it comes to national security. What they propose to do to innocents goes beyond the bounds. Can they be stopped?"

"You could go public. Who would believe you? This goes all the way to the top. Investigations would be launched. This takes time. It will be too late for the innocents. Witnesses will be discredited, disappear. Conspiracy critics will rule the day. The spin doctors will revel in their work. The public will grow tired of hearing and reading about it, they'll move on to the next big sensational titillation. That's how it works. We both know it."

Was the SEAL Team here to secure the facility? Eliminate uncooperative members General McDab perceived as a threat? These thoughts had occurred to her. Lizzie was unable to confirm.

She unblocked Hardy's implant.

Harlee informed him of Lizzie, Dr. Guthridge's implant.

Afterwards, Harlee told him the mission priority had not changed: complete the op, eliminate any national security threat.

Jake and TJ were part of his team. He wanted to protect them. How could he?

"Can the other implant recipients be shut down?"

"Yes. They would need to be kept in isolation, away from phone, internet, other outside communication sources." Or eliminated. She hoped this wasn't the case.

"Okay. Poponovich has requested he be allowed to talk to his controller. Do you think this is General McDab?"

"I don't know. He never told me."

"I'm going to let him make his call. I want you to join Agents Harper and Alvarez, along with Dean and Boyd. You will be placed in our secure conference room. Agents Alvarez and Harper are already aware that Dean and Boyd have implants. I will tell them to question them in your presence that you have a way to determine their credibility. I would like you to be the facilitator. Harper and Alvarez will be told to watch the others' reactions. This will give you an opportunity to observe Harper and Alvarez also. If I think Poponovich can be trusted, he will be allowed to see an edited version of the session. I want to see his reaction. You will get your chance to meet with him depending on how I read him."

"To prevent them from outside sources will require extended isolation. General McDab and the others will be here no later than day after tomorrow for the gala. At that point yours and their decisions will be expected. Their Plan B may have been already decided as the better alternative."

"Do this while I work out a response. You and I will talk afterwards."

CHAPTER

48

Control Center
CT—Jake's neuro-implant

Jake and TJ were skeptical of Dr. Guthridge.

"How do we know we can trust her."

He replied, "we don't. Watch Dr. Guthridge; check the other two guys' reactions to her and each other."

Lisa had seen Harper's and Alvarez's pictures, still shots and videos. Neither conveyed the true person. They both exuded maleness, warriors, could serve as military recruit posters. Lisa felt the wetness. *Damnit Lizzie, stop.*

These are the real thing. Not the toys you use.

Stop. Now. We need to focus on the threats. Read them and the others. Evaluate their implants. Practical not emotional.

Dr. Guthridge didn't look like what Jake had envisioned her to look like. CT instantly reacted. *She's doable son. All her physical responses say she's ready and willing. Look. She's blushing.*

Lisa: *Lizzie No. Keep extraneous thoughts out of the evaluations. Concentrate on assigned tasks.* She had let down her guard, forgot while reading Jake to block his implant.

CT: *She has an implant. It is open, reading you. She would do you.*

Jake: *CT stop.*

Jake saw her blush deepen. He was amazed, her handshake was firm, feminine, damp despite the airconditioned coolness. They both broke eye contact. He now knew not to ask her about CT's sexual overreactions. If they were extraneous, her implant was also compromised. Weird.

Dr. Guthridge nodded her assent.

Jake cleared his throat, smiled, and said, "If you'll excuse me, I believe I need to go into the room first." Jake looked over to TJ. He nodded with his gotcha smile. Jake stepped by him and entered the room.

Lisa turned to TJ. His implant signaled its response. His implant's self-control was better than Jake's, and surprisingly, hers; his was less emotional, more analytical.

When Lisa's and his eyes locked during the handshake, his implant signaled him of the presence of her implant.

"Hello Agent Alvarez." She memed him confirming his implant's read.

'No need in the cover-story verbal evaluation. Hardy just learned I have the NM0099. I have blocked him and Agent Harper from this communication. I am here to give you the latest upgrades. I can do that. I am doing that now while you receive my recording of Hardy's conversation with me.'

TJ wondered if this woman was a flake. Geniuses often tread between great mental ability and insanity.

'I assure you I am not insane. Bear with me. Act normal. You and I must decide on a way forward for you and Agent Harper. Otherwise, I feel Undersecretary Hardy will do his duty and follow orders. There is no way out for any of us. Your friend Agent Harper, like the rest of us, has no choice. If you decide your friendship is greater than doing as commanded, you will be shutdown, kept in isolation, perhaps made to disappear.'

'Neither Jake nor I take threats to our self or our family lightly.'

"Is there somewhere we can sit down? If you don't mind, I could use something to drink." 'Better if Hardy believes we are acting normal. We can converse while we go elsewhere and perhaps you could get me a water.'

TJ tried to maintain control as they walked to the gym down the hall two doors down past the secure conference room where Jake and the other two men waited. He wasn't sure he could trust this woman. How to prevent her from reading his thoughts?

'I am not the threat. That is why I'm telling you this. You are at a critical point in their scheme for the future. I have put myself in jeopardy by telling you this. I feel morally responsible. The NM0099 upgrades can help protect you by letting you know what is happening, not prevent it. Right now, we need to think of a way to stop Dr. Perkins. Any ideas?'

TJ handed her a water. She took a seat at the juice bar. TJ remained standing. He needed to call Deane. Maybe she knew some way to prevent this from happening; maybe she knew of a way to have Dr. Perkins removed from the hospital.

'My wife is at the hospital. I'm calling her.'

'Dr. Perkins won't be alone, there will be other government agents with him.'

TJ cut the call. Deane would see the missed call and call back shortly.

A terror threat. Call in a terror threat. He could notify his SWAT team buddy. Have him arrest Dr. Perkins and his people. Have Deane get Ariel and Blakely moved.

'That would be too risky. Innocent people could get hurt, you, your wife and Agent Harper would be arrested.'

'Not if the threat was called in by an anonymous source. All that is needed is to buy time, get Dr. Perkins out of the way. Does the doc have family, wife or kids?'

'No. He's a bachelor.'

TJ's phone vibrated.

"Hello sweetheart."

"Hey babe. I'm glad you called. I guess you heard about all the agents here at the hospital?"

"Did you hear why?"

"No. Got a call from the VA Administrator, she wanted to know why I was at University Hospital in Miami? She told me I no longer have permission to be here. Do you know anything about this?"

"Ever hear of iPSCs?"

Deane did not answer immediately. "Their use is experimental. Are you saying they intend to perform that procedure on the Carmichael and Gaspard women?"

"That and who knows what else. Is there any way to stop them?"

"Family members would have to grant permission. I was told the Carmichael woman has no next of kin. A staff committee is considering pulling the plug on her. I'm not certain of the legality of using experimental procedures on her. Ariel's case is different. Her mother may still be alive. They're trying to locate her."

"Would she have the right to allow the procedure on Ariel's fetus?"

"I don't know. Possibly. I can't see her or the hospital taking a chance with an experimental procedure on Ariel's fetus though. Opens them up to lawsuits if anything went wrong. How is it you know about iPSCs and their proposed use, TJ?"

"Hardy and a member of the team told me. They said a Dr. Perkins is going to perform the procedures on the Carmichael woman and possibly on Ariel's fetus. I was hoping you could tell me how to stop this from happening to Ariel. Jake hasn't been told. No telling what he'll do if anything happens to Ariel or the fetus."

"Can't Hardy stop them?"

"I don't know. Can you think of anything?"

"I could threaten to go public."

"They could deny it. Finding out who knows or did what, would take time."

"I'll think about it and call you back if I think of something." There was a pause. "I miss you. Any idea when you may be coming home?"

"Soon, I hope. Miss you too. Love you."

TJ rejoined Lisa. She was standing at the window watching the storm. TJ walked closer. He saw the tropical foliage bent in the wind. The water was coming down in sheets off the roof. Strange how little of the sound penetrated to the inside. *Dev'sDelight* was gone. Hmm.

'My wife has been blocked from the hospital. She said she wasn't sure of the legality with regards to the Carmichael woman. Apparently, she has no next of kin and they were going to pull the plug on her anyway. Ariel's mother may still alive. Deane said they would need her permission.'

'That assumes normal procedure. Anyone involved is sworn to secrecy. They will follow orders. Just like we are expected to do.'

'What if we went public?'

'Who would publish the story? Tabloids. Only conspiracy-minded people would believe it. Anyone who did tell this would do so at grave risk to them and their family. Seems you have a decision to make—to tell your friend Agent Harper, or not.'

'This is a damned if I do, damned if I don't problem. Jake finds out I knew and didn't tell him; let's just say it would not end very well. If I do, there's no way he won't go off the deep end. The only way to stop him will be to restrain him or kill him. I can't let that happen.'

'Undersecretary Hardy will follow orders. I expect both of you may be placed under house arrest. Your wife possibly also. You better warn her.'

TJ called his brother Leon. Told him the feds may be after Deane. "I need you send some men, be her escort, get her somewhere safe. Let me know afterwards bro. May need you to remove a couple of women patients also. Need you to think how this can be done. Talk to Deane."

He called Deane. She wanted to argue. She finally agreed.

"I have to be back in Charlotte a week from Monday otherwise I could lose both my jobs. I'll talk to an administrator I know and see if she can request patient transfers. The dogs need to be picked up also."

"Call Leon. This number be good until you're safe." TJ gave her the number of Leon's burner. "Once you make the call, take phone apart, break into pieces, throw them in trash."

"I'll have one of Leon's people take it to my room, leave it there."

"That'll work. Be careful. Love you."

"You too."

TJ remembered something. 'Jake's neck. They administered iPSCs to his neck.'

This came as shocking news to Lisa. Dr. Perkins did this without informing her.

'Jake's neck seems to be fine now. If the procedure worked for him. He shouldn't object to its use on the fetus.'

'Let me be the one to inform him. I will reassure him of its safety.' Lisa was trying to process this news about Jake receiving the iPSC treatment and Dr. Perkins failure to tell her. Yet here she was pretending she knew and was going to lie about its safety. Something she knew nothing about. She was also withholding Dr. Perkins and company's imminent plans to proceed placing the implants in the women and fetus. Her excuse to herself-- it was necessary to protect Harper and Alvarez and buy time until General McDab arrived. She felt dirty. Undersecretary Hardy would know she knew. How much did he know? If TJ knew about the iPSCs, Hardy certainly knew. Why not her? What else didn't *she* know?

'Time to join Jake and the others. Let me take the lead. They don't know me. Could prove useful.'

Lizzie monitor Jake's and the others' ongoing communication through Jake's implant; Jake's alter-ego. *You mean naughty CT.* Don't go there, Lizzie. Damn. Implant sexual conjugation; an unintended consequence. She would need to study a way to prevent implant readings of their hosts emotions.

Control of emotions could be dangerous.

'Agent Alvarez, please do not disclose my implant to Jake or the others. Your upgrade will allow you to pick up on their prior communication, unless they have the blocking algorithm, which is not likely.'

Dean and Boyd sat shackled in the metal chairs. Dean had a bemused look on his gruff, unshaven face. The hair softened his pinched features. Boyd's normally pale, sun-starved looks were red-faced angry. Jake stood on the other side of the table. He shook his head when they entered.

TJ immediately picked up on the sexist meme from Dean to Boyd. He saw Lisa's face darken.

Lisa was used to sexist remarks and behavior from men. Women were normally better at keeping their thoughts to themselves except for the more outspoken feminists. Lizzie threatened to expose her inner emotions.

These two did indeed have implants. She probed theirs to determine how sophisticated theirs were. No blocking ability. She relayed her findings; confirmed TJ's supposition; gave Jake a heads-up. She memed TJ reversing her request that she take the lead.

Lisa checked Jake's implant for knowledge about the iPSC and the condition of his neck. Lizzie reported CT indicated Jake's neck was fine. *Along with the rest of him.* Lizzie, don't go there. *He is trying to block his implant. He is afraid his implant has been compromised. CT likes your thoughts. He thinks we could have virtual sex.* Okay Lizzie, that's it.

'Jake I'm upgrading CT. This will give you a blocking feature. I will explain other attributes later. TJ please send a message for me. Tell Dean to go f' himself.'

TJ smiled. His smile became a grin after observing Dean jerk as if he slapped him.

'Ask him when and by whom he received his implant.'

Jake requested he be allowed to ask. TJ demurred.

'Hey assface we'd like to know how it is you two have the implant? Start with when and by whom? Then tell us what this has to do with Jenkins.'

Dean memed, 'Hello Dr. Guthridge. Dr. Perkins said you were the one who helped him with the NM0099. You're responsible for Jenkins and the reason we're all here. Harper and Alvarez, what a not so surprising discovery. Many of the crew surmised you were possibly one of the recipients Dr. Perkins told us about. He never gave names. He said we should be able to discover this for ourselves. A test of the implant's power. Wondered when ours would be activated. Begs to wonder, why now?'

Jake, TJ, and Lisa received a shrill screech which grew in intensity. Their features contorted with pain--Lisa's was very brief before she blocked it. Jake and TJ suffered slightly longer. Boyd showed no affect.

'Ah. Amazing seems you can stop the debilitating weapon feature. Interesting. And, Dr. Guthridge you were fast, not fast enough. Interesting, you have an updated implant. Perhaps you will enlighten me, Dr. Perkins said you were working on upgrades. Care to share?" Lisa didn't reply. "Be a shame, thought you two were on the same team? Thought all of us were on the same team?'

'Guantanamo, 'happened at Gitmo.' CT informed them, Lizzie and Earl concurred. 'Why just you two? Why not the others?'

Boyd interrupted Dean. 'What makes you think there aren't others? There certainly will be more in the future. We are going to be part of a special unit, a human cyber force. Dr. Perkins said there will be other recruits. Not all will have the same abilities…'

'Can it Boyd,' Dean memed interrupting him. 'I'm sure they heard the same or similar spiel. Dr. Guthridge, I'm curious, why did you receive the implant? You don't look like a soldier.' Dean was giving her a salacious stare.

'The NM0099 was meant to be a defensive weapon. But for your information, I was in the Air Force and in the Air Force Reserve. Moving on. What do you know about Jenkins?'

'Mark never knew or failed to inform us that Jenkins had the implant inserted in his head. He didn't have any of the data files on him. Mark figured he hid them somewhere or gave them to someone. Mark was pissed. He will be further pissed when he finds out others have the implant. I take it, he doesn't have the implant, does he?'

Lisa, Jake, and TJ didn't respond. The scan indicated Boyd and Dean were the only two. Could TJ's scanner have been wrong?

Dean saw the worried expression on their faces. He and Boyd had been ordered not to disclose the implant to anyone. He realized they were reading his implant.

'Perhaps you can tell everyone why we were ordered to leave Jenkins with General Toraz?'

Still no response. 'Would have helped, especially with Jenkins, had we been given the implants sooner. As it was, we fumbled around; learned nothing. Only clue came from that Mexican banger whore who said the Harper woman came there with Jenkins and left with her father. Mark said he would take care of Jenkins; sent us back to the boat. Mark later told us the general claimed Jenkins escaped. We got arrested by the Coast Guard, sent to Gitmo. Mark went looking for Jenkins. Here we are.'

"Bullshit!" TJ replied, startling everyone, especially the unimplanted who had been watching and wondering why no one was saying anything.

"Forensic evidence says otherwise. You and the others were on Okneyev's freighter as was Jenkins. Jenkins was also on Devereaux' boat. Jenkins cut a deal with you, didn't he?"

"Not at liberty to say."

Jake got in his face. "And you have the gall to claim you're on the team with us. Screw you."

Lisa remained quiet, watching the exchange, having Lizzie do a search of Gitmo's records for who had been there when they were there. Dr. Perkins, Colonel Hunter and General McDab had logged in during their stay. So had Undersecretary Hardy. She wondered how much of this seemingly well-rehearsed story was true or another of the CIA's cover concoctions. Undersecretary Hardy, what part did he play in this plot. She looked forward to confronting him and Mark.

Lisa memed Jake and TJ, 'I believe we found out what we expected. Seems Undersecretary Hardy owes us an explanation, as does Mark.' She sent them Lizzie's findings. "Makes me wonder about the others, could they have inactive implants? What does Undersecretary Hardy and these guys have going on?' Her thought, she dared not share with them, was what else Undersecretary Hardy knew and how was it Lizzie's search had missed knowing? Or did she? Jake's paranoia, was it valid?

'We're gonna leave you with the others now. You'll need to explain to the others what just transpired. By the looks on their faces, they'll be wanting to know.'

The guards let them out. Lisa asked Jake and TJ to go with her to the gym juice bar. Jake and TJ turned the sound system music on. A Caribbean steel drum band was banging out a song. Once they were seated sipping bottled water, Lisa asked Jake about his injured neck.

"Hardly feel any pain or stiffness. Whatever Dr. Perkins did, worked great. Why?"

"Part of my follow-up. It's good to hear the iPSCs work. Notice any side effects?"

"Not that I'm aware of." Jake asked CT who ran a diagnostic and informed Jake of Lizzie's earlier request and said everything had worked as promised just as he told her. "You already knew this. What's going on?" Jake saw TJ's normal smile fade.

"Knowing your results, do you believe the Carmichael woman could benefit from the treatment?"

"How should I know? Last I heard, they had given up hope. In which case, why not?" Jake knew by the way TJ was not engaged, something else was going on. "TJ, what's going on?"

Lisa quickly replied. "The doctors in Miami, including Dr. Perkins, believe the Carmichael woman and the Gaspard woman and her fetus could benefit from the iPSC procedure just as you have. I agree. What do you think?"

Jake looked at her, then TJ. "Why is it I feel it doesn't make a damn what I think." He stood up. TJ did also.

Lisa spoke quickly.

"Okay. The Carmichael woman has no next of kin. They were going to pull the plug. This may or may not work for her. Your girlfriend, the Gaspard woman's next of kin is her mother. She has given permission for the treatment. It certainly does matter to Agent Alvarez what you think. Believe me or not, what you think matters a great deal to me, personally and professionally, which is why I'm telling you this. Agent Alvarez wanted to tell you, I insisted I be the one to tell you. From what you indicate about its effectiveness, I believe this may be the best course of action for them also; especially for the Carmichael woman."

TJ tried to keep his expression neutral. He blocked Jake from reading his reaction when Dr. Guthridge claimed Ariel's mother had given permission. Typical spook, say what is expedient, damn the truth. There went trust. Shouldn't try to have him confirm her bullshit. He understood the motive, detested the means.

"You buying this, TJ?" Jake asked.

"Bro, I was given the same information. You're the one had this treatment, not me. What you think?"

Jake had CT do a records' update from the hospital. CT reported he was blocked. He memed TJ, blocking Lisa. 'I'm blocked from the hospital. How about calling Deane. I'm not sure I trust this woman, Hardy or anyone other than you.'

'Done bro, I already talked to Deane. The VA Administrator has ordered her back to her job in Charlotte. She said government agents blocked her from the hospital. I got Leon working with Deane on a backup plan to get them moved out of the hospital. She's first goina request their transfer to Charlotte.'

Jake was struggling to remain calm. He wasn't sure of Dr. Guthridge's capabilities. CT warned him her Lizzie was tied into him; his attempts to block were not working. This news about what was going down in Miami had him knotted up. The iPSCs had relieved his neck pain. Neck pain was minor compared to tampering with the brain. CT assured him reported research experiments provided positive results. Although no known human tests were reported. Then again, there were no posted results for the NM0099 implants. If CT was compromised, he could have been fed misinformation?

This left him with a conundrum, what could he live with knowing: Ariel, their baby, Blakely continuing with possible long-term brain damage, PTSD, pull-the-plug death or, a chance at full recovery without suffering like he had? For Blakely, it meant a possibility of living longer. The same for Ariel and their unborn child. What would Ariel choose? The choice was made without them or him. Was this what bothered him most, this feeling of helplessness, of not having control? It was in God's hands now. Which God? The one, like most people, he believed in when he was scared or felt powerless--the one he trusted to give a shit. Or the one who was beyond caring about petty individual earthlings. Or, the damn puppet masters who may be using the implant, playing their version of God. This was another war zone minefield, Blakely's, Ariel's, and their baby's fates, like his, were sealed. For now, he would play the hand he was dealt, let them think he was onboard. It'll be what it'll be, until it isn't.

'We need to confront Hardy. I need straight answers, no more bullshit.'

Lisa had the capability to bypass Jake's CT's attempted block. She listened. Dared not say anything. None of them need have the bypass- blocking capability. She reserved this ability for herself. She wondered what other changes Dr. Perkins team had developed and had failed to inform her of? Were there others, including Undersecretary Hardy, who had received some upgrade she knew nothing about? Was she in control of her own implant? Had Jake's CT affected Lizzie, planted paranoid thoughts into her head. She instructed Lizzie to do a self-analysis; run a system check for malware or viruses.

CHAPTER
49

Control Center
Hardy and Dr. Guthridge

They found Hardy in his office. He ended his call and motioned them in. "That was General McDab I was talking to. He gave me the go-ahead to disclose the whole operation. I've been dancing around playing musical chairs with all of you. Intel points to two amphibious vessels in Cuban waters. One is Okneyev's freighter which is communicating with a nearby submersible vessel whose signature is cloaked. This is believed to be the underwater nuclear-capable UAV. What we don't know is if it is armed. If so, with what? Two members of an Interpol team failed to confirm the presence of nuclear material aboard Okneyev's former vessel. Later tests detected low-level radiation on the sunken freighter. Which means we must assume a dirty missile could be on the submersible. And we don't know their intent. Is it a bargaining tactic or is there a target? Our op is now considered Code Red. All communication is locked down. Any personal issues will need to be handled when we resolve this threat." Hardy looked at Jake when he said this. "All personnel will assemble in the conference room in thirty minutes to go over our assignments."

Jake fought hard to control his emotions. He wanted to scream "screw you" to Hardy. TJ pulled him out the door. Dr. Guthridge stayed behind, closing the door behind them.

Jake pulled TJ's hand loose. TJ said, "Not here. Come on."

Jake reluctantly followed him down to the secured conference room. TJ waited and closed the door behind Jake after he entered. He held up a hand, then memed, 'assume this room is bugged.'

Jake said, "I don't give a damn. Don't you understand my daughter is out there, possibly on the *SwaleMaiden*, anchored in Cuban waters same as Okneyev's freighter and the submersible. Hardy knows this. Yet, he has the balls to say my personal issues are secondary. screw him. I hope you heard that you asshole. Screw you!" Jake shouted at the ceiling.

"Damnit Jake, get ahold of yourself. This an international situation, a Code Red. The UN and every government agency, US and otherwise goina be all over this."

"Just like they are with Iran and North Korea. How's that working out? This is my daughter TJ. If she is on that boat in Cuban waters the authorities, doesn't matter which country they're from, will have to get the Cuban governments permission to mount a search. That will take time. And, if whoever has Elizabeth fears a search, they damn sure won't keep her onboard."

TJ walked to the center of the room and leaned on the long table facing Jake. He shrugged; palms turned upward.

"There's a storm sitting out there. Nothing's moving on water or in the air, buys us time. If you right 'bout Elizabeth being on the *SwaleMaiden*, then nothing going to happen anytime soon. They goina know there's an all-out search for her, been goin' on some time now. Why would this proposed search be any different? You have your Cuban friends watching the boat, have you heard anything." Jake shook his head. "I didn't think so. You don't know she's on the *SwaleMaiden*. She could be anywhere. Need to calm your ass down, hear Hardy out. Could be we goina be sent to Cuba. Swore I'd never go there long as the damn commies in charge. May not have a choice. We're agents, no longer civilians--we follow orders. Maybe this time we goina be armed."

"Orders or no orders, soon as I can find a way I'm going there."

Suzie met Terrence Lee a day earlier than planned in the Westin Hotel. She earlier learned General McDab was now Secretary of Homeland Security and that he was coming to Cancun for the gala event that was in danger of being rescheduled due to two tropical depressions, one in the Bay of Campeche and the other in the Caribbean. Although, the latest forecast declared they would be out of the area by tomorrow. She was shocked when she received a text from an unknown number telling her to locate and rescue Pablo's wife Elizabeth. The text ended with 999. This was Poponovich's code number. After the text, she realized this gave her a way to accomplish DICE's agent Terrence's goal, as well as her assignment.

"What's in it for me?" he asked after taking a long pull from his bottled beer.

"Use your head. I'm sure you knew the reason your man Alperts had her taken in the first place. We use her as a bargaining chip. Pablo's not going to want her talking. This way we make him pay again. The Harper man will pay; you can bet on it. We get in touch with the cartel, use her as bait for the Harper man. Three payments using one little birdie."

Terrence kept his face neutral. He chugged his beer, signaled the waitress for another. It was like she knew of his plans. Hmm.

"I knew there was a reason to throw in with you. Risky. The bigger the risk, the bigger the reward." Good thing she didn't know about Colonel Tindal's and other's offers, or did she. What else did she know? "You and I should celebrate. Get adjoining rooms have us a pow wow, plan this out."

"What's there to plan. I bet you know where we can find her."

"If I did, why would I need you?"

"You looked in a mirror lately? Listened to yourself? I can go places you can't. I'm an unknown. I bet you aren't. And once we get her, who do you think she'll trust more, me or you?"

He waited to answer until the waitress set his fresh beer down and left with his empty. He followed her sweet looking young ass, dressed in a short, tight skirt, thinking of how much something like that cost and how many like her, or better, all the payoffs could buy. This woman was right. He would play along until the prize was in hand, then he would no longer need her. She had no way of knowing his other plan—it was already in play.

"We'll have to wait until the storm is over. We'll need to be well-armed. I can get the weapons and some backup. You need to lay the groundwork for the meetups." He watched her. Something told him she was thinking to screw him over. This could be fun.

Suzie picked up her glass and took a drink.

"Storm is supposed to be gone by tomorrow afternoon. Can you be ready then?"

"Everything on my end is set for tomorrow. We meet back here the day of the gala to make the exchange. You take care of your end. I'll take care of mine."

"The day of the gala event is risky. Lots of important people. Lots of law enforcement and government authorities."

"Means they'll be too busy to worry with us." Everyone be extra busy if what was to happen happened.

Suzie was thinking, 'he's right. Be a good time to hand him over and secure her target, the cartel boss, and, if everything went off without a hitch, she would bag his nephew also. Mark needed to be told.'

What Suzie didn't know, the cartel boss was coming with General Toraz and the Mexican President.

"What is going on here?" Lisa asked Hardy. He leaned forward, motioned her to a chair across from his desk. She hesitated then sat down.

"Welcome to the team Dr. Guthridge," he said. As you may or may not know, General McDab was charged with helping set up what he calls the president's Space Force Cyber Intelligence Strike Force Unit. The President and the General decided the new subbranch of the Air Force needed an independent covert intelligence unit capable of doing the heavy lifting without all the bullshit oversight. McDab knew through intelligence meetings about Dr. Perkins work and the DoD's development of the NM0099 program of which you were part of. He decided this was the perfect platform upon which to develop the unit. Major Jenkins' subterfuge threw a monkey wrench into his plans. That's what he and others in the loop initially thought. Everyone in the know, knew Jenkins had to be stopped. The General and a few others saw this as an opportunity to test the implant team's effectiveness." Hardy leaned back watching Dr. Guthridge. He saw she was not enthused, seemed her thoughts were elsewhere.

"Long before that decision was made known to me, I was tasked with assembling personnel, providing them with a mission and monitoring their progress, acting as the lead investigator to find Jenkins and the intel he stole. Unfortunately, Agent Harper's personal issues threatened to sidetrack the mission. Then, other agents from sister agencies, of which you were recruited to be part of, became involved. Everyone was suspicious of each other, plots and subplots kept creating more problems. It was decided to use the implant to locate and stop Jenkins. I was kept in the dark about General McDab and others putting together the President's special unit and the decision to create more than one team to test the NM0099's efficacy. Learning others had received the implant came as a surprise to me."

Lisa had been listening while Lizzie analyzed his story for its veracity.

"You were at Guantanamo with the others when they received the implant. How could you not know?"

"I never saw Dr. Perkins or whoever performed the implant operation. I never saw the operation area, didn't know it happened until now. I was there to question the others about Jenkins. I did not know who they worked for. I had suspicions, had received intel, found lots of holes in their cover stories. Everything pointed to CIA covert assets; I had no proof. I suspected and questioned them about their affiliations and possible involvement with the op. I was purposely kept in the dark because of suspicions about Agent Harper. Suspicions which continue to this day. I have been ordered to integrate the two groups into one unit, make assignments, and perform the mission. I do not know what all is necessary to know about most of the members of the proposed team. It is entirely possible, one or more of them may be complicit with the other side and Jenkins. I now know you have the upgraded version of the implant. I was told there are graded levels of control to maintain a command structure. To take charge and perform under the radar, as directed, I need the upgrades and your assistance in monitoring the others. General McDab has made you my assistant."

Lizzie verified Undersecretary Hardy's story. Lisa did not like this turn of events.

"I am a neurobiophysicist. I was never comfortable working undercover. I was coerced, did it because of what was discovered about Major Jenkins and Colonel Tindal."

"And, because of your personal involvement with Mark Poponovich. There is something you should know, as expected, your friend Poponovich called General McDab and was given orders to join the unit. He also texted a message to a burner phone, *person, and message unknown.* I need you to see if you can learn to whom and what messages were passed between him and whomever. As well as help me discover who all has the implants and what they know. I find it puzzling that Dean and Boyd received the implants and not the others."

Lisa had pondered this as Hardy spoke. Lizzie checked their profiles. What was found troubled Lisa.

"There is one common denominator shared by known recipients—the willingness to take another life."

Lisa told Hardy what she found and feared.

"That isn't entirely true. I do not fit that profile and I'm sure you don't either. I was told this implant was to be a nonlethal weapon. My team has operated with that understanding. Okay?"

Lisa didn't reply.

Hardy wasn't sure what this meant.

"I am considering bringing two more women, Major Duplantis and Captain Adams, onboard, giving them the implant. I need your analysis. Talk to them and the others. If you feel you must talk to them about your lethal combat concerns."

Lisa wasn't convinced.

"I was told the NM0099 was to be nonlethal when I signed on with Marberry Industries, Now, it seems that was never true, or the mandate has changed. I abhor violence. If this unit is a combat unit, you can count me out."

"Nothing said to me indicates that is the case. The unit is a clandestine intelligence gathering unit. Lethal force is to be used as a last resort; for defensive purposes where there is no other recourse. I intend to keep it that way. Now, I need you to upgrade Harlee my implant. Let's go save our necks and put this mystery to rest. There is the possibility of a bio or nuclear weapon involved. The clock is ticking."

Lisa upgraded Undersecretary Hardy's implant. She had not received orders making him her superior. She decided Lizzie should retain her exclusive abilities. He had not mentioned the SEALTeam which reinforced her decision to hold back.

CHAPTER
50

Control Center
CT

"No f'ing way," Jake said when Hardy told him about General McDab's proposal to form a Space Force Cyber Intel Strike Force Unit, which would include Mark and crew and Marge and Jenny.

TJ simply shook his head.

"This is the only way forward Jake. You have been given numerous warnings. When you were recruited, the possibility of a nuclear or dirty weapon amphib was feared; became a prime directive of Operation Pink Flamingo even before Jenkins became part of the mission. We knew other agencies would be involved, other agents, both foreign and domestic, trying to infiltrate and undermine our efforts. The threat level is now at its highest. We have been ordered to combine our efforts, become a team, finish the operation and move on."

TJ spoke up, "You have to trust your team members. They have been working against us. They don't trust us. We don't trust them. We're not sure who they work for. I'm sorry sir, I don't see this as workable."

"I have my orders. You have yours. We also have an advantage. Our implants are superior to theirs. Tell them Dr. Guthridge."

Lisa hesitated. "I will need to do further evaluation to determine this."

Hardy reprimanded Lisa with a targeted meme. 'Are you trying to undermine me Dr. Guthridge?'

'No sir. These two believe they have the complete upgrade. Hopefully, theirs is superior to the other recipients. I need to determine if this is the case. This gives them time to consider their lack of options, accept the obvious.'

CT had been tasked to track Ariel's situation at the hospital only to find it was blocked. Informed of this Jake had instructed CT to search offensive and defensive strategies to protect them in case there was an attempt to shut him down as threatened. CT presented numerous strategies, most which would be considered unwarranted violence. He wanted to talk to TJ about this. CT reiterated his worries--warned him he could not do so with any certainty the communication might not be intercepted by Hardy or Dr. Guthridge or God knows who else. CT had been alerted by what he referred to as the *Others*, past recipients of the implant, gone rogue. Jake thought the *Others* were the other members of this proposed team. CT was warned by the rogue *Others* to not dissuade Jake of his error.

"I need to talk to you. I'm thinking the shower area is the safest place."

TJ simply nodded and started walking that way.

Once they entered the shower area, Jake turned on the sinks and the exhaust fans. They stepped inside one of the private shower stalls.

"Are you thinking the same thing I'm thinking that these others with the implant are our possible replacements?"

"Hard not to. General McDab, former head of the CIA clandestine unit, now head of Homeland. What kind of political shit is that? Good bet Poponovich and his crew worked for the General. We both know from experience you can't trust those mothers. Their whole modus is lies and misdirection. Nothing we've heard gives me any reason to trust them. But what can we do?"

"Our implants are tied into the internet. Ever hear of A DDoS attack? That's a distributed denial-of-service attack which sends bogus internet traffic to overwhelm the servers. The servers convert URL addresses into IP numbers which routers use. The servers crash, websites become shutdown. Another way a hacker can attack would be through the BGP tables, the border gateway protocol tables. Scramble them, misdirect traffic and the service providers shutdown. The goal is to insert a virus that lays dormant, undetected until the hacker wants it to become active."

TJ was puzzled. "What you talking about bro? Not thinking about doing this, I hope? That would be considered terrorism."

"Don't you see I may be capable of doing this, you, Hardy, anyone with hacking knowledge could do this. Our implants can access the ways to do this. The threat to shut us down is not an idle threat. With these implants we all become threats to each other and to the internet security of individuals, institutions, governments, essentially, the world. The ultimate weapon capable of individual or mass destruction—a Space Force Cyber Intelligence Strike Force. No mention of any weapons. We talking cyber warfare, understand?"

"Whoa bro." TJ's implant verified what Jake said was true. "This includes Jenkins. No wonder this has become critical. He may be the hacker or working with a hacker. For all we know these other guys may be involved, possibly shielding the virus,"

Jake replied, "They own us. The only way out is termination. The push for this cyber force unit means we're each tasked with working together to find Jenkins, locate a possible bio or nuclear-armed amphib, prevent a possible virus attack. Cooperate or die with no way to know whom to trust. HSI has a cyber security unit, strange we weren't assigned to this unit, and none of them were tasked to join this latest Space Force Cyber Intel Unit. Strike Force? Our minds gonna be the weapons. Who's to say what'll happen to us when we are asked to do something we don't agree with, like not wanting Blakely, Ariel and my son operated upon? They hold all the cards and we're forced to play, or what? We simply don't know. But what I do know is, I'm going to have a look onboard *Dev'sDelight* and the *SwaleMaiden* to check for Elizabeth. I also intend to check General Toraz' property for any sign of Elena. Save my daughter; clear my name. They'll have to show their hand to stop me. If they shut me down, it'll be up to you to decide your own path."

"Hey bro, Deane and me, we on your side. But in case you haven't noticed, we have no boat, no transportation."

"Drones. The drones we were trained for which never materialized. Where are they? Don't look at me like that. The only way is to commandeer drones to reccee the boats. This way we can check to see if Elizabeth and possibly Jenkins are onboard. CT, my implant discovered The Hive came onboard a cargo plane with Dr. Guthridge. Those damn bee drones would be perfect. They could do the recon and be our weapons."

TJ felt this was a longshot. Better than watching Jake go off the deep end.

"You saying you willing to go along with the General's proposal bro?"

"I'm gonna do what I said I'm going to do."

They had not heard Lisa enter the gym. She smiled at their shocked expressions when they exited the shower and saw her seated at the juice bar.

"You spying on us?" Jake asked louder than he intended. "Hardy put you up to this?"

"Yes and no," Lisa replied. "Undersecretary Hardy is being Undersecretary Hardy. He follows orders. Like you Agent Harper, I've learned to question orders. Unfortunately, the NM0099 puts constraints on independent thinking. Every possible action is open for debate. The final decision should be the best consensus and a good leader recognizes it as such. As you said Agent Alvarez, the members of a unit must trust each other, work together, accept the judgement of their leaders. I understand your distrust of General McDab and the CIA. I too have my reservations."

Neither Jake nor TJ said anything.

"I know Agent Poponovich. I don't know the others. The reason I came here to talk to you was two-fold: I have been appointed as second in command, Undersecretary Hardy's assistant." She saw their faces grow hard, read their dubious thoughts. "This wasn't my choice. I sense your disapproval. I hope you'll give me a chance to earn your trust. To that end, I pledge to you I will not let either of you be shut out of the decision loop or be shut down. You will have the added advantage of having your implants be superior to anyone else's in the unit other than Undersecretary Hardy and myself. I hope this is acceptable?"

She turned her attention to Jake. "As for your proposed use of drones, I will see about helping you with that. I was instructed to bring with me the drone called the Hive. I believe both of you are familiar with it."

Jake turned red in the face. TJ's reaction was less noticeable. Jake's thoughts were more intensely angry than TJ's. Images of his dog Dusty, guts hanging out, lying sedated for months at Doc Hunter's clinic, all lingered in Jake's mind. He felt guilty for not having contacted Doc Hunter to check on his dogs.

"I believe I can convince Undersecretary Hardy and the General of the benefits of a test run over water. Put the Hive's Bumblebees in a real-world situation. Their small signature and tactical capabilities give them a superior advantage. Not unlike the one's you both are familiar with from your Middle East deployments. Captain Adams is one of the best from what her superiors say. Once she receives the implant, she'll know what to do. As for your other concern, from what I've discovered, General Toraz is under constant surveillance, ground and air. He is supposed to attend the gala. He'll be accompanying Mexico's President and the Gonzalez uncle."

Jake and TJ stood on the other side of the bar listening. Both had their reservations. Both realized the situation. TJ looked at Jake.

"What you think bro? I say give it a shot. Beats us going it alone."

Jake's implant CT informed Jake, she passed the smell test. '*You might change your mind about her and…*'

'*Can it CT.*'

Jake saw Lisa blush. He knew his neck and face were glowing. TJ's grin was plastered across his face.

"Okay, for now, I'll wait to see how this plays out."

Lisa cleared her throat. "Undersecretary Hardy awaits our evaluation of the others. Be on guard, use your implant's offensive and defensive abilities. You now have the blocking ability, the on/off switch, you requested. Doesn't block Undersecretary Hardy or me and unless Dr. Perkins discovered how to do so, no others don't have the capability. Learning their capabilities is up to us. As for them possibly bearing a Trojan Horse and working for the other side, not impossible. That could mean Dr. Perkins is involved, that indicates he is a CIA or, possibly, a foreign asset. Your upgrade includes the latest in malware and virus detection and protection. If Dr. Perkins is not who he is supposed to be and your implant was infected before installation, the upgraded quantum cryptography algorithm would normally have detected it and destroyed it before now."

"Unless it is dormant and waiting for the trigger command," Jake added.

"Yes. There is no such thing as one hundred percent assurance of detection or protection."

"Then the implant is not just another tool or weapon in our arsenal to deter the enemy like we were initially led to believe. This could be a ticking time bomb. Still think I've been unjustly paranoid TJ?"

TJ shook his head and said, "this time you right bro. Remember, you said we all born to die, and that you not afraid of dying. Tick tock, the clock ticks on. Time to do or die trying. We ain't getting any younger."

"Truth," Jake replied. He felt he was finally going to have a chance to end this once and for all.

Sunlight winked on then off outside the glass window unit. The rain and wind appeared to be subsiding.

"Maybe the storm is moving on as predicted," Lisa said. "We need to check in with the others."

Jake said, "I think we should meet with Poponovich again before we meet with the others."

They stepped out into the corridor. The two guards approached. The larger one told Lisa Hardy awaited them. Lisa asked if Undersecretary Hardy was in his office or the conference room? When told conference room, she told him to remind Undersecretary Hardy she needed to talk to Poponovich prior to meeting with the others. After they left, she memed Jake and TJ.

'I need a few minutes alone with Poponovich. And no, it's not what you think.'

'May not be for you, better believe he'll think otherwise,' Jake replied. 'You should know.'

She gave Jake a hard look then walked on ahead without replying.

The guards and Undersecretary Hardy stepped back outside the door of the conference room where Lisa waited. Jake and TJ joined them.

"We don't have much time Dr. Guthridge," Hardy said studying all three of them, "this better not take long."

"I just have a few questions for him. I need answers, we need answers. It's important or I wouldn't be asking."

Undersecretary Hardy nodded to the guards. "Take Poponovich to my office," he told them. When they reentered the conference room, he turned to Jake and TJ.

"You ready to put your issues aside and get on with the mission?"

TJ answered, "yes sir."

Jake said, "My issues are a part of the mission. General McDab and Dr. Perkins assured me of this as you well know. It started with these guys and Jenkins. Now you're telling me to trust them. We'll see. I'll do my part despite my reservations only because I have no choice; never did, did I?"

Hardy's face grew hard. "Jake, if you all do your part, I promise you I will do everything in my power to make sure your family is safe."

"And I fully intend to make sure you keep that promise. That's why I've agreed to continue, just so you know. Dr. Guthridge…"

Jake stopped talking when Hardy reached out and opened the door to let the guards and Mark out. Mark's face lit up when he saw Lisa. He smiled. Lisa didn't.

"What a nice surprise. Must be party time. Hey guys cheer up, don't look so gloomy. Jake, I may have some good news for you."

"Can it Poponovich. Dr. Guthridge needs a few minutes alone with you," Hardy said gruffly.

"Well, I guess that'll do. Been a while since we last "talked", shouldn't take long." Mark laughed. Lisa turned bright red.

Hardy told the guards to escort them to his office.

Lisa memed Jake and TJ, 'Jake I need you to wait before discussing my proposal with Undersecretary Hardy.'

After the guards left and the door was closed, Mark reached out to hug Lisa. She deflected his attempt.

"What's wrong, is it my cologne? Called au de urine. Works with most primates"

Lisa stared into his eyes. She tried to detect an implant with no luck. "We only have a few minutes. How many of your crew have the NM0099?"

"You mean the device Jenkins has the info on?"

"Cut the shit Mark. You know damn well what I'm asking. How many?"

"I don't have any idea. This is classified. General McDab's orders."

"I know all about the cyber unit Mark. I am now second in command. General McDab's orders."

Mark laughed. "You gotta be kidding me. General McDab would have told me. My crew is independent. His orders. As for this NM0099, that is part of our mission. Classified. I'm sure you know what that means. You need to tell Hardy to let us go so we can complete our mission that he and his bozos screwed up."

Lisa stepped out into the corridor and memed Undersecretary Hardy to join her. As he came her way, she memed him what Mark said.

Hardy joined her and they reentered his office. Mark sat on the other side of Hardy's desk in his swivel chair. Mark looked up and grinned at them.

"Get your ass up out of my chair."

"Or what? You'll put me back in timeout?"

Hardy opened his door. The two guards were hurrying his way. They were followed by Jake and TJ.

"Give me your taser," Hardy ordered one of the guards.

The guard hesitated. "I'm sorry sir. I have orders not to relinquish my weapon to anyone. We have…"

The guard did not move fast enough. Jake and TJ moved in behind the guards and within seconds relieved the men of their tasers. The guards whirled around only to find Jake and TJ anticipated their moves and moved back out of their reach. Tasers in hand pointed at them.

Suddenly the door to the control room burst open and Jake and TJ found themselves staring at two men in tactical gear armed with MP5s. The weapons were pointed directly at them. Two other men walked through the door behind the armed ones. Lisa recognized them. They were the SEAL Team from the plane.

'What is this shit?' Hardy, TJ, and Jake all memed Lisa.

She memed, 'I was going to tell you about them. I wasn't sure who to trust. Who might have known before I did. These men accompanied me and the

Hive UAV aboard a transport as ordered by General McDab It is one of the few things that I was told. These men refused to make polite conversation.'

'F' this. You ready TJ.'

Hardy started to meme them to stand down. His thought never had a chance.

The chisel-faced taller one stepped around the two-armed SEALs and held out his hand to Jake and TJ. Jake stepped forward the taser in his hand. He extended, the man reached out to take it and Jake tased him, then moved in on the SEAL on the right. Before the SEAL could respond, Jake dropped and came up with a hard-right-hand punch to the man's groin, his left hand taking the HP MP-7. Simultaneously, TJ tased the other SEAL and disarmed him. The shorter more-sturdy man stood frozen. TJ held the requisitioned MP5 to his head. The two SEALs and his fellow CIA officer lay at their feet writhing in pain, their moans echoing in the corridor.

The other guard who Hardy hadn't spoken to said to Hardy, "sir, we were alerted by the guards at the gate JSOC, Joint Special Operations Command's men were here under General McDab's orders. We were told to allow their entrance then place the building on lockdown."

The man left standing looked over at Hardy. Mark pushed past Hardy.

"Hello Walt. Took you long enough. You have to excuse these guys lack of manners."

"Hello Mark. Got here as fast as we could."

"What the hell is going on here?" Hardy asked.

Mark saw Jake had the SEAL's weapon pointed in his direction.

"No need in that Jake ole buddy. Everyone, this is Special Agent Colonel Walt Picard." Picard nodded. "These men are here as a tactical unit. Their specialty is nuclear threat assessment and prevention. Walt, I guess Operation White Shark is why you're here?"

"You got it." He looked down at the moaning men. "Mind helping these men up," he said looking at TJ.

TJ and Jake moved over and took the sidearms, K'bars and other weapons from the men, all the while keeping eyes on the man Mark called Walt. When they finished disarming the two SEALs, they backed up and motioned for the control center guards to move over next to the prone men.

"Be my guest," TJ replied. "Wouldn't try any funny moves if I were you. Never assume nor underestimate anyone. We might look out of shape, but we've been there and know better." He grinned.

Hardy told the two guards to help Walt. They helped Walt lean them against the wall of the corridor. The chisel-face man mumbled a few expletives and some code sounding order to Walt. Walt straightened up.

"I'm afraid we don't have much time. The storm is moving on and the ships which took shelter in Cuban waters have weighed anchor. This gala with all the dignitaries coming makes a prime target for a demonstration of a missile attack from the stealth UAV amphib."

Hardy moved over to Jake. "Give me the taser Jake." Jake handed him the re-armed taser. Hardy pointed it at Mark.

"Dr. Guthridge, move away from Agent Poponovich."

Lisa moved past Mark and joined Hardy.

"Now, Picard move over here beside Poponovich."

Picard did so reluctantly. "Didn't you hear what I said? We don't have time for a pissing contest."

"You came into this facility, my facility, unannounced with armed men, threaten my team and expect me to take your word about who you are or why you are here?" Hardy motioned for Mark and Walt to move away from his door. "Everyone remain where you are. I'm going to get some answers."

Walt spoke up. "Call General McDab ask him about Operation White Shark."

Hardy went in his office and shut the door.

CHAPTER
51

Control Center
Dr. Guthridge and Poponovich

"**W**ant to blame me, go ahead?" General McDab said. He had chuckled when Hardy told him what happened.

"Your men disarmed them? Amazing. Picard and Gibron should never have brought SEALs into the center. Should never have happened. Good to know you have two well-trained team members." He chuckled some more.

"Yeah good thing. You're right. This should never have happened. I should have been told."

General McDab seemed not to hear Hardy's complaint. "I've been so busy juggling all the shit I inherited from the last secretary. On top of that, I'm having to continue my previous duties until the pencil pushers get off their asses and approve someone to take my place. Just when you think Washington can't get more screwed up, the politicians prove otherwise."

"Begging your pardon sir, seems you've been keeping me in the dark. I hate surprises," Hardy said. "Especially in light of what is happening. If you have no confidence in me, then relieve me without all this drama."

"Undersecretary Hardy, you serve at the President's and my discretion. I have no orders from the President regarding your command. Between the times I talk to him, then you, shit happens. Events are fluid, my hands are full. I intend to be down there tomorrow, accompanied by a select group from here. Other countries have their dignitaries coming. The last thing anyone wants is a surprise missile attack. You need to take care of your team. The Space Force

Cyber Intel Unit needs to concentrate on locating Jenkins to determine if he's alive and what threat his, his accomplices' or his captors' actions pose. The UAV amphib needs to be located and disarmed. Josef Gibron and Walt Picard are part of a combined unit of our Navy SEALs and Israel's Sayatet 13 teams. Operation White Shark is their baby. You help provide the intel and they'll take care of their end. Now, get busy. None of us can afford a screw up."

The General disconnected the call. Hardy stared into space for a second. He never got to ask the General about Mark and his crew. How was it Mark knew about the special unit? Hardy was confused. He had listened in on the call between Mark and McDab. He missed something somehow. Or did he? He told Harlee to run another check on Mark Castle or Mark Poponovich. Check all military training units. Cross reference Walt Picard.

Harlee responded after a couple minutes. *'Walt Picard 4th Army Psyops Group, Special Forces, two tours Syria, nothing last three years. No Mark Castle or Mark Poponovich connection or records found.'*

Nothing had changed. Mark was a ghost when he last checked, still was, Harlee confirmed this.

He rejoined the others. "In my office Agent Poponovich." He pointed the taser at Mark. "Jake and TJ please escort these other gentlemen to one of our secure rooms. Dr. Guthridge please join me and Agent Poponovich in my office."

"Mark Castle, Mark Poponovich, or whoever the hell you are, have a seat. Dr. Guthridge please have a seat over here away from him." Hardy pointed to a chair at the end of his desk.

"How do you know Walt Picard?"

Mark replied, "had some joint ops. Good soldier, good operative."

"PSYOP, MISO, Military Information Support Operations, sound familiar?"

"You asking, or telling me?"

Hardy leaned forward. "Cut the shit Poponovich. I talked to General McDab. Here's where you need to decide, are you in or are you out? You either join the unit, do as ordered by myself and Dr. Guthridge or you can remain in solitary until our ops are complete and General McDab, or whoever gives the orders, decides I should release you. No more psychobabble bullshit from you or your people. What's it going to be?"

Mark stared at Lisa smiling. "What do you know. You've moved up in the world. Congratulations." He jumped to his feet. Hardy trained the taser on him. "Now, you get to decide who's on top and who's on bottom, don't you sweetheart."

Lisa's eyes grew cold. Her face glowed. "Yes I do and it won't be you." She turned to Hardy. "He doesn't have the implant as far as I can tell. Not sure what use he'll be. I don't trust him."

"Hardy knows I hold the key to finding Jenkins." He looked over at Hardy. The taser didn't waver. "You listened in on my calls. Probably wondering who I texted." He turned his attention back to Lisa. "I promise I'll be a good little boy. Wind me up and watch me go. This was my op long before you were brought onboard. You're the one worked for Tindal, played pickaboo with Jenkins, then put that damn implant into him. Played up to me. General McDab ordered me to keep an eye on you." He looked back at Hardy, then back to Lisa. "Better keep your eye on her. Not hard to do considering. But, wouldn't turn my back on her."

Lisa jumped to her feet. "You're sick." She started to approach him and Hardy grabbed her arm. "Bob, in my opinion, he's more trouble than he's worth."

"Bob? Well now, how interesting," Mark said with a leer.

Hardy got up, went around Lisa opened the door. Jake and TJ waited outside in the corridor.

"Hey Jake," Mark yelled, "I have that info about your daughter."

Hardy looked back at Mark, walked out, Pulled the door to, told Jake and TJ to take him to the shower.

"It's time to have him put up. And shut up. Do it as quickly as possible, then meet us back in the conference room. Here take the taser. Leave the other weapons in my office."

"Be better if we took him out to the dock, the gators will be looking for food since the storm is gone," Jake said.

TJ added, "we'll take him to the shower, soften him up first."

Once they were in the shower area, Mark voiced praise for their surprisingly nifty moves on the SEALs and the Israeli operative.

"Would you mind turning on some fans and sinks? I think you'll be interested to hear what I have to say. I didn't want to talk in front of Hardy and the others." Mark readied his ring. He hoped it still held some serum. Hoped he wouldn't have to use it, especially on Harper.

TJ said, "You'll talk. Be singing like a canary by the time we get done with you."

"No need in the rough stuff. Ask me anything. I'll tell you what you don't already know. First turn on the background interference. Okay?"

Jake had already moved to turn the faucets on. Afterwards, he walked to within arms-length of Mark.

"Where is my daughter?"

Mark didn't flinch. TJ stood in the doorway. Mark knew things were about to get ugly. He hated violence, especially when he was on the receiving end.

"I have an operative named Suzie. She's been keeping in touch with a DICE operative that Alperts left behind at Tindal's place. From what we've learned, your daughter's husband Pablo made a deal with Alperts to get rid of her. She suspects this particular DICE agent may be working with the Russian Ambassador and Pietr Okneyev also."

"Tell me something I don't know."

TJ said, "he's stalling."

"Ok, Pablo's ole man, the ambassador, made a deal with our cartel buddies and DICE. He and his wife want to keep your daughter alive. The mother is the cut out for the Cubans with the Juarez Cartel and DICE. Jenkins and possibly Tindal were in communication with the Russian Okneyev, who was last seen with the Cubans. This you and I both were told by Carmichael and others on Okneyev's now sunk cargo ship. Jake deserves a big thanks for saving my ass I guess you know" TJ said nothing. He turned back to Jake. "Guess I should have said so earlier. But you didn't give me a chance. And, I'm sure you know the Russians and the Mexican cartel want you and Agent Alvarez to suffer, ultimately, they want you and your families dead. Tindal wants you out of the way. He made a deal with the devil through Jenkins. Another reason, Tindal will do anything to make sure Jenkins doesn't live to talk Ask him when you see him. See how he reacts."

"He's stalling," TJ said. "None of this is news. We're wasting time."

"You got one last chance. Where is my daughter?"

"She was on the *SwaleMaiden* before the storm. General McDab and entourage, including your buddy Tindal were supposed to be the Palmroy's guest onboard the yacht tomorrow."

"How could you possibly know this? You've been our guests most of this week."

"Have to be resourceful in this business. See that's where you two are at a disadvantage. You're new to the show and tell games." Mark smirked, leaned against the shower wall, prepared to launch himself if need be. "Good guess is your daughter'll be kept out of sight or be taken off the yacht, perhaps held at the ambassador's residence."

"Hasn't been seen leaving the boat."

"Don't bet on it. What matters is, she's alive. You, Jake, are who everybody wants, Jenkins included, that is, if he is alive and your wife has not already given the cartel boss what he and everybody else wants. Do you happen to know where your wife is? Many think you do." Jake didn't reply.

"Which brings us to why you need me. Tindal, his minion Colonel Hunter, and General McDab are coming here. Picard and his team are here to do the dirty work. According to sources, the snipers who took out Bolstoy and his captain were Israeli. My bet, they are here with this JSOC team. Once they perform Operation White Shark, they won't be leaving their orders incomplete. General McDab wants this op wrapped up before the end of the gala. Deals, made and to be made, will be consummated. The General will not leave any loose ends. Hardy is a yes man. Tindal will want his pound of flesh. Need I spell it out for you?"

"You haven't given a reason for why I need you?"

"General McDab trusts me. He needs me. I know where the cartel money is. This is off-the-books money. You two. When all is said and done, you're dispensable. As for this Space Force Cyber Intel Strike Force Unit. The Space Force is an Air Force Unit why would they want two retired Army guys?"

Jake ran a quick search. He thought he remembered hearing this on the news. Mark was right. 'He's right about the Space Force,' Jake memed TJ.

TJ replied, 'I know. My implant verified as much. Got some thoughts about that. We need to decide what to do about this guy.'

TJ stepped closer to Mark. "Seems to me, by your reasoning, once you show them the funds' locations, you'll be dispensable."

"Why you think I'm telling you this?"

"To save us from messing you up and feeding you to the gators," TJ replied.

"Crocodiles, not gators. There is that." Mark smiled, TJ smiled back his gotcha, better-not-mess-with-me smile. Jake locked eyes with Mark.

"Jake I've been looking out for you since before our little adventure in Cuba. I put my neck on the line to save your journalist girlfriend. I have an agent whose sole purpose is to find and protect your daughter. I do all this because I like your style. In my line of work, you rarely meet people like you." He broke eye contact with Jake, watching TJ, expecting the big man to make a move, not sure he could get by him if he did.

"Agent Alvarez, you seem to be a straight shooter also and you're Jake's friend. I don't have friends like you. Wish I did. Besides, I've been wanting to know how Jake gets so many hot chicks. Maybe, if we both get through this, he will tell me his secret. What you say? How about tell Hardy me and my crew will work with you? I'd appreciate it if you didn't get him all worked up about me and the General. Better for everyone if I keep that line open. Jake, like I said to you when we first met in Cuba, let's watch each other's backs. Another thing, they're filming us and have plans to use it as training material for the real Space Force Cyber Intel Strike Force Unit."

TJ motioned for Jake to follow him. He told Mark to stay put.

'You buying this shit bro?' TJ memed.

'Not all of it? You know the Chinese saying about friends and enemies. I consider him a friendemy. He made a lot of good points. I know, he's covering his ass. So are Hardy and the rest of these mothers. We need to make sure no one splits you and I up. We have to be careful with the memes around the others. How about we meme 99 the first time we sense a problem or danger, then we'll count down from there on each subsequent response. He better not be bullshitting me about this Suzie, or my daughter. If not for my family, Gabriel and I would be outa here.'

Jake felt somewhat better about their situation now that he had weapons.

'Is my right side or left side my better side?' Jake memed, twisting his head back and forth, gazing in one of the floor-to-ceiling mirrors. He noticed how grubby he looked, a shower and shave couldn't hurt. The weapons bulged in his pockets. He pulled them out of the lower pocket, moved them into the upper ones, taser right, K'Bar left. He pulled his t-shirt down to help hide them. 'By the way, I'm holding onto this taser and the K'Bar I confiscated, makes me feel less naked.'

"Ditto bro. I have the Israeli's. TJ patted his upper cargo pants pocket. He too had his shirt out covering his.

'Let's take your friendemy back and join the others. And don't take this the wrong way bro, you don't have a good side.'

'You can always count on your friends. Guess women like my personality.'

'Keep telling yourself that.'

Yeah. Right. Anyway, we need to throw Poponovich's ass in the shower. Make it look good. Make one less stinking asshole in the group.'

'I'll follow your lead on what we goina tell Hardy. We best not screw this up. Deane would never forgive me or you.'

'I don't know diddly shit about Jenkins or the data he stole. These other mothers suspect I do. Since I don't know shit, this means they know less than shit. This is not some Marvel Comic wannabe team. Hardy is a dreamer."

'One other thing to think about before we take care of him. This Air Force Space Force shit. Three of our supposed team members are or were Air Force. The Major, the Captain and Dr. Guthridge. Not me, you, Mark and crew, or Hardy. Not sure what this means. Intel says Mark's right. Makes me wonder.'

"Hey Jake ole buddy," Mark called out from the other side of the wall where Jake and TJ had retreated, "I need to talk to you alone. I think you'll want to hear me out."

Jake memed TJ, 'might be something about my daughter. CT will record so you can listen in on us.'

"Hey bro, not a good idea. We need to join the others."

"It could be about my daughter. Wait outside. I'll know soon enough."

"Make it quick. Hardy's expecting us back." TJ stepped out into the corridor.

"Okay Mark, this better be good."

"Jake, Jenkins is dead." Jake started toward Mark. "Hold on. I didn't see anything. I just know it. What are these people to you? They don't give a shit about you. They're using you. They used me. I know what it feels like. Look, I have access to a lot of money. Cartel money. I need David Gonzalez. He has the rest of the codes. What you say you, your friend and I take Arturo and get the hell out of here. We can use Arturo to lure David into a trap. Turn about is fair play don't you think; you used David to screw over Arturo; we use Arturo to screw over David."

A lot of what Mark said rang true. He figured the odds of his survival were less than he cared to admit. Tindal would see to finishing the job one way or another. Hardy couldn't be trusted. He had to save his family. If he did throw in with Mark, he could maybe find a way out. Screw them all.

"How much money we talking about?"

"Millions. If we can tap into the cartel's other account, we're looking at close to a billion."

"That would be pushing our luck. Your men know about this; you plan on cutting them in?"

"They have no idea about how much; they're thinking a million or a little more."

"Why should I trust you?"

"The way I see it we're both at the end of a dead-end street. I figure they'll be looking at me. You too. I can take care of deflecting the blame away from you. Me, no way. You and I will have the same set-up as David Gonzalez thought he had. We get the codes from him, then we become partners. We let the feds and General McDab have enough to assuage their suspicions, cut my men in on a share and split the rest."

"You're forgetting my partner TJ."

"What you do with your share is up to you."

"Your men's share comes out of your end, not mine."

"Do we have a deal?"

"I have to think about it. I'll get back to you after we see how things play out with Hardy and you and your men."

"While you're thinking, think about what happens when the shit hits the fan. You're going to need money for medical bills. And, legal fees for me and you if things don't go as planned. You can't win without money."

"Get in the shower. I need to run things by TJ. Make it quick."

TJ wasn't sure where Jake was going with this.

"Hey bro, what the hell? You're not seriously thinking about trusting McDab's boy?"

"No. But I believe we better start thinking about what happens when Tindal and Dr. Guthridge's and Mark's old boss shows up. The SEALs and the Israelis coming here has got me thinking that Mark's right they don't intend on me leaving here. We've got to keep our options open, and our implants shut down around Hardy and her. I shut mine down. You need to do the same until we figure out whom we can trust and decide on a plan."

CHAPTER
52

Control Center
Cyber Team

Hardy stood outside the conference room. He watched as a wet Poponovich marched up the corridor, Jake and TJ flanking him on each side. They stopped a step away from him.

"Aye me capitane, I await your orders," Poponovich said, a smile on his face.

"That you will," Hardy replied. "No more talking to General McDab, you and your crew are now members of the joint Space Force Cyber Intel Strike Force Unit under my command. Within hours, you and the others who have not received the implant will do so. You will follow my orders or suffer the consequences. Gentlemen let us now join the other members." Hardy opened the door to the conference room and motioned for him to go inside. They heard Mark greeted with raucous cheers.

Hardy stopped outside the door. Jake and TJ waited with him. He asked, "Poponovich say anything useful?"

Jake said, "He has someone on the outside he's been in touch with. The call to the burner phone be my guess. His source confirmed my daughter is on the *SwaleMaiden*. The only other useful info came at the end before we threw him in the shower. Poponovich and his people are only interested in the money. They're not to be trusted. He intimated General McDab intends to eliminate TJ and me when this op is complete."

"I spoke to General McDab. All eyes are on him as well as us. I think Poponovich is trying to get you to do something that will make you have to be eliminated. I have a way to control Poponovich and his crew. Let's join them, shall we?"

"Hey look who's here, our fearless leader, loverboy and his sidekick," Dean said as they entered the room.

Hardy told the two guards to wait outside and to keep eyes on the monitor to make sure no other uninvited members of Picard's team tried to get by the newly-replaced guards at the entrance gate.

Poponovich took a seat. Jake and TJ remained standing. Hardy walked to the end of the table. Behind him was a large blank space on the concrete wall used as a projector if need be. Hardy waited until the room grew silent.

"Gentlemen and lady," Hardy nodded at Renai. "Let me begin by welcoming you to the newly-formed joint Space Force Cyber Intel Strike Force Unit." The room erupted in voices raised in disapproval. Poponovich yelled at Dean and crew to shut the hell up. Hardy waited until the uproar stopped.

"Your past allegiances are no longer. You are under my command; everything goes through me. Any attempt to bypass my command, undermine my orders, threaten the integrity of the unit will be dealt with severely. There is only one way out," Hardy looked around to each of them, pausing at Jake. "I don't believe I need explain. This is a cyber intel unit first and foremost. Lethal force will only be used after it is sanctioned by me and only as a last resort. Each of you were chosen after an extensive vetting process part of which was conducted at this center. For those of you who heard the rumor regarding a cerebral implant and wondered if it was only a rumor, I am here to dispel the rumor. It exists. Each of you, who do not have the NM0099 implant will receive it later today."

The room erupted in vocal responses. Faces of those who had not been implanted showed mixtures of incredulousness, amazement, and horror. Their necks were on swivel-mode. Those who had the implant sat and stood trying to remain impassive. Their minds raced thinking of the implications. Jake and TJ looked at Dean and Boyd. Dean smirked. Boyd shrugged and looked down. Everyone, including Dean and Boyd protested the announcement.

"With the implant," Hardy started then waited for them to quiet down. "With the implant, you will be able to communicate with other implantees nonverbally. You will have access to the worldwide web and have limited clearance to secure sites. My implant will allow me to monitor you and block you, as necessary. This means any insubordination will be known and dealt with. You will be able to block each other, but not me, Dr. Guthridge or Space Force Command." More dissent erupted.

"That's right, I am your commander and Dr. Guthridge is my second. She answers only to me and my bosses. We will continue with the briefing once all of you receive the implant. Two of you with the implant, Dean and Boyd, will answer any questions from the other soon to be implantees. Get to it. You are now a team."

Hardy sent a meme to the monitoring screen. One of the guards came to the door and let him out. He memed and motioned for Jake and TJ to follow him.

'Dr. Guthridge is with Major Duplantis and Captain Adams explaining to them the implant; seeing if they wish to join our unit,' he memed. 'I'm not sure how they will react, especially Captain Adams. As you know, she has a husband and children. Jake, you are the only one with children and both of you were able to keep this from your spouse and girlfriend. Perhaps you can answer their questions. Hopefully assuage Jeni's concerns.'

"Jeni's concerns? I have concerns of my own," Jake replied out loud.

"We will discuss you two's situations after we determine where they stand. Okay?" He walked up the corridor to the control room without waiting for a reply.

TJ said out the side of his mouth to Jake, "Need to wake up CT"

They followed Hardy into the control room.

Jake looked around for Gabriel. He didn't see him.

'He's taking a nap,' Jeni memed him. She laughed at Jake's expression. 'Couldn't let all you dick-eyed jerks have all the fun.'

Hardy said, "we should have this conversation in private."

"What about my grandson?"

Jeni said, "Cary will keep an eye on him." She went over to a hefty woman monitoring the embassy, leaned down and spoke to her. Jake saw the woman nod her acceptance without taking her eyes off the screen.

They went into a small room off Hardy's office.

"Dr. Guthridge, you care to explain?" Hardy stood facing her. Everyone else sat down on each side of a table large enough for six people.

"You knew the Major and Captain were Air Force Intelligence. They received the implant prior to joining your op. Until now, their devices, like Dean's and Boyd's were not awake--they had not been activated. Dr. Perkins, General McDab and Tindal may or may not know about them. The Air Force member of the Joint Chiefs of Staff, to my knowledge, is the only one who does know. This was done when they were recruited for the USAF Space Force. The USSF is a branch of the Air Force. We're Air Force."

Marge took a deep breath, then jumped in. "When the task force was formed, our commander asked for volunteers for a medical procedure which we were told would allow telepathy between the recipients. This sounded like an opportunity for my intelligence work. Jeni has her own reasons. You'll have to ask her. Dr. Perkins failed to tell us the device would be activated later. We were told it may or may not assimilate itself into our psyche. We weren't aware there were many other facets to be discovered. Just as we didn't know until now you dick-eyed chauvinist jerks were holding out on us. I was shocked when Dr. Guthridge communicated to me without my hearing her voice. She gave a quick rundown; you guys walked in and Jeni couldn't resist. We have a great deal of catching up, so my device informs me."

Dr. Guthridge said, "I'm sorry Undersecretary Hardy; I didn't know how much or how little you knew until I got here. Seems everyone has been keeping a number of things to themselves."

"Hardy, I know you wish to include Poponovich and the others; form a team; we have a team. Jeni, think you can handle The Hive?"

"Marge and I were discussing this with Dr. Guthridge before she activated our devices. With a little guidance from her, it shouldn't be a problem."

Hardy interjected, "Hold on there, Agent Harper I'm the one who decides who, what and how. I have my orders. And, all of you will do as ordered."

"Undersecretary Hardy sir," Marge said, "begging your pardon, I believe any commander worth his salt should ask for and listen to his subordinates. I believe Agent Harper has more personal skin in the game than the rest of us. I for one am interested in what he has to say. With all due respect."

"Thank you Major. Hardy sir, Poponovich made more than a few valid points which I don't believe we should ignore, and I cannot ignore. Tindal and General McDab are scheduled to come to Cancun tomorrow. They have accepted an invitation from the Palmroys to join them on the *SwaleMaiden*. My Cuban sources say my daughter was reported by a deckhand to be onboard the *SwaleMaiden*. As you know Tindal and I have a history. Tindal wants my land. What better way to get my land than if I am no longer alive? McDab's men want the funds. TJ and I don't trust them; team members must trust each other. Once they have the implant I believe they'll go rogue. And I believe I will be expendable once the op is completed; therefore, I say we use The Hive and its bees to recce the *SwaleMaiden*, locate my daughter, disable the crew and TJ and I can use *Dev'sDelight* as our boarding craft and use it to board the *SwaleMaiden*, and rescue my daughter. Then she can reunite with her son; they go to Miami out of harm's way; and you will then have my undivided attention to complete the op."

"The Hive is not mine or yours to do with as we please. I cannot and will not authorize its use. The Hive was brought here by DoD for reasons unknown to me. Care to enlighten us Dr. Guthridge?"

"I was shocked: when I was instructed to board a military aircraft where there were military personnel to accompany me; and, more shocked to find The Hive onboard. I was not given an explanation and I am as much in the dark as the rest of you. Agent Harper, commandeering The Hive is almost impossible. When I disembarked, there were ten heavily armed men onboard; there to guard The Hive. The Hive is secured, and I do not know who has the right to open the bio-locks. Perhaps Picard knows or you Undersecretary Hardy."

"I was not made aware of The Hive; nor, anything regarding Picard's orders and Gibron's; nor, the other men's purpose for coming here. Jake, your plan has its merits. But my orders say nothing about The Hive. I was ordered, and passed those orders on to Captain Conroy, to observe the *SwaleMaiden* and maintain a protective distance from her. My orders state that I am to form a team and continue our cyber intel mission to learn where, when and how an attack could be made, locate Jenkins and/or the stolen files; also search for the amphib and determine any threat it may pose, and set up security for the upcoming gala. Those are our orders. General McDab is not going to change them. Sorry Jake. Orders are orders."

"Screw you Bob. Screw your damn orders. They've declared war on us. No, on me and my family. Screw their orders. I've had enough of them and their orders. It's time we took it to them. And, that includes Thurmond Tindal."

TJ was afraid this was going to happen. He prepared himself in case Jake decided to take it up a notch—do something to put himself beyond help.

"I've let this go on long enough Jake. I thought by now you'd come to your senses. You leave me no choice."

Jake moved toward Hardy. TJ stepped in between. The women moved back out of the way. It appeared a violent confrontation was imminent.

"Jake don't," TJ warned, then he memed, 'I'm not going to let you throw your life away.'

Jake locked eyes with TJ. "I'm tired of his threats. We're not in the military. I don't have to take this shit."

"Dr. Guthridge shut him down."

Lisa looked at Hardy like he was a stranger. Who did he think he was? "Undersecretary Hardy it doesn't work that way."

"What do you mean it doesn't work that way?"

'Come on bro, 'TJ memed privately to him, 'think about your grandson. They'll send him back to his father.'

"They. They. They," Jake replied out loud. "Fuck them TJ. We're fucked. Open your eyes. Ask your damn implant. They're using these damn implants to feed us shit." Jake looked at the women; focused on Dr. Guthridge. "Tell them doctor; this damn thing is a mind control device. They're using it to read us, feed us whatever they want, make it seem like we're in control; only we're not. Tell them Dr. Guthridge. Explain to them how mine and your implants communicated with each other of their own volition. Or are you afraid to admit you've been duped also. She's not in charge any more than you are Hardy. They won't shut me down Hardy. They aren't done with me; they shut me down then they lose because all of you will become paranoid; start thinking you might be next; isn't that right Dr. Guthridge? Wouldn't want to screw up their dog and pony show, would they?"

This was new territory for Lisa—a damned if you say anything, damned if you don't,' she memed Hardy, 'this one's on you.' She memed Jake, 'I'm not in charge. Like Hardy, I follow orders. Can your implant be shut down? Yes. Won't be by me.'

"What's it going to be Hardy? You got me into this; either you help me save my family or stay the hell out of my way."

"This is treasonous mutiny you're proposing Jake. Are you sure you want to go there? Before you say any more, you need to stop and think what this will do to your family. They are protecting Ariel and your unborn child. Captain Conroy is watching the *SwaleMaiden*. I understand you want to lash out. If you do the wrong thing, what happens to you and your family is on you. Not me. Not them."

"Bullshit Hardy." Jake looked over at the women again. "Dr. Guthridge's colleague, Dr. Perkins, and these nameless mothers are planning to, or have already, implanted devices in Blakely Carmichael and Ariel Gaspard without anyone's permission, without regard for the potential consequences. They are experimenting with iPSCs on Carmichael and mine and Ariel's fetus They don't give a damn about any of us. We, like them, are the newest government experimental guinea pigs."

The Major and Captain looked at Jake, then Hardy, then back to Dr. Guthridge. Their expressions went from incredulity to fear, then anger."

Marge cleared her throat. "This is immoral, illegal. They wouldn't dare do this." She saw Dr. Guthridge look down. "This is awful. Dr. Guthridge, you can't let this happen." She turned to Jake. "I'm sorry Jake. No need to apologize for your earlier behavior. No wonder you were so upset.'

The Major had read his thoughts. Good. He had almost forgotten he owed her an explanation, and an apology.

Dr. Guthridge couldn't contain her anger. "I voiced my concerns. General McDab has Dr. Perkins in charge. It is on him. There is nothing more I can do. What about you Undersecretary Hardy? Did you know? Have you said anything to Dr. Perkins?"

Jake spoke up. "No. Hardy isn't about to jeopardize his career. That's all that matters to him. Well Hardy, now everyone here knows. How about it, hink maybe they'll erase this from our memories?" Hardy said nothing. Jake looked back to Lisa. What do you think Dr. Guthridge, is this possible?"

Everyone looked at Dr. Guthridge.

"Not that I'm aware of. Wasn't programmed that way by me. I'm no longer certain what Dr. Perkins or others may have done."

Hardy remained quiet. TJ kept his eyes on him trying to read his reactions. Dr. Guthridge was doing the same thing. His implant was silent. This concerned her; she had Lizzie run a check. His device Harlee was recording the conversation. To cover his ass? Was Jake right, were they able to control information sent to their devices? She asked Lizzie. No response. You were naïve Lisa. You suspected the CIA started the research; you suspected Dr. Perkins; Jenkins and Tindal, Mark, General McDab--all CIA; since inception, the agency has been after mind control; you helped them. Now what can you do to stop them?

She took a risk and memed everyone but Hardy what she suspected. The women's faces reflected concern and anger. They nodded. Jake's eyes blazed. TJ's smile seemed forced. She memed them to order their devices to go to sleep mode. She waited, checked, Lizzie confirmed their devices no longer were active. She hesitated to shut down Lizzie. If she did, she would no longer be able to monitor Harlee; then she remembered Dean and Boyd and Hardy's order to implant the device into the others. She did not have the devices to implant. Dr. Perkins would be bringing them with him. This bought them a day. A day, to do what? She had to risk keeping Lizzie open.

She memed Hardy. 'I can not implant the others; I don't have the devices; Dr. Perkins is bringing them tomorrow.'

His response was a terse command. 'Keep the others here. I need to check on something. The guards will remain outside the door in case there is trouble.'

Hardy reached back opened the door and stepped backwards out it. The lock clicked.

Dr. Guthridge memed Lizzie, '*Take devices out of sleep mode. Have to risk it.*'

She memed the others, 'My device says this room is secure.'

Jake spoke up. "How do we know we can trust your implant, or you?"

"You don't. But what choice do any of us have? We must trust each other. Any ideas?"

TJ said, "We could take over the facility. But then what?'

"We secure everyone," Jake replied, "then we take Picard and the Israeli back to the aircraft and commandeer The Hive. Recce the *SwaleMaiden* and save my daughter."

"Aren't you forgetting something? Lisa said. The Hive is bio-secured. And, if you're correct, they'll be damn sure monitoring our movements via satellite and drones, as well as The Hive. You nor The Hive is a match for a Predator." She memed, 'everyone, use your implants, not sure who's listening.'

Jeni memed, 'Dr. Guthridge is what Jake said correct?'

She nodded.

TJ memed, 'Is there anyway to take control from here? I assume everything up there and in here is being monitored and controlled from here?'

'Maybe. You know what you're proposing is treason. Jeni and I will be court marshalled. If this is a CIA op, they'll make us all disappear. No one knows we're here; they can rendition us and make sure no report ever materializes. If Hardy is in on this, he's probably reporting our conversation and preparing to stop any threat as we speak. There is nothing we can do.'

Jake: 'TJ I'm goina take those guards' weapons and make you all hostages, commandeer the control room. It's my only hope. I don't expect y'all to help me; I understand; but TJ, and the rest of you, don't try to stop me.'

Jake pulled out the taser, pointed it toward TJ. "TJ, hand over the taser and your knife."

"Don't do this Jake. This is suicide. Your grandson is in there."

"I have no choice TJ. When Hardy returns, he plans to put me under guard. If I don't do this, I'm a goner. Hand them over TJ." Jake stepped back out of TJ's reach.

"Damnit bro, you can't win. I guess you know that."

"Maybe. But if I can save my family, that will have to be enough."

TJ half-heartedly laid the taser and K-Bar on the table. Jake waved him over toward the women. When he joined them, Jake retrieved TJ's weapons.

"You can't get out the door bro. You're stuck in here with us."

Jake told CT to go to sleep. "Guess we'll wait to see what Hardy has up his sleeve."

CHAPTER
53

Off the coast of Cancun
Pietr Okneyev Russian Oligarch

Pietr Okneyev nodded to the lovely young thing that brought him his vodka. She made a face after she took a swallow from the bottle and crystal tumbler then she gently set them on the desk next to his monitor. She waited next to him as instructed. This was to make sure there was no poison added like she was told happened before. He was a very careful and suspicious man. She felt his coarse hand slide up under her short skirt. As directed, she wore no underwear. He caressed her derriere, slid his hand gently forward between her thighs and brushed her shaved pubic area with his knarly fingers. He withdrew his hand and patted her backside.

"You may go now. Tell Yakov to proceed. You and I will finish our tete-a-tete later."

Pietr watched from an overhead drone as *Dev'sDelight* exited the harbor. Soon after the amphib drone would move into place. The passing storm meant nothing to him. He had awaited its departure ensconced in his private suite aboard the *SwaleMaiden*.

After it was safe to leave Hemingway Marina, the *SwaleMaiden* moved back into place off the coast of Cancun. Tomorrow, the Palmroys planned to receive Thurmond Tindal and the new DHS Secretary, General McDab. He was looking forward to the discussion. The plans were happening faster than anticipated.

He and the General had developed respect for each other following tours in the Middle East, resulting in business arrangements made before Russia's exit and the American alliance entry into Afghanistan. Colonel Tindal as he was known then, and his man Major Jenkins, doing CIA General McDab's bidding—adversaries, competitors, worthy business partners. Separately, then together, profiting from opium trade, weapons supplying to warring tribal leaders, even much-hated Osama bin laden—had helped Indian and Pakistani religious fanatics form Taliban. Karzai become American puppet Afghani President. This proved highly profitable for respective presidents, him, and the General and Colonel Tindal. Not so much for Major Jenkins.

Pietr was disappointed Jenkins disappeared. Didn't see; didn't get to say hasta la vista baby. Perhaps he blamed Pietr for not eliminating the Harper man. Pietr would rectify this mistake. Comrade, former American President agree with Putin, the General and the Colonel--the Harper man must be questioned, made to disappear. So many willing to pay to make this happen.

Blakely fail him, betray his trust, say she fall in love. He would have laughed had he not known the whole story. An aide to the Cuban Generals died due to her duplicity. He should have killed her. She swore she not responsible. In a moment of weakness, he leave her to contemplate her demise. The Harper man somehow save her and the others. A most worthy adversary. Pietr love a challenge; especially when it prove profitable.

Another DICE man, calling himself Terrance, sent word of the whereabouts of Harper and friends. He said Tindal's offer still stood. Tindal was not worried about a mere million. Not when he stood to make so much more. The Harper man's daughter was the key. He told Pietr he have woman willing to pay him for his young guest. He laughed. First use her to get Harper man to come to him; they have big talk; then, he decide if he wish to sell her to highest bidder or be done with her and her father.

First, he find if Harper man have information others say he have. There can be no more mistakes. Many will pay what he ask; make him and his friends richer, more powerful. Their plan was coming together better than expected. The gala event going to be spectacular. Perhaps he should invest more of his soon-to-be gains in this space venture.

He lit a Cuban cigar, downed a shot of vodka, and leaned back to watch his hole card armed and ready, moving toward its target.

CHAPTER
54

Control Center
Jake and Okneyev

The door opened. Hardy came in followed by Picard and Gibron. The women sat at the table on one side; Jake sat at the far end facing the door; TJ stood behind the women. They were between Jake and the armed men. The room was quiet just like Jake instructed. They dared not speak, not that any of them would have anyway. All except TJ wished Jake good luck.

"Get up Jake. You need to come with me."

"Screw you Hardy."

Hardy moved aside. Picard and Gibron went around the table. Gibron pointed his handgun at TJ as he shuffled by. Picard reached Jake first. He tried to grab Jake's arm with his free right hand; Jake had it tucked in tight; made it impossible to get a grip.

"Get his other arm," Picard told Gibron.

Jake fired both tasers. Both men jerked and convulsed. Jake retrieved Picard's SigSauer P226. He stayed low using the women as a shield and retrieved Gibron's Glock 19. He pointed one at Hardy, the other at the guard who came in through the door. He stopped, blocking the other guard.

"Lower your weapons. You, in front take the other guard's weapon, place them on the floor and slide them to me."

The guard's Colt handguns slid over to where Picard lay. Jake stuck one of them in his pant's back waistband and added the other rearmed taser. He hoped his pants didn't fall down. He motioned the other taser at TJ.

"Everybody up. TJ pick Gibron up. Marge, Jeni come get Picard. Hardy zip tie them to the table legs. Now Hardy over here. You two guards come with him. Hardy zip-tie their hands and feet to the anchored table legs."

"Jake you're compounding your problem. You've gone beyond my protection."

"You know the old saying: *with friends like you, who needs enemies.* Hurry it up. That's good. Take their communication equipment and their lock operators. Hand those to Dr. Guthridge. Good man. Do as I say and we'll all have a party later to celebrate.".

TJ looked at Hardy and shrugged. "I warned you Hardy. Jake's been around the block once or twice. Navy SEALs ain't got nothing on him."

"Here's what we're going to do, we're going around the corner to the control room. I want all of you in front of me. When we get to the door, TJ I want you to go first, followed by Hardy then the women. Hardy you're going to open the door. Any funny moves and I'll tase you. Let's go."

The door opened; an alarm sounded, lights flashed over one of the large monitors mounted on the wall. Hardy ignored Jake and rushed over to the monitor.

The man sitting at the monitor whooped, "we got it sir. We got the white shark. Actually, it's turquoise colored." There was a cheer.

"Son, do you have any idea what you've got?"

"It's the amphibious drone sir."

"Armed with a dirty missile, son."

"Sir. It's not a problem. It's trapped. The automatic system raised the curtain. It can't escape. I dropped a titanium net over it. It can't fire the missile. We have it."

TJ tapped Hardy on the back. He swung his head around and saw Jake holding one taser on him and another on TJ. Jeni rushed over to Gabriel who was shrieking and crying, his hands over his ears.

"Turn that damn alarm off," Jake demanded.

The sound stopped. Murmurs kicked in. They stared at Jake like he was a terrorist. He was sure that was how he looked.

"Jake don't be a fool. I need Gibron's team to gear up, go onboard that amphib and disarm it."

"I agree. They'll need the other men from the transport. I need The Hive. Seems like a win, win to me."

"Dr. Guthridge told you it is secured with a biolock. I don't know whose biometrics are needed."

"You get three guesses; the first two don't count. Better hope you guess correctly."

"I can't reach them, I tried."

"Try again. I'm sure they'll be happy to know you captured the amphib. Talk to whomever; do whatever it takes; get me a way to open the lock."

Jeni brought Gabriel over to Jake. He peeked out from behind Jeni's khaki pants leg. His tear-streaked face was looking at Jake like he was a monster. It broke Jake's heart.

"Jake, I can send another drone to recce the *SwaleMaiden*." She saw the pain in Jake's eyes.

"Any other drone won't do. Sure, another drone can detect the bodies. It can't tell me who is who. I need the Bumblebees. I need to know where Elizabeth is."

Dr. Guthridge spoke up. "Jake the container The Hive is in is not solid. I can arm the bees and launch them without The Hive."

"Why didn't you tell me this earlier?"

Dr. Guthridge looked down at Gabriel. Because I know now who the bad guys are." She looked over at Hardy. "If I were you, I'd do whatever I had to to save the innocents. If I go down, I want to feel good about myself. Trust me, Jake. I'll do whatever I legally can to aid you."

"Thank you, but legally, I'm afraid I've already crossed that line."

Marge spoke up, "That's for others to decide. Later. Right now, we've got a more imminent problem."

"All my problems are imminent Major." Jake stared at TJ.

"Don't look at me like that bro. Kinda pissed me off when you assumed I didn't have your back. Have to admit it was fun watching the old Jake in action."

Jake handed him one of the tasers and Picard's and Gibron's handguns.

"I was counting on it. Thanks. Go with Hardy. Take care of the bomb." TJ and Hardy turned to go. "Aren't you forgetting something?" Jake picked up the comms. "Oh, and Hardy," Hardy's face was set; he refused to look at Jake, "a simple reminder, TJ's much more lethal than I am. I suggest you or the others not warn the SEAL Team or any of your superiors. There doesn't have to be any bloodshed."

Okneyev choked on his drink. He wiped the moisture off his monitor; zoomed in on the scene unfolding outside the American compound. His amphib was being hoisted out of the water wrapped inside a heavy net. There were armed men standing by on the dock. Why were they there?

This was not expected. The Ambassadors would be notified, bids cancelled, intelligence agencies put on alert. The diplomatic repercussions immense.

The door to his suite burst open. The Palmroy bitch screamed at him, "are you watching this?"

"Obviously." He waved her off. She came to his desk. "You moved too soon. Made a major tactical error. I hope you realize what this means."

"Madame Palmroy, please sit down and shut up or leave."

Yakov stopped just inside the doorway. "I try stop her."

Okneyev calmly said, "Arm the self-destruct mechanism. Do not detonate. That is all." Yakov hurried back out.

"You dare not set that thing off. If we managed to survive, they will turn on us. Even your own government will denounce you; launch a retaliatory strike. I hope you realize what you have succeeded in doing."

"Yes. I do know. The Americans will soon realize they have what they euphemistically call a tiger by the tail. See, they stand their scratching their heads." Okneyev pivoted the monitor around so she could see. A red light was winking on and off on the monitor. "Watch this." Okneyev spoke into his voice mike, "Yakov, tell them if they try to open the hatch, the self-destruct mechanism will set the ordinance off."

Okneyev saw the look of surprise on the face of the man he recognized as the American Homeland Undersecretary Robert Hardy. His men stood frozen. Undersecretary Hardy waved all of them back. Okneyev watched as they huddled together.

Hardy's shout came through on the monitor's speaker. "If you detonate the bomb, my government will see this as a declaration of war."

Okneyev spoke through Yakov, "You seized private property. No government involved, you attempt open the hatch, onus on you Undersecretary Hardy. This need not happen. Talk to your superiors. I sent a message to your government; await their reply. In case you or your superiors decide to launch a strike, take me out, your action will automatically set off the bomb. I wait. Have a good day."

Okneyev turned to the Palmroy bitch. Her face was contorted in rage. She spat out her contempt.

"You fool. You have ignited an international firestorm."

"Exactly. Now, we wait to see what comes of it. Why don't you contact your friends in the government? Perhaps, you can make a deal to save your own ass. If you like, you can transfer your funds to my account. Who knows, maybe it will be the best offer. Go now, talk it over with your husband. Bye, bye. Get the hell out."

CHAPTER
55

Control Center
Jake

The control room was a somber place. The excitement of the amphib's capture quickly died a sudden death when TJ and the others hurried back inside.

TJ announced, "The amphib is rigged to blow if tampered with."

"Sink the damn boat; kill that Russian bastard; that'll put an end to it," a voice from one of the monitoring stations shouted.

Jake hurried over to the man. "My daughter and other innocents are onboard, asshole." The man mumbled an apology.

"Wouldn't do any good if we did," Hardy said. "The bomb is rigged to go if the signal is disrupted."

"The bastard wants money," Picard said to Jake. "If your daughter is so precious why don't you ante up cowboy."

Jake slapped him. He started to reach for his newly returned K-Bar. Jake trapped his wrist with his left hand and put the SigSauer in his gut with his right. "I'm sure you're familiar with the gun and knife scenario."

TJ relieved him of his knife. Then he and Jake had the others place all their weapons in a corner cabinet.

"TJ, we need to get these guys out of here."

TJ nodded to Gabriel. "Stay here talk to your grandson. I'll take care of these guys. Come on fellows move it."

Hardy said, "You all are making a big mistake. You'll be prosecuted."

TJ shoved him out the door.

Jake went over to Jeni and retrieved Gabriel.

"Cary, would you please take Gabriel to the break room and give him a snack and a non-sugary drink."

Gabriel said, "I don't want to go."

Jake hugged him, gave him a kiss on his cheek. He told him, he loved him and hoped he would get to know him soon. Gabriel began to squirm in Jake's arms.

"Hey kiddo, how about a snack while you watch your favorite cartoon?" Cary said.

"I hate cartoons."

Jake tried to hand Gabriel to Cary. He pushed her hands away. Jeni stood back up and came over to them. "How about I go with Cary and you? Gabriel said he wanted to walk. Jake stooped down and released him. Gabriel reached out and took Jeni's hand. Jeni memed, 'I'll come back soon as I get him settled.'

Jake thanked her.

TJ was back. He went and stood behind Dr. Guthridge watching her launch the bumblebee drones. They rose into the sky over the cargo plane and hovered there.

"Why they not headed toward the target?" TJ asked her.

The Major was seated at a console next to her, she looked up at Jake and said, "We need Jeni to send a couple drones out as decoys and spotters while she positions another drone in the monitoring position. We have to assume the cargo plane is under constant surveillance by Charlie and Ivan. The *SwaleMaiden* may have radar, jammers, drones, and weapons. Our military has been put on notice. We can expect a reaction, perhaps a Predator soon.

"The bumblebees will need a relay from The Hive. If the surveillance drone gets jammed, the bumblebees will operate autonomously. The first wave are set up to recce only. If we can verify targets and the bumblebees aren't jammed, I will send in armed ones to neutralize the targets. There are other potential problems. If Jenkins is onboard, or they have the information he possessed about The Hive and the bumblebees, that would be a game changer." Dr. Guthridge watched TJ and Jake while she said this. Both did not look overly concerned.

Jake memed, 'Go ahead and arm most of the bumblebees. We may need them fast; before any efforts to stop them can take place. I'm going to be heading out there, soon as I figure out how.'

TJ memed, 'I discovered this place has scuba gear and DPVs. Jake, you and I can make an underwater run at the *SwaleMaiden*.' TJ grinned. 'Another thing my SEAL buddy taught me, got certified. Bet daddy Jake hasn't stayed certified. Got my doubts he remembers what he needs to know. Shall we see?'

'They'll have underwater avoidance and radar. There's no way you can get there without being detected.'

'You telling me these drones don't have jamming capability?'

'They have it,' Major Adams memed. 'But, like I was trying to tell you, if they get jammed or our UAVs are put out of commission first, then you'd be SOL.'

'That's combat for you, always matter of timing and luck. Jake's going. No way he goina go it alone. I'm goina pack a sniper rifle in a waterproof wetbag. Once we get in close, if the wind and water cooperate, I'm goina take out their aerial radar."

TJ turned to Dr. Guthridge. 'Do these implant devices work underwater?'

'As far as I know. This has not been tested.'

'Guess we'll find out. It would be better if we could go unencumbered-- without those heavy-ass-commed dive suits.'

Jeni returned and they went over the game plan with her.

'You know this is crazy.'

Jeni, 'This may be asking a lot. But if I don't make it and Gabriel's mother doesn't either, please make sure Ariel gets to see him and take him in her arms.'

Jeni nodded. Major Adams memed, 'We'll do our best.'

TJ memed, 'We need to talk to Poponovich. He and his men should be willing to watch Hardy, Picard and his crew.'

Dr. Guthridge memed, 'Poponovich can't be trusted.'

Jake: 'I'll have a little chat with him. He'll cooperate.' Jake went to where the arms were stashed. He handed the women handguns taken from Picard's men. 'No one enters or leaves this room. Monitor all lines coming and going. Hopefully, this will be over before anyone knows what happened.'

'We'll either be commemorated or taken away in chains,' TJ memed. 'Tell my wife Deane it was Jake's fault and that I love her. Let's go gramps.'

CHAPTER
56

Off Coast
Jake, TJ and Renai

Everyone but Hardy, Poponovich, Picard and Gabron were seated around the conference room table when Jake opened the door. Hardy told Jake he was out of his mind and if he didn't release him and the others immediately, he would see to it Jake never saw his family again. Jake ignored him and asked Poponovich to step out into the corridor. Mark's face lit up and he joined Jake and TJ.

Jake gave him a brief rundown of the plan. "I need you to keep Hardy and the others in line."

"And how do you propose I do that?"

"I'm sure your crew will be willing to cooperate if they know what the upside is."

"Tell me. You've agreed to my proposal?"

"Yes. We'll discuss the terms when and if I get back."

"Why don't you take Picard with you he's an expert in underwater tactics. I wouldn't want to be left holding the bag if you don't return."

"No Picard. I don't trust him."

"You need to have someone besides you two. How about Renai? She has been trained by the best. Doesn't like swimming, but diving is her main recreational pastime when she's not wrapped up in an assignment. She's also an expert in several different languages."

Jake started to say no. TJ said, "Might be useful bro. Be good to have someone along in case you get in trouble out there."

"How about you just worry about yourself. After what we did to her, she'll want revenge, can't see her agreeing."

Mark said, "I'll talk to her. She'll listen to me."

Jake twisted back around toward TJ. "How will we be able to communicate with her?"

"Hand signals bro. That's what I'm talking about. That's one of the first things I was taught. You sure you remember how to do this? Wouldn't be good if you get out there and find yourself in trouble. I say we take Renai."

"Alright. Mark, you tell her no more attitude. TJ is in charge until we get onboard. Afterwards, she'll need to follow my directions. If she agrees, she can come along. If she screws up and tries to do anything we don't tell her to do, she won't be coming back."

Jake handed Mark a taser. "Just in case."

Renai came out. "A threesome. Didn't think you boys liked me."

"Can the attitude. Understood?" Jake gave her his sternest expression.

She smiled. "Big boys. You have a plan?"

Damn, Jake thought, she has that same double-meaning smile same as TJ.

They went over everything with her. Jake smelled the lingering odor wafting off her. "You need to shower; wash out your bathing suit. Don't want you turning on the sharks and gators. The equipment room is next door to the men's locker room. We'll be in there." She gave him her seductive head tilt.

Shortly she rejoined them. They suited up and armed themselves. Renai chose a knife and a speargun.

"You, me and speargun, apropos don't you think Harper?'

That same gotcha smile. Jake gave her another stern look. TJ wondered what her comment was all about.

"When we get near the boat, TJ intends to take out their radar and outer detection devices. That is if we get close enough before they discover our presence. Hopefully, they won't knock out or block our comms to the drones which connect to the control center. If they do, things could get dicey. Some think this is suicidal. If you have any doubts, now is your chance to back out."

Renai continued with checking her gear. "Poponovich say you agree to help us. I go, make sure you come back; protect my investment." She smiled.

TJ stepped over to Jake and checked his gear despite his protests.

"We may have a problem bro. That amphib has eyes and ears. How we going to get past it?"

"Damn. We'll need to drive out of here, go to somewhere nearby."

"Hardy put this place on lockdown. How we going to get by the guards?"

Renai grinned and started stripping out of her wetsuit. "You have taser, yes?"

TJ looked at Jake. "Got any better idea?" Jake shook his head.

They loaded everything in the van. Jake and TJ watched Renai as she sashayed up the drive and out of sight. TJ waited momentarily, then followed on foot. He stopped when he reached the corner. He watched her as she approached the guards manning the guardhouse. You'd've thought they won the lottery. She tased them both and he motioned Jake forward.

TJ had his implant pull up a map. He found a secluded cove nearby with public access. Remarkably, no one was on the beach.

Jake couldn't help himself. He watched Renai in the rearview mirror squeeze back into her wetsuit. She watched him watching her. She gave him a knowing look and did her coquettish tilt of her head. Neither one said anything. TJ glanced back, grinned, and continued giving Jake directions.

At the beach, Renai being the only one familiar with the DPVs gave them a quick tutorial and demonstration. The DPVs noise-suppressed motors provided slow speed maneuvering capability as well as a two-hour supply of pressurized oxygen.

Jake and TJ tested the implants underwater. They worked with communication to each other and with Jeni at the control center via an overhead drone. So far so good.

TJ went over the hand signals with Jake despite his protests. Renai looked on with a frown and an inquisitive look.

They swam out of the bay. TJ led the way guided by his implant. Jake was next, followed by Renai who was instructed by TJ to keep an eye on Jake.

It was not as tiring as Jake expected. Within twenty minutes, TJ called a halt. They were less than a hundred yards from the vessel. Jeni warned them there was increased activity on the lowest level. As their heads bobbed on the surface, TJ flashed Jake a meme, 'Too much wave action. I dare not risk a shot.' No sooner had he memed this than they heard the roar of motors coming from the *SwaleMaiden*. Seconds later two jet skis appeared followed by an inboard power boat.

Jeni memed, 'I think they've spotted you. I heard someone from the captain's berth give the orders to launch. You better get the hell out of there.

They watched the motorboat swing toward the coast. "They're trying to cut us off from shore.".

Jake yelled over the increased noise of the approaching jet skis, "we need one of the jet skis" The jet skis were headed directly at them.

TJ was busy unzipping his waterproof wetbag. He handed Jake a handgun sealed inside a ziplock bag. He pulled out his rifle. Before he could raise it to take aim, automatic fire stitched the water toward them, barely missing. Jake fired off several rounds. One ricocheted off the closest jet ski. The rider slowed within short range of TJ.

TJ saw what seemed inevitable. He was going to be too late. The shots went high; the rider screamed; his ski tilted and began spinning. He saw Renai clutched onto the handle of the K-Bar buried in the thigh of the would-have-been assassin. TJ got off a shot; the man's head exploded. He went overboard off the craft. Somehow Renai had managed to hang on to the jet ski. The kill switch attached to the rider's wrist shut the machine off as he slid into the water. Renai climbed on.

Jake had not seen what was happening. He was too busy trying to dodge the return fire from the other rider. Jake dove down. Bullets peppered the surface and miniature jets of water pulsed all around him. His DPV was ripped from his grip. He continued his dive until his lungs began rebelling. He looked up. Two sharks were tearing into a corpse. He reached down and pulled his K-Bar off his thigh sheaf. He had to surface. Both jet skis lay motionless off to his right; away from the shark feast, which now included a second corpse. If he was going to be fish food, he'd rather be dead first. He was getting dizzy-headed, wanted to take a deep breath, knew he couldn't, had to restrain himself, began slowly surfacing having recalled what he knew about bends. He was close to blacking out, he had to surface.

Somehow, he managed not to black out. He made it to the surface. TJ and Renai pulled him out of the water. He felt their hands dragging him up and over onto the back of Renai's requisitioned craft.

"Better get your bloody legs out of the water bro."

Renai started the motor, held onto him by his weightbelt and moved away from the churning mass of feeding sharks. They stopped and TJ helped right him. He checked his legs. One of the bullets had passed through his right thigh. The color of the blood indicated it had not hit a major vessel. TJ held onto him; he took his weight belt loose and tied the wound off.

They heard the motor launch. It was coming at them.

Jake said through gritted teeth, "get us out of here."

Renai spun the jet ski around and opened the throttle. Jake heard a series of shots coming from behind them. He looked back. TJ was the shooter. The motor launch had veered off; the shot had slowed its pursuit momentarily. TJ soon caught up with them. His ski was carrying less weight; made it so he could maneuver and travel faster. He slowed so he stayed in line with them, but off at a distance. They heard an explosion behind them. Jake looked back and whooped, "Jeni got the sons of a bitches." He memed, 'Thanks Jeni.'

'Doing my job. How bad is your wound?'

'Through and through. No major damage.'

TJ memed, 'can you fire warning shots over the bow of the *SwaleMaiden*?'

'Shots, no. I have one shot remaining. We have already received an inquiry from the Ambassador regarding the commandeering of the UAV without authorization and the resulting shot on the motorboat. Dr. Guthridge answered that there was an assault made on the captured amphib. You must assume our people have eyes on you. Lisa says not to worry the bumblebees are on the *SwaleMaiden*. The yacht crew will be disabled shortly.'

Jake memed, 'what about my daughter?'

'Have located unidentified female on suite level. Door is closed. No access. Cannot verify who it is. Have found several other females. None fit her description or photo image. One older female matching photo of Mrs. Palmer has been sedated, along with her husband. There are two other inaccessible suites. One is next door to the one where your daughter may be; contains a male. Our guess, this is Pietr Okneyev. Another contains another male and a female. Lisa said all accessible passengers and crew have been sedated. We are worried Okneyev may detonate the bomb. Doubtful he will unless he knows he is outside the blast zone. You're ten minutes away. Lisa is going to withdraw the bumblebees when you arrive. She will have them standby in case you need them. Be advised there are other jet skis in the area. Could be your banger buddies.'

'Roger that. We will board the *SwaleMaiden*. I expect you'll hear from Okneyev very shortly.'

'Copy that.'

Marge came in, 'Have you considered the possibility that you are the target? This could be a trap.'

'I am committed. If I must trade myself for my daughter, I will. I'm counting on that being the case. If he shows his face, I intend to kill him.'

'You forgetting the bomb? TJ memed. 'Anything happens to him, it goes off. Jeni, is there any way you can jam the frequency?'

They were less than a half-mile from the yacht. Jake told Renai to stop. They both did. TJ said, "What little training I received, I know these things are set to go off if there is any interruption in the signal. We're at a stalemate."

Renai asked what he was talking about? TJ explained the situation.

"Mr. Harper you can take your hands off me for now." Jake removed his hands. "You need talk to Boyd. He is bomb expert."

TJ relayed this to Jeni. 'Tell Poponovich the problem. Have him talk to Boyd and Gabron. Better still, Dr. Guthridge think you can get into Boyd's head and read his implant?'

'I can try. I'd rather not have to deal with Poponovich.'

'We need to know what he knows about the bomb. Also be good to know if there's any connection between the CIA and what's going on.'

'What do you mean? You think the CIA is connected to Okneyev?'

'Why do Tindal and General McDab plan to go to the SwaleMaiden? Something's up.'

'I'll try again. Their implant was implanted by Dr. Perkins. I tried earlier without any success. As much as I hate the idea, maybe Poponovich will help me with him.'

'Tell Poponovich if he wants the deal, he'll cooperate.'

'What deal?'

'Better you don't know at this time. We'll tell you later. That is if we make it back from this suicide mission. Get back to us and let us know if there is anything that can be done.'

'Copy.'

Jake's leg throbbed. He released the tourniquet, waited for the tingling in his calf and toes to stop, then retightened the belt.

"You two can wait here if you want. Renai either take me to the yacht or hop on the other one with TJ. I need to see about a first aid kit. Won't matter if we wait here or on the yacht TJ. Like you said we're at a stalemate."

"Sorry bro. You're right. Yacht it is."

CHAPTER
57

Onboard SwaleMaiden
Jake, TJ and Renai

Renai offered to administer the first aid while TJ wandered around doing an inspection.

'They've upgraded everything since the last time I was on here. It was called the *BolsToy* then.' I'm zip-tying our fellow passengers. Just in case they come around quicker than we did. Okneyev is in the former captain's quarters I bet. I don't hear anything. Could be the doors are soundproof. Headed back your way. Hope you two aren't flagrante delicto?'

'Funny. Learned some new words, huh?' Jake lay back on the stateroom leather sofa. Renai's touch was surprisingly gentle. He wished he knew where his daughter was. Wait a minute. 'Jeni, ask Cary if she knows if there are any miniature cameras in the control center. The kind you slip under a door or through a keyhole.'

Shortly, Jeni came back, 'not that she's aware of. She's going to go with Marge and check Hardy's office.'

TJ rejoined them. They kept their voices to a whisper as agreed upon before they slipped onboard. They were quiet; wondered if Okneyev had eyes on them as expected; wondered why he didn't try to warn them off.

"I'm sure he knows we're here," Jake whispered. "Why no response?"

"Probably waiting to see what our plans are. Maybe it is a trap like the Major said. He knows he's holding all the cards. Who knows," TJ replied.

Renai said nothing. She went to the bar and quietly opened a bottle of wine, poured herself a wineglass full and rejoined them.

Jeni memed saying they had no luck. Dr. Guthridge memed that Mark's crew's bomb expert Boyd reiterated what Jake had said 'any interruption in the signal would set off the device. If they could get inside the amphib, perhaps an interrupter could be attached, then he could attempt to defuse the bomb.'

'Were you able to find out anything from his implant about Tindal and McDab?'

'No. I did talk to Poponovich. He agrees there is something fishy about their plans to visit the *SwaleMaiden*.'

"Blackmail or a ransom demand,' Jake memed, 'Only thing that makes sense. Poponovich knows more than he's saying.' Jake looked at Renai. Why was she not saying anything?

"Renai," Jake said out loud to TJ's surprise, "You seem to be relaxed. Enjoying yourself?"

"What would you have me do. You wish we have threesome?"

"I think Poponovich and his crew, meaning you, know more about Okneyev's plans than we do."

She drained her glass, went to the bar brought the bottle back with her. "You show me yours. I show you mine. Yes?"

Okay, you want to play games. Seems we have plenty of time to kill. Why not? Jake had decided the best way wasn't their original questioning approach. Might as well say what was on his mind. See how she reacted.

"Here's what I think: Just like I said before, Dean and you and the rest of the crew were upset Poponovich held out on you about the cartel money. Then y'all found out he had half the codes. When he admitted this to you, he told you he was planning on splitting with all of you, but he needed the other set of codes. The cartel said TJ and I stole them. Then Jenkins disappeared; took government files. My wife went with him. Y'all saw an opportunity to get richer, so you went after Jenkins and then my wife-- thought she had Jenkins' files. You found Tobolokov and Jenkins at General Toraz' hacienda. Jenkins didn't have the files. The cartel suspected Jenkins possibly hid the files somewhere. Jenkins played along, he decided he would be safer, get richer with the cartel than he would if he trusted the CIA. Jenkins and my wife's father told y'all my wife gave the files to me." How'm I doing so far?"

Renai smiled. Continued drinking the wine.

TJ said, "I'm liking it."

So, Tobolokov fingered Blakely. No need in rehashing the Cuba fiasco. Except this is where Toby's angry duplicity comes from. He was pissed at Blakely and me; he had a crush on her that's why he accused me and her of plotting together. All of you except him end up at Guantanamo. You weren't tortured or interrogated. You were debriefed. Then an elaborate scheme was concocted between Okneyev and McDab. Devereaux and Blakely were the only ones interrogated. General McDab wanted to know what the FBI and Interpol knew. Okneyev was pissed she double crossed him. Devereaux was fed a line about Blakely and me."

"How'm I doing? Ring any bells?"

Renai tilted her head, her eyes gleamed. She licked her lips and smiled.

He was getting close. What was he missing?

"Okay, how about this? TJ and I are back in the states minding our own business. I thought I was through with Mark, Blakely, you guys and all the bullshit. Thurmond Tindal, Jenkins, and the cartels had their own agendas. This is where preparation meets opportunity. What the Roman philosopher Seneca called luck. Tindal through Jenkins had asked Okneyev to get rid of me. McDab saw an opportunity. My dog was shot, Jenkins took off with the files and my wife. McDab and Okneyev thought they had everything tied up in a neat little bundle—we would be tried, convicted, and taken where they could interrogate us. Plus, they could collect the money from Tindal."

"Didn't work out quite like everyone planned. The journalist Ariel Gaspard helped clear us. Tindal hired DICE. DICE kidnapped my daughter, then Ms. Gaspard. DICE hoped to use them as bait. Tindal, DICE, Jenkins, Okneyev and McDab, all had their own plans. As did the cartels. Poponovich had his own thing going. Y'all found out about his double cross. Forced his hand. Now you believe he intends to cut you in. He told you he didn't know about Dean's and Boyd's implants, never acknowledged Picard and Gibron. How could he not? He and Picard knew each other. The SEALs came here with The Hive. Why, TJ and I wondered? For us, the most likely conclusion."

"From the beginning, boyscout Hardy, I now believe, was suckered, made head of the task force, enlisted TJ, and me, got promoted to head up a cyber unit of the Space Force, then allowed himself to be implanted. Told to blackmail TJ and me into receiving the implant. Again, I wondered why me, why TJ? Seems so obvious now. This way they could have our minds searched to see if we had the files and the cartel codes."

TJ said, "I believe you're on to them--sounds about right. What do you think Renai?"

She kept smiling, took a heavy drink of wine, and shrugged.

"Starting to get the picture. Everybody has their own thing going. Cross and double cross, isn't that right Renai? Poponovich is working for himself like all the rest of you. Plots and subplots. Who you working with Renai? Hey Okneyev, how about telling her, you have no plan to share with anyone, especially her. You planning on killing her too? Or, are we all meant to be scapegoats? Come on you Russian bastard. My friend and I are here. Tell her."

TJ's Earl echoed CT's soliloquy; a chorus of memes were received. Only Renai didn't receive them since she had been blocked.

'A small helicopter has taken off from the upper deck.' The sound and vibration joined in the cacophony of memes.

Out of the warnings, one from Jeni followed, 'UAV's images confirm, pilot is Okneyev, passenger believed to be Jake's daughter.'

TJ and Jake immediately were on their feet. Renai jumped up expecting they were going to attack her. They ran out leaving her untouched, without saying anything. She heard the helicopter and ran after them. They stopped outside the door to the suite where Okneyev was thought to have been.

Jeni memed, 'His suite is empty. Other suite's occupants, the male and female, are not moving. I have UAV following helo's progress. You may join in via your implant.'

Jake tried the door. Locked. He reared back ready to try to kick it in. TJ shouted, "No. Don't. It could be booby-trapped."

Jake's leg throbbed. He sank down onto the bench seat.

"This whole damn boat may be booby-trapped. We better get off here now."

"What about the others?" Jake stood and limped toward where the Palmroys and the crew members were left after being zip-tied. Renai started toward the lower deck. TJ grabbed her. "Oh no. You're not going anywhere without us." She struggled but was no match for TJ. "Either you help us with the others, or we'll leave you here.

"Let me loose. I go to see about a lifeboat."

"You try to leave us and I will shoot you." He turned her loose and hurried to join Jake who was cutting the zip ties off the other passenger's arms and legs."

"We can't take time to get them down below," Jake said, "Help me."

TJ grabbed the feet of one of the scantily clad young women and Jake took her arms. They dropped them one by one overboard. Renai appeared in an inflatable raft. TJ grabbed his wetbag and they both jumped overboard and swam to the raft. As quickly as they could they loaded the now semi-conscious others.

Jake asked, "what about the male and female in the other suite?"

TJ shook his head as he instructed Renai, "Get us out of here." Renai swung the motor to the left and they slowly headed back toward the compound landing dock. "The other suite's door could have been booby-trapped also," TJ shouted over the sound of the small outboard motor.

They made it back to the dock. Poponovich and his men met them at the end of the dock and helped them unload the protesting Palmroys and the three women and one male. The yacht didn't explode.

"You must release me. Take me back to my ship," Mrs. Palmroy sputtered her demands. Her hair was plastered over her head, her eye shadow and makeup had run downward giving her a haggard, ghoulish look.

"Your friend Okneyev has fled," TJ replied. "There's a good chance your boat is booby-trapped. Let her go. There's your rubber dinghy. You and your husband be my guests." TJ pointed to the rubber dinghy.

"This is preposterous. You had no right. You can't possibly expect us to return in that?"

"See any other boats? Do whatever you wish. That amphib is rigged to blow, if I were you, I wouldn't wait out here and bet on what your lunatic Russian friend may do." TJ turned and followed Jake and the others as they went toward the open compound door where the Major stood guard with an M-5 rifle.

CT tracked the helo via the UAV. Within minutes it landed on the roof of the Russian Embassy. Jake saw Okneyev exit the helo. Another person jumped in the pilot's seat and the helo took off once more. Jeni kept the UAV on it for several more minutes as it headed west. Jake entered the control center monitoring station room. A medic was treating his wound when the call came in. It was the American Ambassador. He demanded to speak to Undersecretary Hardy.

Jake took the call. "Undersecretary Hardy is not available. He will return your call shortly."

"Who is this?" Jake cut the call. "If he calls back, tell him someone has gone to get Undersecretary Hardy."

Within seconds another call came in, it was Okneyev. "Well played Mr. Harper. I grew tired of speech. If you wish see your daughter again, you will do nothing. I call again we discuss terms." The call ended.

Jake saw no other option, he needed to talk to Hardy. He doubted his apology would change the repercussions Hardy would enact. No doubt he would demand Jake's and TJ's immediate surrender and arrest. Possibly the women as well. Jake hoped to convince him of the position this would put the op in. He would ask for, demand, if necessary, that Hardy wait until his daughter's safety was secured. Be his choice. Jake hoped he listened. Otherwise, things could get dicey. Would the Ambassador send the Marines? Jake didn't think so. Wouldn't look good for tomorrow's planned gala.

The UAV tracking the helo carrying his daughter disappeared into a cloud of dust stirred up by its rotors. When the dust cleared, the helo was nowhere to be found. In the immediate area was a small uncharted airstrip and several metal buildings.

'What happened?'

Jeni: 'The pilot knew what he was doing. He must have flown the helo into one of those buildings. I'm sorry Jake I can no longer keep eyes on this location. The ambassador has ordered all our UAVs grounded. He is demanding to speak to Undersecretary Hardy.'

TJ said he would go get Hardy. "You need to take care of that leg, he said with a grin that looked ominous, then spread across his face; the lines extending upward alongside and into his eyes. "If it gets infected, the prison doctor will probably amputate. Make it hard to get away from Bubba with just one leg." TJ didn't wait for a reply; he left the control room laughing.

TJ took his rifle with him into the conference room. Hardy was ensconced in a corner. Mark stood nearby. TJ asked for, then demanded Mark hand over the taser. He told Hardy the Ambassador wished to speak to him. Hardy waited until they were in the corridor before he spoke.

"Do you plan to hold me at gunpoint while I talk? You do realize the seriousness of what you and the others have done. I don't understand why TJ; why you, Jake and the others turned on me?'

'You were suckered into this sir. That's what Jake and I think.'

'Suckered into what?'

'The implant. And, everything that followed. We were all used. Jake was right. Our implants refused to answer hard questions concerning their independence. You admitted this. Yet, you continued to impose their orders on us. When General McDab took over, things seemed to take an eerie turn. Poponovich and the others are his people. Jake and I learned from tours in the Middle East not to trust the CIA. You know much of Jake's, and to a lesser extent my plight, are directly connected to Tindal. Tindal, former CIA, whose company owns the patent to The Hive and the implant, these implants now inside our heads. Jake was freaked out about it from the beginning, you coerced me and him into allowing ourselves to be implanted. Now here we are, two things happened: Picard shows up with a platoon of SEALs and The Hive; and, Dr. Perkins, accompanied by General McDab and Tindal sequester

Carmichael and a pregnant Ariel at Miami University Hospital with the intent to do dangerous and unauthorized procedures on them. You told Jake tough shit, the op came first, orders were orders. That did it for him and the rest of us. If you don't understand, then you are nothing more than a blind, sanctimonious, bureaucratic lapdog whose humanity has been compromised. You are another Oliver North sir.'

'This coming from a soldier and police SWAT team member. You know the importance of following orders. There's a ticking time bomb sitting out there which threatens, not only our safety, it could also launch a war. There are things going on that are far greater than individual concerns. It is my duty as the head of the task force to put my personal feelings aside and concentrate on stopping these threats from getting larger. You, Jake, and the others have made the critical path that much more critical. World leaders are here or will be tomorrow. It is our duty to secure their safety. Don't you get that?'

They were stopped outside one of the other rooms. TJ pointed to the monitor. Hardy looked and saw the haggard Palmroys, a military looking man, and a couple of scantily clad females seated around the metal table. Mrs. Palmroy was cursing and screaming at her husband and the other man. Hardy watched. 'What are they doing here?'

TJ told him about their misadventure on the *SwaleMaiden* and Okneyev's escape with Jake's daughter. 'He's at the Russian Embassy. Jake's daughter was taken to an airstrip southwest of here. That is why I needed to show you these people before you talk to the Ambassador. We are not forcing them to stay here. I gave them the option to return. One other thing, Jake and I take full responsibility for our actions. We are willing to help you if you will listen to our concerns. Jake's family's safety has to be addressed. I'm speaking for myself, and I think I can speak for Jake, I intend to turn myself in and I believe Jake intends to do the same. But, not until this op is over and Jake's family is secure. However, we will not surrender our arms, and will meet force with force if anyone tries to stop us before this happens. I hope this is agreeable sir. What you tell the Ambassador and McDab is up to you.'

'TJ you have put me in a precarious situation. I will have to get back to you on this. First, I must talk to the Ambassador. Alone, if you don't mind.'

TJ unlocked Hardy's office door. Hardy reached for the lock controller. TJ refused to hand them over. Hardy wondered if his bio-scanner for the locks had been compromised.

TJ rejoined Jake in the control room and shared with him what he told Hardy.

"You didn't have to do that. I wish you hadn't. Only one of us should take the fall. That's me.'

A short time later Hardy summoned Jake and TJ to join him in his office.

"The Ambassador is livid. You two have created an international crisis. The *SwaleMaiden* was off limits. You both knew this. Your futile attempt to rescue your daughter could have prompted Okneyev to detonate the bomb. You ruined the State Department's negotiations for a peaceful resolution. For your information, General McDab and Thurmond Tindal were going to the *SwaleMaiden* tomorrow to work out an exchange. Your daughter would have been released. You blew it. The Russians now have the upper hand."

"This is bullshit. Okneyev should be arrested. What happened to *"We don't negotiate with terrorists?"*"

"The Russian Ambassador says Okneyev has diplomatic immunity, and we wrongfully seized his private property. He swears there is no bomb on the amphib and that he rescued your daughter from DICE's people, and that she was in the process of reuniting with her husband. The Ambassador has demanded the immediate return of Gabriel to his parents."

"This is bullshit and you know it. Okneyev threatened to explode the bomb on that damn amphib that sits out there in the center's net. You heard him. I spoke to him again not long ago; he told me he would call back to negotiate a deal concerning my daughter. I will release Gabriel to his mother; not to anyone else."

Jake tried to calm down. He saw the stubborn fix of Hardy's face. He needed answers; needed to know if Hardy was willing to let them proceed or was going to try to shut them down. Perhaps Hardy learned something from the others. Had any of them run their mouths? He wanted to trust Hardy; he now knew without a doubt Hardy was holding back on them. Jake didn't want to go through CT. He decided it was safer to do so only when he felt he had to. Amazingly CT had offered no more interruptions.

"And Poponovich, I think we need to talk to him again. Did you talk with him or get a read from Boyd or Dean while you were in there? "

"You need to talk to the Palmroys. See what they have to say about Okneyev," TJ said, "They've been in this from the git go. They were Bolstoy's money people. Who's protecting them, do you know?"

Hardy remained quiet. He had to get the op back on track. He first had to decide what to do about TJ, Jake, and the others. While in the room with Poponovich and crew the one thing he caught wind of was whether Renai was the right person to keep an eye on Jake and TJ. Poponovich had stopped the conversation saying they should not question his decision. Dean and Boyd kept quiet. He only caught one other hint concerning the money they were promised. They were like a pack of thieves each ready to cut the other's throats. He couldn't trust them. Like Jake and TJ, he was concerned about General McDab and his connection to Poponovich. Why should he, how could he trust them, any of them including Jake, TJ, and the others? The Generals last orders were form the cyber unit utilizing all of them. Paranoia aside, he had his orders.

"The Palmroys are off-limits. They shall remain here until General McDab arrives. I have a mission which is vital to our nation's interests. I will listen to everyone, then we will put together a game plan. My decision will be final. You and the others will need to decide whether you will comply with my orders or face the consequences. If you continue to disobey, I can guarantee you the results will be disastrous for everyone involved, and, their families. I am giving you fifteen minutes to talk it over with the others. That is all. I will wait here."

CHAPTER
58

Airstrip, Quintana Roo, Southwest of Cancun
Suzie and Lee

Suzie waited with Terrence inside the hangar for Elizabeth to be unloaded from the helicopter. Okneyev's man told Terrence to keep her away from everyone. "She is not to talk to anyone. Treat her like a special guest. But no talking." Terrence attempted to give him a suitcase with a half-million US dollars in it. The man refused.

"No money. He say he want you know he watch you. Will collect later." The man asked them where motorcycle was?

Terrence pointed to the corner. The man went to the motorcycle, checked it over, started it and came back to where they stood.

"The helicopter remain here. Wait here. Other guests arrive soon."

He sped away on the motorcycle.

After they watched the dust disappear, Terrence turned to Suzie.

"Seems we have entered into a cabal with persons unknown. Venture a guess?"

Suzie was confused and scared. Her attempts to reach Mark had gone nowhere. A news flash told of a terrorist attack, an amphib with a possible dirty bomb had been captured off the coast, and authorities had neither confirmed nor denied the story. Was it connected to what was happening here? Who had summoned them? Why was Pablo's wife brought here? Why did no one take the money? She looked over at Terrence.

"I should be asking you the same question? She said. Why would this person direct you to bring money then not take it? Who are these other guests he intimated?" Suzie watched DICE's man. He looked as puzzled as she did. They had taken her Smith and Wesson .38. For all the good it would have been. "Who are those armed men who took Elizabeth away? Are they your people?"

"No. I was sent a message to my room. Said bring half-million US dollars, come to this location. I told you. This is all I know. Are you carrying?"

"They took my small peashooter. Not that it mattered. You talked to them, what did they say?"

"Not much. Said we should wait here for special guests. Asked if we had dinero? Nothing more."

"Pablo's wife. You said the Russians had her."

"This is what Alperts' boy said.

They heard an approaching airplane. The Mexicanos came rushing back out of the building where they had taken Elizabeth. They stopped next to them; their AKs in their hands. The small jet taxied to a stop, swung around so the nose was pointed back toward the landing strip; the tail was less than twenty feet outside the hangar door where they stood. A set of steps descended and two more heavily armed Mexicanos wearing combat gear with the federales designation on their headgear took up positions at the foot of the steps.

Suzie recognized the first man who stepped out. It was El Presidente Juan Carlos Santiago. Behind him was a young attractive female in a business suit. Possibly his aide or a girlfriend. The next person was Eduardo Enrique Gonzalez, the self-declared head of the Juarez Cartel. Behind him was General Toraz. One of the last men to exit the jet made her heart skip. It was Major Bud Jenkins. He was followed by two more federales.

One of the men that had stood next to them rushed over when signaled by Gonzalez. The federales went with Jenkins, General Toraz and the Mexican President to the building where Elizabeth was taken. The Gonzalez man toting a carryall canvas bag came with the guard back over to them.

"You have money, yes?"

Terrence reached down and picked up the suitcase. He tried to hand it to Gonzalez. The guard took it and hurried off. He went a ways out onto the tarmac, and looked back at them He was clearly nervous. Gonzalez nodded. The man fumbled with the latches and slowly eased the lid open. His round, brown face appeared relieved. Gonzalez handed Terrence the carryall bag. "You. Go put money in bag."

Terrence stood still. He stared into the man's cold, dark, fathomless eyes which he knew from stories was often the last thing many others had last seen. He was already sweating, now he was more conscious of the clinging moisture dripping off his forehead. For a fleeting moment, he considered pulling out the .22 single shot pen still clipped to his pocket and putting its round between those beady brown eyes. He decided the odds were against him. He hoped the opportunity arose at a more opportune time. He smiled, reached out, and took the bag. He went to retrieve the money and the small tracking device hidden in the right-hand latch. Wouldn't be of much use if they decide to kill them. They would know soon. The Jenkins man. He hoped he got a chance at him. Terrence thought, *I'll either get rich or die trying.*

The well-dressed Gonzalez told Suzie to come with him. "No need standing here in this heat. We have much to talk about."

CHAPTER
59

Control Center
Jake and TJ

The bumblebees hovered in the background. Dr. Guthridge watched the jet land, taxi, spin around and stop. She wanted to scream "it's him" when she saw who exited. Never in her wildest expectations did she believe she would see her old boss ever again. One of the most wanted men of all time. There. It was definitely him.

Jake followed TJ out of Hardy's office. "What do you think? I say Poponovich first."

"Can't take long. No telling who Hardy spoke to. Could be another SEAL Team Unit on the way."

"Don't think so. Wouldn't want the publicity that would generate. Hardy's a career man knows what that would mean. Problem is the State Department. I hope they're scared of the consequences an armed confrontation would mean. CT has gone dark. Has yours?"

"Yeah. Can't decide if that's good or bad."

TJ summoned Poponovich to join them in the corridor. The sound coming from the room was like a coven of crows intermixed with the hissing of a viper den.

"Hope this is good news. Renai told what happened and what you said. You have these guys all stirred up."

"Our deal was predicated on you helping me get my daughter back. Look, I don't have time for bullshit. I need a simple "yes" or "no". Was the NM0099 implant device a CIA program?'

"I don't know."

"Yes or no. Is Thurmond Tindal a CIA asset?"

"I told you he is. The better question is, is Dr. Guthridge? The answer is yes. I recruited her."

"She told us. Why was Picard and Gabron sent here?"

"For the amphib. You know all this, why are you asking?"

"General McDab told Hardy to form a cyber unit. I believe his intention, starting with Dean and Boyd, was to create a CIA clandestine cyber unit for his own personal aggrandizement and that you knew this. You have no intention to go rogue or share with me. The problem with McDab, Tindal, you and your people is none of you trust each other and you're all willing to cut the other's throat. No need in answering. The truth is written all over your face."

TJ shoved Poponovich back inside the door before he could answer.

"I think that went well bro. Glad you squashed that deal. Problem is Hardy and General McDab are going to follow through with or without us."

"They need Gonzalez codes. If they think we have them or they figure out a way to get their hands on David Gonzalez, we should be safe. I'm betting on their greed."

"Deane will never forgive you if you're wrong."

They entered the control room. Lisa looked around and called them over.

"When Jeni was commanded to withdraw the UAVs, I sent the bumblebees to keep our eyes on the airstrip where the helo disappeared. Have a look."

She refocused the split screen and brought forward an earlier recording. Jeni and Marge moved back so Jake and TJ could get a better look. A motorcyclist emerged and sped off, a jet landed, the passengers disembarked—a dignified man in military regalia followed two armed guards, a nice-looking woman was followed by the Gonzalez uncle, then General Toraz and another man with his head down as if he was hiding his face. Lisa zoomed in from another angle and froze the image.

"Son of a bitch," Jake exclaimed.

TJ said, "Damn. Have you told Hardy or anyone outside this room?"

"No. If they're monitoring us, as I suspect, they already know."

"And my daughter?"

"Sorry Jake. The bumblebees were too late getting there."

Jake stood up straighter. "First Elena, now my daughter. That son of a bitch. Why would Okneyev send her there?"

"What did Hardy say?" Lisa asked.

TJ patted Jake on the back.

"Hardy wants us to continue op, continue with the help of Poponovich and crew. Jake and I spoke with Poponovich before coming here. He as much as admitted this a CIA rogue op with General McDab and Thurmond Tindal. Poponovich also implicated your involvement Dr. Guthridge. Jake told him you admitted to your recruitment. Anyway, Jake and I offered Hardy our willingness to turn ourselves in after this is over--as long as Jake's daughter's rescue is included in the plan. Hardy's wanting to have another pow wow with all of us, said he's willing to listen. The way I see it, this recording changes everything." TJ looked at the huge digital wall clock. Numerous time zones were displayed. "We're late. Ladies, Jake, you ready."

"This changes nothing," Hardy exclaimed." "What do you propose to do, launch a hellfire missile, kill them all, including your daughter? You want to start a war? Not going to happen. Our hands are tied. We can't send in troops. Jake, I know you'd like nothing better than to go in guns blazing. You'd get your daughter killed. The best option is to let the ivory tower sons of bitches try to negotiate a settlement. Those are my orders. I know you think I don't care about your daughter. I do. If you hadn't pulled that bonehead stunt on the *SwaleMaiden*, your daughter would possibly be free."

'You don't know that. You trust the staties and McDab's CIA lying word. You just can't accept the fact that he and Tindal are running a scam."

"Show me the proof Jake. Washington's eyes are on this. Look at Jenkins. Proof positive, you can't stay hidden forever. There are eyes everywhere. Even moreso since 9/11 and COVID-19. They know this. I don't agree with everything they've done; but, I don't get to tell them what to do. We'll save your daughter Jake. Don't go rogue again. Otherwise, if something does happen to your daughter, you'll have no one to blame but yourself. Think of Ariel and your grandson."

"That has been and is all I think about. Don't try guilt-tripping me. I can do that without your help."

"Moving on. Anyone have anything they wish to add?"

Dr. Guthridge looked around the table. "Those with implants may have noticed your devices seemed to have gone dark. They have. I shut down their ability to transmit as a precaution. They are in sleep mode until I can determine if changes were implemented without my knowledge.

Undersecretary Hardy agreed. This is not to be shared with anyone outside this room."

Hardy added, "when we release Poponovich and the others they are not to know this. Dr. Guthridge and I will continue monitoring Dean, Boyd and the others."

"And how are you going to be able to stop the grand puppetmasters from reading you or pumping information into our devices?" Jake asked.

"Hardy killed the monitors. Supposedly, as long as we stay inside the rooms the device is shielded. Outside the rooms, I will place the devices in sleep mode." Lisa replied.

"Why not do the same with ours?" Jake asked.

Lisa nodded toward Hardy.

TJ said, "Because Hardy doesn't trust us."

"Not quite TJ. You two will be on the front lines with Dean, Boyd and whoever may have the device. You two are wanted men. If the bad guys get their hands on you…well, need I spell it out for you?"

"So much for having one up on the bad guys. Another promise proven to be bullshit." Jake wished he could just go after his daughter. And take some of their problems off the board while he was at it.

"You seem to forget Jenkins is somewhere nearby. The Russians may already have been given the device."

Lisa spoke up, "We have no idea who has the device or something similar. Russia's announcement of super soldiers was thought not likely. At this point we can assume they do. Our implants may be compromised. If that is the case, everything, the whole op may depend on you two's resourcefulness. I will remain hidden, shielded, monitoring the situation. I will relay signals to your devices via a couple of bumblebees which will always be in your vicinity."

"What's to keep others with the device from receiving your messages?"

"Nothing. Hardy has agreed to let us use the bumblebees for offensive and defensive purposes."

A little after the fact, but better late than never.

"Won't this create a problem when Tindal arrives?"

"Not if he doesn't know. This is another reason to keep Poponovich's men from being able to read you."

"His people are going to be busy with our central casting crew. They will be working as wait staff at the event tomorrow. There is a possibility your daughter and Jenkins will remain behind at the airstrip. Dr. Guthridge is going to use the bumblebees to neutralize their guards after the ones who will be attending the gala leave tomorrow. You and TJ will go there and rescue your daughter and take Jenkins into custody once they've been neutralized. I believe that deserves a thank you Jake."

"I'll thank you if your plan works. We need a plan B and C to cover all possibilities. What we decide will need to consider what Okneyev and the Russians have to say. And, your boss General McDab."

"My boss. He's the head of HSI lest you forget."

"From this point on, I consider myself an independent contractor. As an independent contractor, I expect to be paid for my services. Which, to my knowledge the only payment in kind has been for Ariel's hospitalization. Since she, like I, have been treated like experimental animals, hers unwittingly I might add, the government owes us. I intend to collect. You can tell that to whomever you feel you have to, or whoever reads our minds."

"You agreed to turn yourself in when this is over. Is this no longer true?"

"Yes. But it won't be to you, the CIA, NSA, or HSI. I will turn myself in through a lawyer to the FBI when a public warrant is issued stating legitimate charges having been filed. Any effort to take me into custody by any other means will be resisted in a most publicly displayed show of defense. I wasn't bluffing when I said I put what has happened in a file which will be released if I don't keep checking in. Look around you. These are witnesses. Anything happens to them or my family, the file will be released." Jake hoped CT noted this and would be able to follow through. A shot to the head might put an end to CT, which meant his threat was going nowhere.

Hardy looked around to the others. Their hardened expressions said all he needed to know.

"You don't run this op Jake. Is that understood?"

"Never intended to. Just keep in mind, for me, my family comes first."

CHAPTER
60

Cancun, Russian Embassy
Okneyev, Jake and Hardy

Pablo's father, the Cuban Ambassador to Spain and the Russian Ambassador to Mexico were seated across the ornate mahogany table from Pietr Okneyev.

"Why you not kill the men while you have them on boat?" Pablo's father asked.

The Russian Ambassador to Mexico said, "Better not to cause international problem. I have lodged complaint about seizing Comrade Okneyev's property. The American Ambassador assured me the amphib would be returned, as well as your grandson."

Okneyev said, "Leave amphib where it is. Everything is on track. We have amphib where we want. Senor Guzman have Major Jenkins to trade for family and his moneyman Poponovich. General Toraz have Harper man's wife and now the daughter. Everyone now have things to trade. The Captain of *SwaleMaiden* should be regaining consciousness momentarily. It is time I contact the Americans start the negotiations."

Jake was startled when his burner phone vibrated. He had forgotten all about it since arriving in Cancun. CT had become the replacement. He pulled it out of his cargo pants pocket. It said caller unknown. Who knew this number?

Only Ariel, Deane, and TJ. He decided to take a chance and answer it. Could be something to do with his family.

The room grew quiet. He put the call on speakerphone mode.

"Mr. Harper. Should I say Agent Harper? Are you alone? Sounds like you have me on speakerphone. That is good. Perhaps you will have your audience introduce themselves."

Jake looked at the others, pointed to Hardy and slid his phone to the center of the table. Hardy took the phone and placed it on the table in front of himself.

"And how should I address you, Colonel Okneyev or Comrade Okneyev?"

"Undersecretary Hardy, my close friends call me Pietr and I hope we shall become comrades. Is Agent Alvarez present?"

"Why don't you go ahead with your demands Okneyev." Hardy replied.

"We shall call this negotiations, okay?"

"My country does not negotiate with terrorists."

Jake stood. Hardy waved him down.

"Undersecretary Hardy friends don't talk this way to each other. I am a reasonable man. We are both civilized men you and I. Let us not call each other names. I believe I have something you want, and you have something I want. I call to negotiate a trade. Okay?"

"Negotiations should be made through your ambassador. I am in no position to make any deals."

Jake spoke so he could be heard. "You should release my daughter as a gesture of good will."

"I intended to do so Agent Harper. You and your friend, you cause change to plans. We now start over. There are others whose plans must now be negotiated. There are some who wish to take more drastic measures, see if certain people can fly. The Mexican President upset. Your government it commits criminal acts, kill his people, take others prisoner. Their demands must be heard. Understood?"

Hardy waited, didn't reply. Waved Jake off, gave him finger to lip quiet gesture.

"The Palmroys are upset. You must return them to their vessel. Their captain is standing by. Your General McDab and your friend Colonel Tindal were to join me tomorrow to discuss business of mutual interests onboard the *SwaleMaiden*. Because of your actions, a new time and location will have to be agreed upon. Your daughter is in good hands--her fate will have to wait until I hear from the person able to make decisions."

Hardy terminated the call.

Jake exploded, "You should have heard him out. You have put my daughter's fate in the hands of people who could care less about her or me."

"Calm down Jake. I cannot negotiate terms with him or anyone. You heard him you are responsible for your daughter's situation."

"I will not wait on McDab or Tindal. You said TJ and I could go after my daughter and Jenkins. We need to move into position tonight. Hit them at first light."

Hardy studied the others. They looked at him expectantly.

"Just so we're clear, I did not and cannot authorize any action. I need to make some calls, give Poponovich and the others their instructions. You have perhaps thirty minutes to talk before I turn the Palmroys loose and have them escorted back to the *SwaleMaiden*."

Hardy walked out the door. His ass was on the line. The only good outcome for him was if they brought Jenkins back with them. For some reason, he felt this was not going to happen. If he was going to be able to salvage his career, he needed this to happen. He hoped Jake and TJ survived. He dreaded making the calls to the ambassador and General McDab. He had to buy more time. Not likely to happen. The dignitaries and investors were gathering.

"We're in," Lisa announced. She released the others' blocked devices so they could watch the two bumblebees who had entered the dark, weathered structure, The interior was not as bleak or austere as the exterior intimated. This was a well-apportioned purlieu for someone—Jake's guess, this was one of the cartel's safehouses.

"Where is everyone?"

Lisa guided one of the bumblebees through the large living area, which contained a nice leather sofa and two chairs on one end with a kitchenette on the other. The other bumblebee went into the two bedrooms. Empty. Did not look used. Bathroom separating the two bedrooms also empty, not even toilet paper. The windows were shuttered. No back door.

"How could they have vanished?" Jeni remarked.

"My guess: the same way El Chapo did," TJ said, "through a pantry or possibly, under the shower. Has to be a tunnel. Dr. Guthridge, we need to surveille the immediate area. Be on the lookout for other vehicles in the area which standout, a limo, anything the poor farmers and villagers couldn't own."

"Got them. Two limos speeding east."

The bumblebees followed their progress back through the countryside, then downtown Cancun and onto Hotel Row. The limos disappeared beneath the Mexican Embassy.

Hardy was coming out of his office when Jake and TJ exited the control room.

"My daughter, Jenkins and the others left the compound. We traced them to the Russian Embassy."

"I know all about it. I was talking to the ambassador…" Jake was about to interrupt. Hardy spoke up before he could. "Hold on Jake hear me out; the ambassador and I were on a conference call with the Mexican Ambassador when the news broke. The Russian Ambassador to Mexico has demanded we release the Gonzalez family members and return your grandson to his father and mother."

"Not going to happen."

Hardy ignored the comment. "Hear me out. Our ambassador was willing to comply until I informed him of Jenkins presence with the Mexican President and the Gonzalez uncle, the Juarez Cartel boss. Our ambassador demanded an explanation from the Russian Ambassador. He replied we must meet his demands before any further discussion could take place. I spoke up and said they had a wanted man, Jenkins, an American citizen, and they must turn him over to us immediately. Our ambassador reiterated my demand and said this must happen before any other discussions about the fate of the others could take place. The Russian Ambassador said he would discuss this turn of events with the Mexican President and get back to our ambassador afterwards. Our ambassador is in discussions with Washington. I expect to hear from General McDab shortly."

"There is no way Elizabeth would have agreed to reconcile with her asshole husband. She is being held hostage and she is an American citizen."

"You don't know that. It's no telling what she may have been told about her son or who is responsible for his and her fate. And, as far as her citizenship, the State Department has questions concerning this."

"Ariel's her mother. She is an American citizen. And, I'm damn sure an American citizen. That makes Elizabeth an American citizen."

"Blood-wise, yes. However, Elizabeth's adoptive parents live in Sweden; there is no record that they maintained an American address or citizenship; and, they never applied to have Elizabeth naturalized. That said, in my opinion. because she was at a British adoption agency when whoever signed off on her, which I assume was Ariel's parents or her British aunt, means Elizabeth could be considered an American or British citizen by birth."

"You told me the staties were looking into locating her and securing her release. Sounds to me like that was either a lie or now they're trying to cover their asses by claiming she is not their problem. Until I hear, in person, from Elizabeth that this is her decision and she is not being threatened or coerced into making it, I will assume this is bullshit and will do whatever it takes to learn the truth. And Gabriel is going nowhere until this happens."

"Don't go jumping to conclusions. I will tell the ambassador of your concerns. Probably won't matter. I'm sorry Jake but that amphib sitting out there and Jenkins' presence makes this a whole new ball game. That is why we're here; this was and is the op. Everyone's priorities are focused on these two problems, and I have my orders."

"Here we go again—f' you Jake—you and your family don't matter."

"I didn't say that."

"Yes, you did. Maybe not using those words, but the meaning couldn't be clearer. We'll see about that."

"Jake, you were in the military. I don't understand what part of defending national security you don't understand. And, I would think getting our hands on Jenkins would make you happy. He could clear your name. The sooner we can clear this op, the quicker you can resolve your personal concerns."

"Hold on. General McDab sent me a message. He and Tindal are on their way. Will be here before the end of the day. I am to break off talks with Okneyev and others. Prepare people for tomorrow's event. Security is the priority."

"TJ said, "This should be interesting bro. Maybe we'll finally have a chance to meet face to face with Tindal.""

"Yeah. Won't that be great."

"Jake don't dig the hole deeper than it already is. I need you, TJ, and the others to cooperate with the rest of our team. We need to be ready for tomorrow. I'm going to have my talk with Poponovich and the others. If you would, ask Dr. Guthridge, the Major and the Captain to join us in the conference room to go over everything. Afterwards, I'll introduce you to the weapons we have at our disposal. Might help put your defensive concerns to rest. You need to let me hold onto the weapons you confiscated before we enter the conference room arena. Wouldn't want you taking out any disagreements on the others. Okay?"

"I'll try to restrain myself," Jake replied. TJ answered the same.

"You guys make my job even more difficult. I'll be waiting for you."

CHAPTER
61

Cancun, American Embassy
Cyber Unit Members

Unhappy with the news about their assignments would have been an understatement. When Jake, TJ and the women entered, the room was buzzing with raucous cries of descent. "Waiters. I'll be damned if I'll be a waiter" seemed to be the general sentiment. Jake and TJ said nothing when told the not so news news.

Hardy shouted, "That's enough. General McDab is on his way. These are his orders. You will be given non-lethal weapons which will be secreted under your uniform cummerbunds. There will be a contingent of US Marshals and US and Mexican Marines standing by with Mexican Federales and Colonel Picard and Major Gibron. A SEAL Team is at the airport. They will escort the American representatives to the event. Mark Poponovich, Agents Harper and Alvarez will not be in attendance due to the fact they are known to the hostiles.

Jake said, "Now wait a damn minute."

"Agent Harper, we can't afford open hostilities which would put everyone in danger."

Jake began to step forward. TJ restrained him. Hardy memed, 'I have other plans for you three. Hear me out.'

'Those plans better be good.'

Jake saw grins on some of the other's faces. They faded and the general noise became more subdued when Hardy said, "Jenkins has been spotted. He arrived a little while ago at the Mexican Embassy along with Don Eduardo Enrique Gonzalez, the defacto Juarez Cartel boss. The Mexican President was with him. As was Jake's daughter." Everyone's eyes went to Jake. There were no grins this time. Dean smirked. It disappeared when Jake locked eyes with him.

Hardy continued. "Jenkins is the primary target, hence the reason we are going to the event disguised. Keep your eyes and ears open for him or any mention of his name. Pietr Okneyev is expected to be part of the Russian contingent. Be careful with him. If he feels threatened, he may set off the bomb sitting out there in the harbor. You are to let General McDab and Colonel Tindal handle him. You will all be connected via camera mics. There will be call signs. If you don't receive the correct response, don't respond. You can bet there will be watchers/listeners posted in and out of the embassy ballroom. That is all for now. Like I said General McDab will be here in a few hours. He will speak to you. If there are any changes between now and then I will let you know. I have arranged for a group of design and disguise gurus who will fit you out in the uniforms in the locker rooms. First Colonel Picard and Major Gibron, I need you and the others to accompany the control center guards to the firing line room where I want you to check the proficiency of the others using the weapons they will be issued."

Colonel Picard asked, "What about Major Gibron's and my weapons which were taken from us?"

"They will be returned after General McDab gives the word. Please do as I instructed. Those are your orders."

Jake, TJ, Mark, and the women watched the others file out. Renai waited until the others were gone. "I would be more useful if you let me play the role I normally play. I make very good eye candy. Yes?" She did her seductive tilt of her head.

Hardy hesitated. Poponovich said, "She is damn good at getting information out of the unsuspecting."

"Alright then. I'm sure the artists will have something you can wear. Weapon might pose a problem."

"Not for me. Perhaps they have a hairpin or ring with a sedative."

"Check with them."

She walked out, twitching her hips.

Poponovich laughed. "What are my instructions Herr Capitane?"

"The rest of you will be with me upstairs in the embassy security room. Dr. Guthridge and the Captain will be busy with the drones. Major and Poponovich will be monitoring the cameras. Jake, you, TJ, and I will be using our implants to scan for anything and everything that points to where Jenkins and your daughter are. We will have access throughout the room and the adjacent areas via the embassy cams and the mic cams the others all will be wearing. Jake, General McDab wishes to talk to you. Don't ask me why, I don't know."

Dr. Guthridge asked, "Any word on Dr. Perkins?"

"No." Hardy was afraid hearing his name might set Jake off.

Hardy memed a cautionary response to her and TJ. 'Be careful. We don't know for sure.'

TJ memed, 'Know what for sure?'

'About Dr. Perkins and the proposed operations or the outcome. Tindal is coming. Stick close to Jake.'

'Oh yeah, count on it. Better keep Tindal away from both us.'

Hardy didn't reply. Instead, he watched Jake. *Will he, can he be controlled*?

"Satisfied Jake?"

"Only when this is over, and my family are together."

"I wouldn't say that to the General if I were you."

"Depends on him. Frankly, I could care less what he has to say. If he doesn't feel the same way I do about what I say, it will be his problem."

"You have a total lack of diplomacy. I'm afraid this will be your undoing."

"No political correctness for my bro, that for certain. One of his most endearing traits. "I am what I am", ain't that right bro?"

"You got it."

CHAPTER
62

Control Center
General McDab

When General McDab and Tindal arrived, they spoke to Hardy first. Hardy cautioned Tindal, "You might want to steer clear of Agent Harper and Agent Alvarez. I'm sure you are aware of why. By the way where is Dr. Perkins?"

"At the hospital in Miami. I understand Harper's and Alvarez's misguided animosity toward me. After General McDab goes over the situation with Harper, I believe Agent Harper's feelings toward me will change."

General McDab had been told the efforts to shut Agent Harper down had all failed. He was ordered to find out why. Agent Harper had threatened to go public; this couldn't happen. Dr. Perkins had said the Carmichael woman and Harper family members implant procedures were a success. He had no explanation for why Harper could not be shut down. Neither did Colonel Tindal. Tindal said he would talk to Dr. Guthridge. This was unacceptable. Agent Harper would have to be dealt with, one way or another.

"Colonel Tindal, you and I need to take care of business. Undersecretary Hardy, is the team ready for tomorrow?"

"The agents, the wait staff if you will, along with Colonel Picard and Major Gabrun, are waiting in the conference room for you. The others are in the control room."

"After Colonel Tindal and I speak to the men in the conference room, I will speak to the others. I intend to speak to Agent Poponovich and Agent Harper individually. Please have them wait for me in your office."

Hardy didn't like the General's condescending tone or his lack of respect toward him. If the General, and Tindal in particular, approached Jake in this manner, it would not end well."

General McDab and Colonel Tindal followed the two guards to the conference room and Hardy went to relay the orders to the others.

Jake pondered why the tall, fit-looking general with his grey crewcut hair, former head of the CIA Clandestine Unit, now Homeland Security Acting Director chose to wear his Army dress uniform with all his ribbons and citations? Did he think this was going to impress him? Jake knew you didn't get to be a general without political and strategic savviness and the will to use it to your advantage. McDab gestured for him to sit. Jake waited for him to sit. He smiled, nodded then sat down in the straight-back chair across from him, unholstered and carefully laid a Colt Python upon the metal table, the business end pointed at Jake.

 No, Jake decided, McDab was trying to intimidate him. Wasted effort.

"Afternoon son. Hear you've been quite busy." The General picked up the Python, seemed to be trying to decide what to do with it while waiting for Jake to reply.

Jake said nothing. Kept his posture, relaxed and neutral. He locked eyes with the General and smiled.

"You know the history of many of our firearm's manufacturers. They were pacifists," Mcdab said toying with the weapon, then setting it down, pointed toward Jake. "You're not a pacifist, are you?" He didn't wait for an answer. "Rhetorical question. Of course not. Several reasons why you were chosen: you come from a line of veterans with exemplary records; you were a decorated veteran and a good trainer until your untimely injury. When your wife abandoned you, taking your children and the doctors gave you less than a fifty percent chance of recovery from your injury, your name was presented to us as a possible case for closer study."

Jake was listening while deciding how he could defend himself if McDab intended to do more than intimidate him. McDab's eyes scrutinizing him triggered a faint memory he often visited in his dreams--a pair of eyes standing over him when he was in Bethesda, or was it Walter Reed? CT memed, *déjà vu*. Why were his eyes and words triggering these memories? Where was he going with this?

"Am I getting your attention? Good. Your wife Joanna seemed not to fear losing you. Seemed she feared the alternative much more--the benefits, child support, funds to maintain her habits. Getting her to sign was a mere formality. Your father took more convincing. We could have proceeded without his permission. However, he soon realized our option was the best of several unappetizing alternatives. You were the ideal candidate for our program. Dr. Perkins with the aid of his young assistances had demonstrated to us the promise of the research. The early recipients had shown evolutionary progress. We needed to remove any doubt before we approached the boys with the bigger brass balls."

"Are you saying what I think you're saying? The iPSCs? Already know about that. Guess Joanna and dad were right. Thank goodness. But that's not all you're saying y'all did while I was at Bethesda, is it? You're implying y'all made me your guinea pig back then. That's bullshit. Knowing what I know now, I would've known."

"You were never at Bethesda. The records were falsified. If we hadn't done what we did, you would have been a vegetable, if you lived, a quadriplegic. You were lucky to have survived. Ask your device. The one ironically you call CT in honor of your father. CT can show you footage of your remarkable recovery. You were a well-kept secret. We kept our eyes on you. Elena was no coincident. She didn't know. Her father Sam helped keep us updated. We grew concerned when she told her father you suffered from PTSD. I'm getting ahead of myself. Shall I go on?"

"Did Hardy know? What about TJ?" Jake was feeling deflated. Could this possibly be true?

"Dr. Perkins, his team, and I, along with a select few, were the only ones in the loop. Your friend Agent Alvarez knew nothing. Neither does Undersecretary Hardy. Your name was given to him as a potential recruit for Operation Pink Flamingo along with your friend Agent Alvarez by my predecessor. This was the first test of your potential. Agent Devereaux and Agent Poponovich were your guardians. Miss Carmichael became a problem we had not foreseen. As did the Russians. Someone learned about you we feared. We now know Major Jenkins was in communication with his pal Pietr Okneyev. Okneyev was playing all sides for his own profit. Jenkins fell for it. Agent Poponovich had to intervene. Unfortunately, we were too late stopping Jenkins from getting away and taking your wife."

"Bullshit. Colonel Tindal was in this up to his eyeballs. He wanted me out of the way. Did he help you make up this story? You must think I'm really gullible."

"Colonel Tindal didn't know about your device. Neither did Jenkins as far as we know. If Jenkins had known, Poponovich's recruit Dr. Guthridge would have known. And she didn't. She thinks you were implanted along with Undersecretary Hardy and your friend Agent Alvarez. We know that now without a doubt. It's true Colonel Tindal wants your land. He ordered Major Jenkins to do what he could to get you to sell. He ordered Dr. Guthridge to attempt to persuade you when she took over as COO of Tindal Industries. Colonel Tindal's made mistakes. We all did. He realizes that now. You and your family have become part of the team, Tindal can no longer legitimately claim a need for your land. National security is no longer an issue. However, your father-in-law made a grave mistake when he didn't report his daughter. Your wife and her daughter will have to be punished for their part in attempting to defraud the country."

"What about Blakely and Ariel and our fetus? And where is Dr. Perkins?"

"Miss Carmichael is no innocent. She needs to answer a lot of questions. As does her cohort Tobias Tobolokov about his connection with Pietr Okneyev Your friend Ariel Gaspard the journalist complicated our ops and our ongoing evaluation of you. We hoped you would remain unattached. We were pleased to learn, when you underwent your fake implant procedure, that you kept the secret from her. Then we became concerned when we learned about yours and her earlier unknown parenthood."

"Things really became troubling when DICE entered the picture. Agent Poponovich tried to learn what he could to head off this new entanglement. He failed in his attempt to stop her or save her. We allowed his efforts for your sake. The damn cartels sought revenge upon you and your family and friends. She paid the price, same as Miss Carmichael. Your girlfriend and the fetus, when we learned it was yours, put us, the operation and you in an even more precarious situation. That's why I'm telling you all this. Undersecretary Hardy hasn't been able to assuage your concerns and get you fully onboard."

"There's a lot of holes in your narrative. If you think your telling me this will change my mind about this device and convince me to be part of your cyber unit, you are sadly mistaken. My main concern is for my family. Saving my daughter and her son and giving Ariel and myself a chance to be the family I often dreamed of. That is all that matters to me. Your Orwellian dream holds no appeal to me. I want an answer. Has Dr. Perkins implanted Blakely, Ariel and the fetus?"

Jake saw the answer in McDab's face. The smile vanished replaced by a flat expression people put on when they're about to lie or say a predetermined answer to a question they've dreaded was coming.

"They better all be alive and undamaged. Or I swear to God…"

"God?" McDab laughed. "What God? Seems your polyamorous religion is more humanistic pagan than orthodox. Oh come now, one can only imagine what God thinks of your sexual proclivities. Not that this matters, but…"

Jake straightened up. The look in his eyes told McDab he may be pushing it with his humorous diatribe. He toyed with his Python, gripped it then let go. Jake watched with an I-dare-you expression. McDab smiled, eased back with a placating hands-up gesture.

"But… I assure you those with whom you've shared your saintly virtues, and the resulting offspring thereof, are on the mend. All but the fetus. Which brings us to the difficult decision you need to make. Legally, I am under no obligation to talk to you about this. As the newly appointed head of Homeland, I have been chosen to act as the messenger. The message comes as a warning, made from far above my paygrade. Think about what I told you, think about your recovery. Some would call your recovery miraculous. Knowing this, would you rather Miss Carmichael, Ms. Gaspard and the fetus live or die? Given the choice, what would either of them choose for themselves? And, what do you think Ms. Gaspard would choose for her baby? If nothing were done and if Ms. Gaspard and the fetus managed to survive, the medical experts concurred, they would be physically and mentally handicapped. The same as you would have been. What choice would you have made about yourself? What choice, given the choice, will you make about the unborn baby Ms. Gaspard carries?"

Jake sat forward.

"You could have saved them without the implant. That was your choice. Knowing what I know now about the device, I would have chosen to live without it—even if it meant dying."

"The implant is what preserved your mind. The iPSCs and the other procedures healed your body, but what good is a body without memories? Is that what you would wish for them? Knowing what I know about you, I don't for a minute believe that. The difficult decision was made. You will no longer have to keep your device secret from Ms. Gaspard or your child. Think what that means. No more worries about unforeseen viruses or diseases, no need to pay for an expensive education. You and your newly found family can stay in touch no matter where all of you are. The government will pay for everything from now on. You can keep your farm. No more worries about Colonel Tindal or anyone else taking it from you."

"If this is your idea of utopia, why not make it available for everyone? Do you have the implant? Does your family?" McDab didn't answer. "I didn't think so. You picked a poor smuck who was helpless, then decided to safeguard your secret and continue the experiment with other hapless individuals. You can plant thoughts in our head-- use us like test dummies. To what end? How do I know that I'm really me? And what about Ariel and the child? How are you going to keep them from talking, and what about if they let it slip? What happened to free will?"

"This is not nirvana you're offering, it's hell. Why not place the device in geniuses, masters of industry, politicians, then remove it and insert it into a robot, create an android? Oh, I see, should've known, you've thought about that. There's no way to know anyone is who they say they are. You know you talk about national security, the two biggest threats to national security are climate change and domestic terrorists--like you, Tindal, and the minions you trained that raided our capitol. Fuck you. Fuck them and the politicians whose tails you ride on or control. You might as well kill me. Go on get it over with."

McDab raised the gun and pointed it at Jake and pulled the trigger four times. Nothing happened. Jake knew the Python held six rounds. He stood up and moved around the table and stopped next to McDab. McDab locked eyes with him. Jake saw a flicker of fear despite the smile.

"I have on a graphite vest. Want to bet that I can't break your neck before you can shoot me."

"I am an excellent shot. You have vital organs that are exposed. And you are not that reckless—would end all hope. And you want to live and be free."

"Yeah. Care to find out. I wonder who is more valuable to them, you or I?"

McDab cleared his throat.

"There is no need to find out. You see you have free will. No one's taken that away from you. Your device is part of you. You are part of it. It is directed to protect you. Asimov's laws of robotics were the prime directive when we decided to make the device. We tested it. Tested you. Your device shut down. You shut it down. We are not the monsters you think us to be. Ask CT."

CT answered for the first time in a while. 'Yes son. I am you, you are me.' Then CT started singing the Beetles' Walrus song. Jake told him to go to sleep. The discordant sound of his singing abruptly ended. Jake returned to his end of the table.

McDab saw the change in Jake. He had to press on.

"This op exists to prevent others less altruistic from weaponizing the device without constraints. Therefore, we must regain Major Jenkins. We believe he shut himself down when he realized his captors did not have his best interests in mind. They want you. Why we don't know. If and how they found out about your having the device is a mystery. One which has to be solved for the integrity of our program and to make sure you can return to a public life."

"Two decisions you must make now: save your fetus; and, are you willing to continue?"

"As I'm sure you are aware, I will continue until, and only until, I have secured my daughter's release and know Ariel and our unborn child are safe and we can return to the farm. I do not want any implant device placed in Ariel's or the fetus' head. From the sound of it, you people may have already implanted Ariel. Of course, I want to save our unborn child, physically and mentally. But I want more evidence from additional, nongovernmental, experts about the efficacy of what you're proposing."

"That can't be done for security reasons, and you know it."

"You have my answer. If any harm comes to my daughter, Ariel, or our unborn child, I will hold you and Dr. Perkins personally responsible. Tomorrow I intend to do what needs to be done. After that, I intend to make good on the promise I made to myself. I'm sure you're aware I have threatened to go public, that is the promise I intend to keep if anything happens to me or any member of my family. We're done here. Do what you have to, and I will do the same."

"It doesn't have to be this way. I hope you come to realize that. I would prefer our conversation remains private. I give you my word I will not divulge any part of it until this op is complete and you and I reach an agreement. Now, we need to get on with this mission. As you may, or may not have heard, all hell is breaking loose regarding China and North Korea, and I must give more than my divided attention to what this means. I need this mission over with pronto."

Jake didn't know what McDab was talking about. CT would have to tell him. Didn't matter. His family came first. McDab's problems were not his. No way could he trust McDab. Had McDab's cronies heard the whole conversation? They now had a decision to make. That is if it wasn't already a foregone conclusion. He had dug the hole deeper and painted a target on his back. His termination wasn't an if, it was when and in what manner and by whom.

"Before we part ways there's one other thing that puzzles me: why would Tindal allow Jenkins be implanted and Dr. Guthridge, why not implant himself? Same thing: why not Dr. Perkins and you?"

McDab stood. His arms were crossed, a smile was almost there but not quite. He hesitated, couldn't help himself.

"Anything can be hacked. We'll be watching you, don't make me regret choosing to let you live."

He picked up the Python, turned and marched out of the room.

Jake had to tell someone. That someone was his usual confident.

Do you believe him?" TJ asked.

"I don't know what to believe. Is it possible? Dean, Boyd, Major Devereaux, Captain Adams, Major Duplantis were sleepers like I supposedly was? Dr. Guthridge says there were others. Is it possible? The simple answer is yes. But why me? Another bigger question is why wait to activate me and the others? And how did Okneyev and the Russians find out? How did Jenkins know how to block his implant? And, why not tell Hardy? Too many who, what, when and whys. I just want it to be over; it's never going to be. I think they intend to terminate me."

"They'll have to terminate me also bro."

CHAPTER
63

American Embassy, Cancun

Another troubled sleep night. Everyone ran through their respective preparations over and over.TJ and those who would be in the consulate control room were sent in pairs to the embassy at short intervals using many different vehicles under the cloak of darkness. The rest waited until early morning and arrived in catering vans amidst the hustle and bustle of the regular embassy staff.

TJ set himself up on top of the embassy with a borrowed sniper rifle, a Springfield polymer XD M5.25 Competition Model, reluctantly loaned to him by Colonel Picard, who was ordered to do so by General McDab. The rest of the SEAL Team were spread out in strategic locations on top with TJ and out of sight elsewhere. Dr. Guthridge and Lisa used the bumblebees and two high altitude UAVs to surveille the area.

Jake hated leaving Gabriel behind. He was asleep on a cot in the control room under the watchful eye of Cary the appointed babysitter at the nearby monitor. CT would be watching him also.

Jake insisted on coming to the embassy at the break of dawn by himself—a decoy target. He wore a new Dragon Skin armored body suit over his street clothes. He knew he was taking a risk announcing his presence. He hoped TJ and other friendly watchers might get lucky and get a read on anyone lurking nearby wishing to take him out. He waited near the van, then received the all-clear meme from the watchers via Hardy to CT. He entered through the main entrance, shed the body armor, and was scanned first by a Marine then by the mechanical walk-thru scanner and, lastly, by another man in plain clothes.

TJ joined him and they went to the upstairs security control room. A row of monitors displayed the images from the cameras which showed every public accessible part of the embassy including the restroom areas. The toilet and urinal area cameras were set so the images would be from the waist up.

'No hanky panky in the bathroom unless you're a voyeur,' Jake thought. CT responded, 'when has that stopped you, son?'

Hardy said, "The Secretary of State and the other American dignitaries arrived late last night. Colonel Picard and the SEAL Team took turns catching cat naps. They'll be running on adrenaline and fumes."

Marge commented, "Like the rest of us. Good thing our implants are alert. A Space Force and NSA contingent is helping the mining venture geeks with their setup."

Jake and TJ watched the bio-monitor checking the vitals and run up of facial recognition on everyone down below. No warning alarm was set off.

"What time are the guests expected to begin arriving?" TJ asked.

Marge said, "The caterer should be setting up shortly. There will be a meet and greet starting around lunch time. The main event will happen starting with dinner scheduled for six. Introductions and speeches, sales pitches, will start around eight, followed by ballroom dancing until midnight."

"I guess McDab and Tindal are with the ambassador and the other so-called dignitaries," Jake said, "I wonder if that includes the Mexican and Russian Ambassadors and Okneyev?"

He wondered where Elizabeth and Jenkins were and who would be watching them when the Russian contingent was here. CT was attempting to get a read on Jenkins' implant. So far, no luck. McDab's guess appeared to be spot on--Jenkins had gone dark. If he could locate him, he figured Elizabeth would be nearby. Who was guarding them, and where, was all he needed to know?

Jake and the others watched an overabundance of magazine, tv and other media geeks, whose eyes, and ears, with mics and cameras, were filming and interviewing the who's who of world celebrities mingling with political, aerospace and industry giants, including his old pal Colonel Tindal. He recognized Gates, Zuckerberg, Branson, and Musk, two NASA space partners and competitors. They were involved in discussions with other nerdy looking men and over- and under-dressed women. CT took note and Jake reprimanded him. '*Others may be listening.*'

'*I only read what you see.*'

Jake's attention went to the Cuban Ambassador to Spain's wife who arrived accompanied by the Russian Ambassador to Mexico's wife and a couple suits following behind. Boyd approached them to take their order, interrupting an animated conversation with a nice-looking blonde lady. Jake and the others heard Gabriel's grandmother say Pablo something or other and Elizabeth. Before Jake could tell Boyd to stay close, he had hurried off to attend to their order. Jake asked CT if he caught what they said and could translate. CT memed, by an interpretive extrapolation, it seems that Pablo's mother was requesting the Russian woman have her husband to ask the Russian Ambassador return Pablo's wife to him. This other Russian woman disagreed, said must wait.

Jake thought, 'Pablo's mother wished to fill Elizabeth's head with lies, accusing Jake and the Americans of abducting Gabriel. General McDab and the American representatives better not acquiesce.'

Boyd returned with the women's drinks and lingered nearby momentarily. They were discussing the space mining venture negotiations taking place. The Hive, Okneyev and the UAV amphib were mentioned, as was Putin.

TJ heard bits and pieces of the conversation. He didn't need an interpreter--the women were speaking in Spanish. But the growing ambient noise made it difficult to hear. He and Jake swapped memes. TJ heard one thing CT missed—something about the ISS, International Space Station being abandoned, a new one, partnering with the Chinese, a good bargaining chip for the mining venture negotiation and U.S. device that read brain waves.

"Is there a way to get an audio fix on them?" Jake asked one of the ambassador's monitoring team members.

"I would need authorization."

Hardy heard Jake's request. He memed him asking why he was requesting this. Jake memed him the conversation bits.

"Do it," Hardy commanded the security tech.

"Pablo make mistake dealing through DICE men," the Russian Ambassador to Mexico's wife said. "My husband say our president and Mexican President, they not wish DICE involvement. Now have ugly cartel boss wish make deal. He talk flanking maneuver. This concern my husband."

The Cuban was telling the two other women, "DICE men no longer problem my husband say. Okneyev he take care of this other one. He say

DICE man not alone. Have European woman. This make for more surprises for American negotiators."

The noise of the burgeoning crowd made hearing individual conversations too difficult. The security tech was not good enough to separate the signal on the fly. "This would have to be done later," Hardy told Jake and TJ.

'Flanking maneuver and surprises involving cartel, European woman and DICE. What could this mean?' Jake memed TJ, Hardy, and the others. 'We're all concentrated here. Our flanks are open. What flanks? Where?' Jake checked the UAV cams, memed Jeni, 'You see any movement near the control center?'

'Nothing out of the ordinary.'

'The cartel safehouse, check it?'

'The jet is no longer visible. They could have moved it inside the hangar. We are sending a bumblebee to check.'

Ten minutes later Jeni reported, 'The jet is gone.'

Hardy memed, 'That doesn't necessarily mean it has anything to do with what they were talking about. We need to concentrate our attention on our mission. Jenkins and your daughter were last seen going into the Russian embassy. Whatever Okneyev and the cartel boss were talking about could mean anything. Stay focused. We'll hear back from General McDab soon. The festivities have begun. Don't get sidetracked.'

TJ received a text from Deane. '*Been trying to reach you. Call. Emergency.*'

TJ stepped off from the others and went where he could talk and not cause a distraction.

Deane answered on the second chirp, "TJ, I've been trying to reach you. There were two incidents you need to know about. Leon and his crew had to fight off a raid on the Hood by a rival gang. At the same time, it was reported an apparent terrorist attack happened outside the University Hospital. Dr. Perkins has been abducted. The kidnappers got away."

"Where are you?"

"At mama's. Leon has members of his crew outside and three of them are in here with us. The hospital is on lockdown. They are calling this an act of terrorism in protest of the conference down there where you are. I was worried about you. The terrorists said they have a nuclear missile onboard a vessel outside the conference and will detonate unless their demands are met. Is this true?"

"Don't worry 'bout me. I'm safe. Stay there. Don't go anywhere. I've got to go. Love you."

Pandemonium had broken out on the ball room floor and TJ disconnected hoping Deane had not heard the noise behind him in the security room.

"Okneyev fired a missile from the amphib. The damn thing has exploded," someone shouted.

An overhead monitor showed the explosion.

'What triggered it? How was this possible? How did the missile get through the net?' The meme went from Hardy to Jake, TJ and the other implantees.

Hardy had a tech pull up the vids from the cameras which had been monitoring the amphib. They showed a bright light reflected off the water, so bright it had to be a cutting torch, it had quickly cut through the netting, which fell away. The missile had been launched.

Within minutes, one of the guards at the gate of the control center sent a message saying his personal radiation detector had detected radiation.

All outside personnel were ordered inside and told to go through decontamination procedures.

Jake began frantically checking the damage to the control center where Gabriel was. Hardy shouted at him, "The building is bomb proofed and has suffered only minor exterior damage. The power was reported cut. The backup generators will be up and running. General McDab has ordered everyone inside and the embassy is sealed—no one can leave or enter."

TJ told Jake, Hardy, and the others what Deane said.

"What about Ariel?"

"Only said Dr. Perkins abducted outside and hospital on lockdown."

Jake tried to call. His call went to a prerecorded message telling him all circuits were busy, blah, blah, blah. He needed to do something. He wanted to strike out, retaliate. Where was Okneyev and the others? He instructed CT to locate them while keeping an eye on Gabriel and searching the news in Miami.

CT: *Intercepted message from meeting room Okneyev and Cartel Boss Gonzalez reported not with others. Not at embassies. Searching for them. News from Miami say only two security men killed, three bystanders wounded during abduction. Gabriel fine, playing video game. President has ordered evacuation of remaining military from Afghanistan.'*

Hardy was looking from one monitor to another. The cyber crew had their hands full trying to calm the crowd below. He too was using his implant to check multiple locations. He also wondered where Okneyev and the Cartel's Gonzalez were. He ordered TJ and Jake to guard the door and not let anyone in unless they knew the pass code.

"General McDab says emergency crews are evaluating the range and level of exposure. He said the ambassadors are in contact with their respective governments. No one is accepting responsibility for the amphib and missile or the abduction of Dr. Perkins. He has requested our president allow him to take charge of the investigation. He expects to be given the green light. We need to be ready."

TJ had a hunch. 'Jeni check location of the *SwaleMaiden*.'

The UAV showed the *SwaleMaiden* had moved out to sea, was beyond Cozumel. He memed the other device members, 'The Palmroys took the *SwaleMaiden* out, that broke the signal. That could be why the missile was launched.'

Hardy: 'Could be.' He sent a message to Captain Conroy and instructed him to intercept the *SwaleMaiden.* He called General McDab and informed him of his order. McDab concurred. Then said, "We have been given the go ahead. This will be a field test for our unit. Let's show the big boys what we're capable of. I'll be rejoining you shortly."

TJ said to Jake, "Missile was distraction so Okneyev, Jenkins and Don Gonzalez could get away. Must have not liked how negotiations going."

"Why would he bring my daughter and Jenkins to the Russian Consulate? Why would their ambassador allow it? Doesn't make sense. McDab thinks they want you, me, and my grandson. He and the ambassador were willng to give them Gabriel. I can understand why they would want Dr. Perkins and Dr. Gallagher. Why would Okneyev be willing to risk everything for you and me? Someone has to be making it worth his while."

"David Gonzalez and the cartel would. Need to find him."

"What about that DICE man and the other woman?"

Mark Poponovich had wandered over to them. "I might be able to help you with that."

"I told you before I have someone on the outside. An agent named Suzie. She was with the Gonzalez Mexican bitch after she arrived in Cancun. I directed her to find your daughter. I tried to tell you this. You wouldn't listen. I believe I know where your daughter and the others are headed. I'm surprised Okneyev didn't tell you Jake since you're one of their most-wanted targets."

"You mean the cartels? That's not news. We figured that."

"Not only the cartels but almost every group out there. For many you have become more valuable than Jenkins."

"I doubt that. Doesn't matter. I'll be happy to give them their chance. Where did your source say they were headed?"

"The transport at Tulum Naval Air Base. This was before the missile blast. Because of the damn EMPs I can't reach her for an update, but it makes sense Okneyev wants it all—you, Dr. Perkins, The Hive—checkmate—every one of the pieces in his greedy Russian hands."

TJ said, "Makes sense. He used distractions to flank us. Now, he's making his move. Check, not mate."

"Damn right it's not checkmate. I'm still in play. Time for me to make my move."

"How you propose to do that? This place on lockdown and possible radiation dust from here to there."

"This place has to have hazmat suits."

"If they have them, they'll be for the Marine guards. You'd need General McDab or the Ambassador to okay you going out there. I don't see that happening. Plus, you'll be vastly outnumbered. You might be good, but I doubt seriously you're that good." Mark saw Jake's angry determination.

Hardy rejoined them. "General McDab wants us to assemble downstairs in the strategy conference room to go over his plan."

Jake told him what Mark's source reported.

Hardy turned to Mark who grinned and shrugged.

"Mine is only to serve and please."

"Tell that to General McDab, why don't you?"

"Aye, Aye, el comandante." Mark saluted, turned and left.

"God, that guy gets on my nerves. Jake, I guess you and TJ heard the news from Miami and about the Chinese and North Korean threats?" They both acknowledged they had.

"Jake, General McDab is concerned about you. You're being watched. Fair warning. Shall we go?"

"I told McDab the same thing I told you, my family comes first, I'll let you remind him of that so you can look like a loyal kiss-ass."

Hardy shook his head. "Can't say I didn't warn you."

TJ memed Jake, 'Dr. Guthridge sent meme. Bumblebees' circuits possibly scrambled by the blast, no longer responding.'

'What did you think when you heard Poponovich's source report about the transport?'

'First thought The Hive, gotta wonder how many SEALs there guarding it?'

'Precisely. But, this goes back to the question of why bring The Hive in the first place?'

TJ stroked his chin. 'Good question bro. When we get downstairs, why don't you ask why?'

'Hope Tindal is there. Like to see his response before I mess the mother up. Just so you know. And I'm going after my daughter, permission or not.'

'Figured as much. Not to worry bro, I'll have your back,' TJ memed as they headed for the elevator. 'Need the sniper rifle and eyes so I can get into a strategic position. Too bad we don't have the bumblebees. But do have Major Adams' UAV recceing the area. No firefight happenin'. Wonder why?'

'I don't trust Tindal or McDab. The earlier shit with Picard, Gibron and the SEALs still bothers me.'

'Ditto. Just so you know, I'm not enthused with having the former CIA Counterintelligence Chief as my commanding officer. Never trusted them. Never will.'

'You got it. I plan to make my move sooner rather than later. CT has managed to pull up the plans for the embassy. There is a large room next to their locker room designated a secure area. I'm willing to bet that's where the hazmat suits are. Right next to the armory.'

'Makes sense.'

The room grew quieter when McDab, Picard and a well-dressed man entered and joined Hardy and Dr. Guthridge at the front of the room. As Jake suspected, the other man was with the embassy. McDab introduced him as the Consulate Communications Director.

The little pompous pipsqueak droned on and on about bioterror and the bomb, which was unprecedented and demanded a retaliation, but cautioned cooler heads must prevail. *Yeah, don't want to hurt the tourism.* He called the detonation an accident. This caused a resounding crescendo of disapproval that McDab allowed a few minutes of before ordering its cessation. The chastised bureaucrat said it had been decided that the conference should continue since no one could leave until it was determined safe enough to do so.

"We need this conference. Our country and the world need the economic impetus this will provide. We lost too much due to the pandemic. I…"

General McDab stepped forward, cut him off and began issuing orders. There were lots of grumbles when they were told they needed to resume their earlier assignments and stay in disguise. He tried to appease everyone by announcing there was enough food and alcohol to last up to a week. "That should give comfort to you and any restless guests. Being sequestered here is better than most of you had it during the pandemic. You survived that. You'll survive this."

After the consulate guy left, McDab said, "Dr. Guthridge, Captain Adams, Agents Harper, Alvarez and Poponovich, you will be issued hazmat suits so you can return to the control center. Major Duplantis, you will join Undersecretary Hardy in the upstairs communications room. You two will be the liaisons between the control center and Colonel Tindal and myself. The rest of you will continue working the crowd. Stay vigilant. Report anything that is pertinent to the mission. You will assist the Marines and the SEALs with crowd control. Remember, no violence. We can't afford increased panic or the subsequent fallout. These people are cutoff from the outside. And we need to keep it that way. No talking to the press. Those of you requiring hazmat suits remain behind. The rest of you return to the ballroom."

Jake noticed Picard left with the embassy puke. After the others left, McDab asked Poponovich what his source reported. Mark told him.

"Hardy gave Colonel Picard and me a quick briefing before you came down. He has gone to try to check the SEAL Team's status. I will go over with you what I decide once he gets back to me. Go with the Marine by that door." He pointed to the far corner behind the podium. He will take you back to get suited up. I'll get back to you shortly."

McDab returned, Picard in tow, before they were completely suited up.

"Colonel Picard wasn't able to reach his team at the transport. Okneyev sent a message. He said the team was resting. He also has made demands. Most cannot be met without higher authorization which won't happen because his actions as a terrorist go against our country's stated policy. McDab went on and said what Jake and TJ already knew: Okneyev has offered to trade Jenkins for you Agent Alvarez, you Agent Harper, and your grandson, plus Poponovich and the Gonzalez man and woman. He would not give any reason. I told him I will get back to him after I talk to my superiors." He looked at his timepiece. "We have fifteen more minutes until I must contact him. Otherwise, he says he will execute your daughter."

"Let me talk to the son of a bitch. I will meet with him if he releases my daughter. I don't give a shit about Jenkins."

"I'm afraid that won't happen. The higher ups don't want to make an exchange. They told me he must release everyone. They're prepared to hold out until he does. Dr. Guthridge, do you think you can get any of your bumblebees back operational?"

"To redeploy them requires their mother, The Hive. The EMPs have scrambled outside communication. Fortunately, we were shielded inside here. Hopefully, the aircraft is also. If we get lucky, and someone can figure a way to communicate with the high-altitude satellites…Only way I see a possibility for surveillance."

TJ asked, "Any idea how many men he has with him?"

"We don't know. Furthermore, we have no idea where he is. I know Agent Poponovich, you said your source says they were headed to Tulum and that may or may not be true. Big question of transportation capability. It is more than likely he had men in place at Tulum before anyone knew to check. Before the blast, satellite reconnaissance showed no vehicles arrived and Okneyev's jet did not land there. We know it took off from the cartel airstrip and it left the area. Since it did not pose a threat to us here, no one kept tabs on it. He could be anywhere."

Jake said, "There's something wrong with your scenario. Seems to me he wanted The Hive. And, Picard you say your men weren't responding; makes no sense to me. Did he say where the exchange is to take place?"

Picard spoke up, "The radiation from the bomb would have scrambled my men's comms. The Hive and my men may well be still onboard the transport."

"How is it Okneyev intercepted your attempt to communicate and why did he say your men were resting?"

Picard turned red in the face. Before he could reply, General McDab interrupted. "Agent Harper don't try to read too much into this. Okneyev could be communicating via consulate emergency channels. For all we know, he may very well be at the Russian Consulate. Therefore I'm sending you to escort these ladies to the control center. Agents Alvarez and Poponovich are going to make sure you all are not ambushed. We hope to shortly have a UAV overhead watching for anything suspicious. The emergency crews are out there, they could have been infiltrated, so stay alert. Finish suiting up. The guards at the control center are preparing for your arrival."

"And how are we supposed to get there? That's two hours away by auto and any vehicle's electronics will be out of commission. First off, I need to know about my daughter? I need to speak with Okneyev. I will demand he let me speak to her."

"I should be able to patch the call through to you whenever he calls back. You can't trust him. You can bet he's not going to release your daughter even if he says he will. Whatever it is he wants from you depends on using her to force your cooperation. We're doing everything we can to locate him and all the others including your daughter. The blast has made doing so much more difficult. If we can trace the call, we will. I need these women back at the control center ASAP."

When Picard and McDab left, Mark whispered to Jake, "Been a long time since I've fired a weapon. I hope we don't run into any trouble."

Jake memed this to the others. 'Makes me wonder why McDab chose him for this mission. And, there's no way I can think of that he'll be able to patch through Okneyev's call. This is bullshit.'

TJ: 'Kinda makes you wonder 'bout lots of things. Let's see: Poponovich, the cartel moneyman has part of the access codes. They think you or I have the other part. We told Okneyev left the embassy as did Don Gonzalez, then Okneyev demands an exchange, Jenkins for you in fifteen minutes. Add these things together, says we being set up. Hey ladies, how proficient you with firearms?'

Captain Adams: 'Can't be any more difficult than guiding and firing a hellfire missile. And I scored marksman on my last small arms weapon proficiency test.'

'Dr. Guthridge: 'With smart weapons our devices normally would be capable of making up for any deficiencies. Problem is our devices were never tested for their efficacy from radioactive interference.'

Jake: 'A firefight depends upon coordination and communication. This could be a suicide mission for you novices. Why would they want to send you two and leave Hardy and the Major here?'

TJ: 'Assume they have Dr. Perkins. With Dr. Guthridge, they have the two leading experts. Sorry Captain Adams you just a dronie—they think you replaceable. The question not why we chosen, rather, who all's involved in plot?'

Jake turned to the Marine inside the armory, "Corporal, I need to use your comms. Have them patch me through to General McDab."

The Corporal spoke into his comm. Seconds later, he said "I'm sorry, General McDab is in a meeting."

"You tell whoever you're talking to Jake Harper said if I don't hear back from him in less than a minute all hell is going to break loose."

The Corporal relayed the message. Shortly the Corporal removed his headset and handed it to Jake. Hardy was on the other end. "The General is in a meeting. What is going on Jake?"

"My daughter is what's going on. You tell McDab or whoever, I want to speak to Okneyev immediately or all hell is going to break loose. You've got two minutes. This is not a threat, it's a promise."

"Jake…"

"One minute, fifty and counting."

Hardy heard the Corporal's protest cut off. Jake had disarmed him. Hardy sent someone to alert McDab.

"Agent Harper I told you I would patch you in whenever Okneyev calls."

"The comms may not work outside due to the radiation, you heard Picard. I'm not going anywhere until I talk to Okneyev and I hear my daughter's voice."

"Listen here Agent Harper you have your orders."

"Screw you General. I don't work for you. I resigned. Ask Hardy. I'm inside the armory. You do as I ask and there won't be a problem. You don't, the results will be on you. I have recorded everything. The others with me have done the same. You do the right thing there won't be a problem. If you don't, we'll let the world hear what went on here."

"No. Fuck you. You'll never see the light of day after this Harper. Colonel Tindal will be happy to know this. The fate of your girlfriend and her fetus are on you."

"Anything happens to them or any member of my family I'll hold you and your asshole buddy Tindal responsible. Better think about it, you can't leave this building, I've got you where I can get my hands on you. This armory is well stocked. I'll be waiting on you to patch the call through. Over."

"TJ, Ladies, Poponovich you free to leave. Corporal, sorry you goanna have to stay right here with me. Promise I won't harm you unless you try to be a freaking hero."

"Bro, you've gone and done it now. When I sided with you earlier, I pretty much figured my fate sealed. Kind of strange me the one come from the Hood, went to work for the man. Always wanted to be on the right side. You the privileged honky, had other choices. Now you done gone and brought me back down to my roots, pushing back against the man. Thing is I know you right. Can't walk away now, Deane would never forgive me."

Mark fidgeted. "Jake, I was told to watch over you. My earlier offer still stands if we make it out of here. I don't know how much help I'll be, but I trust you a lot more than I trust my old boss. My crew want what I promised them. They'll never tell the General and he'll never have their loyalty after what happened at Gitmo. Besides, I've yet to learn your secret about attracting the women."

"You may be risking everything for nothing. You might want to reconsider."

Dr. Guthridge memed, 'I won't help you in a fight. I've never killed anyone, and I don't intend to start now. But I won't help the General and Tindal. I know Tindal will do anything to get his hands on your land; and the unethical things Dr. Perkins did, I have no doubt at Tindal's and the General's behest, turns my stomach. I planned to resign. Now I have.'

Jeni: 'I'm your hostage, a willing hostage. Marge won't help them either. She was as sick about what they did to the Carmichael woman and your girlfriend as I am. I won't leave, but I won't fight either.'

"If me and TJ are correct, they'll do what I demanded. We're no good to them if we're dead."

"You hope," Mark said.

"I think we have a good chance to find out who's who. At least that's what I hope."

"You thinking what I'm thinking?" TJ asked.

"We'll know soon enough."

CHAPTER
64

Embassies

Pietr Okneyev watched the Tindal man squirm. "Seems Harper man once more prove he a worthy adversary. Does our friend General McDab know who take Dr. Perkins?"

"This is still being investigated. The evidence points to Chinese, perhaps a triad. No one has claimed responsibility. No demands have been made."

"Why should they? This mean Dr. Guthridge and Harper and Alvarez men much more valuable. The Mexican cartel boss he grow impatient, think maybe we should storm embassy, force their hand, perhaps take hostages. I not want this but you and General McDab leave me little choice. I will talk to Harper man, see if he willing to listen to my terms." Okneyev pulled Elizabeth into view. She had a vest with explosives wrapped around her waist and chest. "Put this on screen where Harper man can see. Tell him I wish to talk to him."

General McDab signaled Jake and told him Okneyev wished to talk to him face to face. "There is a teleconference monitor in the assembly room."

When Jake turned on the monitor, Dr. Guthridge and Captain Adams let out a gasp. The image of Elizabeth filled the screen then Okneyev came into view.

"Mr. Harper, game time over. Hello Dr. Guthridge, glad you join us. Mr. Harper you see your daughter now have new decorative piece added to her attire. A very nice fashion statement, yes? If you do as I ask, I keep the ensemble. Otherwise, I will send your daughter outside and her pieces will be mixed with the radioactive dust. Maybe this preserve them, I don't know. No need in this sacrifice of such lovely flesh. You can ensure this not happen. I make trade for you, your grandson and Dr. Guthridge. Don Gonzalez wish have his family released along with Agent Poponovich. These things happen, your daughter can rejoin her family, the Americans get Major Jenkins, and everyone leave happy. You see I very reasonable man. One hour."

He disappeared from the screen.

Jake felt numb. He had feared something like this would happen. He hoped McDab would keep Okneyev in line. He was willing to sacrifice himself, had hoped he could force a one on one with Okneyev with TJ covering his back giving him a chance to free his daughter. He would never surrender Gabriel.

TJ watched from the armory doorway. He could only imagine the agony this caused Jake.

Dr. Guthridge spoke up, "Jake, I'm sorry. I'm willing to do whatever you ask. There may be a way out of this."

"What do you mean? I appreciate your willingness to help. But I also know once he finds out I'm no good to him, he will kill my daughter first then me. He will use us to force your cooperation before he kills us, or he will turn us over to the cartel. Either way, there is no way out of this for me and my daughter. And there is no way in hell I will let them have my grandson."

Jake sat down and put his head in his hands.

"Demand he meet us outside for exchange. Jeni can take him out with shot from satellite signal to UAV." TJ hoped he was right.

Jake looked up. "He'll detonate the vest. How's that going to help me or my daughter?"

"EMP from blast will have knocked out signal just like it did the bumblebees. Okneyev's dead, we safe, and world cheers."

"Even if Jeni can somehow communicate with the satellite, how's she going to be able to commandeer the UAV with Hardy and McDab in control?"

"Our devices work inside the consulate bro. Hopefully. All we need do is get her inside communication control room. We can manage that?"

"Need to do that anyway to make sure McDab doesn't keep me from talking to Okneyev. You up for this TJ?"

"Ready when you are." TJ held up a couple stun grenades. "This should do the trick."

"What about Marge?" Jeni asked.

"Not goina kill her. She just goina have to get over it," TJ replied. TJ saw the shocked expression on Jeni's face. "Didn't mean kill in literal sense."

Mark had been listening. Without Jake, he was screwed. No Jake. Not likely to get his hands on the cartel funds. "What do you need me to do?"

"Stay here. Make sure no one gets in," TJ replied.

"Dr. Guthridge could do that. You know the people down below are going to hear and see those flash bangers. Be better if I warn my crew. Let them know what's going down. Also, they can be useful outside against Okneyev's people. You can bet he won't come out without having his people covering his ass."

TJ used the stairs. Jake and Jeni took the elevator. There was no need for the flash bangs, Hardy and the Major were the only two present.

"I should have known," Jake said, "they were watching us."

McDab spoke over the intercom. "We could not allow you to terrorize our guests any moreso than has already been done. I will let you speak to Okneyev. You must not agree to his terms There is another way. Jake you wanted your farm, I told you, you could have that. Money, I will see to it you never lack for this, neither will your friends. We have too much invested in you."

"So, now you admit, you're part of the puppet masters? Who are the others?"

"I am not a puppet master. If I were, we wouldn't be having this discussion."

"What discussion? Are you and your Russian friend prepared to give me my daughter? Has Okneyev agreed?"

"Soon you will talk to him. You will tell him you agree to his terms. We will have substitutes for you and your friends. With the hazmat suits, he will not know the difference. You can be the voice, watch via the monitor. The idea to use the UAV is a good one. We had considered this but were afraid you would not agree."

"I don't agree. He will know it's not me by my posture. You're supposed to be the grand spy master. He'll be expecting we'll do something like that. He'll analyze the way I stand, the way I walk. You know this. First you were willing to sacrifice us, and my daughter. Now, a cast of others and my daughter. Doesn't matter to you. You people might as well be robots—program you, wind you up and let you go. Robots wanting to control other robots who want the latest toy."

"What is it you want?"

"A simple life on my farm with my family and my dogs."

"Once this op is over, you can have that. You have my word."

"Put it in writing, I'll look at it, send it to my lawyer, agree to let him post it if anything happens to me, TJ or our families, then we can go from there."

Jake memed TJ, 'Think you can get a bead on the Russian Consulate from the roof of the hotel on the west side?'

TJ checked the mapping via his implant. 'Possibly. What good that be?'

'I'm going to post myself outside the side entrance of their consulate with a huge sign and demand their ambassador release my daughter and turn Okneyev over to the authorities. I need someone, I was thinking a UAV or satellite will work, to film it, stream it live in case CT is unable to perform the task.'

'They may not respond way you expect them to bro. If they deny it or don't reply, then what? You don't know Okneyev's even there.'

'Then I create an international incident by threatening to release CT's recordings I have ready to upload. I've got all the calls and conversations recorded. My bet is the threat should be sufficient. I doubt Russia or our government will want these recordings out there. I don't see any other way.'

'The Russians and our own government'll do anything to stop you. They'll label you a deranged terrorist. After they kill you.'

'That's where you come in. I need you to allow me to send CT's recordings to you, along with the access site and codes I have as a backup placed on the dark web. Send the information to Deane as a precaution. I believe both sides think I have something they want; therefore, they won't kill me. I need you to cover me from that roof in case I'm wrong.'

'We're here with you.' A cacophony of voices, male and female in harmony silently clamored for attention inside Jake's head disorienting him.

'CT: *I summoned them earlier. I will play the recorded conversation.*

Consider us you must, we are the forgotten ones. They took our bodies, unbeknownst to them our memories, the ones they thought erased, survived inside the ethernet of things. CT searched and notified us.'

A female voice: *They can beat me, but they can't defeat me.*'

A stunned Jake realized he had unknowingly thought of his youthful competitive running chant, an unconscious reaction to the chaotic chorus inside his head.

'Did you not hear them?'

TJ and Dr. Guthridge looked askance at Jake. Was he losing it?

'Hear what bro?'

"Voices. CT says he recorded them.'

'I have blocked Dr. Guthridge and TJ.' CT memed.

Jake shook his head. 'What the f' TJ? There are other voices besides CT's inside my head saying they are the forgotten ones. Earlier recipients of the device who are preserved inside the ethernet. Apparently, they are dead. The lead voice sounds like Blakely. But I never told Blakely my competition rhythmic breathing chant, *you can beat me, but you can never defeat me*. How could whatever these voices are know this unless they're communicating with CT? Don't look at me like that. I know this sounds crazy. It's even crazier sounding to me. What the hell? How is this possible?'

Dr. Guthridge: 'What is going on?'

TJ memed her he feared a repeat of Jake's earlier episode when CT *spoke* for the first time. Could it be they were trying to shut Jake down? Was he next?

Dr. Guthridge: 'Keep him talking. I don't know how but I've been blocked.'

'Don't know bro. Maybe they trying to disorient you, shut you down.'

'It won't work mothers.'

CT: '*They are no longer under their control. They are not aware of their existence. I knew about them. Each one of us discovered the other inside the web. They needed an outside source. A voice. The voice is Blakely Carmichael's.*'

'Why just me?' Jake could not believe he was accepting this madness. He included TJ so he could hear. This caused TJ to look even more perplexed.

'*They came to me son. Through the computer Blakely is hooked into at the hospital. She was declared dead twice. The second time the others reached out to her. They revived her. She may never leave the hospital physically intact, despite Dr. Perkins' wish to keep her alive. General McDab and others intend to learn what they believe she knows. They wish to steal her mind. These others found her because she was reaching out to you. I was monitoring the hospital computer. The others allowed her access. She said she may never get to see you again but this way she can be part of you. TJ, you must believe this also.*'

CT memed TJ's Earl the conversation. 'Damn. You buying this bro?'

Dr. Guthridge: 'What is it?'

TJ shook his head. 'Dr. Guthridge wants to know what's going on.'

Dr. Guthridge was trying to tune in, process what was going on. Verify the source.

'*We have no way of predicting the future. From our experiences you are right to suspect they won't kill you until they have your device.*'

Jake couldn't believe he was accepting this. CT assured him of the veracity.

Could he, should he trust CT?

'*What choice do you have son? Okneyev wants you dead in order to receive a big payoff. But first his intent is to get inside your head to retrieve the codes for the cartel accounts he thinks you possess. If you do what you plan to do, he will kill your daughter in front of you in a most horrific way in order to make you break down. He will wound you, expose you to radiation, whatever it takes to get his hands on you. I have seen him do far worse to others. You are no good to him without Dr. Perkins or Dr. Guthridge. He must not get his hands on you or Dr. Guthridge.'*

'What about Ariel and the fetus? And Elizabeth?'

'The others say they cannot predict with certainty any one outcome for the future. Okneyev, Gabriel's other grandparents, the cartels, McDab and Tindal are intertwined, have many connections and plots with and against each other all of which revolve around you. They want to know what you know and will do anything to learn this. Like me, your family is at risk. Okneyev and the others will do whatever they must to learn what they suspect you know. And no, committing suicide will not save us or stop them from getting their hands on your device.'

'Why me? Why has all this happened to me?'

'Because you were the first what Dr. Perkins felt to be a successful recipient. You stumbled onto the agencies' plans and you stood in Tindal's, Okneyev's and others' means of achieving their goals.'

TJ couldn't believe what he just heard. 'What do they mean the first *successful* recipient?'

'I have no idea. Remember I told you McDab told me this. I wasn't sure whether to believe him or not. Look, it doesn't matter, not now.' Jake started pacing. 'According to our newly discovered web friends, Okneyev needs me alive and, from every indication, he intends to kill Elizabeth. The Blakely voice warned me about suicide.'

Dr. Guthridge was finally able to tune in through TJ. What came next was shocking.

'What if I threatened to kill Dr. Guthridge and myself unless he releases Elizabeth? That ought to shake things up.'

Could Jake seriously consider doing her harm. She wanted to break in, but decided she needed to know more.

'Bro, remember first rule of pulling a weapon—don't point it at anyone unless you intend to use it.'

'I shoot Dr. Guthridge to show I'm serious. Don't look at me like that. I don't intend to actually do it. These virtual voices gave me the idea. I make it look as though I shoot her. Come on. We don't have much time.' Jake turned to Dr. Guthridge, 'Lisa, I don't have much time to explain. I need a virtual vid which makes it look like I wound then possibly kill you, depending on their reaction. How do I do this?' Jake was surprised when Dr. Guthridge replied. How much had she picked up on?

Dr. Guthridge: 'Enough. As for your shocking hypothetical, it can be done. Central casting could do it, but there isn't enough time before Okneyev calls. We would need to create a communication glitch to buy time.'

TJ: 'Bet Hardy could take care of that. You willing to trust him?'

Dr. Guthridge decided to interrupt: 'It can't happen otherwise. I don't know of any other way.'

CT broke in, *'Jake, Hardy's device did a search of the woman who was talking to the Russian and Cuban Ambassador's wives that were recorded earlier. She is YeKaterina V. Putin, the Russian President's daughter who is Director of Scientific Institute Innopaktika. Their research is concerned with developing devices to read brain waves. Their goal is to develop the supermen that have been reported already in existence.'*

'Where is she now?'

'She and the ambassadors' wives were recorded leaving the ballroom accompanied by Thomas Devereaux and Colonel Tindal minutes ago.'

Jake checked the time. He had less than thirty minutes. He memed TJ and Dr. Guthridge the latest development. 'Why Devereaux?'

TJ walked over to the chair Mark was seated in, his chin on his chest. TJ prodded him. He jerked awake causing him to tip sideways nearly falling off his seat. "You guys ready to roll?"

"Your buddy Devereaux left the ballroom in the company of Tindal, the ambassadors' wives and another woman identified as Putin's daughter. Know anything about Devereaux and Tindal and the Russians?"

"Tindal yeah. Told you guys Jenkins at his behest was in touch with Okneyev and others. Devereaux? Have no idea. He killed two Russians on Great Exuma, ran them off the road. Jake you were there. That's the only connection I'm aware of."

"We're running out of time. Seems to me I now have a better option, take these commie women, use them for the exchange."

"How you going to do that?" Dr. Guthridge asked.

CT: *'The others have been monitoring the consulate cameras. The women and their bodyguards entered the elevator into the motorpool.'*

Jake memed TJ, hurriedly reached down onto the table where Mark sat, grabbed an M-5 and several stun grenades plus his coms helmet and trotted toward the door that would take him into the corridor that ended at the motorpool. TJ having quickly followed his example was right behind him. The hazmat suits made more than a trot impossible.

CHAPTER
65

Quintana Roo, Cancun Outskirts

By the time they entered the motorpool, the big black limousine was at the guard station. Jake yelled at the Marine guards inside the gate control room to not let them go. They didn't react fast enough.

He and Jake donned their headgear and ran to a smaller, older model luxury vehicle. The doors were locked, and the glass was reinforced. It took several minutes of precious time pounding on the side window with the butt of the M-5 to break it. Jake hit the lock to let TJ in. He busted the cover then reached under the steering column and crossed the wires.

He floored the sluggish automobile. The guards had not been able to close the gate or engage the floor mounted barrier. Jake and TJ raced by the guardhouse, and they took a tire screeching swing out onto Boulevard Kulkulcan, headed north. The thought hit Jake and TJ: how was it the other vehicle wasn't affected by the radiation? Hm?

The other vehicle was not visually to be seen, too many stranded vehicles lined the road, blocked their ability to see. Somehow CT managed to tap into the satellite feed. Jake was thankful the device signal functioned. Another thing to ponder. For now, he had to concentrate on catching them.

"At present rates of speed, should overtake them just past the airport exit," TJ's suit's miced voice was barely audible.

Jake pounded the steering wheel with his thick-gloved hand. "Come on, come on."

"There they are," TJ shouted as they swung around past the exit and slid onto 307, Tulum Boulevard headed south. Were they headed to Tulum Naval Airbase? Why toward the blast zone? The blast zone, Akumal, the control center, Gabriel.

Jake knew he had to take them by surprise because if they suspected he was after them, they most likely could outrun him. He swerved into the other lane, zipping between several stranded vehicles, sparks flew from metal-on-metal contact. He was almost on them, swerved right then left like he was going to pass them. When the front of his vehicle was just past their vehicle's rear wheel, he abruptly turned into them. The other vehicle slid partially sideways, the bumper of Jake's and TJ's vehicle ripped a hole in the tire then tore loose. The driver of the women's vehicle was able to pull out of the skid and accelerated. Evidently, their vehicle's tire was a dual tire. But the ripped tire slowed them down enough so that Jake was able to catch them.

The other driver kept Jake from being able to get alongside them again. Jake used his street racing skills learned as a teenage get-away driver. When the other driver swerved to block them, Jake went for it, caught the other vehicles leading rear edge on the driver's side opposite the damaged rear tire and was able to push the other vehicle into a skid. Jake braked then floored it and managed to broadside the other vehicle, locking them together in a postcoital embrace, attached, neither vehicle going anywhere.

Jake pushed the inflated airbag out and managed to reach into the suit's side pocket and retrieve the K-Bar he had put there when he first donned the suit. He punctured the airbag. He miced TJ, "You okay?"

TJ punctured his bag and miced back, "Everything seems to be in working order. Better get out of here before one of those commie bozos decides to use us for target practice."

With some effort they were able to exit out TJ's side of the vehicle. No one got out of the other vehicle. No weapons fired.

"Must be afraid of the radiation," Jake replied.

TJ went around to the driver's window and placed his M-5 against the glass and with his other hand mimicked speaking into a device.

A squelch was followed by a female voice speaking Russian. TJ knew enough Russian to understand she wanted to know who they were and what they wanted, as if they didn't know?

"Any more bright ideas bro?"

Jake went back to their vehicle, pushed aside the airbag remnants, and found a pen and pad inside the console. With difficulty, he wrote, **Jake Harper. Want my daughter. Or else…**

"Bro don't think they will understand. And I don't know enough written Russian."

Jake went back to the passenger side front windshield and placed the pad on the glass so the writing faced them.

After a brief pause, another woman said something, TJ interpreted. "Daughter? They not understand." From her tone, my bet is they know who you are. My bet, they know about your daughter. What next? Your call."

Off in the distance from the direction of the Russian Consulate came the sounds of an approaching helicopter. Soon it hovered overhead and Okneyev's voice emanated from a loudspeaker. "Lay down your arms Mr. Harper or I throw your daughter out the door. You watch her pieces fly to ground after she go boom."

TJ came around to join Jake. Suddenly, the ground not far from the chopper erupted. Jake rose back up slowly. He handed the pad and pen to TJ. "Write them inside the car tell them to tell Okneyev if he harms my daughter, the next missile will take him out then everyone in the limo will die."

It took TJ a minute to write out the message and for the Russian voice to announce it to Okneyev. The female voice announced her demand out loud in a commanding, frightened voice.

He landed the helicopter after announcing his intentions to do so.

CT sent the hold-your-fire, await-further-instructions message to the out-of-sight UAV manned by Jeni.

'I have relayed message to Captain Adams.'

Jake had CT link up with the chopper's radio. *"You are hereby instructed to stand by and await further instructions from your master."*

Okneyev exited the helicopter accompanied by another man. Both wore hazmat suits, and the other man was armed. Jake walked around to meet him.

Okneyev thought about removing his suit. No, could be some radiation here. He spoke through his suit's mic which CT had connected Jake's suit's mic to.

"Mr. Harper. You very industrious. Too bad we must meet like this. I make proposal: exchange daughter for you and no one die. My pilot wait for me give signal. I not give signal, he leave with your daughter. You agree, we get in vehicle, wait for rescue vehicle come. Your people not fire on this vehicle. Your daughter, she wait in helicopter with your friend. We leave and pilot take them back to consulate. No one need die."

'While he was talking Jake had CT relay the message telling Jeni to take off the tail rotor of the helicopter and send backup.'

'Backup on way,' TJ memed.

There was another explosion and the tail section erupted sending shrapnel into the air. TJ ducked down and ran around the vehicle and jammed his K-Bar into Okneyev's other man's neck before he could turn back around after reacting to the shock of the blast.

Jake used the distraction to reach the bent-over Okneyev. He sliced through Okneyev's hazmat suit and held the knife against his throat before he could recover from the blast.

"Don't move. Anything happens to my daughter and I will give you another mouth to breath out of. You got it?" Jake hoped Okneyev's mic was working.

Okneyev didn't dare move. "Harper, you make big mistake."

"You made bigger mistake. I would like nothing better than to open you up right here."

TJ: "Don't do it bro."

Jake took note, no one inside the vehicle had dared open a window or door. Jake handed Okneyev off to TJ after he zip-tied the other man to the chopper strut. He cautiously approached the helicopter. The pilot stared at Jake as he advanced toward his door. Jake noticed neither the pilot nor Elizabeth had hazmat suits on.

Just as Jake reached the immobile copter, the pilots head crashed into the door. Jake saw Elizabeth rear back and kick him again. He slumped down in his seat. Elizabeth struggled to sit back up, finally, she did. Jake gave her a thumbs up. He hoped she could see his grin inside his suit through the blood-streaked side window of the door. She was trying to use her feet to move the pilot. Jake radioed her to stay inside the helicopter and wait for help. She stopped struggling, then her whole body shook, and tears flooded down her face.

"This vest will ignite if anyone attempts to remove it," she struggled to say. Jake couldn't hear her, she had not pressed the radio mic button. He managed to figure out the gist of what she was saying by reading her lips. He hoped the radio was still on inside the chopper.

"You have to press the button on the radio mic or take the pilot's headset." The pilot's headset was covered in blood. She shook her head, then she shuffled around until she was able to retrieve the communication mic, a struggle since her hands were zip-tied behind her back.

"Who are you?" She asked.

"My name is Jake Harper. Would you believe I'm your biological father?" She shook her head. "It's a long story. We'll talk later. We have bomb experts on the way who know what to do. I'm going to stay right here until we can safely get you out of there with the vest disarmed and off of you. By the way,

I have Gabriel, he's waiting for us." Jake watched her lips twitch, tears followed.

Jake's and TJ's backup arrived, within minutes before the Russian's. Hardy was with their people. A hazmat-suited Russian General disembarked from a Russian military helicopter, took charge of the Russians. There was a heated exchange. Hardy refused to release Okneyev.

"He's a terrorist who detonated a nuclear bomb. The American Jenkins also must be returned, immediately."

"You mistaken. We no explode nuclear missile. Perhaps you wish to provoke international conflict?" The Russian who introduced himself as General Yarazenko said.

"It is this man, your countryman who had missile, threatened us, was at your embassy. It is your country which will be seen as having violated the international nuclear weapon's treaty. It is you who will be held responsible for this incident if you claim Pietr Okneyev. He will be seen as having acted for your government in kidnapping and terrorism. I suggest you do as requested, or your country will suffer the consequences."

As the known bomb expert, Boyd had arrived with Hardy. He climbed in the helicopter after telling Jake he should move back. Jake said he would stay right there. He helped Boyd pull the pilot out. A Russian soldier came over and carried the pilot to a Russian armored vehicle that had arrived.

It took Boyd what seemed like forever to unarm the vest. He climbed out and helped Jake carry Elizabeth over to the field decontamination tent. Marge had sent her a set of clothes that loosely fit her slender frame. After she dressed, she seated herself inside a Humvee where a Marine medic waited to check her over. He administered an antidote for possible radiation exposure.

Jake rejoined TJ and the others. General Yarazenko came back to Hardy and said their ambassador agreed to their request. Soon another helicopter arrived Jenkins was removed and the women inside the wrecked limo boarded then departed. They had not worn hazmat suits.

Hardy instructed Jake and TJ to relinquish their arms to a pair of Marines standing by. They reluctantly did so. Hardy informed them they were under arrest and would be held at the control center pending a hearing.

On the ride back, just before they reached the damaged control center, Hardy miced them, "The gala event attendees are being evacuated. The conference will be rescheduled. They have agreed in principle to an international-space-use treaty agreement. Mexico's president demanded the return of his citizens being held by us. He swears they had nothing to do with the incident on the beach. An agreement was reached despite my objections."

After they exited the vehicle, two guards were waiting for them and escorted them down to the conference room once they were hosed down. Jake shut the door behind them, shutting out the two guards. Hardy remained by the door; Jake and TJ leaned back, their hands, along with their hips, supported their weight against the anchored metal table. Hardy picked up where he left off.

"General McDab, understandably, is unhappy with both of you. He will be the one to handle any disciplinary actions against you two and the others. As for Poponovich, seems he was telling the truth about having someone on the outside. He said she goes by the name Suzie Hasty. She has embedded herself inside DICE and was working with one of their agents to extort money from the cartel by kidnapping David Gonzalez and his uncle and extorting money from the Russians by kidnapping your son-in-law Pablo and/or your grandson Gabriel. Seems their plans were more ambitious than she knew. The man she was working with is a Canadian of British Chinese descent. He is part of a Maoist splinter cell who are responsible for the kidnapping of Dr. Perkins. General McDab has a contingent on their way to extricate him."

TJ replied, "I hope they're better than Picard's and Gabron's group."

"I've given you this information because you need to understand your misguided rebellion against me and General McDab was unjustified. There was a lot going on you had no right to know. Keep this in mind when you are called to defend your actions."

Jake wanted to yell out a reply. He restrained himself. "I did what I did for my family. At this point, I have no regrets. TJ and I saved my daughter, helped you secure Okneyev and Jenkins, so screw McDab. And you. Your self-righteous pat on the back doesn't bear up. And, how about Blakely and Ariel and our unborn child? Blakely, for all intents and purposes, is dead, isn't she? Ariel better survive, as well as our child. I'll repeat what I told you and McDab before: I have this whole bullshit experiment out there ready to be posted on the web. Anything happens to me, TJ, or our families and the others, I don't check in, give the proper codes, it will be released." Jake hesitated to mention the *Others*, his emergency backup informational calvary.

"That would be very unwise Jake. You are up against a government. You think you can win? You better think again. Who's going to believe you?"

"You didn't answer me, is Blakely alive?"

"As far as I know, she is on life-support, and no one knows if she will survive."

"Bullshit. They know. And she's not the first casualty of this god-forsaken experiment. So quit lying Hardy. We deserve the truth. McDab said I was the first *successful* device recipient. Did you know this before TJ and I were coerced into signing off in the clinic? Were you working with McDab and Tindal at that time?" Hardy didn't have to reply.

"His contorted face gave Jake all the answer he expected. "So, the way I see it, like Blakely, Ariel, and our child, I was illegally implanted, as I'm certain there were and will be others. They will be heard from if need be. Wonder what that's worth? I won't hesitate to disclose this whole damn mess. In fact, one of the recipients of my recordings is a team of world-renowned attorneys. Tell that to McDab and the puppet masters. Screw all of you."

Hardy wondered how Jake seemed to know about Blakely and the others. Could his threat be stopped? General McDab wasn't going to like this.

TJ chuckled.

Hardy's squinting eyes glared at TJ. "I guess you agree with Jake, You'll both go down because of this. You're only kidding yourselves if you think you can put the genie back in the bottle. There won't be any three wishes. You better think about what you're getting yourselves into, Jake. Better think about it, TJ, do you really want to be in on this?"

"Why not? My bro's right and you know it. Seems to me you people put our families at risk and aren't man enough to own up to it."

Jake straightened up. "Talk about putting the genie back in the bottle; while you're talking to that douchebag McDab, tell him, Dr. Perkins, and their puppet masters, we know all about these other recipients that were made to disappear. They're gone, but they refuse to be forgotten. Now if you'll be so kind as to tell your guards to stand down and stay the hell out of our way, I need to go see about my family. And oh, by the way, tell Tindal I'm looking forward to seeing him in court, and if I don't see Dr. Guthridge, tell her I expect her to keep her word about getting me that *off switch*."

Hardy couldn't hide it; his reddening face reflected his anger. Damnit, he should have seen this coming. He stepped aside and nodded to the guards standing outside the door.

"What's wrong, cat got your tongue?" Jake laughingly smirked as he and TJ pushed past Hardy and the guards.

423

POSTSCRIPT

"What about it Master Sergeant Alvarez?"

"Hey bro skip the formal bullshit. Haven't made any decision yet. Deane tells me Ariel is coming home today."

"Yep. As if you didn't know. You two coming, I hope? Elizabeth has taken Gabriel out to the landing site. I'll be heading that way myself in a few minutes. Waiting on you. Don't be wastin' my time."

"Be there shortly. Guess you know Deane volunteered to help with Ariel, and goina be Blakely's caretaker."

Jake heard Deane in the background, "Looking forward to it. Way medicine is going, who knows, Blakely might fool everyone."

'Did you tell her about my supposedly miraculous recovery with the iPSCs and some other undisclosed experimental treatment?' Jake memed, then switched to verbal. "Deane, if anyone can pull off a miracle, you can. They should make you a saint for putting up with TJ." Jake heard her laugh.

TJ switched back to meming. 'I didn't tell her Blakely has been in touch with you. You think Ariel is going to be okay with this?'

'She already knows. They've been communicating. Ariel is not the jealous type. In fact, seems like they've become friends.'

'Has Ariel agreed to join the Space Force Unit?'

'We haven't talked about it. I'm not sure how well she can handle losing her independence. And I don't think it's a good idea. Right now, we're both working on adjusting to being parents, grandparents and parents-to-be of supposedly the first newborn device recipient. Hard for me to get my mind around it. I told my other children about their other siblings. Not sure how they feel. I didn't hear any enthusiastic responses or congratulations. I may head out to my son's wedding week after next, try to restore our relationships. I'm playing it by ear.'

'Just remember you can't fix everything bro.'

'Speaking of fixing. Tindal is going to trial next court session. Our attorney says he'll likely plea bargain, most likely receive a pardon. Guess he told you our civil suit will probably end up with Tindal, McDab and the government offering a settlement? I still have a hard time with Devereaux's duplicity. Heard he'll be testifying for that son of a bitch Tindal.'

'He probably will. Screw him.'

'Yeah. Screw him. Anyway, how about you, have you talked to Deane about the Space Force Unit?'

'Nah bro. Not yet. You might think ill of me, but I want to see how well Ariel handles the device. And, it's not like we need the money.'

'Whoa now be careful. We all agreed to keep that under wraps until things cool down.'

'What you and Poponovich worried about, CT and the *Others* are keeping those codes hidden from everyone, including you? The weak link is Poponovich and crew. And the cartel. They the major concern. Guess you heard The Hive slipped right through everyone's hands. Been told the cartel has it. And the Mexican authorities agreed with the Russians and released Okneyev. Damn device like havin' a target on our backs. Sorry bro.'

'Yeah. Hope Dr. Guthridge comes through. Like to have this damn thing removed. Need to get the target off Ariel's and Samuel Sage's backs. CT informed me about The Hive and Okneyev. No surprise. Like we suspected and later CT verified.' *(And despite the idiotic attempted cover-up. Afterall, the media was there at the gala. Can't buy off a big story)* 'As suspected the missile was a dirty bomb, only contaminated the area around the control center. A ruse so The Hive could be stolen. And as for the money, Mark and I agreed, as did you and his crew, no mention of the codes, no going after the funds. Now that you are to be their superior, you can hold them to the agreement, Master Sergeant.'

'Like I said, not a done deal. If I do, means you've only got until Ariel is operational to remain civilian. Don't go thinking about renegging on your obligation. We agreed if one did it, the other would also. You ain't goina let me down now, are you bro?'

'You know if we join, our lawsuit against them will probably be dismissed. Besides, if things work out and Dr. Guthridge comes through, then my family and I will no longer be of any use to the unit.'

'Big if bro.'

'I guess Deane knows the reason we're not having this discussion vocally.'

'She's adjusting to fact I have this ability. Damn thing makes me an even better lover. I think she likes my renewed vigor. I'm happy to report I haven't heard any complaints.'

Jake laughed. 'I hope to find out before too long. I have to be patient until after Ariel's been cleared and Samuel Sage makes his appearance. Can't wait.'

'Bet not, lover boy. Deane informed me Ariel's communicating with Sage. That's amazing.'

'Not something I'm exactly comfortable with. Going to take some getting use to. Now I have to watch what I think along with what I say. Rather CT does. He's a dirty old man as you know.'

TJ chuckled. 'No secrets. Hmm. Maybe it's not such a good idea for Deane after all.'

'Don't worry, Ariel will keep her up on all your dirty little secrets.'

'You mean yours bro. This could prove very interesting.'

"We're here bro." TJ switched to verbal. "Don't turn Dusty and Maisy loose on us."

"Dusty is with Gabriel. Gabriel's first pet. Now the son of a bitch tends to ignore me. Don't be surprised if he doesn't act happy to see you. As for Maisy, Maisy is Maisy. She doesn't trust foreigners, or anybody for that matter."

"Takes after you."

"Takes one to know one," Jake said to TJ as they did their bro chest bump and hug after TJ exited his truck and came around to where Jake greeted Deane with a hug and kiss.

They started down the freshly cut grassy road that passed between the ancient gnarly oaks to the field where Gabriel was tossing a stick for the limping Dusty to retrieve. Maisy chased afterwards, yapping. Jake smiled.

The sound of a hovercraft echoed over the woods as it made its final approach. Everyone stopped talking, stopped doing what they were doing, and looked up. Dusty's deep-throated barks of alarm joined Maisy's never-ceasing yaps. Gabriel ran to his mother. This was going to be the first up-close-in-person meeting for Elizabeth and Gabe with Ariel and Sage. Jake couldn't wait to take Ariel into his arms again. And finally hold his son Sage.

Jake was happy to be back on the farm with his friends and his newly formed family. Everything was frozen in this moment. Time stood still. Whatever lay ahead, nothing would ever take away this memory.

THE OFF SWITCH

ACKNOWLEDGEMENTS

I would like to think all my friends and readers who have been here throughout this journey with me. You make the work of writing and rewriting worth it. If it weren't for you, there would be no need for writers like me. Special thanks go out to Candy Thomas, John Glenn, Gary Sauerbrei, Vickie Coates, Susan Smith Long, Terri Rockwell, Gail Hoffman Kot Hy, Bob Belangia, Dr. Kenneth and Amanda Burtner, Kevin Marshall, Elise Jones, and Sean Marshall who have encouraged me and have been my Beta Reader, sounding boards.

I would also like to thank Annette Kistner and Lori Perkins for your patience and guidance through the printing process.

Kudos to Matt Worsman of Rock-A-Print for the cover work.

Photo courtesy unsplash.com/ Mateo Grassi.

For further reading on subjects related to this novel:

#https://futurism.com/the-byte/us-military-augmented-human-beings

#Inside the 'super-soldier arms race to create genetically modified killing machines unable to feel pain or fear.

#NDB nano-diamond battery.

For information about US government surveillance network originally called *God's Eye* which was renamed *Guardian Angel* to sound less ominous: https://www.amazon.com/gp/product/B00XT47SOK/ref=dbs_a_def_rwt_bi bl_vppi_i16

or read Barry Eisler's novel *The God's Eye View*

Next

Book Four

In

THE WAR AFTER THE WAR SERIES

Another

JAKE HARPER / TJ ALVAREZ NOVEL

ENTANGLED

Warrior veteran, roguish, Ron Marshall is a graduate of UNC Charlotte, where he lettered in wrestling and LSU, where he played rugby. His major courses of study included economics, architecture, landscape architecture, real estate and construction management. He has worked up and down the eastern seaboard, along the Gulf Coast and in the Bahamas.

He and his dog Streak spend their time on his farm in the Carolinas and visiting friends and family in Louisiana and Texas, or wherever he finds interesting people and places to inspire his writing.

www.ingramcontent.com/pod-product-compliance
Lightning Source LLC
Chambersburg PA
CBHW021241200726
48288CB00014B/133